Romantic Suspense

Danger. Passion. Drama.

Cold Case Kidnapping
Kimberly Van Meter

Escape To The Bayou
Amber Leigh Williams

MILLS & BOON

MIX
Paper | Supporting
responsible forestry
FSC® C001695
www.fsc.org

Published by
Harlequin Mills & Boon
An imprint of Harlequin Enterprises (Australia) Pty Limited
(ABN 47 001 180 918), a subsidiary of HarperCollins
Publishers Australia Pty Limited
(ABN 36 009 913 517)
Level 19, 201 Elizabeth Street
SYDNEY NSW 2000 AUSTRALIA

Cover art used by arrangement with Harlequin Books S.A.. All rights reserved.

Printed and bound in Australia by McPherson's Printing Group

Cold Case Kidnapping

Kimberly Van Meter

MILLS & BOON

Kimberly Van Meter wrote her first book at sixteen and finally achieved publication in December 2006. She has written for the Harlequin Superromance, Blaze and Romantic Suspense lines. She and her husband of thirty years have three children, two cats, and always a houseful of friends, family and fun.

Books by Kimberly Van Meter

Harlequin Romantic Suspense

Big Sky Justice

Danger in Big Sky Country
Her K-9 Protector
Cold Case Secrets
Cold Case Kidnapping

The Coltons of Owl Creek

Colton's Secret Stalker

The Coltons of Kansas

Colton's Amnesia Target

Military Precision Heroes

Soldier for Hire
Soldier Protector

Visit the Author Profile page at millsandboon.com.au for more titles.

Dear Reader,

Cold case stories are my secret love. There's something about stories that involve solving painful or violent mysteries that will always engage my muse.

While my story is fictional, there are far too many real-life stories without resolution—and crimes against Indigenous women have been happening without consequence for too long.

The time is now to end the cycle of violence.

As always, "see something, say something" and you might just save a life.

Hearing from readers is a special joy. Please feel free to find me on social media or email me at authorkvanmeter@gmail.com.

Kimberly Van Meter

Chapter 1

The hallway at the Bureau of Indian Affairs office was filled with the faint hum of fluorescent lights overhead as agent Dakota Foster mentally steeled herself for the meeting she'd been dreading since her superior, Isaac Berrigan, dropped the file on her desk last week for review.

Unlike her first case, which involved a drunken cheater who got whacked by his wife one night when she'd had enough of his bullshit, this case had a real chance to make a difference—and she was hungry for a personal victory.

She didn't even mind that it was a co-op with the FBI, until she read who the FBI agent assigned to the case was and her heart sank like it was tied to a bucket of cement and tossed into Flathead Lake.

Of all the FBI agents who could've been assigned, why Ellis Vaughn? The last time she saw that train wreck was two years ago and the memory still had the power to make her wince.

Sometimes, late at night, when her brain refused to shut down, her thoughts wandered into forbidden territory—opening that tightly sealed locked box where she'd stuffed memories of Ellis—and it still hurt when she thought about what could've been.

But doing so felt like weakness and she couldn't abide such a slip in her self-control.

Her drive had pushed her to become the first in her family to graduate from college—a hard-won accomplishment for an Indigenous woman who grew up on a Montana reservation—which then propelled her into the world of law enforcement, before transitioning to the BIA. There, she quickly gained a reputation for her unwavering commitment to chasing justice for the Indigenous people even when it meant going head-to-head against bureaucratic red tape and relentless opposition. She was ambitious and efficient, and she prided herself on being organized and no-nonsense.

Which left little room for self-indulgent pity parties.

Besides, Ellis was her polar opposite and a relationship with someone she had little in common with was an exercise in futility. Something she should've known better years ago.

It wasn't that Ellis was lazy or lacked ambition, but he operated in a state of chaos that made her head spin and Ellis never found a rule he didn't mind bending or breaking.

But some rules had serious consequences for breaking—a tough lesson he learned the hard way.

Whatever, the past is the past, she told herself, drawing a deep breath before pushing the door open to the debrief room. She was early but her colleague Shilah Parker was already there. She looked up as Dakota entered. "I just finished going over the file… The original vic, Nayeli Swiftwater, was from the Flathead Reservation. That's your neck of the woods, right?" she recalled.

Dakota nodded and slid into the seat beside her. She and Shilah had worked the drunk case—and in doing so, had become tight friends. She recalled the Swiftwater case with a subtle wince. "Yeah, I remember when that hit the news. I was sixteen at the time, but it'd only been three years since my older sister, Mikaya, was killed so I was following the case as much as a kid could."

"Ouch, that had to have been rough," Shilah commiserated. "That would've hit too close to home for me."

Dakota remembered being hyperfocused on Nayeli's case for that very reason. "Each time the case came up in the news, it was like swallowing razor blades, but I couldn't stop watching or reading anything that popped up. I think I was clinging to the hope that if Nayeli's case got solved, maybe that would mean there was hope for Mikaya's case. Naive of me, I know, but I couldn't help myself. I needed something to make the pain manageable."

"The pain of hope," Shilah murmured, understanding, returning to the case. "Well, it's been a long time coming but I'm happy to see a cold case like this getting some attention. Maybe with some luck, eventually there will be answers for Mikaya's case, too."

Dakota had long since abandoned hope for answers in her sister's case but the resurgence of Nayeli's case renewed her sense of purpose—the reason why her job was so important—even if the memory dredged up the inevitable pain of losing her sister.

"Maybe," Dakota agreed, blinking away the tears that were never far whenever Mikaya's name was brought up. She gestured to the case files. "This case was so brutal. Nayeli was nineteen and a single mother when she was killed, but her baby was never found. Cases like these never fail to punch you in the gut. I'd always held out hope that the baby would turn up."

"If you don't find an infant within the first forty-eight hours..." Shilah trailed, shaking her head.

It was a heartbreaking statistic that they wished wasn't true but even if the kidnapped child wasn't harmed, their faces changed so much in the first year, even with age progression software, they were difficult to recognize without an identifying mark or feature.

Unless a twist of fate intervened and seventeen years later that infant reappeared out of nowhere, creating an all-hands-on-deck frenzy to reopen the case.

Isaac Berrigan, the task force leader, walked into the room, along with Sayeh Griffin and Levi Wyatt, and not more than two minutes later, Ellis Vaughn, catching the door with a flash of that charming grin that made most women weak in the knees, followed.

"Looks like I just made it," he said, shaking hands with Isaac and Levi, nodding to Sayeh, before swiveling his gaze to Dakota.

The moment their eyes locked, the tension between them was immediate and palpable—and hard to smother.

When Isaac had broached the subject of putting her on the case with the FBI agent, she hadn't disclosed that she and Ellis had history and she wasn't about to do that now, either, which meant she had to stove her natural reaction to seeing him again.

Dakota studied him for a moment, taking in the dark circles under his eyes and the faint lines etched into his features—signs that the years that'd passed since their breakup two years ago hadn't been a cakewalk. Despite the lingering tension between them, she couldn't deny that Ellis was brilliant at his job, and his troubled past only seemed to fuel his determination to bring criminals to justice, something she'd always admired.

It'd taken a long time to get over Ellis and seeing him again wasn't doing her any favors, but this case was bigger than her feelings.

Isaac, a man who hated politicking and posturing, made short work of the introductions in a gruff voice before taking his seat at the head of the table.

"Agent Vaughn," Dakota said, managing a tight smile as she extended her hand, ignoring the flutter in her stomach the second their palms met.

"Agent Foster," Ellis replied, shaking her hand firmly before finding his seat opposite her. There was a time when his hand in hers had been the calm in the storm, no matter what life had thrown their way. Now they were strangers and that's the way it would stay because the past needed to stay in the past. The sudden prick at her heart only focused her resolve that much more.

"I assume you've all read the brief," Isaac started, opening the file. "The gravity of the situation is only outmatched by the sense of urgency to find out how a six-week-old infant that's been missing for seventeen years just showed up as a coma patient in a Butte hospital."

Seventeen-year-old Cheyenne Swiftwater was admitted into Saint James Hospital after a solo rollover car accident, suffering a major head injury. According to the police report, the teen overcorrected on a turn and flipped the car. She was ejected from the vehicle and was put into a medically induced coma to bring down the swelling in her brain.

"It's a miracle she survived the wreck," Sayeh murmured, surveying the crash scene pictures. "It's not often that getting thrown from a vehicle actually saves your life. If the seat belt hadn't failed, she would've been crushed."

"Situations like these make idiots say that seat belts don't save lives," Isaac grumbled, but added, "Luck was riding shotgun with this girl, that's for sure."

"No ID found at the time of the accident," Shilah said, reading over the report. "How'd they get an identification?"

"They had her listed as Jane Doe until her fingerprints were put into the system, tripping the FBI database for Missing and Exploited Children," Ellis answered, adding, "Imagine our surprise when Cheyenne Swiftwater popped up."

Nayeli's baby. The sixteen-year-old Dakota wanted to sob with relief that the child was alive, but the adult BIA agent had to stay focused and detached. She wouldn't dare do anything that would cause Isaac to side-eye her involvement with the case. "Did Cheyenne say where she was headed?" Dakota asked.

"She's awake but she doesn't know who she is or where she was going," Ellis said. "Doctors are saying it's short-term memory loss due to the head injury and there's no telling how long it might last but we need to find out where Cheyenne's been all this time."

"There's also no guarantee she's been in Montana. For all we know she could've been anywhere. Who's the car registered to?" Levi asked.

"An eighty-year-old Stevensville man who's been dead for at least five years. No surviving kin," Ellis answered, shaking his head. "If he was the one who abducted Cheyenne, he took the truth to his grave."

"We can put the media to work—area newspapers, news outlets, even social media—to see if anyone recognizes her," Dakota suggested. "Someone out there is bound to know something."

Isaac nodded with approval. "Good call. Dakota, you and Agent Vaughn will go to Saint James Hospital and speak with the girl first thing tomorrow. Talk to her doctors, see what you can find out. Levi and Sayeh, you'll handle the press, get the word out. Shilah, run background on the girl's mother. See if there's anything from the past that might've been missed."

The debrief room's fluorescent lights hummed overhead, casting a harsh glare on the case files spread across the table, a visual reminder that emotions didn't matter in this situation. The import of this case was huge but Dakota fought a well of complicated thoughts and feelings at the reopening of Nayeli's case. Solving what happened to the stolen infant of a murdered Native mother was the kind of case that would make all of her sacrifices worth it, but it didn't change the fact that Nayeli's case was located too close in her heart to Mikaya's for her to remain completely unbiased.

And Ellis had to know this, but he hadn't raised the alarm, so she'd give him that.

Perhaps Ellis's silence was a sign that he was willing to keep the past buried if she was—and Dakota was determined to prove that she could.

If she had to work side by side with Ellis, she'd do it as a professional should.

"We can drive together," Ellis offered but Dakota shut that down real quick.

Oh, hell no. Just because she was ready to show that she could keep the past in its place didn't mean she wanted to ride shotgun with the man like they were buddies. "I'd prefer separate cars. We can meet at the destination."

Ellis accepted her counter with a nod. "I'll call ahead, let the hospital know that we're coming. Let's meet at the hospital at eleven hundred. Does that work for you?"

Dakota put the time into her schedule with a short, "It does," and quickly added her own checklist into her notes for tomorrow.

Berrigan nodded. "Good. All right, you have your assignments. Let's bring home another win—and it goes without saying, stay safe." The last case nearly cost them Sayeh and Levi but a win was a win and their case had given the task force the added weight they'd needed to go harder on more complicated cases.

Such as this one.

The team started to disperse but Ellis hung back, which made Dakota want to run from the room, but they were officially on the same team for the time being so being professional was her emotional armor.

"It's been a while," Ellis said in an attempt at small talk, which she didn't want or need.

Since they were alone, Dakota dropped the act that they were strangers meeting for the first time. She turned to Ellis, addressing him in a low tone. "Look, I'll only say this once—our past doesn't matter. What matters is this case. We're adults. I can handle being civil and professional but don't try to charm me into anything more. Whatever we once had is now dust and ash with zero hope of resurrecting. Got it?"

"Geesh, Dakota, all I said was *It's been a while*. I wasn't trying to resurrect anything," he assured her, shaking his head as if she were overreacting, but there was the tiniest flicker of something else behind his eyes even as he added, "I was just being polite. That's a thing, you know."

"Don't do that," she warned, hating how he was trying to turn this into a problem on her end. "I know how you operate and I'm not interested in playing your games. Focus on the case, keep the past where it belongs and we'll do just fine."

Ellis looked away, accepting her terms with a stiff nod, but as she started to leave, he added, "Well, it's still good to see you, even if you don't share the sentiment."

She'd eat her shoe before admitting that she missed Ellis, but damn him for even saying such a thing to her. The time for sharing such thoughts was long gone. She ignored the heat flushing through her body and blurted, "I'm seeing someone." Which was a complete lie but she needed him to know that she wasn't pining for his stupid ass. "And it's pretty serious."

That subtle arch of surprise in his brow as well as the micro-expression of hurt before he smiled with a congratulatory, "That's great. I'm really happy for you, Dakota," made her instantly angry. He wasn't supposed to be nice about learning that she'd replaced him in her heart but how else was he supposed to react? What did she want, for him to fall to his knees and publicly humiliate himself with an overt display of a broken heart?

That might soothe her bruised ego but would create major turmoil affecting their case, so no.

"Thanks," she returned stiffly, clutching her files to her chest. "So, tomorrow, then. Eleven hundred hours. I'll see you at Saint James."

"Don't get the wrong idea but we should probably exchange numbers..." he suggested as Dakota started to walk out the door, adding, "Unless, your number is the same, because mine hasn't changed."

She swallowed, hating that she hadn't changed her number. At the time, when her heart was still weeping, she'd desperately hoped that her phone would ring in the middle of the night and it would be Ellis begging for another chance. That call never happened but she also couldn't bring herself to change numbers. She lifted her chin. "I never got around to changing mine," she said, hoping to convey that he hadn't been important enough to warrant top priority.

If her statement hurt him, his brief smile and short nod didn't show it. "Great. Eleven hundred, then."

Dakota didn't trust herself to stay in that room a moment longer. She left without another word. Ordinarily, working with a new partner—especially interagency co-ops—she would've been more accommodating, maybe even offering to take them to lunch to get better acquainted, talk shop, the usual, but she already knew all she needed to know about Ellis Vaughn.

He'd grown up with a sadistic "one-percenter" outlaw biker father who'd kicked the crap out of him whenever Ellis had even sneezed wrong, and who'd eaten a bullet from a rival gang when Ellis was a teenager, which was the best thing that could've happened.

Ellis, determined to be different from his old man, went into law enforcement, taking great pleasure in taking down violent dirtbags with similar MOs as his father but his maverick style had rubbed his superior the wrong way. After the last assignment had barely gone the right way, Ellis was unceremoniously kicked out of the narcotics unit and sent to the missing persons division.

She remembered that day all too well.

"They demoted me!" Ellis had roared, slamming into the kitchen with all of the rage of a man wronged. "That son of a bitch Carleton demoted me to the goddamn missing persons division!"

Dakota, alarmed at seeing this side of Ellis, tried to call him down. "It's not exactly a demotion. Missing Persons is an important division with a lot of opportunity for growth... You might even say that Carleton did you a favor."

"It's a paperwork division with no action," Ellis had shot back, his narrowed gaze hot with scathing mockery. "He did it on purpose because he knows I need to be where the action's at. This is punishment, Dakota. Don't insult me by trying to make me think it's not."

She'd tried to empathize with Ellis's situation but she'd warned him that he had to stop playing fast and loose with the rules or else it was going to backfire on him. It was the lowest-hanging fruit of an "I told you so" but facts were facts.

"I'm not trying to do anything but point out a perspective that you might've missed," she retorted, stung. "And if you didn't want to leave the narcotics division, you shouldn't have pressed your luck when Carleton told you to cool it. A dead agent is the last thing anyone wants and that's exactly what was going to happen if someone didn't put you in check. I'm sorry, Ellis, but I agree with Carleton's decision."

It might've been true but it'd been the wrong thing to say at that moment.

Ellis was a powder keg of rage, guilt and self-recrimination that only needed the slightest spark to ignite—and Dakota had just lit the match.

Ellis had grabbed the first thing his hand could grasp and the crystal cookie jar shattered into a million pieces against the wall.

In her life and career, Dakota had seen too many red flags go ignored only to grow monstrous with time and she couldn't let the incident slide. It would've been easy to chalk up the situation as a moment of anger that got out of hand and might never happen again but Dakota didn't play with those kinds of odds.

The memory of the shattering glass echoed in her mind—as did her decision to leave. At the time, Dakota had been grateful that Ellis neither tried to make excuses for his actions nor did he try to stop her from leaving. Did Ellis ever think of that night? Or did he walk away from everything they'd shared without a backward glance? It wasn't her business to know or ask but the questions poked at her during quiet moments.

Or not-so-quiet moments—like now.

After the breakup, she'd rationalized they'd been kidding themselves from the start. Their relationship had never stood a chance. Compartmentalizing the reason for their breakup had helped manage her grief but it didn't stop the sting when he was standing in front of her.

Dakota knew that Isaac had picked her to work with Ellis because of her connection to the Flathead Reservation. She appreciated that he cared even when he acted like he was insensitive to anything but the outcome of a case, but working side by side with Ellis was going to take its toll.

She might put up a good front, but privately, seeing Ellis again had just taken a sledgehammer to that carefully sealed box. The thing was, they never had any closure over what'd happened and why they broke up.

It'd been more than the crystal cookie jar—it was the explosion of unfettered rage that'd scared her.

Even if they'd both agreed it was for the best, neither had actually had that conversation, which, in hindsight, was probably necessary to process the pain, but Dakota couldn't handle seeing him again for fear of slipping in her decision to end things. So, when she walked away, she hadn't looked back—and he hadn't come looking, either.

In her mind, that was further confirmation that he'd agreed.

But seeing him again was going to put the strength of that mental box to the test. What might happen if it finally sprang open after all these years of being tightly shut?

Don't go there, Dakota. Focus, focus, focus—all that matters is the case.

It would have to be the mantra that got her through this.

Chapter 2

Ellis knew seeing Dakota again would be like a punch to the solar plexus but two years' absence should've been enough time to get over the woman.

The immediate heat flushing through his body at first sight was proof that a hundred years might not be enough.

Dakota had an energy that vibrated with intensity; that inner passion for justice vibrated from her core in a way that drew him straight to her. He'd always admired her tenacity and stubborn will but her rigid sense of fair play had ultimately cleaved their love in two.

Well, that and his stupid temper. The last year of anger management classes had taught him a lot about his triggers and why he'd erupted that night at the one person who'd been the straightest shooter in his life. It hadn't been her fault that his actions had cost him but he'd taken his rage out on her—and an unsuspecting crystal cookie jar that'd been a gift from her grandmother.

Even with two years between him and that excruciatingly embarrassing moment, the memory still had the power to make him want to fall through the floor and disappear. He'd made it his life's mission to be different from his shit-bag father and yet, in a flash, he'd channeled his violent spirit, erupting with vicious rage at someone who didn't deserve it.

And it'd scared him. That's what he hadn't been able to admit.

So, instead, when Dakota had walked—and with good reason—he'd let her.

That was then. This is now. It was time to move on.

Which was all well and good, except they had the kind of chemistry that couldn't be ignored, which should make working side by side interesting.

Similar to working with a hungry lion—death by snapping jaws could be imminent but at least it would never be boring.

Was he worried? Hard to answer. Dakota was a consummate professional and damn good at her job. She wouldn't let anything stand in her way of solving a case—especially one like this. But there was something between them still, he could feel it—and she did, too.

For both their sakes, he'd do his best to smother it. Neither could afford a messy break in their focus when each had something big riding on the outcome of this case.

Just as he knew she would be, Dakota was already in the parking lot, waiting. She didn't waste time on pleasantries, or even a half-hearted, perfunctory smile. God, his memory hadn't embellished the woman's beauty. Even in conservative street clothes, hair pulled in a tight ponytail, she was still stunning. He remembered with sharp clarity how it felt to let those long dark, silky strands slide through his fingertips. There wasn't a thing he *didn't* remember about Dakota Foster, but her hard-as-nails, zero-bend attitude was something he didn't miss.

They walked into Saint James Hospital, signed in with their credentials and made their way to the ICU department to meet with Dr. Patel before going into Cheyenne's room.

Dr. Patel, a man with a slight build and sharp, intelligent brown eyes, said with a subtle South Asian inflection, "I understand you're here to question my patient," he said, eyeing Ellis and Dakota warily. "But I must insist that you proceed with extreme caution. She's still very fragile. She's stable and her memory is improving but she struggles with details. She also tires easily so please keep your questioning to only what is necessary. Also, she doesn't respond to the name Cheyenne. She says her name is Zoey."

Ellis appreciated the information, asking, "Last name?"

"Grojan."

Ellis shared a look with Dakota, both thinking the same. Time to run background on the name Zoey Grojan. If she attended public school, went to the doctor or otherwise used public aid in anyway, that would give them a place to start looking for her whereabouts the past seventeen years.

"Thank you, Doctor," Dakota murmured. "We'll be mindful of her injury. Can you give us any guidance on how best to approach this?"

"Of course," Dr. Patel replied, softening slightly. "Try to avoid causing her too much stress or asking her to recall anything traumatic. Her brain is still healing, and we need to give it time."

That was like asking the sun not to rise. Everything surrounding the girl's existence was traumatic but Ellis would try. "Understood," Ellis said, his focus unwavering as he confirmed with Dakota. "We'll do our best to keep this as painless as possible."

Dr. Patel nodded and led them into the sterile room.

The seventeen-year-old girl looked small in the bed. She was petite with light brown hair, the bruising on her face standing out in a garish purple, black and blue across her cheekbones. The swelling had gone down, leaving behind a mess as the injuries continued to heal, but he supposed it was a small price to pay for being alive. The crash photos were pretty gnarly.

"Miss Zoey? These are the agents I told you were coming today. Are you up to talking to them?"

"Yes." The girl regarded them with wary apprehension, but in the same gaze, Ellis saw a flicker of resilience. The girl was a fighter. Ellis recognized the innate strength despite her battered body. She gingerly sat upright, wincing at the motion. A large bandage covered half her forehead and the steady beep of the machines monitoring her vitals punctuated the silence.

While some people purposefully angled for a position within the missing persons division, it was too far removed from the action he craved. In the two years since being unceremoniously dumped in the division, his opinion hadn't changed—there was too much desk work when he preferred to be in the field.

The narcotics division had been constant action—the threat

of danger around every corner had fueled his need for adrenaline in a way that Missing Persons never could. Not that it wasn't important work, but he was working his ass off to prove to Carleton he was ready to return to the action.

To prove that he'd changed in the ways that mattered.

Carleton seemed receptive to the idea, hinting that a win with this case might go a long way. So, he was going to throw everything he had at solving this case—through any means necessary.

The doc warned about pushing too hard, but the urgency of the situation made it impossible to tread too lightly. They needed answers—where had Zoey/Cheyenne been for the past seventeen years?

Might as well start at the obvious. "Hey, Zoey," he started in a soft, soothing tone, "my name is Ellis Vaughn and this is my partner, Dakota Foster. We're here to talk to you about your accident."

Zoey cast a nervous glance at Dr. Patel. "I don't remember much. Everything is kinda murky in my head."

"That's okay, we'll just see what we can get. Don't worry if you can't remember, okay?" Ellis said, purposefully hiding his impatience with a smile. "Just tell us whatever you can remember, no matter how small."

Zoey nodded, nervously fidgeting.

"You're not in trouble," Dakota assured the girl. "We just need to ask you a few questions about what happened and try to put together some missing information. Think of it like a puzzle and each piece has a place. Let us figure out where the pieces go."

"I'll try," she said.

"Anything you can tell us will help," Ellis said.

"Okay," she murmured, her voice barely audible.

"Zoey," Dakota began again, gently taking her hand. "Can you tell us anything about where you were going? Any details at all?"

The room seemed to hold its breath as Zoey considered the question, her brow furrowing in concentration. Finally, she said in a halting tone, "I don't remember where I was going but I... remember a farm of some kind? The sound of cows, chickens and maybe goats? I'm not sure… I remember firewood stacked on the side of the house."

"Did you live there?"

"I think so?"

"And your parents… Do you remember them?"

Zoey frowned, confusion creeping up on her expression. "Sort of? But I can't see their faces."

"That's okay," Ellis said, encouraging her. "What else?"

"I wanted to get away," she continued, slowly recalling, "I felt…closed up, like stuck in a bubble or something. That doesn't make sense, though, does it?"

"We're not sure yet, but you're doing great," Dakota assured her. "The doctor says your name is Zoey Grojan… But we know you as a different name."

"What do you mean?"

"Does the name Cheyenne Swiftwater mean anything to you?"

Zoey's expression crinkled into a baffled uncertainty. "Should it?"

They had to be careful how quickly they presented the facts of her case. She might not be ready to hear that she'd been kidnapped as an infant. "We'll get back to that," Dakota said quickly, moving on. "Do you remember the names of your parents?"

Zoey shook her head, her eyes welling with tears. "What if I never remember who I am?"

Dr. Patel intervened, shooting them a warning look for agitating his patient. "Don't worry, Miss Zoey, your memory will return. Your brain is still healing. Give it time."

"I'm sorry, I'm trying to remember," Zoey said to Ellis and Dakota as if needing their approval. "I'm not trying to be difficult."

Beneath the resilience there was a sweetness to Zoey that reminded Ellis of kids that were homeschooled. No shade against public school systems but homeschooled kids were just different, somehow softer than those exposed to a wide range of personality types and social situations, both good and bad.

"You're doing great," Ellis reassured her with a smile. "Rest

now. We'll be back to talk more tomorrow. You focus on getting better."

Dr. Patel followed them out and away from Zoey's doorway.
"Every day she gets stronger but brain injuries are unpredictable. I'll permit you to see her tomorrow but I need your assur-
ances that you won't push harder than she's ready."

Both Ellis and Dakota agreed, even if they were both guilty
of wanting to push a little harder.

They left the hospital and returned to their cars.

"Looks like we'll need to get a hotel because we'll be here
for a few days at least," Ellis said, checking his watch.

Dakota agreed but added unnecessarily, "Separate rooms,
of course."

"Of course," Ellis confirmed, slightly annoyed that she felt
compelled to make that point. She'd made it pretty damn clear
that she'd rather give a feral cat a bath than be anything more
than passingly civil with him.

Fine by me. He wasn't going to chase someone who didn't
want to be caught. Like he didn't have a phone full of women
who wouldn't mind some private time with him. He didn't need
the emotional scraps from an ice queen. *Whoa, was that called
for? She left for a good reason, remember that, buddy.* The
downside to going to therapy? Your therapist's voice was always in your head. "Closest hotel to the hospital is the Wayfair
Inn," he said.

"I don't need anything fancy. Just a decent bed and a shower.
I packed a suitcase just in case we ended up needing to stay."

Of course she did, Little Miss Always Prepared. He'd actually always appreciated that about her. Glad to see some things
hadn't changed.

"Yeah, same," he lied. He'd have to run over to the mall and
grab a few things.

"Great," she said, moving to unlock her car. "Let's get
checked in, then."

Dakota climbed into her sedan and punched the address into
GPS, then, she was gone.

Damn—it's like that, then.

Ellis sighed and climbed into his own car. This case, and

working with Dakota, was going to be like serving penance before transferring straight to hell.

Dakota couldn't get away from Ellis fast enough. Maintaining a professional distance hadn't prevented her from getting a whiff of his cologne—a signature scent that complimented his personality in a way that was intoxicating—and it brought back a slew of memories best forgotten.

Memories with the power to burn.

Put it away, Dakota growled to herself, irritated that she was even thinking of those things. Refocusing with fierce purpose, she navigated to the Wayfair Inn, which, as Ellis said, wasn't far from the hospital.

Ellis was only five minutes behind her. He entered the lobby just as she was finishing with her registration. She received the key, saying, only for safety and professional purposes, "I'm in room 218, second floor. Debrief tomorrow at 0700?"

"Only if it involves a copious amount of coffee and a doughnut," Ellis returned, reminding her that he wasn't an early riser.

She supposed they couldn't get to the hospital too early and grudgingly changed the time to 0800, which would put them back with Zoey by ten hundred, a more reasonable time.

Ellis agreed and she left him at the registration desk to sign in.

Once in her room, door firmly locked, she did a quick safety check of the room, making sure there weren't any two-way mirrors or loose locks on the windows, and that the door didn't have a gap between the frames. Being in law enforcement had completely corrupted the way she saw people. The complete depravity of humankind was too much to leave to chance. Although, if someone was stupid enough to try anything with her, they'd find themselves in a world of hurt. In her spare time, she volunteered at the women's shelter teaching self-defense. Maybe if her sister had known how to defend herself, she would still be here.

Removing her gun from its holster, she set it on her nightstand, always within grabbing distance when she traveled.

Grabbing her cell, she called Shilah to let her know she was checked in and what she'd learned from talking to the girl.

"She's pretty banged up," Dakota said, pulling her shoes off and wiggling her toes in relief. She hated wearing shoes. As a kid growing up on the reservation, she'd rarely worn shoes during the summer and into late fall, even. The bottoms of her feet had grown so calloused she could withstand almost anything without wincing, but she had "city feet" now.

Even so, she loved being free of the restrictive shoes. "Her face is bruised and her brain is still healing but I think a few more days of rest and she'll be ready for harder questions. Refresh my memory about the details on her biological mother."

"Not a whole lot beyond what was originally printed when she was killed," Shilah shared. "Let's see, the basics—Nayeli Swiftwater, nineteen, formerly of the Flathead Reservation, was found dead in her Whitefish apartment April 8, but there was no sign of her six-week-old infant, Cheyenne. Nayeli was working for one of the bigger chain hotels as a housekeeper and sending as much as she could to her disabled mother back at the reservation. Her mother has since been moved into a subsidized, long-term care facility in Missoula. Nayeli had a younger sister, Nakita, who got into trouble with drugs but has since cleaned herself up and lives in Missoula as well, presumably to be close to her mother."

"No other family?"

"Nakita has two kids but they're pretty young, only ten and six."

"Okay, thanks. Can you email me all of that information?"

"Sure." There was a beat, then Shilah asked, "Am I imagining things or was there tension between you and the FBI agent? Do you know each other?"

Dakota mentally cursed her inability to hide her emotions better. She'd always been accused of wearing her feelings on her sleeve and anyone wanting to know how she felt could just look at her face. She didn't want to lie to Shilah but she also wasn't ready to share. Still, it was hard to get the words out. "Uh, yeah, we have some history, nothing serious, but I don't really care for the guy."

"How'd you meet?"

A bar of all places. She hadn't known he was FBI, and he hadn't known she was BIA. They'd just been two people blowing off steam who happened to click one night over too many beers. And possibly a few shots of tequila. "It was casual. Like I said, nothing serious." The white lie tasted bitter but she and Ellis weren't planning a reunion tour of their relationship so it wouldn't matter. "But we're both professional so it shouldn't be a problem."

But then Shilah said, "Well, he's damn fine," and Dakota wanted to howl at the moon for the immediate insecurity that crawled up her throat. Of course Ellis was fine, that was his superpower. Women flocked to him like geese looking for something tasty to nibble. Shilah added, "I know you're too straitlaced to play like that but, girl, I wouldn't fault you none."

Dakota forced a chuckle she didn't feel, saying, "Well, if you knew his true personality, you'd understand. Ellis Vaughn is a hot mess."

A thread of concern replaced Shilah's playful interest. "Is he going to be a problem? Isaac could probably have him replaced if he's going to be a detriment to the case."

"No, Ellis is actually a really good investigator," Dakota said, "I can handle his personality. It'll be fine. If I thought he was a threat to the integrity of the case, I'd say something immediately."

That much was true. Dakota wouldn't let anything derail this case—and that included her personal feelings, one way or another.

Shilah relaxed, saying, "All right, so you're heading back to the hospital tomorrow?"

"Yes, hopefully, we can push a little harder."

"Sayeh and Levi sent out press releases to all the news outlets. You should start seeing the bulletins on the evening news in the area."

"Good. I don't think it'll take long before we start getting traction once the media does its thing," Dakota said, hoping that was true. The faster they got answers, the faster they could close this case.

She didn't want to spend a moment longer with Ellis than she had to.

For a number of reasons—not all of which were professional.

Chapter 3

Ellis arrived at the hospital a few minutes early, just as Dakota pulled into the parking lot. Was he trying to prove to Dakota that he'd changed since they'd broken up? No, but he also didn't want to hear her gripe at him for showing up a few minutes late. Some things weren't worth the hassle.

Whomever she was dating now, he wished them luck if they weren't cut from the same rigid piece of wood because Dakota didn't bend for anyone.

Dakota noted his bakery bag with a frown. "What's that?"

"Chocolate doughnut," he answered, adding, "For Zoey. Hospital food is the worst."

"How do you know she can have a doughnut?" Dakota asked. "Did you clear it with Dr. Patel?"

"It's a doughnut, Dakota, not drugs."

Dakota wouldn't budge. "She could have a food allergy. You're not giving her that doughnut," Dakota said with a stern shake of her head. "Absolutely not. It's unprofessional."

"The kid just went through something terrible. Something sweet might go a long way toward getting her to feel more comfortable around us. Did it ever occur to you that she's been conditioned to distrust strangers? She needs to trust us enough for her subconscious to open up to talking."

"And you think a doughnut is going to do that? You're putting a lot of faith in the power of a pastry."

"The power of chocolate," he corrected with a wink. "But if it puts your mind at ease, I'll ask her doc if it's okay before offering it to her. Does that meet with your approval?"

Dakota grudgingly agreed but he could tell she didn't like it. Of course she didn't like it. His methods weren't detailed in the manual in some obscure subsection of code that could be studied and analyzed. Sometimes you had to listen to your gut—and the kid felt lost and alone. Chocolate hit the center of the brain that controlled endorphins. Endorphins were the feel-good hormone. The kid needed something to make her feel safe.

Hence, chocolate.

"Let's keep the off-roading to a minimum," Dakota said stiffly before they walked into the hospital, going through the same motions as the day before. He ignored that bit of advice as unnecessary. She didn't need to school him like a rookie. He cut her a short look but otherwise kept his mouth shut.

As they walked to Zoey's room, Dakota debriefed him. "Shilah didn't find much more about the birth mother aside from what was already known but I forwarded the information to your email. Also, last night I caught a news report from the local stations with Zoey's information and photo. We should be wary of any crackpots showing up claiming to be Zoey's parents. This situation is ripe for human traffickers looking for an easy target."

Ellis nodded in agreement. "Hopefully, Zoey remembers a bit more today."

"Here's hoping," Dakota said, crossing her fingers.

They knocked softly on the doorframe before entering Zoey's room. Same as yesterday, Dr. Patel hovered like an over-protective helicopter parent, reminding them to be conservative in their questioning.

"Good morning, Zoey," Dakota said with a warm and engaging smile. "How are you feeling today?"

"A little better," she admitted, casting a glance at Dr. Patel, assuring him that she was okay. They must've had a private conversation prior to Ellis and Dakota arriving, establishing some kind of code. She saw the bag in Ellis's hand, suddenly curious. "What's that?"

Ellis smiled, holding the bag up. "This is a chocolate dough- nut from the mom-and-pop doughnut shop I found near my hotel, and if it's okay with your doc, it's got your name all over it. That is…if you like chocolate."

Zoey's eyes widened with excitement as she looked to Dr. Patel. "Please?"

Dr. Patel was uncertain. "We have no way of knowing if you have any food allergies," he said, to which Ellis knew in his bones Dakota was smugly saying in her head, "That's what I said," but in light of Zoey's hopeful expression, he relented, saying, "I suppose you're in the safest place if it turns out you're allergic. Go ahead."

Ellis handed Zoey the bag and she gleefully pulled the dough- nut out, taking a deep sniff of the pastry with complete delight before sinking her teeth in for a huge bite. Her squeal was worth any pushback from either the doctor or Dakota, although he had to admit, even Dakota smiled at the simple happiness the doughnut created for the girl.

"I *never* get to eat chocolate," Zoey admitted, savoring the bite. Then her eyes widened at the admission, realizing she'd remembered something. "Oh! That's right, chocolate was a big treat in my house. I remembered something!" She quickly took another bite as if it had magical powers. "My mom was real strict about sugar because 'sugar rots your teeth,' she said. We used honey or agave to sweeten things but nothing compares to this. Oh, this is sooo good! Thank you!"

Strict parents who didn't believe in letting their kids have sugar could be a clue.

Even the doctor smiled, losing some of his watchful stance. When it became apparent no allergic reaction was imminent, he said, "You seem to be tolerating the pastry without any ill ef- fects. If you think you'll be okay, I'll leave you with the agents but if at any point you feel taxed, don't feel bad about ending this little visit."

Zoey smiled and nodded. Ellis waited for the doctor to leave the room before whispering out of the side of his mouth to Zoey,

"I don't think the good doctor likes us very much. Maybe I ought to bring two doughnuts next time."

Zoey's small, tremulous smile was a win he'd take. Operation: Win Zoey's Trust seemed to be working. He dragged a chair to her bedside, saying, "I don't blame him, I blame the media. FBI agents get a bad rap. We're either the bad guys running over the little guys or we're the larger-than-life badasses that no one can relate to. I promise you, I'm no badass. The real badass," he shared in a conspiratorial whisper as he cast a glance in Dakota's direction, "is my partner. She can probably twist my spine into a pretzel without breaking a sweat but no one's going to think that because at first glance, she doesn't look strong enough to break a breadstick in half. Looks are deceiving, though."

Dakota chuckled in spite of herself—probably killed her to crack a smile at his joke—but he secretly enjoyed getting her to smile. Old habits died hard, he supposed.

Zoey's grin widened, until she winced from the pain and she sobered again, reminded of why they were there in the first place. "I think I remembered something new last night after you left," she shared.

Both Dakota and Ellis were all ears. "Yeah? What was that?" Ellis asked.

"Well, you asked me about my parents and I can't remember their names yet but I do remember my bedroom."

"Can you share what you remember?" Dakota prompted, pulling out her notebook.

"I remember my bedspread has a patchwork quilt and there are pencil sketches on the walls that I think I drew. The window overlooks a farm with all sorts of animals, but people, too. That's the part that's confusing to me."

"Maybe they're working the farm?" Dakota suggested.

But Zoey shook her head as if that didn't quite fit what she felt as true. "No, there's a lot of people…like entire families? Does that make sense?"

The wheels in Ellis's head started to turn faster. Was it possible Zoey lived in a commune? That would explain why there was no record of Zoey in the public school system and why she gave off a sheltered vibe. It also connected with the newfound

information about her parents' strict stance on sugars. Many
communes shied away from foods known to create dental issues as they had limited access to dental health. "Is it possible
you lived with a bunch of families?" Ellis asked.

Zoey frowned as she tested that theory in her head. She
winced but nodded even though she couldn't really be sure. "I
think that might be right."

"Do you remember going to school at any point?" Dakota
asked.

Zoey nodded, adding, "Yes, there was a room with a bunch
of kids, different ages though, and we all did our own thing...
I guess I was homeschooled?"

Bingo. Ellis nodded. "It would seem so. Nothing wrong with
that, though," he assured her when her expression dipped into
embarrassment. "Lots of kids are homeschooled these days."

"Yeah?"

Dakota chimed in, "Oh sure, with the internet, almost anyone can open a charter school these days. It's nothing to be
ashamed of."

"But is it weird? Seems weird. Why wouldn't my parents
want me to go to public school?"

Probably because you were kidnapped at six weeks old. But
she wasn't ready to hear that just yet. "I'm sure they had your
best interests at heart," he said with a disarming smile. "But
let's celebrate the fact that you're starting to remember things.
That's a great sign."

"You think so?"

Dakota immediately agreed. "Oh yes, absolutely. Your brain
is healing quickly. Before you know it, you'll be back to normal."

But that caused her expression to falter, as if she wasn't sure
she wanted to go back to what she'd known and that was another important key.

Ellis had a feeling the girl had been running for good reason.

Dakota hated that Ellis had been right to bring the doughnut,
but also hated that she couldn't seem to let him have the win
without feeling uncharitable. Maybe it was because she knew
how slippery a slope it could be when Ellis started breaking

rules. Not every means to an end was worth the risk. What if Zoey had been allergic to chocolate and started going into anaphylactic shock?

Then her doc would've sprung into action, logic reasoned, refusing to let her cling to a bullshit argument for the sake of her ego. The fact was, Ellis's instincts had been spot-on and she needed to let him have the win.

And it was something she wouldn't have thought of.

Ellis had once accused her of being too stiff to bend with the wind, which ultimately kept her rooted in one spot without hope of any growth.

She'd found his comment ridiculously unsupported by fact.

But maybe there was something to being able to bend a little.

She swallowed, forcing a bright smile for Zoey's benefit. They needed her to trust them. She grabbed a chair and pulled it closer, sharing, "If you like chocolate, I'll have to introduce you to my absolute favorite dessert—chocolate cheesecake. Now, I'll be honest, it's so rich, you can only eat a few bites before you tap out, but ohhh, those bites are worth it."

"I would love to try it," Zoey said, her eyes shining, admitting, "I think I have a sweet tooth."

"That's okay, there are worse things to have," Ellis said. "And I have to agree with Dakota, chocolate cheesecake is the best. We'll bring you some tomorrow."

Dakota ignored the flutter of memory that popped unwelcome in her head of the night Ellis had surprised her with a mini chocolate cheesecake and they'd shared it, feeding it to one another between kisses during a rain-soaked night, sitting beside a cozy fire while the storm raged outside the apartment.

Shaking off the feelings that rose up to choke her, Dakota said, "So, is it possible you lived in a commune?"

"What's a commune?" Zoey asked, confused.

"It's a small, tight-knit community that share like-minded belief structures, living on one property," Dakota explained, trying to lessen any stigma. "In this economy, we're seeing more people returning to that kind of community living."

"Um, yeah, I guess so," Zoey said, chewing on the side of her cheek. "Seems like that might be right."

Dakota tried to keep her excitement hidden. They were on the right track. All signs pointed to Zoey being raised off-grid somewhere, which would explain why the girl just disappeared after being abducted.

"Is there anything else you can remember? Any detail, no matter how small, might help," Ellis said.

Zoey stilled, pausing to wipe at her face with the small napkin, her gaze darting as if fighting the urge to share yet understanding the need to divulge certain information. Dakota wondered if Zoey's memory was better than she wanted to let on. If the girl was running from something bad, it made sense that she didn't want to be found.

Yet, there was a softness about Zoey that didn't lend itself to the suspicion that she was being purposefully deceitful. Dakota sensed Zoey was a sweet girl at her heart but there was definitely something she didn't want to share.

"Zoey...we're here to help you," Dakota assured her in a gentle voice. "I promise you, we can protect you if you're in some kind of trouble."

Zoey held Dakota's stare before flitting to Ellis's and Dakota could feel her wavering. The tension in the air was palpable. *C'mon Zoey, you can do it...* Dakota held her breath, sensing Zoey was close to revealing something important.

But then an anguished voice at the door caused them all to swivel their attention to a man and woman staring at Zoey with tears in their eyes. Both Dakota and Ellis rose to their feet in a protective stance, halting their rush toward Zoey's bed. Ellis immediately demanded, "Stop right there. Who are you?" with his hand resting on his holster, beating Dakota to it.

The woman, dressed in a simple cotton dress, her graying hair pulled into a severe bun, skidded to a shocked stop, drawing herself up as if offended by their mistrust, her chin lifting as she answered, "We're Zoey's parents and we're here to bring her home."

The hell you are—but you might just be the ones who killed her actual mother.

Chapter 4

"I beg your pardon?" The woman's confused expression mingled with the shock of being denied access to Zoey. The reaction seemed genuine enough but Ellis knew people to be very good actors when it suited them. The woman looked to her husband for backup, urging him to take control of the situation. "Ned, do something!"

The man, small-framed with a balding pate, tried to settle his wife. "Now, now, Barbara-Jean, they're just looking out for Zoey," he said. Introducing himself to Ellis, he said, "My name's Ned Grojan and this here's my wife, Barbara-Jean. We've been looking for Zoey since she run away and we came as soon as we saw her picture on the news."

"We're going to need to see identification," Dakota said firmly.

Ned pulled an old driver's license from his wallet and handed it to Ellis. Ellis didn't need to see the expiration date to know that it'd expired a long time ago. He narrowed his gaze. "This expired ten years ago. Do you have current ID?"

"We don't drive and we live off the grid," the woman replied stiffly as if it were none of their business how they lived and wouldn't stand for any judgment.

"How'd you get here if you don't drive?" he asked, returning the useless ID to the man.

"We have friends who brought us," Ned answered. "They're waiting in the lobby while we sort this all out."

"I hate to be the bearer of bad news but you're not leaving with Zoey anytime soon," Dakota said. "It will take time to process your identification seeing as you don't have current ID."

"This is preposterous," the woman sputtered indignantly. "Zoey is our daughter and you have no right to keep her from us."

Ellis turned to Zoey and saw the anguish and fear in her eyes. She definitely knew the couple but had she been running from them? Wordlessly, Dakota picked up the same vibe and stepped into action. "Why don't you come with me? We'll talk about this in private," she said, ushering them from the room, despite the woman's protests.

Ellis turned to Zoey. "Do you recognize that couple as your parents?" he asked.

Zoey hesitated, tears filling her eyes, her mouth working as if she didn't want to answer but felt compelled to. "I think so," she finally admitted in a small voice. "They look real mad."

"Have they hurt you?" Ellis asked quietly. "I can't help you if you're not honest. Tell me why you're afraid right now."

"I don't know," she said, shaking her head. "I'm so confused. I ran away for a reason but I can't remember why. Why would I run from my own parents unless they did something bad?"

It was solid logic. Ellis appreciated her attempt at reasoning things out under extreme circumstances. "I don't know but we'll help you find out," he said. "I promise you, you're not going anywhere with anyone until you are ready and able."

Zoey sagged with relief, her shoulders dropping from around her ears. "Thank you," she said. "I'm sorry if I'm being too much trouble."

"No need to apologize, Zoey. We're here to protect you and to find out what happened." *Such as how a six-week-old infant was kidnapped from her murdered mother.* That was at the top of his list. "I'll be back. Try not to worry."

Ellis left Zoey, found Dr. Patel, informed him of the situation, and everyone was taken to a private conference room for questioning.

"This is a travesty," Barbara-Jean exclaimed, pacing like a trapped cat. "My daughter suffered a major head trauma and I'm stuck in this room with you instead of by her bedside. I want to talk to your supervisor," she said, stabbing a finger in Ellis's direction. To Dr. Patel she said, "And shame on you for keeping a mother from her child. You should know better."

But Dr. Patel took the woman's judgment with barely a blink, saying, "Madam, my concern is for my patient, not your feelings. I will tell you the same thing I told the agents—if you stress my patient, you will be escorted from the premises."

Ellis was starting to appreciate the doctor's blunt manner. He gestured to the empty chairs around the conference table. "Let's all have a seat and talk," he said.

"I don't want—"

"Barbara-Jean!" the man cut in tersely. "Sit down. You're making things worse. Zoey is safe, that's what matters. The agents are just trying to make sure we're not deviants or something."

"Deviants?" Barbara-Jean gasped, sinking into the chair. "That's an obscene thought. We're her parents. And since when do FBI agents get involved with a runaway girl involved in a car accident? Something isn't right and if I don't start getting answers real soon..."

Might as well get to the meat of things. Ellis swiveled his gaze straight to the indignant woman. "Great. I'd also like answers. Where were you on the night of April 8, 2006?"

The woman balked with confusion. "What? What kind of question is that?" She looked to her husband, who was equally baffled by the sudden shift in direction. "What does that have to do with our daughter's accident? What's going on?"

"That's the night Zoey's *biological* mother was murdered in her Whitefish apartment and her infant daughter—the one you claim is your daughter—was kidnapped," Dakota provided flatly, watching for their reaction just as he was. "So you can imagine how we're not so keen to just let you waltz in and take custody of Zoey."

Neither reacted in a way that betrayed guilt, only deep, horrified bewilderment.

Ned spoke first, reaching over to clutch his wife's hand in support. "I'm sorry but I think you've got us turned around a bit. What do you mean?"

"My partner was pretty clear," Ellis said. "Before Zoey was Zoey Grojan, she was born Cheyenne Swiftwater. Did you know her mother, Nayeli Swiftwater?"

"I'm her mother," Barbara-Jean shot back in a watery tone as she tried to hold herself together. "She's my daughter. You can't take her from me."

"Did you know Nayeli Swiftwater?" Ellis asked again, ignoring the woman's declaration.

Barbara-Jean's lip quivered as she looked to her husband but she shook her head in answer. "I've never heard of that name before in my life."

Dakota looked to Ned. "And you?"

He also shook his head. "We adopted Zoey in a closed adoption. We never knew her birth parents and preferred it that way. We thought it best to raise Zoey without the burden of knowledge that she was adopted."

"Do you have paperwork supporting the adoption process?" Dakota asked.

"Of course," Barbara-Jean answered, but her lip continued to quiver as if she were barely holding herself together. "Back at home."

"We're going to need to see that documentation," Ellis said. "What was the name of the adoption agency?"

"It wasn't an agency," Ned admitted, looking uncomfortable, as if just now realizing that there might be some truth to the horrific story they were investigating. "It was private. We didn't ask a lot of questions because we were so happy to finally have a child to complete our family."

"Did you think a baby just dropped out of the sky?" Dakota asked. "You didn't think it was a little odd that a newborn just showed up as available when it takes years for people to get a newborn?"

"I hear the judgment in your voice, Agent Foster, and I don't appreciate it. You don't know our story or our journey, so please keep your judgment to yourself," Barbara-Jean snapped, in spite of her husband's attempts to keep her under control.

Dakota's cold smile had the power to put the fear of God into the most hardened criminals but Barbara-Jean was oblivious to the danger she was in. "I'll ask one more time—where were you on the night of April 8, 2006?"

"Not murdering people in a Whitefish apartment, if that's what you're asking," Barbara-Jean shot back, her chin lifted. "This is…outrageous. We have the documentation. We did everything we were asked. You have no right to keep us from our daughter."

Ellis rose and Dakota followed his lead. "Until we can determine whether or not you had anything to do with the murder of Nayeli Swiftwater, we're taking you into custody for further questioning."

"What?" The word escaped Barbara-Jean's mouth in an explosion of incredulity but Dakota was already pulling her arms behind her and fastening the handcuffs. "What is happening right now?" she gasped in a shrill tone, looking to her husband. "Are you kidding me? You're arresting us?"

The husband, shaking his head, realizing it was futile to argue, calmly allowed Ellis to handcuff him. "We'll get it sorted, Barbara-Jean," he assured her. "We've done nothing wrong. Just calm down and don't make it worse."

"It can't possibly get worse!"

That cold Dakota smile surfaced again as she quipped, "Oh, I assure you, if we find out you had anything to do with Nayeli's murder, it most certainly can and will."

Dakota knew the kind of woman Barbara-Jean Grojan was the minute she walked into the room—overbearing, stubborn and rigidly certain her way was the only way—so it didn't come as a huge shock that Barbara-Jean put up a fuss as soon as she realized they weren't going to let her get near Zoey.

Their story might be legit—desperate people willing to look the other way when a baby became available wasn't farfetched—but Dakota would never understand how anyone could just accept an infant without question and expect nothing illegal was involved.

Babies didn't just fall from the sky.

It seemed the height of selfishness that people would turn a blind eye to the possibility that their precious bundle might've been ripped from the arms of its birth mother without consent.

Coordinating with local police, the Grojans were transported to the police department where Ellis and Dakota could continue their questioning in a more controlled environment, which was a relief to the hospital staff as their presence on the wing was already a disruption.

Dakota sent the Grojans' details to Shilah to run background and Shilah was quick with the information.

"According to public records, the Grojans were your typical American couple, paid their taxes and otherwise were pretty average until 2006 when they simply dropped off the grid," Dakota shared with Ellis. "Ned Grojan was an accountant and Barbara-Jean a dental hygienist. One day, they both quit their jobs, liquidated their accounts, including their 401(k), and disappeared."

"That's not suspicious," Ellis joked. "Totally normal."

"Exactly. Something tells me there's more to the Grojans than meets the eye," Dakota said.

"Mmm, my favorite kind of suspect. Let's see how long it takes for them to spill their secrets."

"My money's on Ned. He looks the least likely to cling to a story."

Ellis agreed. "My guess is that after being married to Barbara-Jean for almost twenty years, a nice long stay in a quiet cell might feel like a vacation."

Dakota chuckled and followed Ellis into the room where Ned awaited. He was still handcuffed and secured to a special bolt in the metal table. His wife was in a holding cell elsewhere in the building.

"Where's my wife?" he asked as soon as they entered the room. "She gets anxious in new surroundings. She's probably very upset right now."

"Probably," Dakota agreed, settling in the chair opposite Ned and continuing without a missing a beat. "Okay, so let's get back to the truth. If you're truly innocent, you're going to need to be more forthcoming about how you acquired a stolen baby."

"Please stop calling Zoey a stolen child. It makes me feel sick to my stomach," Ned implored. "To us, she was a gift from God. We had no idea that she'd been taken from her birth mother."

"Sure, that's possible but it doesn't negate the facts—*Cheyenne* was *taken* when her birth mother was murdered and given to you and we need to know by whom."

Ned's eyes sparkled with tears. "I swear to you, we didn't know anything about that."

"Who facilitated the adoption?" Ellis asked.

Ned hesitated, torn between saving himself and protecting the person involved. Impatience sharpened Dakota's tone. "In case it wasn't clear, without information proving your innocence, you're our number one suspect in a murder/kidnapping case, so I suggest you find your way clear to giving up some names."

"We're not guilty of murder or kidnapping," Ned stubbornly maintained.

"Prove it," Ellis countered.

"How?" Ned asked, licking his lips, confused. "How can I prove I didn't commit murder?"

"Let's start with the basics. Explain to us why you went off-grid at the exact time, or near to it, that Nayeli Swiftwater was killed,"

To refresh Ned's memory, Dakota said, "You liquidated all of your accounts and basically disappeared. Why? In our experience, the only people who do that are usually running or hiding from something or someone. Why would an accountant and a dental hygienist leave behind everything they'd worked for—" she snapped her fingers "—like that unless they were trying to run from something?"

"You've got it all wrong," Ned said, shaking his head. "We weren't running from our lives, we were closing a chapter and starting a new one, a fresh one with people who shared our values. Do you believe in God, Agent Foster?"

Dakota hated that question. After her sister's gruesome murder, she'd lost a lot of her faith. "Get to the point," she warned.

"Barbara-Jean and I realized a long time ago that the world

had lost its way and we were tired of trying to right the ship. We prayed about it and realized the best use of our energy would be to find those who shared our faith and start over. That's when we met Zachariah."

That was a new name.

"Zachariah who?" Ellis asked. "Is he your pastor or something?"

"He's so much more than a pastor. He's our mentor, leader, friend, trusted confidant…and miracle worker."

"Tall order for a single man. Does he walk on water, too?" Dakota quipped.

"You joke because you can't possibly understand our calling. Zachariah formed The Congregation in the hopes of creating more space for like-minded people who simply want to be left alone to live cleanly off the land, supporting one another and raising our children to love God."

Dakota suppressed the shudder. In her line of work, often when cults reared their ugly head it was never as innocuous as it sounded on paper. There was always something dark working in the background. She suspected this would turn out to be no different. "Sounds like paradise," she quipped. "We need a name."

"If you could just let me make a phone call—"

"Name," Ellis cut in, getting impatient. He had just as much tolerance for zealots as Dakota. "Give us a name."

Ned clearly didn't want to but when he realized neither Ellis nor Dakota were interested in playing any games, he relented with a sigh, sharing, "Zachariah Deakins."

"Great," Dakota said. "And an address for Mr. Deakins?"

"10045 Sommerset Road. The Congregation owns a thirty-acre place outside of Stevensville."

"See? That wasn't so hard, was it?" Dakota said, rising and knocking on the door. A uniformed officer appeared. "Officer, please escort Mr. Grojan back to his cell and bring Mrs. Grojan in."

"Wait—I thought—"

"You thought wrong," Ellis cut in as the officer took Ned down the hall. To Dakota, he said, "You thinking cult?"

"Yep." Dakota was already texting Shilah the details so she

could run backgrounds on Zachariah Deakins. "And those are rarely as 'Kumbaya, my Lord' as people want others to believe."

Ellis grinned. *"Amen* to that, sister."

Chapter 5

Barbara-Jean's eyes, red and puffy from tears, blazed with indignant fire the instant she was ushered into the room and restrained to the metallic table. Her voice, although strained, boomed with a fusion of frustration and demand. "This is outrageous. We have rights! This is America, not a third-world country, and I demand to speak with my husband. You have no right—"

Ellis interjected, curtailing her tirade with a firm yet calm demeanor, allowing little space for her to further erupt. "Let's streamline this discussion for the sake of efficiency," he advised, maintaining unflinching eye contact with the older woman. "You are being lawfully detained while we conduct an inquiry. We aim to ascertain whether you should be charged with the murder of Nayeli Swiftwater and the kidnapping of her infant daughter, Cheyenne. Your cooperation would be in your best interest."

In the silence that ensued, the weight of Ellis's words hung heavily in the air, trapping Barbara-Jean in a predicament where her next words could dictate the path forward and one wrong move could land her in hot water.

Deflated, Barbara-Jean whimpered, her eyes flicking between Dakota and Ellis, attempting to discern the sincerity in his statement. After a moment, she gave a terse nod, signaling her reluctant agreement to cooperate. "Ask your questions. The sooner this charade is over, the sooner I can be with my daughter," she declared with a shaky voice.

"Great. We appreciate your cooperation," Dakota responded, flipping open her notebook. "Can you tell us how you came to adopt Cheyenne?"

"Her name is Zoey!" Barbara-Jean snapped back, her voice laced with a mixture of defiance and protectiveness. "You will call her by her proper name. Do you understand? Her name is *Zoey.*"

Barbara-Jean seemed on the verge of losing her emotional stability. Ellis recognized that if they pushed her too hard, she might collapse under the pressure and they would lose any opportunity to extract answers from her. He exhaled softly, choosing to employ a gentler approach. "Mrs. Grojan, may we get you something to drink?" he offered, presenting a disarming smile. "Perhaps a coffee or some water?"

"A water would be nice," she admitted with a stiff upper lip, shooting Dakota a sour look. "You've no cause to treat me so poorly. I didn't have anything to do with the death of that woman."

Ellis glanced at Dakota, prompting her to exit the room. She returned shortly with a bottle of water, which she opened before handing it to Barbara-Jean. Accepting the water with an air of it being the bare minimum they could do, Barbara-Jean nevertheless took a sip with apparent gratitude. Her hands trembled as she awkwardly lifted the bottle to her lips, the handcuffs inhibiting her movements.

After a drawn-out moment during which Barbara-Jean seemed to regain some composure, she began to speak with a reluctant tone. "For years we tried to have a child naturally, but God didn't bless us that way. We attempted to adopt through the foster care system and various charitable organizations but couldn't find a suitable match. We were looking to raise an infant, while most available children were part of sibling groups or were older."

The foster care system was brimming with children in need of stable homes, but many of them came with emotional challenges that numerous prospective parents were ill-equipped to handle. Securing an infant for adoption was considered the pinnacle, often unattainable without substantial financial resources—the damn Holy Grail of adoptions.

Given this context, Ellis queried, "So, understanding the challenges of being placed with an infant, didn't you find it peculiar when one miraculously became available to you?"

"No, we believed God had answered our prayers," Barbara-Jean responded, her voice devoid of deceit. She seemed to sincerely believe that they had been recipients of a divine miracle.

Blind faith gave Ellis indigestion. He didn't need to see Dakota's expression to know that she felt the same. They were different in a lot of ways, but the same in others.

"And who was this miracle worker?" Dakota asked, looking to cross-reference what Ned had shared.

But unlike her husband, Barbara-Jean didn't hesitate. "Zachariah Deakins," she shared with a hint of reverence in her tone. "He came to us with our beautiful Zoey, blessing us with the most incredible gift, and we'll forever be grateful. She's been the brightest blessing of our lives and I will never apologize for that."

Ellis didn't sense any subterfuge from the woman or guilt. She truly believed what she was saying, but why would Zoey run away from a happy home?

Dakota picked up his mental thread without missing a beat. "Let's set that aside for a minute. Help us to understand why Zoey was so anxious to get away from your *blessed* home that she ended up wrecking in her haste to escape?"

Fresh tears filled Barbara-Jean's eyes as she broke down. "We never wanted her to know she was adopted but she found those blasted papers in Ned's desk. I told him we should've burned them but Ned insisted that we keep them, saying they were official documents that Zoey might need at some point in her life. I told him it was unnecessary because Zoey's life was with us, on the farm, not out with the worldly people."

"Zoey was upset at discovering she was adopted?" Dakota asked.

"Terribly," Barbara-Jean admitted mournfully. "I think her

heart was shattered. She was so angry with us for keeping that secret. I thought it would pass but then we woke up one morning to find the car and Zoey gone. We've been looking for her ever since she left. You have to believe me, we were devastated to learn she'd gone and we were worried sick. Zoey had never left the farm in her life. She had no idea what horrors awaited her out there."

"The car was registered to a man who died years ago. Why did you have possession of the vehicle?"

"The car belonged to The Congregation," Barbara-Jean said. "Everyone had access to it, should they need it."

"But it hasn't been registered to anyone in five years. The original owner is listed as deceased."

"The car was gifted to The Congregation and Zachariah handles the finances and paperwork. You'll have to ask him about the registration details. All I know is that when we needed transportation, we all had use of the vehicle but we rarely went to town unless it couldn't be avoided."

"And why is that?" Dakota asked.

"Because worldly people are a contagion of the spirit. Godlessness can be catching. It's best to limit contact."

Dakota looked like she was biting her tongue in half and Ellis couldn't blame her.

"So Zoey ran away because she discovered she was adopted?" Ellis summarized.

"Yes."

But was that the whole story? Seemed likely not. Zoey didn't seem the dramatic type. "Are you sure that's all that sent her running?"

"What are you implying?" Barbara-Jean asked sharply, her gaze narrowing. "If you're asking if we abused our daughter, you're out of line."

"You've never hit Zoey?" Dakota asked.

"In anger? Absolutely not. But discipline is not abuse. We disciplined our child, in accordance with God's law, and I won't be made to feel as if I've done anything wrong. It's our job as parents to raise our child to be kind, loving and respectful of God's word."

"And what does that mean exactly?" Ellis pressed. "Because some of the Old Testament stuff is pretty harsh."

"I'm not going to justify my parenting decisions. I've answered your questions and now I wish to see my husband or a lawyer. One or the other."

Barbara-Jean was finished cooperating and there was little point in keeping her. The officer returned the woman to her cell while Ellis and Dakota traded notes.

"She's clearly rigidly religious and some of those types of people have been known to be physically abusive in the name of God, so maybe we need to go back to Zoey and see if she remembers being abused at the hands of her adopted parents," Dakota said, scribbling down her notes. "What do you think?"

"Agreed. Although her husband seems more levelheaded, more mild-mannered. I'm not getting a killer vibe from either of them, though."

"Me, either. More's the pity," Dakota quipped. "That woman could do with a little time behind bars. I think it might humble her into being a nicer person."

He chuckled. "Maybe, or it might make her meaner. I've seen it go both ways."

Dakota sighed. "Well, at least we have a lead. Shilah is running background on this Deakins character. In the meantime, we don't have anything we can hold the Grojans for so we're going to have to let them go but they aren't leaving with Zoey. I'll take that as a small victory."

"We gotta take them where we find them, right?"

She smiled in response, adding, "I'd like a guard posted to keep them from having access for the time being. Until we know more about the quality of Zoey's childhood, I don't want them around her."

"Fair enough," Ellis agreed, pausing before sharing, "You're still sharp as a tack in interrogations. Impressive."

Dakota shifted against his praise, as if uncomfortable with how it made her feel, and he immediately wished he'd kept his feelings to himself, but she moved on quickly, saying, "I'm going to head back to the hotel and do some more research on this Congregation and see what I can find. I'll let you know if anything important pops up."

"Great. I'll let the officers know they can release the Grojans for now," he said, taking her lead.

Dakota didn't linger. She scooped up her notebook and left him behind.

The picture of cold efficiency.

Damn it, Ellis, should've kept your mouth shut.

It was such a small thing—a compliment between colleagues—so why was her heart hammering to a wild beat inside her chest?

It shouldn't matter what Ellis thought about her personally. She didn't live for or need his praise. And yet, a sweet warmth spread beneath her breastbone at the simple words as if it *did* matter to her how he felt about her.

Get a grip, you're embarrassing yourself.

She detoured to the grocery store to pick up something to eat—the hotel room had a tiny refrigerator and she disliked eating out too much when on assignment—and then after changing, headed to the hotel gym.

The best way to calm a disordered mind was to sweat out the extra noise.

Shilah was still running background so she had time to kill.

She went straight to the treadmill, popped her headphones in and set the pace. The best thing about most hotels was that it was easy to find an open station on the gym floor. Most people didn't go on vacation to sweat unless it was beneath the hot sun while sipping a margarita. The only people using the gym were like her, traveling for work, and on the job.

There was only one other person, another woman, using the facility and after perfunctory smiles, they were happy to leave each other in peace.

The treadmill helped her to think. There was something calming about the rhythmic motion of her feet slapping the high-grade rubber belt as her pace ate up imaginary miles.

The case immediately came to mind. As much as it would be an easy win if the Grojans were guilty of murdering Nayeli, her gut didn't support that theory. They might have extremist beliefs, but they didn't give off a killer vibe.

And her gut was always right.

Sweat rolled down her temple as the first wave of heat flushed through her body. She welcomed the punishing pace she set for herself, accepting the discomfort of fatigued muscles because it meant she was feeling something.

She started running after the death of her sister. Not on purpose, but one morning a week after Mikaya was found brutally murdered, she stepped outside her mother's house and, suddenly, she was running barefoot down the dusty road, numb to the fact that rocks were digging into her feet and tearing her soles. Tears had streamed down her cheeks as her rage and grief coalesced into fuel for her muscles and running had helped her manage the pain churning inside her.

After that moment, she became addicted to the release that running provided for her emotionally. She ran track in high school and later college, but now, she laced up to deal with stress that came with the job.

The other woman finished her run, wiped down her machine and left. Minutes later, a large man entered, choosing a treadmill uncomfortably close to her own when there were plenty of available machines.

Dakota's sense of awareness sharpened, dampening her enjoyment of her run. "You're quite the runner," he observed, trying to make conversation while he started his own jog. "You staying here at the hotel?"

Dakota ignored the man, giving him the cold shoulder to communicate that she wasn't here to chitchat, but at the same time, she was highly aware of his every movement. The red flags were flapping and Dakota never ignored what was flapping in her face.

"Oh, I see how it is, too good to talk to me, huh?"

Dakota swore beneath her breath and cut her run short. Shutting down the machine, she hopped off and wiped down, going to the hang bar to do some quick pull-ups before returning to her room.

One of the largest failings of ingrained patriarchal conditioning was women's reluctance to appear rude, which often caused them to ignore that inner voice when something wasn't right. Dakota didn't give two shits about seeming rude. Maybe if Mikaya had been a bitch to whoever killed her, she'd still be here.

From her peripheral vision, she caught movement and saw that the man had left his machine to head her way. His energy was arrogant and mildly predatory. Dakota summed him up within minutes. Older, traditionally good-looking, accustomed to getting what he wanted because of his looks, probably frequently told women to "smile more" because their worth was based solely on how screwable they appeared to him, and his ego was bigger than his sense of self-preservation.

And he thought Dakota was an easy target because she was a petite woman alone in a deserted gym.

Wrong.

"I love a woman with muscle," he said, openly leering at Dakota as if ogling a complete stranger without invitation was appreciated. "Pretty strong for such a little girl. I bet you're tight all over."

Final straw.

Dakota met his gaze, staring him down. "If I'd wanted to talk to you, I would've when you first interrupted my gym time. Take the hint and leave me alone."

He chuckled as if Dakota's firm warning was cute. "I find women like you just need a man to show them how to be soft, how to be feminine. You don't want too much muscle, sweetheart. A man wants a soft lady to cuddle up with at night."

"Last warning, mind your business, and stay out of mine."

"Or what, Pocahontas?" He made the mistake of trying to caress her cheek as if it was his right to touch her and Dakota reacted with the lightning-quick reflexes of a feral cat. She snatched his hand away from her jaw and cranked his fingers in the opposite direction they were made to go and drove him straight to his knees. He garbled a sharp yell, the agony keeping him locked in place as one more move and she'd snap his fingers in two.

"I get that you're from a generation that embraced casual misogyny, classism and blatant racism but let this serve as an educating moment—if a woman isn't interested in your attention, don't force it on her. Also, Pocahontas was a real person who suffered unimaginable horror as a child at the hands of a white man, who probably looked a lot like you, so keep her name out of your mouth unless it's spoken with the respect it's due. Now, my guess is that you've gotten away with this kind of disgusting behavior in the past, which has emboldened you—"

The man interrupted her with a wild swing with his free hand, shouting, "You stupid whore!" landing a lucky glance against her cheek, but it was only enough to throw her momentarily. Dakota snapped the fingers in her grip, breaking the bones like cracking a carrot in half, sending him writhing to the floor.

"Never mind. You're too stupid to learn," she said, rubbing at her bruised cheek. "You messed with the wrong girl. I'm a BIA agent and you assaulted a federal officer. Hope you didn't have plans for the evening because your ass is going to jail."

The man groaned, cradling his mangled fingers, and Dakota used the gym phone to call the front desk for security.

As the man was hauled off by two burly uniformed security officers, Dakota was surprised to see Ellis walk into the gym facility, apparently with the same idea of blowing off some steam, but when he saw Dakota, his expression darkened. "What the hell happened here?" he asked, his gaze going straight to the gathering bruise on her cheek.

She shook her head. "Nothing. Some jerkwad thinking he could get handsy with me. He'll think twice about doing that again."

"Did you break his fingers?" Ellis asked with a knowing expression.

"Yep."

"You okay?"

There was that warmth again. She stuffed it down and away, jerking a nod, shrugging as if it was no big deal. "I'm fine. I'm more embarrassed than anything that he got a lucky shot. I was off my game."

A smile curved the corner of his mouth, as if he were impressed and proud, even if he wasn't supposed to acknowledge that kind of thing between them. "Go put some ice on that bruise," he said, shaking his head. "You don't want to scare Zoey tomorrow."

She grinned in spite of her resolve to keep it professionally distant between them, then winced as the bruised flesh protested the motion.

Ouch. Ice was a good idea.

"See you tomorrow."

"Bright and early, Mike Tyson," he quipped, heading for the treadmill.

She chuckled and left him to his workout.

Chapter 6

Zoey wouldn't be available until later in the afternoon, so Dakota and Ellis decided to convene in Ellis's room for a Zoom meeting with Shilah.

Dakota, with a faint purple-and-blue bruise subtly discoloring her cheek from the gym altercation the previous day, opted to ignore her better judgment and brought along Ellis's favorite muffins—poppy seed. She did this as a self-assurance that she wasn't treating Ellis any differently than she would other colleagues in the field. Admittedly, the choice of poppy seed might have been slightly indulgent.

Ellis's eyes sparkled at the sight of the muffins. "How did you read my mind?" he inquired, eagerly reaching for one.

"You've never encountered a poppy seed muffin you didn't want to devour," Dakota said. "No matter the place or its source. I've watched you eat a muffin from a gas station convenience store, even when it was past its sell-by date."

"Are you implying my mind is easy to figure out?" he quipped, relishing each bite of the muffin with unabashed enjoyment.

The essence of Ellis lay in his steadfast appreciation for life's simple pleasures. While far from a simple man, the things that brought him joy were endearingly uncomplicated: the innocent sound of a child's laughter, the serene blue skies on a summer day and the taste of a freshly baked poppy seed muffin.

Dispelling a moment of nostalgia, Dakota pivoted toward the task at hand, opening her laptop for the scheduled Zoom meeting with Shilah. "I was thinking last night—"

"Was that before or after your impressive Special Ops takedown of that dumbass in the gym?" Ellis interjected, his grin teasing.

Suppressing a chuckle, she shot back, "You have seeds in your teeth," gracefully deflating his jest. "And for the record, he got what he deserved. I regret nothing."

Her words lingered in a space where lighthearted banter met the underlying pulses of their shared past, a balance that felt dangerously delicate. It was too easy to fall into a comfortable place with Ellis and that's what made her pull back.

"How's your boss gonna feel about it? The paperwork will probably be hitting his desk today."

Dakota laughed ruefully because she didn't know how Isaac would react but she still didn't regret a thing. Some men remained predators until someone made them stop. Dakota was happy to be the stopping point. "He thought it was okay to touch me without my consent. He learned the hard way it wasn't."

"No argument from me. I'm kinda tempted to get the surveillance footage just so I can watch the show."

"Surveillance footage of what?" Shilah broke in, sliding into her window screen. "What am I missing?"

"Just Dakota breaking fingers and righting social injustices one misogynist at a time," Ellis quipped.

Shilah laughed. "Well, that sounds like fun. What happened?"

Dakota rolled her eyes, giving Shilah the quick summary, and when she finished Shilah was hooting with appreciation and support. "Yesss, girl! Although, I probably wouldn't have stopped at his fingers. The man would've been sporting a broken jaw, too."

Dakota chuckled. "Well, hopefully, he's learned a valuable lesson and it'll encourage him to be less of a shit person in the future."

"Not likely, too old at this point, but worth it, I say," Shilah said.

"You're probably right," Dakota agreed, adding, "Still not sorry."

"I don't blame you. All right, I did some digging into your Zachariah Deakins but I don't think you're going to like what I found."

"What do you mean?" Dakota asked, frowning.

"I mean, he's seemingly clean as a whistle. Not even an outstanding parking ticket. I was really hoping to find some tax evasion or something but nothing juicy. It's pretty boring. Definitely not the picture of a crazy cult leader getting ready to pass out spiked punch."

Shilah put up a picture of Zachariah Deakins on the screen and Dakota agreed. He looked like the host of a children's television show about nature, meditation and respecting the earth.

"I don't trust anyone who can pull off a haircut that should've been made illegal after the seventies," Ellis said. "I mean, c'mon, who is this guy? That bushy beard should be a crime in itself. There's probably birds nesting in that thing."

Dakota barked a laugh, forgetting how funny Ellis could be. She sobered quickly. "Looks can be deceiving. We have an address for The Congregation. We'll have to schedule a meeting."

"You're not worried about leaving Zoey alone?" Shilah asked.

Ellis quipped, "Even if we didn't have an officer on guard at her room, I doubt anyone could get past Dr. Patel. The man is very protective of his patients."

Dakota nodded. "No one is getting past the good doc. We're going to talk to Zoey later this afternoon. Hopefully, we can get a better idea of why she was truly running away in the first place."

"Didn't the mom say it was because she discovered she was adopted?" Shilah asked.

"Yeah, but that seems flimsy. I don't know, something seems off. I'm hoping she can trust us enough to tell us what really happened," Dakota said.

"How's her head injury?" Shilah asked.

"Better each day. I think she's holding back because she's

afraid of something," Ellis answered. "She's really a sweet kid. Now that we know a bit more about The Congregation, it makes sense that she seems a little naive. The kid has lived her entire life isolated on a farm with a bunch of people who believe outsiders are bad."

"Exactly, so why would such a sheltered kid run like a bat out of hell away from the only life she's ever known?" Dakota pondered, then decided, "Yeah, something's not adding up."

"I emailed you both the Deakins background details. You can go over it and see if anything stands out that I might've missed."

"Thanks, Shilah," Dakota said. "We'll be in touch."

Shilah waved and ended the meeting.

Both Ellis and Dakota took a minute to peruse the file from their email. Ellis asked, "Ever wonder what makes a person go from completely typical to 'I think I want to create my own cult'? Do they wake up one morning, eat some cornflakes and decide, 'Today is the day I walk away from normal society and rewrite the rules to suit my personal vision of how the world should be run.' Honestly, if it were me, I think I'd come up with a better name than The Congregation."

"Is that so? And what name would you pick?" Dakota had to ask.

The second she saw his immediate grin, followed by his answer, "Ellisville, of course," she didn't even try to stop the laugh even though nothing about their case was funny.

Still, it felt good to joke with Ellis again.

Even if it shouldn't.

That laugh, her smile, the way the corners of her eyes crinkled with true amusement, it was like a lightning bolt straight to his heart.

Man, their breakup still hurt. He missed her more than he was allowed to say. She left for a good reason but he should've been honest about why he didn't fight to keep her.

No one ever talked about how being noble sometimes sucked ass. He'd like to say that nobility had kept him from chasing after her, but that would be a lie.

His pride had stuck in his craw, too.

He'd been embarrassed by his lack of control and scared of being too much like his old man to drag Dakota down with him while he figured things out.

But, damn, the last two years evaporated in the sunshine of that smile.

Dakota sobered and their gazes met. That electricity that seemed to spark whenever they were around each other started to snap. He wanted to kiss her. The pull to taste her lips, to feel that familiar brush of her soft mouth across his, created a physical ache that shouldn't be real but he felt in his bones.

Shake it off. Don't blow it. She doesn't want you and she's made herself pretty clear on that score. Focus on the case.

It took superhuman strength to pretend that he wasn't feeling a damn thing as he pulled away on the guise of cleaning up his muffin crumbs, saying, "All right, so we have about an hour before we can head to the hospital. I'm going to run some errands beforehand and meet you there, yeah?"

Dakota blinked as if momentarily caught off guard by his not-so-subtle hint that it was time for her to go but she recovered quickly. She gathered her laptop and stuffed it in her bag with a short nod. "Yes, sounds good," she said and quickly left.

The energy between them was palpable. There was no way she didn't feel it but she'd made it very clear that she wasn't interested in the reunion tour of Ellis and Dakota and he'd never disrespect her boundaries.

He liked his fingers the way they were.

Speaking of, he wasn't joking when he said he'd love to see the surveillance footage. The thing was, Dakota was a badass. She didn't look it but she was tougher than anyone gave her credit for. A compact package of lean muscle and hard attitude with a mouth that—yeah, best not to revisit those memories.

But the memories were riding him hard.

His body buzzed with pent-up energy with nowhere to go. Was it too late to run down to the gym and punish himself with a quick workout? No, he couldn't take the chance of running into Dakota when he said he was going to run errands. He'd just have to let it dissipate on its own, knuckling down on the urge to catch up with Dakota and spill his guts in the hopes that she'd forgive him and they could repair what he'd broken.

Ah, hell, what a pipe dream and a waste of time. Dakota wasn't like any woman he'd ever known. She didn't waver, didn't give second chances, and once her mind was made up, it was a steel trap that nothing could force open.

Give it up, man. What you had was great, but it's gone. Focus on the case.

Grabbing his keys, he resigned himself to hitting the mall. Perhaps he could find something for Zoey. Everyone liked getting gifts—especially sheltered kids who rarely got chocolate and never left their compound.

He didn't know the details of Zoey's life on the compound but it was hard to imagine it as anything less than dull. Kids were meant to go to Disneyland, have sleepovers, play sports or something. Childhood was over in a flash. Why shorten the experience by sucking all the joy out of it?

Not that he'd know what it was like to have an idyllic childhood but maybe that's why he felt so strongly about it. He knew what it was like to live in fear, not knowing if that uneven footfall down the hallway would stop at your door, as the old man swayed on his feet staring into your darkened room, deciding whether or not he had the wherewithal to deliver a random beating to the kid shaking silently in his bed.

Had Zoey's childhood been like his? Was the Grojans' idea of parental love peppered with harsh discipline?

He thought of Nayeli, the young mom who'd been doing her best to be a good provider for her infant, only to have her life cut short for reasons they didn't understand yet.

His cell rang and it was a buddy still in Narcotics. He hesitated to take the call. When he was forced out and demoted, he'd cut off most ties, believing everyone had turned against him from his old division, but that'd been his pride whispering lies in his ear.

Thankfully, Harlan was a stubborn son of a bitch and he hadn't let Ellis off the hook so easily. If anything, the man had stalked and harassed him until he agreed to talk, ultimately saving their friendship.

Picking up, he answered, "This better not be a call bragging about your latest case or as soon as I'm back in town, I'm going to kick your scrawny ass."

"Dream big, kid," Harlan returned with good humor. "You couldn't kick my ass if I came to you half-broken and drunk from the night before."

Maybe so. Harlan was about ten years older than him but he was built like a brick shithouse. The man was unnaturally strong, an ox with a badge and laughing eyes that perps often underestimated right before he rearranged their face.

"So, how's it going?" he asked, going straight to the very topic Ellis didn't want to touch.

Ellis deliberately misunderstood. "Not much to go on just yet. The girl is still suffering from head trauma so her memory is spotty but we've got some leads to chase down."

"Not the case, dumbass. Your girl."

Harlan was also there when it all went sour with Dakota. He also was a secret romantic with a bleeding heart. The man should really get a hobby.

"She's not my girl," Ellis reminded Harlan. "Just a colleague and it's going fine. Dakota is a consummate professional."

"Aw, c'mon, don't feed me that crap. You've been holding a torch for your lady since the day you crawled out of her life with your tail between your legs. You can't tell me that the second you have a chance to actually say your piece, you've gotten all tongue-tied."

"What can I say, I'm a shy guy," Ellis quipped darkly, to which Harlan called immediate bullshit.

"And I'm the pope," Harlan countered derisively. "You've always been in love with the sound of your own voice so there's no way you've suddenly found the value in silence."

"People change," Ellis said, but Harlan wasn't buying it, nor should he because Ellis was lying. "Look, even if I was of a mind to crack that book open, Dakota ain't having it. She's not interested and I don't blame her. It's been two years, she's moved on, and I respect her for it. We're colleagues working together and that's all we'll ever be again. I'm good with it. Really, I am."

"Who you trying to convince? Me or you?"

"Stop busting my balls. The day I take advice from a man who's been married and divorced three times is the day I have my head examined," Ellis groused.

"I'm exactly the person you should take advice from—I know what don't work. Each wife teaches me something different. I can't wait to find out what wife number four has to teach me."

Ellis shook his head. Harlan was impossible but you had to love the guy for his irrepressible optimism. Or was that stupidity? Sometimes it looked the same.

On a whim, Ellis asked, "Carleton mention my name at all lately?"

"Sorry, not to me," Harlan answered with a touch of understanding. He knew how badly Ellis wanted to get back to Narcotics and how Carleton was dangling that carrot. Maybe Ellis was delusional in hoping that Carleton wasn't just stringing him along so he'd stop pestering him. "Hey, what you're doing... It truly matters. Remember that. You and me both know that there ain't nothing that's going to change the flow of drugs on the streets. It's a game of whack-a-felon. But what you're doing... That shit's real. Kids, man. And you're good at it. To be honest, I think you're where you're supposed to be."

That wasn't what Ellis wanted to hear. Frustrated, he exhaled and bit down on his urge to snap at his friend. Instead, he said, "Hey, man, I gotta go. I'm supposed to meet Dakota at the hospital in an hour and still have to run an errand. Stay safe out there."

"Yeah, yeah, of course. Right back atcha."

They clicked off and Ellis fought the wave of anger that always threatened to swamp him when he thought of how he'd been kicked from the job he loved the most.

He didn't believe for a second he was where he belonged and it pissed him off when Harlan said shit like that.

He was doing everything he could to get back to Narcotics—and nothing was going to stop him from getting there.

Chapter 7

Dakota and Ellis, united by a shared mission yet carrying unspoken memories, headed toward the hospital's private room section, their steps shadowed by the looming visit to The Congregation compound the next day.

A knot of anxiety twisted in Dakota's stomach as they prepared to unveil harsh truths to Zoey, a girl who'd already been through enough in her young life. Their goal was clear: navigate the difficult waters of revelation with utmost empathy and care.

Upon being cleared by Dr. Patel, whose firm reminder of Zoey's vulnerability echoed in their ears, they ventured toward her room, where the security, a silent sentinel, verified their credentials before permitting entry.

Zoey, her eyes momentarily brightening at their appearance, greeted them with a small smile, her spirit temporarily lifted by Ellis's predictable gift-bearing.

He handed her a soft, stuffed raccoon, its neck adorned with a shiny red bow, offering a gentle, "In my experience, something soft and cuddly goes a long way when you're feeling crummy." Ellis, always thoughtful in peculiar ways, found an odd charm in what Dakota playfully deemed "trash pandas," much to her initial amusement. "I hope you like *trash pandas*. I feel like they have more character than a regular teddy bear."

Dakota smothered a laugh, only because she'd given Ellis a

hard time for picking a raccoon of all animals, saying a teddy bear was traditionally cuddlier. Then she'd quipped, "No one looks at a trash panda and says that looks soft and sweet and lovable. No, they usually think about throwing something to get it out of their trash can."

To which Ellis had countered, "Speak for yourself. Raccoons are just misunderstood night bandits with a bad rap."

"They bite," Dakota returned flatly.

He'd shrugged. "So do bears—and bears do a lot more damage."

As Zoey clutched the raccoon, Dakota, despite earlier jesting at Ellis's unconventional choice, surrendered a genuine smile, recognizing his uncanny ability to read the emotional pulse of the young victim. Zoey's approval—"I love it!"—further validated Ellis's gift choice.

Dakota smiled, shaking her head with a subtle motion, realizing Ellis had the jump on her when it came to understanding the emotional nuance of their injured teen victim and she'd just have to go with whatever he thought was best in this case.

The room, dimly lit and carrying the faint sterile scent characteristic of hospitals, seemed to pause as Ellis broached the topic of Zoey's healing, his voice an attempt to blend cheerfulness and admiration. "The doc says you passed all your tests with flying colors. Of all his patients, he said you're top of the leaderboard. Personally, I think you must be some kind of superhero with how fast you're healing. Pretty incredible."

Zoey's innocent curiosity surfaced with, "What's a leaderboard? Is it a sport thing? Father Zach didn't approve of open competitiveness. He said competition created negative energy." Her upbringing under Father Zach's strict, competition-adverse doctrine shadowed her understanding of such concepts. The shared glance between Dakota and Ellis carried unspoken agreement: it was time to delve deeper.

Father Zach. Cue the all-over ick shudder. Dakota shared a look with Ellis, silently giving him the cue to start the real reason they were there.

"Yeah, it's a sport thing. Suffice to say, you're winning," Ellis answered as he dragged a chair to Zoey's bedside. At Zoey's grin, he prompted, "Tell me more about Father Zach and what it was like to grow up with The Congregation."

"What do you want to know?"

"Anything you'd like to share," Dakota offered. "It's something we're not familiar with and we'd like to know how it's different. Such as… You mentioned you were homeschooled. Did you enjoy it?"

The purposefully soft entry into their questioning served its purpose as Zoey's shoulders lost some of their tension as she nodded with a genuine smile. "I didn't mind it. We had one schoolroom so it was all of the children at the same time but the older kids were able to help the younger kids and I liked that part. We're not supposed to have favorites but Georgia and Wesley were my little shadows. They're six and seven."

"Are you the oldest child in the Congregation?"

Zoey nodded, admitting with a touch a guilt creeping into her gaze, "I wasn't thinking about how my leaving would affect the little kids who look up to me and I didn't mean to crash the car. My actions were selfish and I'm embarrassed by what I've done. My parents must be so ashamed of me."

"We all make mistakes, kiddo," Ellis said, sharing, "One time I stole a tractor and drove it down the street because my buddy dared me. Definitely not my finest hour—or my best driving, either. I crashed into a neighboring fence and part of my punishment was spending my summer repairing it."

A giggle escaped Zoey, even if she knew he was commiserating to cheer her up. Even with the past between them, Dakota was humbled by Ellis's innate ability to empathize.

Dakota shared a smile with Zoey, saying, "Your parents seem to love you very much. I'm sure they're more relieved that you're okay than concerned about what happened to an old car."

Ellis nodded, his easy smile fading as he tackled the bigger issue. "Zoey, I need to ask you something that might be difficult to answer. I need you to know that you're not in trouble and nothing you say will be used against you, okay?"

"Okay," Zoey acknowledged in a small voice. "What do you need to know?"

"Did your parents or anyone within The Congregation ever hurt you or any of the other children?" Ellis asked.

Zoey's expression of shock was genuine. "Hurt us? How? No."

Dakota explained gently, "Sometimes in our line of work, we see organizations such as yours that normalize the abuse of children, both sexually and physically, and we want to make sure that's not happening where you live."

Zoey shook her head vehemently. "No, nothing like that. No one has ever hurt me like that. I swear it."

Ellis absorbed her answer, murmuring, "That's good to hear," but added, "When you first saw your parents, you looked scared. Are you sure you're telling us everything? I promise we can protect you if you're in danger or afraid."

Zoey swallowed, hesitating for a minute, chewing on the side of her cheek as if trying to decide how much to share. "My mom… She has a temper but she's never hurt me like what you're asking. My dad has never even spanked me."

Dakota was relieved but surprised. Switching gears, she said, "Your dad said that you found something that upset you. Can you talk about that?"

Zoey nodded, tears welling in her eyes, her cheeks flushing as she admitted, "After everything that's happened, it seems so awfully terrible on my part but I was so upset I couldn't stand being there another minute. Everything I'd ever known felt like a lie and I needed to get away." She paused a minute, staring down at her fidgeting fingers. "I never meant for all of this to happen, though. I should've taken a minute to breathe and calm down before I let my emotions get the better of me. Father Zach is always saying I need to be more mindful of my actions." She looked guilty, adding, "Sometimes, I can be very thoughtless and a terrible example to all of the littles that look up to me."

Dakota didn't believe that for a second and was instantly defensive on Zoey's behalf. "I'm sure that's not the case," she assured the girl, making sure Zoey didn't take on unnecessary blame. "Big emotions sometimes bubble up and cause us to do things that we might not otherwise."

As the words left her mouth, she instantly flashed to the

night that ultimately destroyed her relationship with Ellis. The sound of shattered crystal echoed in her memory and she had to drag her focus back to the moment. Forcing a gentle smile, she reached out and squeezed Zoey's hand. "What matters is that you're okay," she reminded her.

Ellis agreed, though the somber set of his jaw suggested that he remembered that night, too. It was the elephant in the room between them no matter where they went—reminding them that some things were too big to ignore for long.

Shame over his actions from that night washed over him. His anger management therapist always reminded him that no one could go back in time and change something that already happened so beating yourself up over what's been done was a waste of energy. Focus on moving forward, changing behavior for the future, was the win.

But it still didn't lessen the guilt.

He'd lost the love of his life that night.

C'mon, man, there's a time and place and this ain't it.

Shaking off his inner turmoil, he focused on Zoey. The poor kid was twisting herself inside and out for acting out over something traumatic. He knew better but he was starting to feel a soft spot for the girl and he felt protective over her well-being. "Zoey, I want you to know that we're not going to let anything bad happen to you. We're here to protect you. You know that, right?"

She nodded.

Ellis drew a deep breath, preparing to drop a bomb on her. "But we'll also always be honest with you, even if it's hard. Do you understand that?"

Zoey nodded again, though she seemed apprehensive. "I know you say it's nothing to worry about but resources in The Congregation are shared with everyone. We only have two cars and now we're down to one." She shook her head with a heart-broken expression that made Ellis want to slay dragons on her behalf. "Leaving like I did was so selfish. My parents are probably embarrassed, too."

Ellis stopped her from spiraling with a grave shake of his

head. "That ain't it, kiddo. I can promise you that the car is the least of your parents' concerns."

"What do you mean?"

Ellis drew a deep breath, meeting Zoey's gaze. "I'm going to need you to be brave and strong because I have to tell you something that's going to change your life going forward."

Zoey paled but bravely waited for the other shoe to drop.

Ellis shared a look with Dakota before he continued. "The reason we're here isn't because you crashed your car. Seventeen years ago, a six-week-old infant girl was kidnapped from her mother in the dead of night. Whoever took the baby also killed that poor young mother. She was only nineteen, working as a housekeeper at a Whitefish hotel. Authorities never found the baby girl." He paused and Dakota finished for him.

"Until you crashed your car and ended up here."

"Turns out, you're that baby girl that disappeared seventeen years ago," Ellis said.

"What?" Zoey shook her head in denial, unable to wrap her head around the information. Ellis didn't blame her—it was a lot to take in, especially after everything else that'd happened. "No, that can't be. There has to be a mistake."

"Hospitals take blood and fingerprints of newborns when they're born. When emergency personnel brought you to the hospital with no identity, they ran your DNA. It flagged the FBI database. It's definitely, without a doubt, you," Dakota explained, gentling her tone. "DNA doesn't lie."

"I don't understand," she said, her voice barely above a whisper, as if invisible hands were curled around her throat. "What are you saying? My parents…did they…" Her voice caught and she struggled to get the words out. "M-my parents…"

Dakota rushed to ease the panic she saw building in Zoey's gaze. "Honey, we don't know enough about your parents' involvement to say for sure. They could be victims, too, if they didn't know anything about how you came to be available for adoption. Let's not jump to conclusions just yet, okay?"

"That's why you asked me if they were abusive?" Zoey asked.

"Well, we had to cover all our bases," Ellis said. "There are still a lot of questions that need to be answered but when you were strong enough to hear it, we wanted to be honest with you about your situation."

Zoey jerked a nod, visibly gathering her courage. She clutched the stuffed raccoon to her chest, asking in a tremulous voice, "Can you tell me about my biological mom?"

It was a big deal to discover you were adopted and then in the next breath that your biological mother was murdered, but Zoey was brave and strong and as far as Dakota was concerned, handling the news like a boss.

Unexpected tears jumped to Dakota's eyes as she looked away under the guise of pulling up the one photograph they had of Nayeli Swiftwater from the file on her phone. She handed the phone to Zoey and watched as the girl laid eyes on the woman who'd given her life.

After a pregnant pause, Zoey looked up, her eyes sparkling with tears as she half laughed, half cried as she said, "I have her eyes," and Dakota nodded in agreement, realizing it was the first thing she'd noticed, too, but couldn't say anything.

"She was beautiful," Ellis said. "And so are you."

But even more important than that, Dakota said, "She loved you more than anything—and we're going to find out who did this. I promise."

Chapter 8

Dakota's grip tightened on the steering wheel, her knuckles turning an eerie shade of white as the car sped through the seemingly endless stretch of road toward Stevensville while Ellis sat in the passenger seat, glancing her way every now and again, his sharp gaze flickering with a mixture of trepidation and concern.

Agreeing to ignore the past and only focus on the here and now was like sliding a bucket beneath a dripping pipe and expecting the bucket not to overflow at some point.

Shouldn't they at least get some things out in the open, share apologies even as a start? Although, Dakota might say she had nothing to apologize for—and maybe she was right—but he'd sure like to know what was brewing behind those dark eyes.

Dakota was the kind of person who internalized her emotions, whereas he wore his feelings on his sleeve. When they'd been together, they'd served as a complementary yin and yang, balancing each other out. An unpleasant memory came to him— she'd told him on day one that she was seeing someone but he hadn't seen any evidence to that claim.

Not that he expected her to parade her man in front of him— Dakota was too private for that kind of show—but she hadn't mentioned her relationship since that day, which led him to believe she'd been lying.

And why would she lie?

Because she wanted him to feel that she'd moved on? To make him jealous? Maybe both. How screwed up was he that he took that possibility as a positive sign that she wasn't over him. *Pretty damn screwy.*

Frankly, he was surprised Dakota agreed to carpool when he'd half expected her to meet him at the compound, leaving him in the dust like she'd been doing this whole time.

The tension in the vehicle was palpable, underscored by the distant murmurs of the radio, spouting occasional weather updates and soft rock tunes.

"We could talk about it—" he ventured but she shut him down real quick.

"Unless it's about the case, there's no need to dredge up the past," she cut in with the short, polite smile she reserved for waitstaff. "No need to add water to a dried-up patch of mud."

"I guess not," he conceded, though he was just keeping the peace. He wanted to talk about it but if she wasn't ready, it would just be him talking to an unresponsive brick wall.

Throwing him a conciliatory bone, Dakota said, "I had my doubts but I think we're working well together. You're not half-bad as a partner."

That was high praise given their painful history. Hell, he'd take it. He released a short chuckle, forcefully shelving his feelings for the time being. "You're not half-bad yourself. I was worried you might've gone soft since I saw you last."

She barked a short laugh that ended with an indelicate snort. "Sure. Just ask Mr. Touch-A-Lot how soft I am. My boss said the guy needed surgery to reset his hand."

Ellis felt no sympathy. "Well-deserved," he said, but even as they bantered, there was a pocket of pain that remained lodged between them and he didn't know how much longer he could pretend it wasn't there.

They fell back into silence as Dakota's car ate up the miles between them and Stevensville, pulling into the compound property before noon. A wooden painted sign advertising fresh fruit, vegetables and canned goods directed them down a long dirt driveway. Ponderosa pines flanked the driveway, swaying in the cool autumn breeze. The crisp scent of pine, spruce and fir rode on the fine layer of dust from the tires as they rolled slowly into the compound.

The Congregation's compound, enshrouded in lush greenery, radiated a peaceful, idyllic ambiance that belied the underlying suspicion that both Ellis and Dakota shared about communal living in a cult-like environment. Some might say they were jaded but they'd seen too much in their line of work not to be.

"One thing's for sure, it's not hard on the eyes," Ellis murmured, surveying the area, taking in every detail, realizing that the compound had possibly served as a summer camp, back when it was in fashion to send your kids off for a few weeks in the care of complete strangers. The wooden cabins were equally spaced apart and a large main hall veered off to the left. They parked and headed to the tables laden with seasonal vegetables and fruits, as well as rows of canned items.

"Welcome to Eden's Bounty," a sturdy middle-aged woman of Hispanic descent with soft brown eyes greeted them with a gentle, engaging smile as they approached her table. "My name's Lina. Are you looking for anything in particular? We have butternut squash that'll melt in your mouth and honey crisp apples that will make you see stars. We also offer samples of anything you see here."

"Actually, we're here on official business," Dakota said as she flashed her credentials. "We'd like to speak with Zachariah Deakins."

Lina's smile faltered in confusion but she nodded, flagging down a passing member. "Howie? Can you take our guests to see Father Zach?"

Howie, a tall and lanky man of roughly seventy, could have passed for a decade younger if not for his wild, coarse white hair. He nodded and gestured for them to follow, saying good-naturedly, "Promise me you won't leave until you try our homemade grape jelly. Or take some dried figs for the road." Patting his trim stomach, he added, "Good stuff. Keeps you regular."

"I'll keep that in mind," Ellis returned with a congenial smile as they walked to the main building. Howie opened the wooden door as it creaked on its hinges, gesturing for them to follow.

The hall was busy with various people doing individual jobs, while the sound of children playing echoed off the thick walls.

They detoured to another room where the smell of incense pricked his nose and a group of people sat on ornate matted squares while another man, similar to Howie, sat cross-legged in a meditative pose, breathing in and out in a measured and purposeful way.

A burning stick of Nag Champa incense clouded the air with a single curling ribbon of scented smoke from a brass dragon holder while a gurgling water fountain created a calming white noise that immediately reminded Ellis's bladder of the long drive.

It was a peaceful room if you liked that sort of thing.

Howie bent down and whispered in the man's ear and then said to Ellis and Dakota, "He'll be with you in a few minutes. Intentional prayer is nearly finished."

Intentional prayer? That's a new one.

The short delay enabled them to observe as the man finished whatever it was they were doing. While Howie and Zachariah Deakins were likely similar in age and build, there was something about Deakins that was wildly different.

Ellis wasn't the woo-woo type but Deakins definitely had something about him, like an aura of energy that commanded respect yet at the same time elicited calm, which Ellis found distinctly dangerous. He was the kind of man who could sell ice cubes to an Inuit.

It was men with this particular gift that often turned out to be the worst kind of people.

Dakota's investigative instincts kicked into overdrive as they awaited an audience with Zachariah, a man of unassuming stature and disarmingly gentle demeanor. His long gray beard flowed like a river from his chin but his blue eyes glittered with a shrewdness that sent a chill skittering down her spine.

Ellis, always keenly perceptive, sensed it, too—an insidious undercurrent beneath Zachariah's charismatic exterior.

Or maybe they were seeing what they wanted to see. Maybe he was just a magnetic man grown weary of a broken society trying to create a better one for his pocket of people—it wasn't a crime to want better than what you had.

It would be great to be wrong, but her flagging faith in humanity put her squarely in the pessimistic side, especially when her gut turned out to be right.

Finished, Zachariah murmured, "Namaste," bowing low and dismissing the group. As the people filed out of the room, Zachariah climbed to his feet, smiling in welcome. "Agent Foster, Agent Vaughn." Zachariah's voice was smooth, honeyed and a particularly low dulcet that aimed to relax and disarm. "Welcome to our home. How may I help you?"

Dakota took the lead. "Is there somewhere we could talk in private?"

"Of course, though we hide nothing here. All of The Congregation are equal as we shoulder the burden and the bounty of our people. However, we have a room over here if *you* would feel more comfortable."

"Yes, I think that would be best," Dakota said, smothering that all-over ick that threatened to further color her bias. Just because it wasn't her cup of tea didn't mean they were up to no good.

The idea of living like this gave her immediate hives.

Zachariah led them to a quiet room down a long hallway, which seemed to be the old director's office, and Ellis commented, "I can't help but notice the vibe to this place… Am I off-base or did this used to be a summer camp of some kind?"

Zachariah smiled and winked, approving of Ellis's observation. "Good eye. This place was once Camp Serenity Pines, a beloved summer spot for families and youth groups from 1969 to the late eighties. A variety of factors caused its gradual decline over the years." His expression turned somber as he continued. "A string of misfortunes, including a tragic drowning and a fire that ruined the main recreation hall, marked the end for this magnificent place. Lawsuits, financial hardships and falling enrollment buried it until we stepped in. It had been closed for five years when we bought it in 1995."

"I'm surprised it was still standing," Dakota murmured, thinking of how much it must've deteriorated in that time.

Zachariah chuckled ruefully, recalling, "Oh, it was barely standing at all. A pine beetle infestation had nearly wiped out the surrounding trees. In fact, one damaged tree had fallen and crushed one of the southern cabins to bits. We had to rebuild it from the ground up."

"So you've lived here since 1995?" Ellis asked.

"Indeed. The old place had good bones but it needed a good, firm hand to put it to rights again. Much like people. Every person here in The Congregation has come to us with the need for healing—and we deliver with God's help."

"You're Christian?" Dakota asked, surprised. "I thought, with all the meditation and incense and general vibe—" she gestured all around "—you might subscribe to a New Age metaphysical, earth-based belief structure."

"Religion is man-made. God, Great Spirit, The Creator—is everywhere and everything. I prefer the term *spiritual* rather than religious. We embrace spirituality and follow God's laws at the same time. It's a blending that works well for us."

Ellis smiled and said, "It seems very peaceful here." His smile faded as he continued, "Unfortunately, I wish we were here to buy some of your homegrown goods."

But Zachariah already knew. "Ned and Barbara-Jean Grojan. You have questions regarding their daughter, Zoey."

"Yes," Dakota responded, her expression revealing surprise. Both she and Ellis were caught off guard by Zachariah's composed demeanor, which displayed neither indignation nor shock at their statement. "How did you know?" she inquired, her curiosity piqued by his smooth transition in the conversation.

"I told you, we have no secrets here. The Grojans called as soon as they were prevented from seeing their daughter. We've been apprised of the situation from the start. How can we help so that the Grojans can reclaim their daughter and come home?"

"That depends," Ellis returned, regarding Zachariah with a keen eye. "How did the Grojans come to adopt Zoey?"

"From what I understand, the circumstances of Zoey's birth were sad and tragic but the Grojans have blessed that child with an enviable life of security, spiritual wellness and happiness. A silver lining in an otherwise heartbreaking situation."

Dakota's eyes narrowed, her breath held in anticipation, hoping Zachariah would confess to knowing something about Nayeli's murder. But instead, he said, "Drugs are the nation's scourge and the true poison afflicting our humanity. If only more resources were devoted to recovery rather than punishment, maybe stories like Zoey's mother's would have different endings."

"Are you saying you knew Nayeli Swiftwater?" Dakota asked.

"Sadly, no. I like to think that if I'd been there, she might have found salvation instead of exiting this world in the way she did," Zachariah responded.

"Murdered?" Ellis interjected, his eyebrow arching. "Because that's how she died. Someone took her life. Are you implying that drugs were involved?"

This time, Zachariah was the one caught off guard. "Murder?" he echoed, his brow furrowing in confusion. "What are you talking about? Zoey's mother was a teenage drug addict. She died from an overdose." His voice reflected genuine surprise, revealing that the notion of murder was new and unexpected to him. "I'm sorry, I need a minute to process this information. Sweet Zoey, her poor mother. There must be some kind of mix-up. This is horrifying." Zachariah bracketed his head with his fingertips, taking a full minute to collect himself. When he finally composed himself, he said, "Now I understand why the FBI and BIA are involved with the Grojans' case. I can assure you, no one from The Congregation had anything to do with the death of Zoey's biological mother. We're a peaceful people who abhor violence. Just ask anyone here and you'll find happy, wholesome families living clean lives."

Dakota's gaze fixated on Zachariah. "Ned Grojan informed us that you played a key role in facilitating Zoey's adoption. Could you provide more details on how you helped make the adoption possible?" she asked.

Zachariah nodded in agreement, though he appeared distinctly rattled. "Of course," he said, trying to maintain a composed demeanor. "I have a copy of Zoey's paperwork in my office. I'll retrieve it for you." He gestured around them, adding,

"In the meantime, please feel free to converse with anyone here or try a sample of the pear jam. It's a personal favorite of mine."

"Thank you," Ellis responded, his eyes tracking Zachariah as he walked away, navigating past a long line of cabins before vanishing into the distant building.

Dakota swiveled toward Ellis, her voice taut with skepticism. "Do you think he's bluffing?"

Ellis fell into a pensive silence, pondering for what seemed like an eternity. Eventually, he shook his head, his voice carrying a trace of begrudging admiration. "I don't think so. Unless he's the most skilled liar I've encountered in a while. He seemed genuinely taken aback about Zoey's birth mother."

A tense pause lingered between them, laden with unspoken thoughts and speculations, as they wondered whether Zachariah's shock was a masterful performance or a genuine reaction.

Either way, getting their hands on Zoey's adoption papers was the first step in discovering how little Cheyenne Swiftwater became Zoey Grojan after her mother breathed her last breath.

Chapter 9

Ellis's boots crunched on the gravel as he and Dakota strolled through the compound, the sunshine casting warm, inviting light on families playing together, groups of people chatting and children laughing as they ran across the open spaces. It was a serene picture, yet a knot formed in Ellis's stomach.

"Everything here seems so...happy," Ellis murmured, his brow furrowed slightly as he took in the scene.

"Yeah, too happy," Dakota replied, glancing around suspiciously. "Nothing's ever this perfect."

"How do they pay their bills? How did they pay for this property? Where's their income coming from?" Ellis mused, his gaze resting on the outdoor market that seemed to be catching a few buyers but wasn't exactly bustling with patrons. "We had a saying in Narcotics that seems to track here, too—follow the money. To run a place like this, they'd need more than what their little fruit stand can provide."

Dakota nodded, murmuring, "I'll have Shilah run financials and see what pops up," just as a young woman with a cascade of chestnut hair and a warm, albeit practiced, smile approached them. She wore a flowy summer dress, the kind that perfectly matched the carefree atmosphere of the compound, and a daisy tucked behind her ear.

"Hi there! You must be Dakota and Ellis, Father Zach's

guests. I'm Annabelle Turner," she said, extending her hand graciously. Her eyes flickered ever so briefly when she mentioned Deakins's name.

Dakota shook her hand cautiously. "Pleasure. I'm BIA agent Dakota Foster and this is my colleague, FBI agent Ellis Vaughn. Mr. Deakins said we could take a look around the compound."

Annabelle's smile seemed to widen, but her eyes didn't quite match the enthusiasm. "Absolutely, I'd love to be your guide. Everything you see here, we're all one big, happy family. No secrets, no worries."

"The vibe here does seem that way," Ellis returned with a brief smile, adding, "I don't know how you do it, though. Managing all these different personalities would be a challenge for me."

"We're all like-minded so it's not that hard," Annabelle said brightly. "When you're bonded by love and respect, conflict is relatively easy to resolve. I've never been happier than when I pledged to The Congregation."

"Pledge? Is that like a baptism or something?" Dakota asked, curious.

"In a way, I suppose," Annabelle answered but didn't elaborate. Instead, she enthusiastically pointed toward the community garden. "This is our award-winning vegetable garden. Our zucchini and butternut squash took Best in Show at the Stevensville fair five years running. Honestly, sometimes it doesn't even seem fair to the other contestants when our produce is in the mix. We always win." She whispered conspiratorially, "I've been told the secret is in our composting. High-quality nutrients produce extraordinary results. Our carrots are sweeter than candy."

"Not really a vegetable fan," Ellis apologized. "I never met a vegetable that could make me overlook a chocolate bar."

Dakota smothered a snicker; she knew all about his sweet tooth and his general disdain for vegetables. Annabelle didn't miss a beat, saying, "Well, then, you have to try our pear jam, it's to die for—and very sweet."

Despite her skepticism, Dakota couldn't help but be swayed slightly by Annabelle's charm. "Your community does seem quite peaceful."

Annabelle didn't hesitate, saying, "Oh, it truly is. What you see is what you get. We're all happy and content. Father Zach has made the success of The Congregation his life's work because quality of life matters. That's what's missing in today's world—true happiness."

"And that's what you found here?" Dakota said, gesturing around them. "By gardening and living in old cabins?"

Annabelle chuckled. "I know it's hard to imagine that giving up your material comforts could result in a better way of life but being free of the punishing drive behind late-stage capitalism is a gift you can't see but you can feel in your heart."

It all sounded bonkers to Ellis but Annabelle almost made it sound worth it. *Almost.* "What did you do before you came here?" he asked.

"Same thing that I do here—art," she replied cheerfully. "I'm a freelance graphic artist. I help create The Congregation's pamphlets and printed materials for Eden's Bounty."

"Don't you need technology to do that?" Dakota asked.

Annabelle offered an understanding smile, clarifying, "We don't shun technology here at The Congregation, but I know it's easy to assume we're *that* kind of group because we try to be as self-sufficient as possible. We have solar panels, we grow our own food, have our own livestock and school our children right here on the property, but high-speed internet is something we haven't figured out how to create on our own terms. We have a community Wi-Fi hub but in keeping with our beliefs, the hub is shut down by nine each night. Nothing is so pressing that it interferes with time that should be reserved for family, or personal wellness. There are studies that support the theory that too much technology actually dulls our brains."

"Believing what you want to see can be dangerous," Dakota commented softly. Annabelle heard her and replied with a faint, somewhat condescending smile, "Changing one's perspective is challenging, but worth it."

Ellis jumped in before Dakota got them kicked off the compound. "Sounds very healthy," he said, shooting Dakota a quelling look. "And I definitely want to try that pear jam."

Suddenly, Deakins found them, a folder in hand. "Got the paperwork," he announced, handing it over to Ellis. "Everything we have on Zoey's adoption is here."

"What are you doing?" Annabelle's demeanor shifted to concern. "That's private information."

"Whatever we can do to dispel any shadow of guilt on The Congregation, we're eager to provide," he replied with an even smile but his sharp look to Annabelle quieted any further protest. "Belle, would you mind helping Lina at Eden's Bounty? It looks like she could use a hand."

Annabelle didn't look happy being dismissed but she didn't refuse. Turning to Ellis and Dakota, she murmured a brief, "Pleasure to meet you," and then hustled off in a swish of her flowing dress to do as she was directed.

Deakins watched her go with a mix of indulgent pride like that of a father figure but his gaze lingered a bit too long on her backside to be completely innocent and Ellis was willing to bet the older man was sleeping with the younger woman.

Finally, something typical in situations like this. Primal human nature was hard to fight, especially when people were removed from the public eye and left to their own devices.

"If there isn't anything else I can provide..."

Ellis shook his head. "We appreciate your cooperation. We'll get this verified and returned as soon as possible."

Deakins nodded, clasping his hands together in a prayer motion, bowed and left them with a solicitous, "Lina has prepared a basket for the road. Enjoy."

"It's not often we're given gift baskets by potential suspects," Dakota said quietly as they trudged over to the open-air market. "Think it's safe to eat?"

"It's probably fine. It wouldn't be very smart to send agents home with a poisoned gift basket. Deakins is too sharp to make such a careless mistake," Ellis returned in a low voice before they reached a smiling Lina as she produced a beautiful wicker basket packed to the brim with a little bit of everything available for sale. Ellis accepted the basket with a smile. "This is very kind of you."

"We hope you enjoy," Lina said with a warm smile. "Perhaps when you return, it will not be under the guise of official business."

Dakota and Ellis just smiled and walked to the car. "You can drive," Dakota surprised Ellis, tossing him the keys.

Ellis chuckled, "You feeling all right?"

"Just drive," Dakota returned, the corners of her mouth turning up. "How else am I supposed to rummage through this gift basket?"

He laughed. "Ah, the true reason. You never could resist a good gift basket."

It was true. Every banquet with a silent auction Dakota was there, putting in her bid if there were gift baskets on the line. She was also enamored with trial-sized items. If something came in trial-sized, she'd buy it. A weird compulsion, but not the weirdest.

As they left the compound, the laughter and chatter of the people behind them seemed to fade into an eerie silence. Ellis broke it. "All right, first impressions on The Congregation?"

Dakota barked a short laugh even as she rummaged through the huge basket of goodies. "My opinion stands—anyone trying to sell the myth of a utopia is usually hiding something else. Also, I'm pretty sure that Annabelle is sleeping with Deakins, which gives me an all-over ick but she's of legal age so it's not a crime."

"I'm surprised Deakins handed over Zoey's paperwork so easily," Ellis remarked, as Dakota took a careful bite of a carrot. "I was expecting him to make us get a warrant first."

"I thought the same," Dakota responded, chewing thoughtfully. "Either he's confident in the paperwork or he genuinely has nothing to hide. There's something off about The Congregation, though. I can't tell if it's just my bias against groups like these."

Ellis nodded in agreement. "Pass me one of those carrots," he said, intrigued by its supposed taste.

Handing him a freshly picked carrot, Dakota teased, "Never thought I'd see the day where you willingly eat a veggie, Ellis. Who are you now?"

Taking a bite, Ellis was pleasantly surprised by the taste. "It's definitely good. I get the hype—but it's no chocolate bar."

Dakota finished her carrot and her stomach growled loudly as if to protest such a paltry offering. "Let's stop in Stevensville for some food," she suggested.

Ellis, however, seemed preoccupied, his gaze fixed on the rearview mirror. Sensing his unease, Dakota glanced to the side mirror, spotting an old sedan trailing them. "Problem?"

Ellis's eyebrows knitted. "That car pulled in right after we left the compound. The consistent distance and speed... It's suspicious."

"Do you think they're from the compound?" Dakota inquired. "Could be."

She swiftly moved her basket to the floor, drawing her side-arm. "Why would they tail us?"

Ellis looked thoughtful. "Deakins might not have been as forthcoming with those documents as he'd like to appear."

"Are they planning to chase us and retrieve them? Seems like a foolhardy move on their part." Dakota's body tensed, ready for any scenario.

"I doubt they're exactly criminal masterminds," Ellis remarked. Just then, as if to challenge Ellis's comment, the sedan closed in, tailgating aggressively.

Ellis kept his cool, noting, "They're really pushing their luck and testing my patience," he said, as the sedan pushed in so close they were practically in the back seat.

"Can you see the driver?" Dakota asked.

"The sun's glare is in the way. All I see is sunglasses and a hoodie."

"Tap the brakes," Dakota said.

"And brace for impact? No thanks. I don't have plans to spend the day nursing a whiplash headache." Ellis remained steady, unrattled, but they both knew the situation could go sidewise on a dime.

Before they could decide on a course of action, the sedan suddenly rammed into the bumper of their car, the impact causing the back end to get squirrelly. "Shit!" Ellis exclaimed, fighting to gain control of the vehicle.

Dakota braced for impact as a curve in the road worked against them. They were both trained in defensive driving techniques but sometimes all you could do was react in a way that would keep you alive.

The car left the road and skidded onto the shoulder in a spray of dirt and gravel. They narrowly missed slamming into the thick oak tree and their aggressor sped past them, leaving them in the dust.

Dakota coughed, waving away the dust cloud. "You okay?"

"So much for trying to avoid a whiplash headache, but yeah, I'm fine," Ellis groused, rubbing the back of his neck. "How about you?"

"I'm fine," she assured him, more irritated that she hadn't managed to catch the license plate. "Damn sun was in my eyes. I couldn't see the license plate numbers."

"A fact they probably knowingly used against us," Ellis said as he scanned the road ahead but whoever had run them off the road was long gone. "Maybe we can get a sample of paint transfer from the bumper, match it to the VIN and registered owner."

"I wouldn't get my hopes up. The Congregation doesn't seem real big on keeping up-to-date financial records."

Ellis agreed, saying, "Here goes nothing," as he tried to turn over the car. Miraculously, the engine sparked to life and Ellis was able to pull away from the soft shoulder and back onto the road with a grin. "I take back anything I've ever said about import cars not being able to take more than a tap without folding."

Dakota chuckled as she rubbed the back of her own neck. She was going to need a massage at some point. She remembered Ellis having good hands but pushed that memory aside as Ellis growled his next statement.

"I also amend my earlier statement—Deakins *is* a damn good liar. The man sent us off with a fruit basket and a smile all the while planning to send a couple of his people to run us off the road."

"We don't know for sure it's Deakins but yeah, I'd put money on that theory. You think it was just to scare us?"

"Probably," he answered with a dark glower. "But all it did was piss me off."

"Same," Dakota agreed but she switched gears quickly now, her stomach still growling. Nothing like a quick crisis to remind her belly that food was a priority. "Now I'm really hungry. Let's find a spot in Stevensville."

"You still want to get something to eat?"

Dakota blinked at his question. "Why wouldn't I?"

Ellis shook his head ruefully, his lips curving with amusement. "I mean, the whole car crash thing comes to mind..."

"It barely qualifies as a crash," she teased. "And maybe if you hadn't overcorrected when the other car tapped our back end..."

"Ohhh, those are fighting words," he shot back with a grin.

She laughed. Being able to joke with Ellis lessened the adrenaline rush of being run off the road. In their field, sometimes being able to joke about a bad situation made the reality of almost dying on a country road less daunting.

"All right, make yourself useful and find us a place to eat."

They entered Stevensville, a town exuding the charm of many settler-founded locales. Dakota found a cozy diner that boasted a country dinner for a reasonable price, and Dakota knew how much Ellis loved homemade meat loaf. While Dakota was unfamiliar with Stevensville, she knew of its history with the Indigenous people uprooted by missionaries in the nineteenth century. Everyone who called the Flathead Reservation home knew of its sad origin story, which wasn't much different from most reservation beginnings. Land stolen equaled people displaced. End of story.

"Isn't your mom's place nearby?" Ellis asked.

"About two hours out," she replied, grabbing a menu. More than the past or her family, right now, she craved a juicy burger and a plate of fries. Dakota's relationship with her mother was complicated. Following the loss of her sister, family dynamics had shifted dramatically. Her mother had changed from an independent single mom to two daughters to an overprotective and paranoid parent of a surviving child.

The day Dakota shared she was leaving the reservation for college and a career in law enforcement was the day her mother broke down and begged her to stay and find a career less dangerous.

So, yeah, their relationship was strained to this day.

And it hurt to remember what it'd been like before.

Chapter 10

Ellis understood the delicacy of Dakota's relationship with her mother. It wasn't a lack of affection but the aftermath of tragedy.

Dakota seldom discussed the sensitive topic of her relationship with her mother, given the pain it evoked. Ellis quickly reported the incident to start a vehicle swap-out while Dakota pulled the file on Zoey's adoption as they awaited their server. Finished with the incident report, he clicked off and Dakota handed him the adoption paperwork, noting with a frown, "Everything seems legitimate."

Ellis quirked an eyebrow. "Yeah, I doubt they're going to list murdering the biological mother to get their grubby hands on an infant. We need more info on this agency."

Dakota shared, thinking out loud, "With the property's size, even if it was falling down like Deakins claimed, it must've been pricey. The land alone would've been worth a pretty penny. How does The Congregation fund such acquisitions? I don't care how good the pear jam is, I doubt they're selling enough to drop a couple hundred thousand."

Their young waitress, with her dark hair pulled in a disheveled bun with the name "Cora" blazoned across the dull surface of her name plate, piped up, "I know how they do it… They steal it."

That got their attention. "What do you mean?" he asked. Despite her initial quip, Cora suddenly seemed reluctant to elaborate until Ellis quickly flashed his credentials. "We're federal agents investigating a local case. Anything you can share with us about what you know about The Congregation would be a big help."

Cora pressed her lips together for a minute before divulging, "My aunt Lina is with them. She left her normal life, gave away all her assets from her divorce to The Congregation and basically walked away from everything."

Ellis remembered the name but wanted to make sure they were talking about the same person. "Short, dark-haired Hispanic lady in her midforties?"

"Yeah, that's her," Cora confirmed. "Plus, there aren't many Linas around here."

Fair enough.

"We met her at the compound. She made us a fruit basket to take with us," Dakota shared. "Your aunt just…left everything behind?"

Cora's eyes sparkled with a mix of frustration and bewilderment. "Yeah, just like that. One day she's celebrating Sophie's sixteenth birthday, and the next, she's packing up and leaving, saying she's found her 'true calling' and she's going where people understand her. It was so abrupt, so out of character, but no one could stop her."

"Were there any signs—possible mental illness, depression—anything at all that could've hinted at this?"

Cora snorted, her tone bitter. "Hints? No. Shock? Absolutely. She abandoned a good job, her family… My cousin Sophie was devastated. My uncle? Broken. And for what? To live on a compound with strangers and give everything to that Deakins guy so she can can peaches and grow asparagus all day? C'mon, my aunt was an ER nurse. She thrived in crisis situations—always the cool head—but then this guy comes along, and suddenly she's walking away from everything and everyone she's ever loved and cared about? What would you do if it were your family member that did this? Would you just let them go without question?"

"Not at all," Ellis said. "I'd probably chase them down and make sure they weren't being coerced."

"Well, we did that and I think that was worse. She was doing it of her own free will. Like, it would've been easier to swallow if she'd been tricked or something, but no, she was happy to do it. I think that's the part that crushed my cousin."

Ellis tilted his head, "But why? There must've been something that drew her in, something they offered her."

Cora shot a glance to the manager, who was giving her a warning look, then defiantly turned back to them, lowering her voice. "Honestly? I think they prey on vulnerability. My aunt was going through something at work, a situation where someone died and she took it real hard. It changed her. And then her marriage started falling apart. So, I don't know, maybe he just said all the right things when she was in a bad place."

"You think they manipulate emotions, then?" Dakota queried, scribbling something in her notebook.

"Yes!" Cora exclaimed, slightly louder than she intended. The manager's stern gaze snapped to her again, and she lowered her voice. "*Absolutely.* It's like they have a radar for the vulnerable. And once they're in, The Congregation becomes their new family, their new world. It's creepy as hell, if you ask me."

Ellis looked deep in thought. "It's classic cult behavior, playing on insecurities and creating a sense of dependence."

Cora's face reddened, saying with a flash of spirit, "It's infuriating! And the worst part is, everyone just stands by. Even when they see families torn apart. It's like they're blind. I literally don't understand why I'm the only one who sees it around here."

With a slight twitch of her lips, Dakota empathized, "It must be hard, seeing someone you love get pulled into something like that and feeling powerless."

"It is," Cora said, a mix of anger and sadness evident in her eyes. She then cast a defiant glance at her manager. "But I won't stay silent. People need to know."

Ellis smiled, admiring her spunk. "Stay strong, Cora. And thanks for sharing. It gives us more to work with."

The manager had reached her limit, motioning for Cora to

get a move on, but Cora ignored her. "I hope you find a way to shut that place down. It's ruined enough lives already."

She gave a tight nod, her eyes conveying gratitude for being heard, and headed off to attend to other tables, every so often throwing annoyed glances at her disapproving manager.

After she left, Dakota speculated, "It's plausible. If all members give their wealth, coupled with smart investments…"

But for Ellis the numbers didn't add up, countering, "Given the compound's size and the modest potential assets, there must be another income source."

The manager approached, addressing Ellis with an apologetic smile. "I'm so sorry for Cora's behavior. We've talked to her about bringing her personal issues to work but she's young and sometimes she just does what she wants."

"I hope she's not in any trouble," Dakota said.

"Not any more than she usually is." The manager's reply suggested underlying tension. Ellis sensed that Cora could provide further information, given the right circumstances. He then ordered his meal, subtly shifting the focus.

"I'll get the double bacon burger with no tomatoes, lettuce or pickles, please."

"So, basically meat, cheese and a bun?"

"You got it," he said with a flirty wink. "And extra fries a little on the crispy side would make life worth living."

The manager, probably older than him by about ten years, reacted with a blush and a smile and Ellis hoped he'd distracted her enough to forget about chewing out the young Cora. He had a feeling Cora had plenty more to say about The Congregation and he was interested in hearing it.

The sight of Ellis ordering his usual "heart-attack special" stirred a pot of memories in Dakota. She had always chided him about his dietary choices, but that was just Ellis—stubborn and set in his ways about food.

As she contemplated teasing him, memories of their shared past rose to grab her by the throat. He might have a finicky taste in food, but his zest for life was contagious. And she had come to realize that maybe it wasn't just his energy she missed.

Maybe she missed him more than she cared to admit.

Don't muddy the waters, Foster.

She tried to refocus, but Ellis seemed to be on the same wave-length, looking nostalgic. "You remember that weekend we went camping at Glacier National Park? We'd set everything up, only to realize we forgot the ice chest with all our food."

Dakota chuckled at the memory. "Oh, that ancient granola bar at the bottom of my backpack? It tasted like cardboard but we were so hungry, we didn't hesitate to wolf it down."

Ellis laughed. "Yeah, but neither of us wanted to pack up and leave. We were determined to enjoy our rare free weekend to-gether, even if it meant surviving on a stale granola bar."

Being federal agents with demanding jobs meant getting away for some quality "reset time" hadn't been easy.

"And the next morning, we ended up paying triple at a con-venience store for food that was already waiting for us back home," Dakota remembered with a short laugh.

Ellis raised his eyebrows, playfully pointing at her. "It was your turn to remember the ice chest, wasn't it?"

She shot back, "No way, you were on ice chest duty. I packed the bedding."

His laughter was infectious. "All right, all right, you win. I should've known better than to try and question your memory."

Tapping her temple with a smirk, she quipped, "Like a steel trap, right?"

His soft chuckle resonated with her in an all-too-familiar way, tugging at memories of a shared past, and her cheeks flushed with warmth. That weekend, nestled in the cozy embrace of na-ture and the sanctuary of their tent, had created a red-hot con-nection that still had the power to burn.

Damn it, why couldn't she move on from him? She may have claimed to have a boyfriend, but the reality was no one since Ellis had barely registered and she wished it were different. It was a special kind of hell to be stuck in the past and unable to move forward to a new future.

But everyone else in comparison with Ellis was as enjoy-able as the prospect of eating stale toast left out all night on the counter for breakfast.

Ellis's eyes danced with mischief, teasing her, "If my memory serves me right, didn't you leave some rather…wild marks on my back? It looked like I'd gone a few rounds with a bear. Or perhaps, a very hungry wolverine."

"Ellis!" she shot back, her cheeks burning, but yes, she remembered all too well. One thing they'd never fell short of having—chemistry.

He shrugged casually, unapologetic. "I'm just sayin'…"

Just as a playful retort danced on her lips, the demanding buzz of her cell interrupted them. As she glanced at the screen, Dakota's playful demeanor vanished, replaced with a mask of professional concern. "It's the hospital," she whispered before answering, "Agent Foster speaking."

"Agent Foster, we're facing an urgent situation." Dr. Patel's voice was grim. "Zoey's parents attempted to forcibly remove her from the facility."

A cold rush of panic hit Dakota. "Is Zoey all right?"

"She's safe now, and we've detained her parents with our security," Dr. Patel responded. "I think you ought to come to the hospital and assess the situation."

Drawing a deep, relieved breath, Dakota exchanged a brief, worried glance with Ellis, her eyes relaying the gravity of the situation. "I'll get the Butte Police to reassume custody. We'll be there in a few hours. Thank you, Dr. Patel," she said, ending the call.

She turned to Ellis, urgency in her voice. "We need our order to go. After being released, Zoey's parents headed straight for the hospital, trying to get her out by force."

"Damn it," Ellis muttered, "I had a feeling that woman wasn't going to let things settle before doing something stupid. She thinks she's above the law because of that all bullshit Deakins and his church has been shoveling down their throats."

"Yeah, well, she's just earned herself a night in jail to help her reevaluate her life choices. In the meantime, we need to secure a better place for Zoey for the time being. With jails as crowded as they are, I don't see Butte police holding the Grojans much longer than they did before."

Ellis agreed, signaling the manager to put a rush on their order. The faster they hit the road, the better.

Chapter 11

Dakota and Ellis arrived at Butte Hospital later that night, pausing briefly to speak with security before making their way to Zoey's room. Dakota's patience was wearing thin. "How did the Grojans get past your security?" she pressed. "There was supposed to be a guard at her door, always."

The security administrator, Mr. Forsythe, looked as if he'd swallowed a lemon. "Agent, we've gone above and beyond to safeguard your patient. Our team is overwhelmed and understaffed without adding additional work."

Dakota's temper flared and her words came sharp. "Overwhelmed or not, Mr. Forsythe, a breach occurred. How?"

Shifting uncomfortably, he admitted, "There was an unexpected lapse during the shift change."

"How long was the lapse?"

"It...lasted forty-five minutes."

Ellis' jaw clenched. "Nearly an hour? How is that even possible?"

The security manager shifted with discomfort as he struggled to justify an indefensible argument but in the end, he gave up and shrugged, lifting his hands with frustration, offering a weak, "We're reevaluating our shift change protocols to ensure this doesn't happen again," as if that should be enough to cool their anger.

But Dakota wasn't so easily mollified. "Zoey's bravery is the only reason she's still here. If the charge nurse hadn't been alerted, she'd be gone. Do you even comprehend what kind of danger you put Zoey in?"

Forsythe's face reddened, words caught in his throat as he garbled a mumbled apology of sorts. "As I said, we're reevaluating our policies and making changes going forward. It was an unfortunate incident that won't happen again."

"You're damn right it won't happen again," Dakota growled, locking eyes with Ellis. "We have to move her. Can we get federal custody?"

"I can probably make that happen," Ellis said with a short nod, in lockstep agreement. "I'll make arrangements." Then, with a steely gaze to Forsythe, "We appreciate your...'help.' We've got it from here."

As they exited the security office, Ellis sensed the storm of emotions within Dakota. She was on the brink of explosion. He grabbed her arm, making her face him. "Zoey's okay," he whispered, seeing right through her guilt and fear.

Her voice broke slightly as she said, "The what-ifs are killing me, Ellis. If they'd gotten to her—we don't even know the full involvement of the Grojans. What if they're more than what meets the eye and actually killed Zoey's mother? It makes me sick to my stomach to think of how close they came to snatching Zoey."

"You know the drill—the what-ifs will kill you if you let them," he gently reminded her. "We deal in facts, not speculation or fiction. We're back in control. Zoey needs us to be exactly as we've been from the start—calm, cool and collected. She's counting on us to feel safe when her entire world has been upended."

"But she was unprotected for *forty-five* minutes," Dakota protested. "Anything could've happened in that time and it would've been both our asses, not to mention how it could've affected Zoey. Zoey's been missing for seventeen years. It's not far-fetched to assume the Grojans would've disappeared into the wind if they felt threatened."

"But that's not what happened," Ellis said sternly. "Take a

deep breath. Roll your shoulders. We're back in the driver's seat, okay?"

His words resonated. God, he was right. She was catastrophizing out of uncontrolled anxiety. *Get a grip, Foster.* She inhaled deeply, regaining her composure. Dakota had always been the overthinker and Ellis the one who shrugged off most challenges. She'd needed his perspective on this before she spiraled. She jerked a short nod as she sucked in a big breath and pushed it out with determination. *Calm, cool and collected.* She cast Ellis a grateful glance and by the time they reached Zoey's room, Dakota was the picture of composure and determination.

Zoey looked up as they entered the room, a combination of trepidation and relief in her wide eyes as she ventured, "You heard, didn't you?"

"Are you okay?" Dakota asked. "That had to be quite upsetting."

"You have no idea." Zoey looked miserable as she admitted, "I feel like I don't even know them right now. I've never seen them act like this before. It's like strangers took over my parents' bodies, forcing them to say and do things that are out of character. I know it's hard to believe but that's not how they acted back home."

"Your parents seem to be…unpredictable right now. Big stressors can alter people's personalities if they don't have the coping skills to manage the situation," Ellis said. "Try not to take it personally."

Zoey winced as her voice quavered, "Are they…in jail?"

Ellis hesitated, but Dakota answered, feeling honesty was best. "Yes," she said gravely. "But I don't want you to worry about that."

"How can I not worry? It's *jail.*"

"I know it's probably upsetting but sometimes adults need time-outs, too. They can't just do whatever they want because they don't like how things are being handled. The fact of the matter is you're an important piece of a tragic puzzle that's been missing for far too long, and whether they like it or not, they're going to have to cooperate."

"My mom's pretty stubborn," Zoey admitted, the corners of

her mouth lifting as if to say she didn't think her mom was capable of cooperating. "Even within The Congregation my mom was known for being rigidly stuck in her own ways. Father Zach was always counseling her to soften and bend but she struggled with the idea."

Dakota didn't like the idea of having anything in common with that shrewish woman but she could relate to not wanting to bend when she was certain her way was better. "Well, that's a problem for her to sort out."

"Why are you going to so much trouble for me?" Zoey asked, bewildered, clutching her stuffed raccoon to her chest. "I'm nobody."

Dakota's heart ached, feeling her isolation and vulnerability. No one should ever feel as if they were nobody. "You're the opposite of nobody, Zoey. I can promise you that your birth mother thought you were everything worth fighting for. That's another reason we need to make sure you're safe. Tomorrow, Agent Vaughn and I are going to talk with someone who knew your birth mother, Nayeli. We don't want to leave town until we know you're going to be well taken care of."

Zoey's eyes teared up. "Who?"

Dakota knew there was no way to soften the information. "We're going to talk with your biological aunt, Nakita. She lives in Missoula now."

Zoey shook her head trying to cope with the flood of information. Dakota couldn't imagine how jarring it must be to realize you have more family than you ever knew, especially if you were raised in such an insular bubble your entire life. "I have an aunt?"

"And a grandmother," Ellis added. "And when the time is right...and if you're interested in doing so, we'll arrange a meeting."

"Do they want to meet me?" Zoey's voice was small, vulnerable.

The first rule in investigations—don't let it get personal—used to be stamped on Dakota's spine but she felt herself slipping. There was something about Zoey that pricked at her sense of justice in a way that made being impartial almost impossible.

It probably had something to do with the trauma of Mikaya's death but Dakota didn't have the time to puzzle it out.

"I'm sure as soon as they're aware of you they will absolutely want to be part of your life, but that will be your choice. It's a very complicated situation and we're all treading cautiously forward but I promise you, everything we do will be done with your safety and well-being at the heart."

Zoey nodded, wiping at her eyes, admitting, "I don't know how my parents will take me wanting to know my biological family."

Given their current instability, not well—but that was a problem for a different day. "Your parents need some cooling-off time. Meanwhile, we're moving you to a safer spot to help everything settle."

Zoey's eyebrows knitted in confusion. "Moving? To where?"

"We believe it's safer for you, considering everything, to be in a federal safe house," Dakota explained. "A nurse we trust will be with you. And your parents… They won't know where, for now."

Zoey's eyes shimmered with unshed tears. "I don't get it. My mom's never been this…unhinged. She genuinely scared me."

A pang of suspicion hit Dakota. How far had Barbara-Jean been willing to go for a child of her own? Desperation led people down dark paths. Had Barbara-Jean lied about knowing who Nayeli was? Had she and Deakins orchestrated the entire adoption scenario as a way to cover her tracks?

Too many questions and not enough information.

"I wish I never took that car," Zoey admitted in a hoarse whisper, practically disintegrating beneath the guilt. "This is all my fault."

Dakota reached for the girl's hand and squeezed it gently. "No, it's not. You're not responsible for the actions of others. I never used to believe that everything happens for a reason but sometimes it does. If you hadn't taken that car, crashed and ended up here, we never would've found you. That's something to hold on to. I don't know how your parents are connected but we're going to keep you safe, okay? That's a promise."

"My head is a mess. I don't know what or how to think about

this entire situation. Suddenly, my life is so much more complicated than it ever was and I just want to crawl under the blankets and hide."

"Don't sell yourself short, kiddo. You might not believe this but you're handling things pretty well," Dakota said. "But let's prioritize getting you settled. The other pieces we'll fit together later."

As Ellis approached, signaling a successful call with a thumbs-up, he quipped, "Five-star relocation service ready to roll. Just a quick chat with your doctor, then it's lights and sirens for you."

Zoey's expression crinkled into an unhappy frown. "Do I have to go in an ambulance?"

Dakota quickly jumped in. "I get it. Ambulances aren't the most fun. But we need to ensure your safety, especially with your injury. Think of it as a medical limousine—a sort of privileged transport. Ready to roll?"

Zoey sighed. "As ready as I'll ever be, I guess."

Dr. Patel signed off on the transfer with stern instructions for her aftercare as well as arrangements to get cleared by the FBI for weekly check-ins and Dakota felt a grudging respect for the crusty doctor. He might be grumpy and unfriendly to everyone else but he genuinely cared for his patients and that was a good quality for someone in charge of others' well-being.

Ellis pulled the car into the dimly lit parking garage of the boutique hotel, the weight of the day pressing on his shoulders. His head and neck ached from the accident but he wasn't going to complain. He'd take some aspirin when he got to his room. Dakota, eyes shadowed but determined, glanced out at the darkened streets. He could practically hear the wheels grinding in that busy mind that probably had the same pounding headache as him but she'd never admit it.

He knew how she shouldered the blame of the Grojans' failed hospital heist, even though it wasn't her fault. It was in her nature to be the one in charge, the one with the answers and solutions—a consequence of losing her older sister too young and ending up being the responsible one when her own mother crumpled.

"Zoey's safe now," he murmured, cutting the engine. It was late and they were both dragging at this point. All Ellis wanted now was his bed and at least four hours of solid shut-eye but Dakota was pensive.

"For now," Dakota murmured, already trying to prepare for the next obstacle or challenge, even though they didn't know how or when it might happen. "We're far from done and if anything, we're just as far from an answer as when Zoey first popped up on the radar. I can't explain it but I feel this sense of urgency that's pressing on my shoulders, whispering in my ear that we're running out of time."

"But we're not," Ellis said. "Aren't you the one who was always advocating slow and steady wins the race?"

Dakota's half-hearted smile as she quipped, "Don't use my words against me," gave him hope that Dakota would come around. For some reason this case had her spinning on her axis in a way he'd never seen before. He suspected it had something to do with her sister's death, but he was reluctant to go there if she wasn't ready. "But yeah, you're right," she chuckled ruefully, before admitting in a weary tone, "I'm off my game and that worries me. I've never felt so unsure of my every move like this. I don't know why this case is affecting me so much. I mean, I do know but that bothers me even more. I should be able to put everything in its place but I'm wildly off-balance right now."

Ellis drew a deep breath, hoping he was doing the right thing. "Nayeli's death was too close to Mikaya's and you were so young when it all happened. You're human, Dakota. You're allowed to have feelings."

"Not if they get in the way of my judgment," she returned with a frown. "I can't let my feelings muck up this investigation."

"You won't," he assured her. "If there's anyone I would never worry about in that regard, it's you. Don't be so hard on yourself."

He hated seeing her look so dejected and lost. He wanted to shake her and tell her to snap out of it, but also he wanted to hug her tight and reassure her that it was going to work out. He split the difference, playfully admonishing, "I never pictured you as the pity-party type, Foster. Even off your game, as you say, you're still a damn good investigator so cut yourself some slack, okay? Your instincts are sharp. You just have to listen to them. You're too busy second-guessing every move and you're smothering that spark that made you the right person for this case."

She was ever the overthinker, and he couldn't imagine the chaos inside Dakota's brilliant mind.

Dakota cast him a look full of grudging appreciation, murmuring her acknowledgment. "You're right. I am second-guessing myself and I need to stop."

"Sometimes things get messy even when we know to keep it clean," he said quietly and wasn't entirely sure that he was only talking about the work. The more he worked side by side with Dakota, the harder it was to remember to keep it professional.

If she caught on to the parallel, she didn't comment. Instead, she exhaled a long breath, taking a minute to recalibrate.

They'd gotten Zoey transferred to the federal safe house, a fortress hidden in plain sight. But even as he cautioned Dakota to be wary of putting the cart before the horse, he knew there was more to the story, more threads to unravel. He felt it, an itch at the back of his mind.

Rubbing the grit from her eyes, Dakota shared on a yawn, "Shilah called while you were signing the paperwork for the transfer. She's got something worth looking into on Deakins."

"Yeah? What's she got?" He unbuckled his seat belt, turning fully to face her. "Anything good?"

"Possibly. I mean, it's definitely odd. The Congregation compound? It was purchased by a company that traces back to Montana senator Mitchell Lawrence."

Didn't expect that intel. "I've met Lawrence once before, some FBI benefit dinner. He was one of the VIP guests." Ellis's eyebrows shot up. "But Deakins and Lawrence? You're right, that's an odd pairing. But why? What's his play?"

Dakota ran a hand through her hair, tension drawing her features tight. "I don't know but it seems weird that a senator would have ties to a cult compound in the middle of nowhere."

"I'll add it to the list of questions attached to this case," Ellis said.

There was a moment of heavy silence as fatigue warred with

restless energy born of too much adrenaline. Dakota's gaze was sharp, assessing. "If Deakins has enough influence and power to convince a senator to pony up the cash for the compound, we're not just fighting a cult. We're up against a system with deep pockets and dangerous connections."

Ellis grunted in agreement. Working in Narcotics for as long as he had taught him that dirty money found itself in many different hands, regardless of social stature, but the more powerful the connection, the more determined people were to keep their secrets hidden. Had Nayeli been mixed up with the wrong people, collateral damage in a dangerous game?

A yawn found him in spite of his restless thoughts and he knew he had to hit the sheets. "Look, it's been a helluva day and we need to get some sleep—and some aspirin. We're no good to anyone if we're dragging ass in the morning."

"Second on that aspirin. Damn my neck is sore," Dakota agreed with a nod as she climbed out of the car and he followed. "Thanks for driving," she said with a hint of a weary smile. "I'll drive tomorrow if you want," she offered with a wave before leaving for her room without a backward glance.

Of course, that's how it should be. No lingering looks, or hint that there'd once been something passionate and tender between them. Now, it was all about the job.

Why was he struggling to follow her example?

As ready for bed as he was, he stood for a minute, allowing the cool night air to kiss his face. Call it a moment of weakness but he'd give anything to be invited into Dakota's hotel room so he could fall asleep with her body beside him. That wasn't going to happen, but it didn't stop the longing from punching him in the gut.

How could he have lost such an incredible woman? He sighed inwardly. Those were not the questions to entertain when the tank was nearly empty, and self-control was low.

Because if he went down that rabbit hole, he'd end up doing and saying something he regretted and potentially screw up this case—and he wasn't willing to do that.

Too much was riding on the success of this case and he wished he could say it was only Zoey's well-being that mattered but his career was on the line, too.

Chapter 12

Ellis maneuvered the car onto the highway, making the journey from Butte to Missoula under a canvas of thickening clouds. Fall always brought unpredictable weather patterns. One minute it was sunny and warm; the next, a storm boiled on the horizon. Ellis kept his eyes on the road, his focused expression matching the tension Dakota felt.

Even as tired as she was, sleep hadn't come easily to her last night. Sitting in the car, enveloped in the cocoon of the car's shadowed interior, Dakota struggled against the powerful pull toward Ellis. His voice soothed her ragged nerves—something she hadn't realized she'd been sorely missing—and the simple scent of his skin made her want to lay her head on his shoulder and close her eyes for a brief moment.

Ellis had always had a way of making her feel emotionally safe—until that night had shattered everything between them.

She couldn't explain to anyone who hadn't experienced trauma in their life how precious a gift that feeling of safety was to someone with a soul torn in half, but it was equally traumatic to lose that security when it meant so much to you.

But there was a saying, "Dating someone you've already broken up with is like biting into an apple you already know is bad and being surprised when you eat a worm," that stuck in

her head whenever she ventured too close to considering another try with Ellis.

Not that she should assume he was open to another try.

Needless to say, she tossed and turned, punched her poor pillow, kicked her bedding around a bit, all in effort to find sleep
that didn't come until almost one in the morning.

Which made getting up bright-eyed and bushy-tailed when
the alarm went off a challenge.

But caffeine paired with her driving sense of responsibility
was a godsend because today was too important to waste on
poor life decisions.

They were meeting Nayeli's younger sister, Nakita, not only
to learn about Nayeli's past but also to share that her long-lost
niece had been found. It was bound to be an emotional meeting
and she needed all of her faculties on point.

Even though she'd offered to drive, Ellis had taken one look
at the dark circles beneath her eyes and wordlessly pointed to
the passenger seat. Any other time she might've pushed back but
today she was silently grateful for his innate protective nature.

They pulled into Missoula in good time, making their scheduled appointment with a few minutes to spare, which was just
how Dakota liked it as it gave her time to prepare.

"Ready?" Ellis asked.

She inhaled deeply. "Yes."

The modest suburban neighborhood was typical with tidy
tract homes lining the streets and city-approved landscaping
that looked copied and pasted from one house to the next.

They parked and walked up to the home, Ellis taking the lead
to rap sharply on the front door.

Nakita knew they were coming, but not the full purpose of
their visit. Dakota shared they were investigating new leads on
Nayeli's case and asked if Nakita wouldn't mind talking to them.
It was a way to gauge Nakita's interest and to see how open the
family would be to finding out about Zoey.

Nakita had been eagerly open to talking about her sister's
case and quickly invited them to talk, which was a good sign.

The door swung open, revealing Nakita—a petite woman
with long dark hair that hung in two braids, and even darker

eyes that were kind as a smile wreathed her face. "You must be Agent Foster and Agent Vaughn," she said, before they could even flash their credentials. Her dark eyes lit up as she ushered them in, anxious to hear details of the case. "I can't tell you how happy I am that you're reopening my sister's case. It's been so long I'd almost given up hope."

"Thank you for agreeing to talk with us on such short notice," Dakota said, showing her credentials even though Nakita didn't seem to need it. She was too excited to hear what they'd come to share.

She motioned for them to sit. "Can I get you something to drink? I have coffee, tea, juice boxes…"

Ellis waved away her offer with a smile. "Please, have a seat, Miss Swiftwater. The kind of news we have to share is best heard sitting down."

Nakita swallowed and sank into the chair opposite them. "Please tell me you've caught who killed my sister."

"Not yet but there's been a development in the case," Dakota said. "A pretty big one."

Nakita nodded imperceptibly, steeling herself for the news.

"A week ago, a seventeen-year-old Jane Doe was brought into a Butte hospital with major head trauma from a solo car accident. DNA revealed the teen to be your niece, Cheyenne."

Nakita cried out, her shaking hands going straight to her mouth as if trying to keep the storm of her emotions from spilling out further. Tears leaked down her cheeks as she tried to find the words. "Are you sure?" she asked, her voice choked. "Without a doubt?"

"The DNA match was conclusive," Ellis confirmed.

"Is she…okay? You said major head trauma?" Nakita said, her bottom lip quivering.

"She's recovering," Dakota said, hoping to ease Nakita's fears. "She suffered some short-term memory loss, but the doctor feels confident she'll make a full recovery with time."

Nakita nodded, relieved, but the floodgates opened and the questions came tumbling out. "I don't understand. Where has she been all these years? What happened? Does she know about her family? Where was she going when the accident happened?

When can I see her? Oh my God, I have to tell my mom." She rose sharply, her hands fluttering as she tried to prioritize what to do first. "I need to make arrangements for my sons but I can be ready to leave in about an hour—"

"Miss Swiftwater—"

"Call me Nakita, please."

Dakota smiled. "Nakita, I know this is a lot to take in but I need you to take a breath. Your niece has been moved to a federal safe house given the circumstances of her abduction. We can't take you to her just yet, but I promise, when Cheyenne is ready... We'll facilitate that visit. For now, we need your help finding who killed your sister."

Sharply disappointed but trying to be cooperative, Nakita returned to her chair, sniffing back tears. "Of course, whatever you need. I'll help in any way I can." She glanced up, her eyes still watering. "But... Can you tell me something about her?"

Dakota nodded, pulling out her cell phone. "I can do you one better." She brought up a picture of Zoey holding the stuffed raccoon Ellis brought her. The smile on Zoey's face was similar to Nakita's, showing strong genes ran in the Swiftwater genetics. "This is Cheyenne...although she goes by Zoey now."

Nakita accepted Dakota's phone with trembling fingers, tears splashing down her cheek as she stared at the photo. "She's beautiful," she breathed, her voice clogged with tears. "She looks just like Nayeli."

"I was thinking she looks a lot like you," Dakota said with a smile.

"People always used to say that me and Nayeli looked a lot alike," Nakita admitted with a watery chuckle. "I guess they were right." She reluctantly returned Dakota's phone. "Is she okay? Does she know about us, her real family?"

"She knows now," Dakota answered with a kind smile. She could only imagine what was going through Nakita's head right now and it made Dakota freshly angry over the cruel nature of the situation.

"Does she...want to meet us?" Nakita's halting question pierced Dakota's heart.

Dakota chose her words carefully, trying to navigate a tricky situation. "Zoey's been through a lot and she's a bit over-whelmed. Until we can determine that her adoptive parents are innocent of any wrongdoing in regards to your sister's case, we're keeping Zoey in protective custody and they haven't responded well to that situation."

"I don't understand. My sister was killed and her baby abducted. Of course they had something to do with Nayeli's murder," Nakita returned, flabbergasted. "Why aren't they in jail?"

"Technically, they are, but for other reasons, and they're likely to be released within a few days," Ellis said.

Nakita didn't understand and Dakota didn't blame her. Logic and reason were difficult to manage when emotions were running high. She tried to return Nakita to the current situation. "Traumatic brain injuries take time to heal and it's best if Zoey focuses on what she needs for her health. It's all very confusing for her and we want to minimize the stress. I know you want what's best for Zoey, and right now what's best is trying to find out who killed her biological mother. I'm hoping you can help us find the clue that might've been missed the first time around."

That pierced through the fog of Nakita's pain and she nodded. "Yes, of course. Whatever she needs." She wiped at her eyes and rubbed the moisture away on the thigh of her jeans, drawing herself up and straightening. "What would you like to know?"

Ellis admired the strength of women. Time and time again, he saw instances of women rising to the occasion despite physical or emotional pain and it always awed him.

Today was no different. He just watched Nakita Swiftwater discover her niece was alive after being missing for seventeen years and in the next breath, shelve her emotions so she could help find her sister's murderer when he knew all she wanted to do was hop in the car and drive straight to the child who represented the last living piece of her sister.

Seeing such emotional strength was humbling.

"Can you tell us about Nayeli's relationships, friendships?" Dakota asked.

"I can try," Nakita said, taking a minute to search her memory, a flicker of pain crossing her gaze as she confessed,

"Sometimes my memory isn't so good about remembering my childhood. After Nayeli died, I spiraled, lost myself in addiction." She swallowed hard, her eyes glistening. "It was the birth of my first son, born addicted, that was my wake-up call. I got clean. For my child. For Nayeli, who would've been an amazing mom. Once I was clean, I poured myself into bettering my life. I went back to school and got my counselor credentials. Now I'm a substance abuse counselor, helping others overcome similar challenges with addiction and loss."

"That's incredible," Dakota said. "I'm sure Nayeli would've been proud."

"I hope so. For a long time I didn't think I could pull myself out of the dark place I was in but somehow I found the strength. I liked to think that Nayeli was there beside me in spirit, lifting me up when I stumbled," she shared with a mild blush. "We were raised to believe that the Great Spirit is everywhere but it was my sister's spirit I needed most."

Dakota's own belief structure leaned more toward science, finding solace in the tangible rather than in faith. After Mikaya was killed, it was hard for Dakota to embrace the concept of a higher power when there was so much evil in the world.

Shaking off her personal thoughts, she murmured, "I understand," shooting a glance at Ellis. "Anything you can remember might point us in the right direction."

Ellis pressed gently, "What about Nayeli's romantic relationships? Perhaps a past boyfriend we could talk to?"

Nakita chuckled, shaking her head. "Childhood friends, yes, but a boyfriend? Nayeli was very shy around boys. She wasn't like some of those girls who are so eager to get attached. She was quiet, kind and always had her nose in a book. She loved to read. Me, not so much. I used to tease her that she was going to end up an old auntie with nothing but cats to keep her company when she got old. She said she didn't care because a cat in her lap wouldn't stop her from reading whenever she wanted." She chuckled at the memory, recalling with a pained frown, "That's why when she told us she was moving to Whitefish for a job, we thought she was joking."

"So that seemed out of character for Nayeli?" Ellis asked.

"Well, yeah, a little bit. She was painfully introverted and preferred to stay home than go out and she knew our mom needed her help here," Nakita said.

"Did she give a reason for leaving?" Dakota asked.

"From what I remember, she said it was the only way to make more money. She said there wasn't enough opportunity in Flathead and she knew that she'd need a better career if she was going to be able to take care of us."

"So Nayeli was trying to improve your family's financial status," Ellis said.

"She got an interview at that fancy hotel and said she wanted to work up the chain to manager." Nakita nodded but guilt remained in her expression. "She told me it was up to me to help Mom while she was gone and that she'd send money each pay period. I was supposed to help with the groceries and day-to-day stuff but I was a kid and I didn't want that kind of responsibility. I resented Nayeli for leaving."

Ellis digested that information. "Did she follow through and send money?"

Nayeli nodded. "Like clockwork. She would even send extra if we were short. Nayeli never complained or said no. She just fixed whatever problem happened. Especially if I was the one being the problem," she admitted.

Ellis could read between the lines. Nakita, a resentful kid unable to understand why she was being asked to shoulder a heavy burden for the sake of her family, probably helped herself to some of the funds as compensation but then that created a shortfall in the family budget.

Dakota asked, "Once she moved to Whitefish, did she mention having a boyfriend?"

"Not that I knew of," Nakita said, shaking her head, pausing as she recalled something. "Though she mentioned a frequent hotel guest. Always polite, always kind, even helped her out a few times. She got a flat tire one time and he bought her all four new tires. I think... I think she had a crush on him. But she never named him. I was too young to think about pressing any harder, and honestly, I was selfishly preoccupied with my own stuff."

"You were a kid being a kid," Ellis reminded her. "Being asked to carry a heavy load for an eleven-year-old." But his thoughts were stuck on the mysteriously generous stranger in Nayeli's life. Four tires were costly. Whomever Nayeli was talking to, they had money to throw around.

Nakita cast a grateful smile his way. "That's what my therapist told me, too. It was a long time before I accepted that truth. It's still hard, to be honest. It always feels like somehow it was my fault what happened to Nayeli, even though I've processed that it wasn't. Emotions are tricky."

"That they are," Dakota agreed with a murmur. "Thank you, Nakita, for talking with us today. We'll be in touch," she said, handing Nakita a business card with her personal number scrawled on the back. "As soon as we know more, you'll be the first call."

They left Nakita's with a list of old contacts and possible connections back at the reservation and climbed into the car, but Ellis was still thinking of the mysterious hotel guest.

"We need to find out who Nayeli was seeing," he said. A connection, however faint, gave them a direction to investigate further. Human beings, no matter how private and reserved their personality, craved connection. Nayeli was seeing someone long enough to get pregnant. It was possible whoever got her pregnant…was also the killer.

Dakota was on the same page. "Beautiful, shy Native girl with a kind heart and a generous soul alone in a city full of predators… Yeah, I have a feeling someone took advantage of a naive girl and then snuffed out her life when she became inconvenient."

Ellis agreed. Did a younger Zachariah Deakins set his eyes on Nayeli or was there someone else lurking in the shadows of the past thinking they got away with murder?

Chapter 13

Taking advantage of the fact that Flathead Reservation was only an hour and a half from Missoula, they immediately returned to the road after leaving Nakita's place.

Again, Dakota let Ellis drive but this time it was so she could put her emotions in check. She rarely found reason to go home again, and the guilt always sat like a stone in her stomach.

The rusty hues of fall painted the landscape, accentuating the beauty of Montana's sprawling vistas. However, the trees shedding their golden leaves only served as a stark reminder of time passing, of seasons changing, and of the wounds that never quite healed.

She rested her head on the open window frame, closing her eyes as the wind blew her hair back and caressed her face. The sun bathed her upturned cheeks and the scent of evergreen, wild things, and the hum of nature plucked at her soul.

As she knew they would, the memories hit her hard and fast. Her home was beautiful but a well of grief simmered beneath the pretty picture, creating a lump in her throat even as she tried to push it away.

When would the pain end? Shouldn't there be a statute of limitations for the sharp stab of emotional damage?

She saw herself, at sixteen, lost and shattered, needing the strength of her only parent—but her mother was drowning in her own pain and had nothing left to offer her youngest—and remaining—daughter.

Dakota reopened her eyes in time to see the diner where Mikaya used to work—a sad shack off Highway 93, closed and boarded up for a long time now—yet still standing as a painful relic of the past. If it were within her power, she'd bulldoze the place to the ground and scorch the earth where it stood. *Oh, Mikaya, I miss you so much.*

Nineteen was too young to die. Dakota blinked back tears. It was always this way when she came home. The tears lay in wait, bubbling in her heart, just waiting to spill over at the first opportunity.

Ellis, sensing Dakota's internal struggle, squeezed her hand. "You okay?"

Not even a little. She took a deep breath, letting the cool fall air fill her lungs. "Yeah, just... It's a lot coming back here."

He nodded. "I know it's hard to be home."

Hard to be home. Bittersweet was more like it. Flathead Reservation was good-sized with more employment opportunities than the nearby Macawi Reservation—the casino and the sale of timber drove the economy—but there remained an undercurrent of inequality and financial insecurity that fueled much of the social problems affecting the tribes.

Alcoholism, domestic violence, drug abuse—they were common enough among the Native people as an aftereffect of generations of subjugation at the hands of settlers and missionaries with an inflated sense of entitlement.

But home was still achingly beautiful to eyes that misted from a bone-deep homesickness that no amount of avoiding could smother.

A sigh escaped her lips but not Ellis's notice. "How long has it been since you've been home?"

"Too long and not long enough," she answered wistfully watching the scenery pass by in a colorful blur. "It's been about five years, I think."

Saying it aloud made her feel worse. It was easy to lose track of time when you were busy with your life and that life included a time-consuming career but it was so much more than that simple answer. She avoided this place—and her mother—because this place held her dreams and her nightmares clutched tightly in its fist.

Being honest with herself, she didn't know if she'd ever be able to return home without suffering the feeling of being smothered beneath the weight of the past.

But today wasn't about her—it was about Nayeli.

She realized the same hope she'd harbored as a young, grieving teen following Nayeli's case still burned inside her. In seeking justice for another, maybe she could find some semblance of closure for Mikaya.

"What's the best memory you have of living in Flathead?" Ellis asked, his arm crooked out the open window.

She shook her head. "I don't want to play that game."

"C'mon, it could help. Sometimes we let our minds paint over the good times and all we end up remembering is the bad stuff. I need you to hold on to something good so you can stay focused."

Dakota shot Ellis a dark look. She didn't like being managed, but there was a certain level of logic to his suggestion. She'd never returned to Flathead on a case and it mattered how she reacted to being home again. She needed her head on straight, not struggling to breathe because the memories were being shoved down her throat.

Drawing a deep breath, she pulled a memory free—something she hadn't dared to think about since she was a kid.

The dappled sunlight peeked in and out of the passing clouds, casting dancing shadows across her face.

"It was one of the hottest summers I can remember," Dakota began, smiling grudgingly. "We were wilting like houseplants left in the sun. Mikaya talked our mom into letting her borrow the car, even though she didn't have a license yet, so we could go swimming at Flathead Lake. We packed the car with a blanket, some towels and sandwiches, and headed out. We played the music loud, laughed and felt like grown-ups. That day on the lake was almost perfect. I thought my sister was the coolest person on the planet and I wanted to be just like her. I still remember her purple bikini top and how beautiful she was. I thought, if I turned out to be half as pretty as my sister, life would be damn good. I idolized her." She trailed off, weathering the inevitable wave of pain that always followed a memory of Mikaya. "The smell of coconut suntan lotion always reminds me of that day on the lake." She wiped at a sudden tear, nodding. "It was a good day."

That day had been the catalyst of Mikaya getting a job at the diner. She planned to save enough money to buy her own car. She'd been $300 shy of her goal when she was killed.

A cold chill shook Dakota's frame, and she shot Ellis a short smile. "A goose walked over my grave."

"Those damn ghost geese are a menace," Ellis joked, teasing a more genuine smile from Dakota.

"I'm glad you're here with me," Dakota said, ignoring all of the boundary rules about keeping things professional. "I think you're the only person who would truly understand how difficult returning home is for me."

Ellis sobered, acknowledging her comment with a grave nod. Words would just muck things up and he seemed to understand that. *Let the moment be, whatever it needed to be, and then move on.*

They had a list of contacts to start with, all of whom had remained in Flathead, so they wasted no time in going down the list.

First up, Evelyn Redhawk, one of Nayeli's closest friends growing up. Evelyn and Nakita had remained in contact over the years, the initial connection being Nayeli, but they'd since grown close on their own terms. If anyone would know about a boyfriend, it would be Evelyn.

Evelyn worked as a tourism and hospitality manager at the casino, an integral cog in the tourism machine that drew people to the area, infusing much-needed cash into the region.

Nakita gave Evelyn a heads-up that they were coming and as soon as they arrived, Evelyn was waiting for them. A tall, graceful woman with long hair pulled into a stylish bun held in place with a beautifully beaded hairpiece, she ushered them into her on-site office and closed the door for privacy.

Her office was smart and tidy with enlarged historical photographs of Indigenous people at the turn of the century hanging on the wall. She smiled as she gestured for them to take a seat as she sank into the large leather chair behind the expansive desk. "Nakita called and told me you were coming and why." She inhaled a breath and shook her head, amazed at the turn of events. "After all this time...for Cheyenne to pop up like that... It's something of a miracle."

Dakota smiled. "Definitely a stroke of good luck at work. Nakita said that you and Nayeli were best friends growing up."

"Like sisters," Evelyn said. "I always liked to think we were perhaps soul sisters. The day she died, a piece of me died with her."

Dakota knew that feeling. "Nakita said it was a surprise when she took that job in Whitefish, out of character, even. Do you know if she was seeing someone there? Perhaps secretly?"

Evelyn chuckled, admitting, "It was a surprise to her family but not to me. We'd been talking about going into the hospitality business since freshman year in high school. We had a plan— I'd handle the tourist stuff, she'd handle the guest services. In a way, my job today is because of our long-ago dream."

"Why didn't Nayeli share her aspirations with her mom and sister?"

Evelyn smiled, shaking her head at the memory of long-gone squabbles between loved ones. "Nayeli was so close to her mom and little sister but she always knew she'd have to leave Flathead in order to make her dreams come true. She wanted to manage a large hotel chain. She'd been planning to take college courses in hotel management when she found out she was pregnant. Still, even realizing she'd have to work twice as hard, she always planned to return to school after the baby came. People always underestimated Nayeli because she kept her thoughts and plans to herself, but that girl had ambition."

"So Nayeli wasn't seeing anyone in Whitefish?" Ellis asked.

"Not anyone serious," Evelyn answered, though a troubled frown creased her forehead and there seemed to be something she wasn't sure if she should share, but upon Dakota's encouragement, she admitted, "It feels like gossip and that feels like a betrayal to my friend, especially when nothing became of it when I shared the information with police, but there was someone she was seeing casually that I thought might not have been a good idea."

Ellis and Dakota perked up. "Who?" Dakota asked.

"Someone we grew up with who always held a torch for Nayeli, though she never really saw him as more than a friend. However, he started visiting her on weekends, and then she admitted that one night they'd ended up sleeping together. She felt really bad and cut it off."

"And how did he take the news?" Ellis asked.

"According to Nayeli, not well," Evelyn admitted with a wince. "He got a little physical with her—I guess he pushed her against the wall but she kicked him out before things got worse. As far as I know, he never came back around, which was a good thing."

"Is he the father of Nayeli's baby?" Dakota asked.

Evelyn was unsure. "I never asked and Nayeli didn't say. I figured it was her business and if she wanted me to know, she'd tell me. Or maybe she didn't know herself and didn't care to know. We never really talked about the paternity of her baby."

"Curiosity never got the better of you?" Dakota asked. "That kind of secret would've driven me crazy."

Evelyn shrugged. "A lot of us were raised by single mothers. Sometimes all a man does is get in the way. I supported her decision and her secret."

"So, who was the man she rejected?" Ellis asked.

Evelyn hesitated, conflicted. "He's a good man and I'd hate to rehash old hurts for nothing, plus his father is an important member of the tribal community. If I tell you, I'd ask that you handle your questioning with sensitivity. At the end of the day, we all loved Nayeli in our way and losing her was a huge blow to the community."

"If he's innocent, he'll have no worries about talking to us. Ultimately, finding Nayeli's killer is our main concern," Ellis said, saving Dakota the trouble of sounding hard-hearted. "A name, please."

Dakota smiled, supporting Ellis.

Evelyn huffed a short breath and pulled up a name on her phone. "His name is Leonard Two Eagles but we all called him

Lenny. He works odd jobs, as a handyman of sorts. His father is a tribal elder, and well-respected."

"Do you have a contact number for Leonard?" Dakota asked.

Evelyn sighed. "Yes." She scribbled down a number quickly and handed it to Dakota. "For what it's worth, I don't think Lenny was capable of hurting Nayeli. He truly loved her but it just wasn't meant to be."

Dakota pocketed the paper, appreciating the lead. "You said you shared the information with authorities?"

"Yes, I felt terrible doing it but it seemed the right thing to do." Evelyn's solemn answer seemed genuine, then she added, "When nothing became of the information, I was relieved. Like I said, Lenny is a good man who's had his struggles but he's worked hard to put all of that behind him."

Dakota shared a look with Ellis. There was no mention of Leonard in the original investigation. The follow-through on the case seemed half-hearted at best but there was nothing that could be done about that injustice now. All they could do was move forward.

"What if Cheyenne is Leonard's biological daughter?"

Evelyn held her ground. "If Nayeli wanted that information known, she would've shared it. It's not my place to do so. Not then and not now."

Dakota realized the woman was strong in her convictions but they had a lead to chase down. "We'll be in touch."

They left the casino and returned to the car, realizing they were going to have to spend more time in Flathead than she'd planned—another sign she was off her game.

Ellis, reading her mind, squinted into the slowly setting sun. "Well, I say we get a hotel, grab a pizza and regroup tomorrow. We're both tired, need to debrief and check in with Shilah about Deakins. Sound like a plan?"

It was a good plan. Solid. Except, there was one place she needed to visit before calling it a night—the one place she dreaded—and she didn't want to go alone. "I...uh...should probably pop into my mom's place before calling it a night," she said, her mouth suddenly feeling dry as dust. "I can drop you off at the hotel..."

Ellis regarded her with compassion, knowing the painful history between Dakota and her mother and how it tore at her. "Do you want to go alone or do you want backup?"

It was a simple question.

But somehow it felt heavy between them.

Her eyes welled up as she admitted in a barely audible voice, "I'd like backup."

And that's all he needed. Nodding, he tapped the roof of the car and said, "All right, let's do this," and Dakota never felt more supported by the man who didn't have to care anymore.

But he did anyway.

Chapter 14

Ellis could almost see the agitated energy rolling off Dakota in waves. He knew what it took for Dakota to admit she needed him to do this with her and he wasn't going to make it harder on her by drawing attention to her request.

Dakota had shared her childhood experiences with him when they were first dating, and he'd shared his, bonding through trauma and finding a kindred spirit in the shared pain. While his dad had been an abusive drug addict/alcoholic with no redeeming qualities, Dakota's mom had once been a good mother until tragedy ate her from the inside and the soothing burn of alcohol became her only solace.

Ellis thought that was the hardest part for Dakota—knowing that her mom had once been different. Being the child of an addict, sometimes the hope that they'll get better was the thing that broke you.

Except in Ellis's case, his dad had always been a piece of shit and he'd never harbored any delusion that he'd ever be anything but a worthless waste of oxygen.

When he died, Ellis hadn't shed a tear.

Best day of his life, actually.

"Does she know we're coming?" Ellis asked.

"No. I wasn't sure she'd be home if she knew I was coming. My mom pretends like she's not avoiding me, but I'm not

the only one who can't handle the past. Aside from the obliga-
tory phone call on birthdays, and the major holidays, mostly
Christmas and Thanksgiving, we don't talk and we definitely
don't visit."

"So, why today?"

Dakota shrugged, admitting, "I don't know, seems like the
right thing to do. I mean, I'm here. I don't really have an excuse."

"Maybe she'll be happy to see you. Time has a way of healing old wounds."

Dakota's wry expression revealed her opinion on that adage.
"We'll see. I'll just apologize in advance if she's not exactly a
welcoming hostess. We won't stay long," she promised.

But he was willing to stay for as long as she needed. Dakota prided herself on being self-sufficient, independent and
strong, but he knew the side of her she protected like a Dober-
man against intruders.

Ellis reached over, entwining his fingers with Dakota's. The
gesture was silent, no words exchanged, yet it spoke volumes of
the support and understanding he was offering her.

The drive continued in a quiet solidarity, the world outside passing by as the landscape gradually changed. The road
stretched out, weaving through an expanse of open land with
occasional clusters of homes and cabins as the beauty of the area
exploded in brilliant colors like spilled paint from God's palette.

Every so often, Ellis would shoot Dakota a glance. Not the
curious or probing kind, but the reassuring ones that said he
was right there with her, ready to face whatever awaited them.
Maybe he was overstepping but he felt Dakota's need and responded, damn the supposed rules.

Dakota took a deep breath, her gaze focused on the road
ahead. "It's just past this bend," she murmured.

As they rounded the curve, a modest house came into view.
The paint was peeling off in places, but it was tidy and well-kept,
showing a certain level of attention to the small garden spilling over with bright, red tomatoes and large cucumber leaves
shadowing green cucumbers ready for harvest.

"Your mom's a gardener?" he observed as they parked in the
driveway beside an older sedan.

"Yeah, she's always had a green thumb," Dakota answered, climbing from the car, squinting against the sun as it played peekaboo with the passing clouds. "Something I didn't inherit."

Ellis chuckled. He remembered Dakota's black thumb. RIP to any plant she'd brought home until she finally accepted that silk plants were her only option.

Dakota bounded up the two short steps to the front door, but hesitated, her hand on the door handle. Her gaze darted toward the window of the house, as if half expecting her mother to appear. "You know, I've been preparing myself for this moment for so long, but now that it's here... I'm not sure if I can go through with it."

"Whatever happens in there, just remember you're not alone. I'm here with you."

Dakota met his gaze, her eyes glistening with unshed tears until she straightened her spine and cautiously opened the door, calling out, "Mom? You home?"

From his vantage point, Ellis could see a bedroom door slowly creak open to reveal a woman with salt-and-pepper hair, lines of age and hardship etched on her face. Her eyes, the same shade as Dakota's but weighed down by years of sorrow, widened in shocked recognition.

"Dakota?" Her voice was barely above a whisper, thick with disbelief.

Dakota swallowed hard, her posture straight yet hesitant. "Hi, Mom."

An uncomfortable silence stretched between them, as if each were stuck in a loop and unable to move past the glitch.

Attempting to bridge the gap, Ellis cleared his throat slightly and stepped forward. "Hello, Mrs. Foster. I'm Ellis, Dakota's... partner."

Dakota snapped out of her funk and picked up the slack with quick introductions. "Ellis, this is my mom, Amara Foster. Mom, meet my partner, FBI agent Ellis Vaughn."

"Partner..." she queried, sizing him up for a moment "...in life or work?"

"No, he's my colleague," Dakota answered for him. "I mean,

we dated once before but that ended and now we're just colleagues...working a case."

One thin eyebrow shot up. "Oh, well, that sounds complicated."

Dakota's chin lifted, as if readying for a fight and preparing
to counter any sling or arrow. "It's not. Perfectly professional
between us. No problems whatsoever."

"Hmm...well, nice to meet you, Ellis," Amara said, gesturing toward the living room. "Come, sit. I have sun tea. Brewed
this morning."

Both Ellis and Dakota declined as they sat on the faded ging-
ham sofa. Time had frozen some moments; pictures of a younger
Dakota with a bright smile, some with her sister and a few with
all three in happier times.

"So," Dakota's mom began, her voice quavering with forced
casualness, "how's the city? Still as busy and loud as ever?"

Dakota chuckled softly, "Even busier, I think. But it's home,
you know?"

Her mom nodded, sinking into a chair, awkward in the space
between them. "And the job?"

"Good. I made the new BIA Task Force. That's why we're in
Flathead. We're working a local case so I thought I'd pop by."

A subtle frown of interest crossed Amara's features. "Local?
Which case?" The faint burgeoning unsaid hope caused Dakota
to hastily clarify.

"It's not Mikaya's case, a different girl. Her name was Nayeli Swiftwater. She was killed—"

"In Whitefish," Amara finished with a subtle stiffness of her
mouth. "I remember."

Dakota didn't hide her surprise, murmuring, "I didn't think
you'd remember much of that time period. It was only a few
years after Mikaya died."

Amara didn't flinch as she said, "I remember far more than
you think, far more than I'd like to. Being a drunk didn't save
me from remembering a lot."

Dakota shot Ellis a look as if reaching her breaking point already, unable to bridge the gap between them. It killed him to

see her trying to find common ground yet failing. "Well, speaking of... How's your sobriety going?"

"Each day has its struggles but I have my support group, my work and my garden. I'm managing."

"I'm glad to hear that, Mom," Dakota said. "You look good."

"Your garden is impressive," Ellis said, trying to find an inroad to a less painful topic. "Those tomatoes are better than what you can find in the store."

The first genuine smile wreathed Amara's face as she said, "I'll send some with you when you go. I always end up with more than I can use." She cast a hopeful look Dakota's way, adding, "I've been pickling, too. I can send you with a few jars of homemade pickles. I remember them being your favorite."

Dakota shared with Ellis, "I used to eat so many pickles as a kid. My mom makes the absolute best." To her mom, she said with a smile, "That would be great, Mom."

The air in the room seemed to lighten, as if the room itself released a deep breath, and conversation started to flow more easily.

By the time they wrapped things up, Dakota actually seemed glad they made the stop.

True to her promise, Amara fetched the jars of pickled cucumbers and a bag of ripe tomatoes. "For the road," she said, handing them to Dakota.

Ellis read the body language between the two women and he sensed something had shifted between them. It was small but it was a good start to something even better in the future.

They lingered longer than anticipated, sharing memories and skirting around certain topics. As the sun cast a soft glow over the garden, Dakota knew it was time to leave. She sent a silent, thankful look to Ellis and said, "We need to get to our hotel. Early start tomorrow."

Amara's eyes moved between the pair. "Had I known you were coming, I would've cleaned up your old room. It's currently storage for my craft supplies. I've a dream catcher workshop at the tribal center next week. Your room is filled with beads and frames."

Dakota smiled. "It's okay, Mom. We have reservations. Plus, I like sticking to routines during a case. Helps keep me focused. Tomorrow we're talking with Leonard Two Eagles and a few other people and I want to be mentally sharp."

Amara's eyes showed recognition. "Why Lenny? Is he all right?"

"I can't share case specifics," Dakota began, "but any insights about him you'd like to share?"

"He's turned his life around. Did a great job tilling my garden. I even hired him to paint the house next week. If you need a character reference, I'd back him."

Smiling, Dakota replied, "Noted. Thanks, Mom." They hugged awkwardly but what could you expect after a five-year hiatus from the mother/daughter dynamic? It was a start and Dakota would take it.

En route to the hotel, the atmosphere in the car was quiet, punctuated by the soft music on the radio. Pine Ridge Inn, their last-minute choice, was an old yet charming three-story building.

Pulling into the parking lot, Dakota spotted an oddity—a black sedan with dark windows. A sense of déjà vu hit her; she'd seen it near Amara's house earlier. As if on cue, the sedan exited the lot in a rush.

"That car seemed familiar, didn't it?" Ellis questioned.

"It was near my mom's. I found it peculiar then and now," Dakota admitted with narrowed gaze.

Her phone buzzed, displaying a chilling message: "Stop digging before someone gets hurt."

"Damn it," she swore under her breath. "Look at this," Dakota said, showing Ellis the message. "Brave keyboard warriors. Now I'll have to change my number."

"Forward that to your IT," Ellis said, surveying the surroundings. "You think it's Deakins's men tailing us?"

"Zoey mentioned they have two cars. Zoey took out one in the accident and the other was probably tailing us after we left the compound. That sedan might not be Deakins's," Dakota said.

"Which implies someone else is getting real uncomfortable about us asking around about Nayeli's case."

"That's always a good sign we're on the right track," Dakota quipped, shaking her phone playfully. "Thanks, anonymous keyboard warrior, for the validation."

Ellis chuckled and collected his key card. "I'd offer to share a room for safety's sake but I wouldn't want you to get the wrong idea that I was trying to get frisky."

"Frisky?"

"Yeah," he returned with a grin that sent butterflies dancing down her spine. "I said what I said."

A familiar warmth spread across her skin as memories of their "frisky" adventures flooded her brain and nearly stole her breath. A charged, playful silence grew between them and Dakota felt the tug to close the distance but she held back. The mantra "Keep things professional" seemed a distant echo as her fluttering heartbeat drowned out the good sense of that decision.

She'd underestimated the power of their chemistry when she'd naively assumed she could just ignore it.

Right now, ignoring the urge to reach up and pull him straight to her lips was like trying to yell into the swirling winds of a tornado to "back off," but that's what she needed to do.

Clearing her throat and breaking the spell, she scooped up her key card, joking, "Well, nice to know we have fans," and acted as if she hadn't been scorched by the sudden heat kindling between them.

They parted ways and Dakota let herself into her room, leaning against the door to take big, calming breaths, reminding herself that *she* was in control—not her hormones. Once she was sufficiently right in her head again, she focused on doing her usual safety checks before settling in her room for the night.

But alone in her hotel room, Dakota's emotional armor crumbled as she realized the threat might not be for her, but for the only family she had left behind on the reservation. And that thought was chilling—and aggravating.

Come for me all you want but leave my mom out of it.

She chewed the side of her cheek, sinking into the realization that she didn't want to be alone tonight but there was only one person she wanted beside her in that moment.

And she couldn't fight it.

Chapter 15

Ellis was barely settled when a soft knock echoed through the room. His pulse quickened, hoping it was Dakota. When he saw her, a rush of warmth surprised him, a surge of relief and happiness all at once.

"Is something wrong?" he asked, trying to appear chill when all he wanted was to pull her close and forget the world outside.

Dakota hesitated. "Could we…maybe get some pizza?"

It wasn't just her words, but the depth in her eyes that caught him off guard. The vulnerability there mirrored his own tumultuous feelings. They stood on the precipice of something deep and irreversible, and he felt his resolve waver.

From the look of it, so did hers.

It wasn't pizza she hungered for—and he was caught between giving in to what they both wanted in that moment and being the stronger person and shutting her down.

Dakota saved him from making that choice—taking control herself.

"I know we've agreed to keep things professional and I know I'm going back on my word but I don't care. I need you right now. Can we just pretend for a minute that the last two years didn't happen and just be who we used to be with each other?"

Was it possible? Was it wise? Hell, he didn't know the answer to either of those questions. All he knew was that his body needed hers like his lungs needed oxygen and he was tired of pretending otherwise.

Ellis reached for her hand, drawing her slowly into his room and shutting the door. "Are you sure?" he asked, their fingers intertwining. "It's not too late to change your mind."

Dakota lifted on her toes, pulling his hands and hers around her back as he drew her close. "I'm not changing my mind."

Ellis felt a spark of something familiar, something electric that made his heart race. He leaned closer, their faces just inches apart, their breaths mingling. This woman knew him like no one else, understood the private pain he carried from his childhood and gave him space to be who he needed to be. She was a kindred spirit, even if life had wedged them apart.

He didn't want to waste another minute second-guessing what was between them. He wasn't naive enough to think there wouldn't be consequences but his brain stubbornly refused to let that voice into his mental theater.

His lips found hers in a kiss that was soft at first but quickly intensified. Dakota's lips parted, welcoming him in with a moan that escaped her throat. Their tongues tangled, danced, as if they'd never stopped kissing. Heat built between them, igniting the desire they'd both done their best to smother.

Hands explored each other's bodies, as if reclaiming what had been lost. She shivered as his rough stubble scratched against her soft skin. Her nails dug into his shoulders, leaving small marks of possession. It was intense, passionate and all-consuming.

He'd dreamed of this moment but his imagination paled in comparison.

Dakota's small gasps poured gasoline into his soul as he devoured her from head to toe, lingering on the swollen peaks of her upturned beautiful breasts, suckling the areolas, using his tongue to swirl the tightened tips until she writhed beneath him, thrusting her hips toward the hard shaft between them.

"Ellis," she cried in a breathy groan that sent powerful surges throughout his body until he was nearly mindless with the need to feel her clasp around his length.

The scent of their sweat-slicked bodies drove him mad, desperate to sink deep between her hot wetness. Ellis pushed himself inside Dakota, instantly groaning with pleasure as she tightened all around him as her legs wound around his waist, drawing him deeper inside. He could die right now and leave this plane a happy man.

God, he'd missed her. Not only the sex—but her. Everything about Dakota made his heart sing. Even when she was being a stubborn ass, he missed her presence in his life.

He thrust against her with deliberate care, remembering the exact angle that always sent her straight to that sweet place of total oblivion.

"God, yes, Ellis," she groaned, clutching at him with mindless pleasure. "That's the spot…"

Pride and pleasure mixed with overwhelming emotion as he ground into her, rocking her body with each push. Dakota stiffened as she cried out, the sound of total abandon releasing his own climax.

"Uhhhh, Dakota…" Tears blinded him as her name exploded from his lips as he came hard, creating a confusing explosion of ecstasy and loss that he was helpless to stop. Burying his face against the sweetness of her neck, he gasped as he finished, his soul leaving his body as he lay completely spent.

He reluctantly rolled off her, surreptitiously wiping at his eyes. The last thing he needed was Dakota knowing that having sex with her had brought him to tears. He rose and grabbed a towel, handing it to her, much like old times. She smiled shyly, accepting the towel, but asked, "Would you mind if I showered instead? You could join me if you want."

"I'll start the water," he said, not about to give up the chance to be naked with Dakota a few minutes longer. They both knew they were acting on borrowed time. What existed outside of this moment wasn't a reality where they ended up together, but in this bubble, they were free to do and be whatever they wanted.

The intimate memories of Ellis filled her senses. Memories she'd tucked far away, though they lingered close to the surface. She missed being a part of his life and vice versa. People liked to say that you don't know what you've got until it's gone but

Dakota always knew that losing Ellis would hurt for a lifetime. And so far, she hadn't been wrong.

While Dakota had moved on in the years apart, no one had made her feel quite like Ellis did. No one understood her like he had, or seemed able to hear what she was saying, even if she hadn't said a word. He had a special kind of magic that caressed her soul with the soft touch of a lover and she desperately missed that connection.

"I need to tell you something," she whispered as they stood close in the shower, her fingers tracing the contours of his body. His gaze remained fixed on her, expectant. "I don't actually have a boyfriend."

A soft chuckle escaped him. "I figured."

She raised an eyebrow, handing him the soap. "How?"

Ellis, gently lathering her skin, replied, "You are honest to a fault—and because of that—you're a terrible liar."

She accepted that judgment. "Guilty as charged." A weighty pause filled the air before Dakota murmured, "Being with others never felt the same. You were hard to replace."

Ellis's expression softened. "The feeling was mutual." Pulling her under the spray, he continued, "But we can't change the past. That incident, my outburst... I saw myself turning into my father. I needed help. You were right to leave."

Dakota's voice was laced with pain. "You're not him." And she believed that, but she'd been so shocked by the sudden explosion of violence from him that it'd thrown her world into a panic. "But I was afraid in that moment," she admitted quietly.

"I'm not him," he agreed, adding somberly, "but I was on that path."

Had he been, though? She'd had a lot of time to think about that day and sometimes she questioned whether she'd thrown in the towel too early. No one was perfect, so why had she given up on Ellis so quickly? She drew a deep breath, admitting, "Maybe I was too harsh that day. You'd been under a lot of stress—"

"No, don't do that, Dakota," he cut in with a warning, shaking his head adamantly. "I won't have you make excuses for what I did. There's no justification for that kind of behavior, ever. You knew that then, and deep down you know that now.

Don't second-guess the right decision just because it hurts to remember what we had."

What we had. Past tense.

"But what if it was a mistake?"

"It wasn't."

How could he say that so easily? Was he relieved that they weren't together anymore? The thought stung. "You seem pretty sure that breaking up was the right thing to do," she said, trying to keep the hurt from her tone. "I wish I had the same confidence."

"Dakota, I saw myself through your eyes that day and I was sick to my stomach. I swore I'd never be like that bastard and yet, in that moment, I was just like him."

"You could never be like your father," Dakota protested, hating that he was carrying that guilt. "Never."

"You don't get it. I was him in that moment. My rage blotted out everything. I didn't care about anything. I reacted and I broke something that belonged to you—something irreplaceable. My dad did that shit all the time but it all starts somewhere. One act leads to another and then another. You were right to leave me. I deserved it."

"But you've changed, I can see it," Dakota said. "One mistake shouldn't ruin any chance in the future, right?"

"Dakota… What if it's a part of me and it's just lurking beneath the surface? As much as I've worked to change the parts of myself that are too much like my dad, he's still in there. I can't stomach the thought of you seeing me like that again. I just can't."

What could she say to that? Nothing. She wasn't going to argue the point but she shared in a small voice, "Being without you, it's been hard. I feel like a piece of me is missing. When does that feeling go away?"

"I wish I could say. Maybe it never does."

God, she hoped that wasn't the case. Dakota didn't like admitting a weakness but Ellis was her Achilles' heel. She needed to find a way to get over him if this was all they'd ever have. "How did you do it?"

"Do what?"

"Forget about me."

Ellis swore beneath his breath, shaking his head as if she were being deliberately difficult. He bracketed her against the cold shower wall, leaning in, kissing her hard and almost desperately. Their tongues tangled in an emotional dance that rang of heartbreak and loss but never new beginnings, and it was enough to split her in half. "Does that feel like I've forgotten about you?" he asked huskily, pulling away, his gaze tortured but laced with frustration. "You're the one person I'd do anything for. I'd give you my last breath if you needed it. Don't think for one second that I'm over you or that I ever will be because it ain't happening."

Dakota knew it was wrong of her to need to hear that from Ellis but the idea of suffering alone made her twist in on herself. Misery loved company, she supposed. "So, what does that mean for us?" she asked.

"It means if you ever need me, I'll be there."

Her eyes watered. What if she needed him right now? But what he wasn't saying was that there was no putting the pieces of their life together. She should've been grateful for his wisdom but she wasn't. If anything, she felt her heart cracking all over again and that made her want to howl at the moon for opening a box that should've stayed closed.

"You're an incredible woman. I'll always cherish what we had," he said.

That was the last thing she wanted to hear but she nodded, accepting the sentiment at its face value.

"So what happens now?" she asked, her voice choked.

"We solve this case and we go back to our lives. If this case goes well, I could return to Narcotics. It's what I've been working toward since Carleton bounced me from the division."

Dakota felt a pang of dread. Narcotics had changed him before, dragging him into dark places where his demons felt too comfortable to play. She knew this was a touchy subject for Ellis but the idea of him returning to Narcotics made her sick to her stomach. She had to try and be the voice of reason. "But you're doing so well in Missing Persons," she argued gently. "Maybe that's where you're truly supposed to be. You're a bril-

liant investigator with a warm heart. I didn't say anything before but I peeked at your record since joining Missing Persons
and you've received nothing but accolades from your superiors
for your investigative skills. At least with Missing Persons you
can see the good you're doing, unlike Narcotics, where it's just
a day-in and day-out, never-ending stream of drugs hitting the
streets and killing people."

"What are you saying? Narcotics doesn't do any good for
the general public?"

"No, of course not, but you've got to admit, no matter how
many drugs you take off the street, there's another shipment
coming in on another boat. The war on drugs is never going to
end. Hell, sometimes I think they ought to just legalize everything and tax the shit out of it like a legitimate business. That
might be the only way we make any progress on the epidemic
of drug trafficking."

Under normal circumstances, the conversation would've been
entertaining. It wasn't the first time they'd joked that legaliz-
ing drugs might be the answer, but that was during better times
when they were together.

Now, it felt like she'd insulted him and thrown a gauntlet by
the way a curtain slammed down behind his eyes. He stiffened,
shutting off the water. "Narcotics is where I belong. Even if you
don't think we're making a difference, I believe that we are, and
the work is important."

Dakota knew his narrow-minded vision to return to Narcotics had everything to do with the hatred he harbored for his dad.
Before Ellis's dad ate a bullet, he'd been a street dealer and he
hadn't been discriminate about whom he sold drugs to. Ellis
had shared that his dad had thought it was funny to watch kids
get high for the first time. One kid had OD'd. He'd only been
twelve. "I'm not saying the work isn't important," she persisted,
struggling to say the right thing. "I'm just saying—"

"Let's let it go," he said, wrapping a towel around his mid-
section and handing her a towel, but gone was the warmth and
tenderness of only a few moments ago—as was any hope of
grabbing a pizza and eating it together while watching a movie
like they used to.

Damn you, Ellis. Sometimes you're as stubborn as a mule.

Silence hung between them as they dried off. The emotional gulf was palpable. Dakota backed down reluctantly. "I guess you know what's best for you."

Looks like it was vending machine surprise and a heart full of regret for dinner tonight.

Chapter 16

Ellis slept fitfully, haunted by dreams of a future that never had a chance to happen. When the alarm pierced the darkness, he rose unsteadily and went through the motions of starting his day. Over bitter coffee, he pushed aside tangled thoughts of last night with Dakota and tried to focus on the case.

They'd agreed to be professional, but the charged air between them in the lobby said otherwise. Dakota's eyes were shadowed, proof she'd fared no better rest-wise.

"Shilah got the warrant for Deakins's financials," she said as they walked through the lobby and into the parking lot. Her distant tone held zero warmth, a complete 180 from the woman she'd been in his arms last night. "She said we've got enough to pull a warrant for The Congregation's financials but it wasn't easy. The judge said we were walking a fine line and we'd better have a good reason for poking into Deakins's church business. Now that we know that Deakins has friends in high places, makes me wonder if Deakins was tight with the judge, too."

"Probably a coincidence but I'll file that away as a possibility," Ellis said, pausing as Dakota purposefully went to the driver's side. It was a silent but loud assertion that they were going back to professional mode, and he couldn't say that he was glad, but he knew it was for the best.

He hated the distance between them but it was better this

way. Did he want to be with Dakota? Hell yes. Was it healthy for either of them to forget the past and go blindly into the future when he couldn't promise the ghost of his father wouldn't show up again? No, he couldn't take that chance. He loved her too much to bank on a hope and a prayer buoyed by good intentions. Dakota deserved so much better.

Besides, what she said about him going back to Narcotics really punched him in the gut. She was wrong about Narcotics being a never-ending cycle that didn't do any good. Every shipment they took off the streets was potentially someone who didn't get addicted or die trying it.

When he was fresh on the detail, a case stuck with him that to this day chased his sense of duty. A sixteen-year-old kid died after trying meth for the first time. What the kid didn't know was it was laced with fentanyl and the tiny dose was enough to put the kid into the ground. He'd been the one to tell the kid's mother that her child was gone. You never forgot the sound of a mother's heart breaking.

That case had triggered the memory of the twelve-year-old who'd died because of his dad and it'd nearly crushed Ellis. Another street kid who died on a dirty couch in an abandoned warehouse, whose body wasn't found until two days later by construction workers getting ready to demo the building.

That kid had had a name, a future.

How could he explain that being on the streets, fighting the war on drugs helped him keep the darkness inside him in a manageable place? She knew his childhood was shit—but she only got the highlight reel. He'd never told her all the bad things that happened and he probably never would. Some things needed to stay private.

But every time he dragged a drug dealer off the street, confiscated a shipment of product or stopped a kid from throwing their life away—he was giving his old man the middle finger.

He wouldn't give that up—his sanity needed it. His therapist had suggested too many times he needed to share those dark things because light chases away shadows, but burdening Dakota with his bullshit past seemed unfair then and definitely not appropriate now.

"I also talked briefly to Zoey this morning."

At the mention of Zoey, he shoved his personal thoughts aside. "Yeah? How's she doing?"

"She said the food is much better at the safe house and the nurse is really nice but she's worried about her parents. The kid has such a heart of gold. Even though she knows her parents screwed up and lost their minds for a minute, she doesn't want them in jail."

"She's a good kid," he agreed, hating that Zoey was in the middle of a war she didn't start. "I really hope her adopted parents didn't have anything to do with Nayeli's death. Maybe they're victims in all of this, too, and just overreacted to the stress of the moment. I've seen it happen before."

"Yeah, maybe. I'm trying not to let my personal feelings get in the way. I really don't care for Barbara-Jean. Just goes to show there are difficult people anywhere you go—even off-grid."

He chuckled. No argument there.

"I called ahead. The receptionist said that Leonard Two Eagles always mows the grass on Wednesdays. He should be easy to spot."

As they pulled up to the parking lot, they saw a man on a riding lawn mower, wearing large ear-protecting headphones and focusing on the task. They exited the vehicle and headed toward him, waving to get his attention.

Leonard cut the engine warily and removed his headphones. His dark eyes were hard, distrustful. "Main office is down that way," he directed, but before he could replace his headphones, Ellis caught his attention.

"Leonard Two Eagles?" he asked, and the man nodded slowly, regarding them with suspicion. "I'm FBI Agent Ellis Vaughn and this is my colleague, BIA Agent Dakota Foster. Can we talk for a minute?"

Leonard nodded, though he didn't look like he trusted either of them, which wasn't surprising given his record. When he couldn't sleep last night, Ellis had logged on to his laptop and accessed Leonard's file.

A garden-variety criminal—drugs, petty theft, vandalism and

assault and battery—the man had been through some things, but according to Evelyn and Amara he'd turned his life around. Ellis was more concerned with what might've happened seventeen years ago between him and Nayeli. Sometimes guilt was a powerful motivator for change, too.

"What do you want?" Leonard asked.

"We understand that you were once close with Nayeli Swiftwater. Can you tell us what the nature of your relationship was?"

"Haven't heard that name in years," he said. "She's with the spirits now."

"Are you a spiritual man?" Dakota asked, curious.

"I didn't used to be," Leonard admitted, wiping at his forehead. Even though it was brisk, he was sweating. "But when I was in trouble a lot my father told me I needed to sweat out my demons, to ask the ancestors for help. I had nothing to lose at that point so I started going to the sweat lodge ceremonies. Each time I came out a little bit stronger. Now, I go regularly. Does that make me spiritual?" He shrugged. "But I know I'm better because of it." Leonard used the break to resecure his long dark hair in the hairband away from his face. Tribal tattoos crawled up his neck and spilled onto his chin. "So, why are you asking about Nayeli?"

"The case has been reopened," Dakota answered. "And your relationship?"

"We were friends."

"Just friends?" Ellis queried. "We heard you were dating."

"And what if we were? Are you talking to all of her friends?" he asked defensively. "Or are you coming at me because I have a record? I haven't had no trouble with the law in five years. Not a single thing. Ask my probation officer—he'll tell you. I've been toeing the line like I'm supposed to."

"No one is accusing you of anything," Dakota clarified, regarding him without emotion. "Is there a reason you feel attacked?"

"Yeah, because that's all you cops ever do. Doesn't matter what badge you're wearing, you're all the same. You see my record and assume I'm the problem."

"No one is assuming anything," Ellis returned calmly. "We heard that you and Nayeli had a romantic relationship that ended badly. Can you tell us about that?"

"Yeah? What about it?"

"Tell us about the last time you saw Nayeli," Ellis said.

When he hesitated, Dakota said, "If you have nothing to hide, you have nothing to worry about."

"I know what you want me to say—"

"We only want the truth," Ellis said.

"No, you want someone to take the rap for what happened to her, that's what you want. Well, it isn't going to be me. I didn't kill Nayeli. I would never. I loved her. You want the truth? That's the truth, I loved her more than anything on this earth but she didn't feel the same way about me."

"How'd you handle that?"

Leonard's mouth seamed as if ashamed. "Not real good. I was still drinking and stuff then. I think that's why she didn't want to be with me—and I really don't blame her for that—but at the time, it really crushed my heart, you know what I mean? And I didn't know how to handle my feelings."

"Did you hurt her?" Dakota asked.

"I pushed her around that night but I never hit her or nothing like that."

"And that night, was that the last night you saw her?" Ellis followed.

Leonard nodded solemnly. "Sometimes I think maybe if I'd cleaned up before it all happened, she might still be here and we'd be together."

"Do you remember when that was? The date, specifically."

"Of course I remember. It was August 25—I remember because I was arrested for drunk driving on my way back from her place that night."

Ellis did the math. That would've made Nayeli about two months pregnant.

Ellis and Dakota exchanged a glance. If the dates matched up...

"One more thing," Ellis said casually. "Would you consent to a DNA sample?"

* * *

They left Leonard with their contact cards and instructions to stick around town or else they'd have a talk with his probation officer. Leonard looked visibly shaken by their question about the DNA sample. Had it never occurred to him that the kidnapped infant could've been his?

"I don't think it's him," Dakota admitted, disappointed. "I mean, I've seen plenty of guys guilty of killing their significant other trying to play it off as innocent, but Leonard doesn't give off that vibe. He looked genuinely stricken at the idea that he might have a child he didn't know about."

Ellis agreed. "He's got a chip on his shoulder from years of being on the wrong side of the law but that doesn't make him a murderer. Plus, he doesn't strike me as the type of man who could kill a woman in cold blood and sneak off in the night with a baby. It doesn't add up. He might be Zoey's biological father but I doubt he's Nayeli's killer."

"Well, DNA should clear up a few things at least. I'll have Shilah get the warrant for his DNA."

"I don't even think he'll fight it. I think he wants to know, too," Ellis said.

Dakota nodded absently, but her thoughts kept drifting back to last night—the same thoughts that'd kept her from falling asleep at a decent hour and made waking up a Herculean effort. The way he'd kissed her, touched her… It had resurrected feelings she'd spent a long time burying. But it was a mistake, one they couldn't repeat, and she was frustrated with her own lack of self-control for practically jumping into his arms when he gave her a chance to reconsider.

At least Ellis had been trying to do the right thing.

She forced herself to focus. "You're right, he seemed genuinely shocked about the baby. I don't think he's our guy."

Ellis agreed as they got into the car. Dakota gripped the steering wheel tightly, hyperaware of his presence next to her. The interior still held traces of his scent, evoking memories of heated passion in that cramped motel bed. She shifted in her seat, willing the memories away.

"You okay?" Ellis asked.

"Yeah, fine," she said sharply.

An awkward silence filled the car until it threatened to smother her. Dakota's mind raced as she drove. Why couldn't she find that professional distance that she'd mastered before? She wanted to hate Ellis for complicating things, but the truth was she'd created this mess and that bothered her a lot.

Was it her fault that they had a combustible chemistry, no matter how hard they tried to ignore it? *Deflecting and justifications. Nice, Foster. C'mon, you're better than that.*

Okay, so it happened, and it can't happen again. She refused to lose herself to him like she had all those years ago. This case was too important to let emotions get in the way. *Shake it off, put it in its place and move on.*

"About last night…" Ellis finally began and she nearly jumped out of her skin. Was the man psychic or something? Or was she just that transparent?

"We don't have to go there," Dakota said tightly. "It was a mistake. We can't change the past. Let's just focus on finding justice for Nayeli."

Ellis looked like he wanted to argue but finally just nodded. Dakota swallowed hard against the ache in her chest. She had to stay detached, despite her traitorous heart begging her to fall into his arms again.

The ghosts of the past would just have to wait in line.

This case came first.

Chapter 17

The drive back to Missoula was quiet, the air still thick with unresolved tension from last night. Ellis was glad when they pulled into the hotel parking lot. He needed space to clear his head.

"I'll get us separate rooms," he told Dakota. She nodded, her face unreadable. It was possible fatigue made her seem unreachable but it could also be because they were both struggling with the aftermath of what they'd done.

Without much further discussion, they got their keys, made quick plans to meet in the morning as usual and then went their separate ways. Once in his room, Ellis sat on the edge of the bed and scrubbed a hand over his face. Last night had been a mistake, but damn if it didn't feel good at the time. He wished they could go back to how it used to be, before life got so goddamn complicated.

Maybe in a different timeline, he and Dakota were living their best lives, married with a couple of kids, making the dream work, but in this timeline? Shit, they'd made a huge mess of things.

His phone buzzed with a message from his work email. He frowned as a photo of Senator Mitchell Lawrence, arm in arm with Zachariah Deakins, popped up on his screen. The message was sent anonymously through the FBI tip line. Senator Lawrence was known for hawking family values loudly and obnoxiously whatever chance he could get. Ellis always gave guys like Lawrence the side-eye. No one was that virtuous. If you had to yell it to the rafters how rigidly you walked the line of morality, chances were you were playing fast and loose with the rules.

But the anonymous tip was clear—the men were definitely connected somehow. What role was the senator playing in this little mystery?

He probably should've just called but he headed over to Dakota's room, rapping on the door.

She answered cautiously.

"We got a lead," Ellis said without preamble, showing her the photo. "Senator Mitchell Lawrence is tied up in this somehow. We need to talk to him."

Dakota's jaw tightened as she studied the image. "Guess we're taking a trip to Helena," she said, adding, "Oh, and Shilah told me that the threatening text came from an untraceable burner. Looks like whoever my keyboard warrior is was at least not stupid enough to use their actual phone."

Ellis expected as much. "I had a feeling that was going to be the case. You're definitely going to need to swap out your number."

Dakota looked annoyed but nodded. However, she waited a beat before saying, "You could've just called me about the photo. You didn't have to tell me in person."

Right, yeah, I know that. I'm just stacking up stupid mistakes by the bushel.

"I needed to get ice and it was on the way," he lied gruffly.

"Oh, sorry. I shouldn't have assumed anything," Dakota said, her cheeks heating. "My mistake. Good night."

He acknowledged her sentiment with a jerked nod on the pretense of heading to the ice machine but as soon as Dakota closed her door, he changed direction and returned to his room, feeling like an idiot.

Ellis closed the door to his room and leaned against it with a sigh. Dakota was right—he didn't need to tell her about the lead in person. He just wanted an excuse to see her again, even though he knew he shouldn't.

Groaning quietly, he berated himself for acting like a love-sick teenager. They had a job to do. Personal feelings had no business on the playing field right now.

Still, seeing the faint flush on Dakota's cheeks threatened his resolve. He stood by his reasoning to keep things professional but that was his head talking, not his heart. That thing between them was a fire that couldn't be extinguished and was impossible to ignore but they had to try.

With a grunt of frustration, Ellis pushed off the door. A cold shower and a good night's sleep. That's what he needed to clear his head. In the morning, they would be focused, professional partners again—and they'd wash, rinse and repeat until this case closed.

Yet as he stripped down and stood under the frigid spray, he couldn't stop his thoughts from drifting back to Dakota. The silken warmth of her skin, the taste of her lips...

Get it together, man, he scolded himself. He ticked off the priorities: justice for Nayeli, answers for Zoey and getting back to Narcotics where he belonged. Too much was at stake. He couldn't afford distractions throwing him off course.

Ellis toweled off and sank onto the edge of the bed, dropping his head in his hands. Unwanted memories from two years ago surfaced, when he'd finally worked up the courage to see a therapist after Dakota left him.

After he'd acted like a psychotic toddler and destroyed her grandmother's crystal cookie jar in a fit of misplaced rage.

"Anger is a natural emotion, but violence is a choice," Dr. Singh had told him gently. "You cannot change how you were raised, Ellis. But you can choose to break the cycle of abuse. Be better than what came before."

At the time, her words had given him hope. But now, as his feelings for Dakota resurfaced, so did his deepest fears. What if the monster his father tried to turn him into was still lurking underneath the surface? Waiting to lash out and hurt those he cared for most?

Dakota had been right to walk away. She deserved someone uncomplicated, without so many broken pieces. Ellis was a chronic work in progress. Despite his best efforts, shadowy remnants of his father's cruelty still haunted him.

Although he no longer went to regular sessions anymore, Ellis kept Dr. Singh's number in his phone. Sort of like an "In case of emergency, break glass" situation.

He was proud that he hadn't yet had to use that safety lever but the fear that he could lose control again haunted him.

Again, he heard her voice, reminding him, "It's a process, Ellis. There will be setbacks. What matters most is that you keep getting back up."

Dakota was his weakness, but he had to stay strong—for both of them.

Dakota lay awake, staring up at the dark ceiling as sleep evaded her, yet again. The ghost of Ellis's touch still lingered on her skin, raising goose bumps. Her body ached for more, even as her mind pushed against her longing. She was stronger than this, wasn't she? She'd never been the type of woman to pine after a man, nor did she allow anything or anyone to cloud her judgment when it came to holding a personal boundary.

What made Ellis different from any other man she'd cut ties from in the past?

With a frustrated sigh, she kicked off the covers and went to stand by the window, gazing sightlessly over the parking lot. She shouldn't have let things go so far. She was to blame for what happened. Sure, it took two to tango, but she'd gone to his hotel room knowing full well what she was truly asking. She'd poked the sleeping bear and she couldn't be shocked that now that it was awake, it was hungry.

Well, what was done was done, right?

They had a job to do, and letting themselves get deeper involved would only end in heartbreak. Hadn't she learned that lesson already?

Resting her forehead against the cool glass, Dakota replayed every searing kiss, every hungry caress in her memory. Ellis had always been her weakness, a fire in her blood that nothing could quell. Much as she tried to resist him, desire won out.

But it was more than physical attraction. When Ellis held her, she felt a sense of homecoming, like the missing piece of herself had been restored. She had never stopped loving him, despite the bitter pain of their breakup years ago.

Dakota squeezed her eyes shut, remembering the shattered cookie jar, Ellis's uncontrollable rage. The yelling, the tears. Her heart had broken, but her will remained unbendable. She'd done what she had to and Ellis had agreed the decision had been sound.

But risking sounding like someone in denial, she could sense the change in Ellis. Was he the same man with a toxic well of rage percolating inside him, just waiting for the right moment to explode? Her gut told her that he wasn't but Ellis was afraid to test that theory. They'd never actually talked about that night, only the repercussions.

Resting her palm on the cool glass, Dakota considered reaching for her phone. One call, and she could feel the reassurance of Ellis's voice again. One call, and all her doubts might be silenced.

But she stopped herself. Tomorrow they would be professional partners once more. She was Dakota Foster—independent, uncompromising. Her spirit had been bruised but never broken. This was about justice, not burned bridges or second chances.

Dakota left the window and returned to bed. She would build an emotional wall between herself and Ellis, even as their bodies yearned to come together once more. Her heart had chosen self-preservation over the man who offered both boundless love and bottomless pain.

Dakota stared up at the dark ceiling, unable to quiet her racing mind. Could people truly change their nature, she wondered, or did the past leave permanent scars? Even though they both shared dark childhood moments, Ellis's childhood was the stuff of nightmares. His father had been a true villain, a man without any redeeming qualities from Ellis's point of view, and it took a lot for a kid to truly hate their parent.

Going through that kind of pain left trauma that never went away, no matter how you tried to bury it. Dakota still believed that working Narcotics had kept dredging up that poison until it was all that was left in Ellis's cup. She hated the idea of him returning to the very place that'd aggravated those wounds, but it wasn't her place to insert her feelings anymore.

She wanted to believe Ellis was a different man now—kinder, gentler. But a dark voice whispered warnings she couldn't ignore. What if she was wrong?

Being near Ellis again was emotionally exhausting. She had to remain hypervigilant, continually tamping down her desire while keeping her walls up. The work of constantly analyzing her every word and action to maintain that professional distance was wearing on her in ways that she hadn't seen coming.

Yet she was drawn to him like a moth to light, despite the risk of getting zapped. His laugh made her heart clench. His subtle scent stirred memories that left her aching. Shutting out the truth was impossible—she still loved him, after everything.

Which left her guarded, confused, oscillating between hope and fear. Part of her yearned to melt into his arms again, rekindle what they'd lost. Another part wanted to run, to protect the still-mending pieces of her heart before it was shattered beyond recognition.

Could she ever let go of the past? Did she even have the right to, when Nayeli's spirit still cried out for justice? The fact that she was even losing sleep over this was selfish. She had to stop.

Exhaustion seeped into Dakota's bones, but sleep would be difficult to find. Too many ghosts jostled for prominence in the darkened bedroom for any decent shut-eye. For now, she could only take things one moment at a time. And try to quiet the ceaseless chaos in her heart.

In her misguided youth, she'd dated an older man in college. At the time he'd seemed so much more emotionally intelligent and wise than the men her age. She'd been awestruck by his solid sense of self and she'd eaten advice from the palm of his hand—which he was fond of feeding her at the drop of a hat.

One thing about Silas that'd been incredibly alluring was his unwavering sense of always knowing what to do in any given situation. She'd asked him his secret, and feeling intellectually superior—something she came to learn was his ultimate failing—he'd shared his method.

"Baby girl," he'd drawled, smiling down at her with indulgence as she rested on his bare chest, "it's simple."

She gazed up at him with pure adoration. "Yeah, how so?"

"I'm always right—even if I'm wrong."

Dakota had chuckled, believing him to be joking, but he was completely serious.

"When you believe your way is right, it always is."

"But no one is always right, all of the time," Dakota had protested, lifting up to peer at him quizzically. "At the end of the day, you're only human and humans make mistakes. Even you."

Silas just shook his head as if she were adorably simple and unable to grasp the concept that he was sharing but before they could dive into that discussion more deeply, he'd distracted her with an epic lovemaking session that'd lasted into the wee hours of the morning.

She'd been too exhausted to return to the topic, but eventually she realized Silas wasn't the man she thought he was and broke it off without ever looking back.

However, she wondered if maybe Silas had influenced her more than she realized.

When she made a decision, she never changed her mind, even when she was wrong.

Chapter 18

The bitter hotel coffee did little to wake Ellis as he and Dakota left early to make the long drive to Helena where Lawrence kept an in-state office. This case had him in the car more than any case he'd ever been assigned and it was starting to wear on his nerves.

"Sleep okay?" he asked, making conversation, but one short look from Dakota told him, no, she hadn't and she wasn't up for small talk, which suited him fine. He didn't want to chat about the weather, either. "Are you driving or me?"

"You," she responded, pulling her sunglasses from her bag, pushing them farther up on the bridge of her nose as she slid into the passenger seat. "I have a splitting headache and the sun is stabbing my brain."

Yeah, same. A tiny reluctant smile tugged at the corner of his mouth. He'd be willing to bet Dakota would sleep the entire way to Helena while he drove. Dakota had slept through more road trips than he could count, rising refreshed and ready to roll while he, on the other hand, had to prop up his eyelids with toothpicks. He didn't mind, though—not then and not now.

True to his prediction, Dakota was lightly snoring before they'd even cleared the city limits of Missoula, but knowing that no matter what lay between them, she still felt safe enough in his company to sleep like a baby when she needed it gave his masculine pride a much-needed lift.

They arrived at the slick, executive building in good time and an aide ushered them into Senator Lawrence's expansive office.

The heavy oak door swung open to reveal an office that looked more like a luxury hotel lobby than a public servant's workplace. Plush cream carpeting swallowed their footsteps as they walked past framed photos of Lawrence with other dignitaries.

Behind an imposing desk of highly polished mahogany, a wall of built-in bookcases stood packed with leather-bound volumes. Ellis noted the complete works of Shakespeare and other classics one would display to look cultured but likely never read, and he immediately started to get a vibe from the man that didn't bode well.

The sitting area held a crystal vase bursting with fresh lilies and ornate antique sofas upholstered in brocade.

Everything about the office shrieked of old money and privilege. Ellis wondered how many donations from struggling families could have furnished this ostentatious space. He glanced at Dakota and knew she was thinking the same.

The distinguished senator rose from behind his desk to shake their hands with a polite, concerned expression.

"You're lucky I'm in town this week. How can I assist the FBI and BIA today?" Lawrence asked mildly as he settled into the leather chair behind his imposing mahogany desk.

"We appreciate you making time for us on such short notice," Ellis said. "We'll try to make this as quick as possible."

"Anything I can do to help," Lawrence said.

Ellis opened by sliding the photo of Lawrence and Zachariah Deakins he'd had printed across the desk. If the senator recognized it, he didn't let on. Lawrence's stare was blank as he said, "By the looks of it, this is a publicity shot," Lawrence replied easily. "I've taken countless of these over the years. Is there a reason I should know this person?"

"His name is Zachariah Deakins. He's the pastor/leader of a minimalist group called The Congregation in Stevensville."

"Hmm, can't say the name rings a bell," Lawrence said. "Has he done something wrong?"

"Not that we know of, yet, but personally, I think people who run cults are always hiding something," Dakota said.

"You said it was a group, like a church," Lawrence said, confused. "Why are you calling it a cult?"

"Because it's very cult-ish," Dakota returned simply. "We visited the compound and it seemed deeply cult-like, and history has shown that cults are rarely a good thing, no matter how they like to paint the picture otherwise."

Lawrence chuckled with amusement at Dakota's judgment. "I see you have some strong personal feelings on the subject, but have they actually done anything wrong?"

"Not that we can tell," Ellis answered calmly. "But there are connections to the case we're working that are potentially serious."

"What case is that?"

"Seventeen years ago, a young Indigenous woman named Nayeli Swiftwater was found murdered in her Whitefish apartment and her six-week-old infant daughter, Cheyenne, was missing. The trail went cold and the case gathered dust until Nayeli's missing daughter showed up at a Butte hospital."

One brow went up. "Interesting. Where has the child been this whole time?"

"She was adopted by a family within The Congregation and living on the compound," Dakota shared. "But we haven't determined yet if the family who raised her are guilty of anything more than unknowingly adopting a stolen child."

"What a terrible tragedy," Lawrence murmured, shaking his head. "That poor girl. I hope she's all right."

"She's recovering," Ellis said, wanting to steer the conversation away from Zoey. "But that brings us back to you."

"Me? How?"

"Well, the compound was formerly a bankrupt summer camp known as Camp Serenity Falls, which was purchased by a company that traces back to you."

"Ah, I see," Lawrence connected the dots, quickly explaining, "my investment advisers are always making financial decisions without my involvement. All aboveboard, of course, but I leave the heavy lifting to the professionals. I own several companies, all funneled through my investment group. I couldn't even tell you all of the businesses in my portfolio. All I know is that my investments are robustly profitable, and for that I don't mind paying the exorbitant amount each year to my investment group for their labors." At that Lawrence smiled widely, unruffled and unconcerned.

But Ellis's investigative senses tingled.

"So you don't remember Nayeli's case?" Dakota asked. "It was pretty big news at the time. Being an upscale community, Whitefish isn't known for its violent crime."

For a split second, Ellis thought he saw Lawrence's genial mask crack. But the senator quickly composed himself, spreading his hands regretfully. "I'm embarrassed to admit that I don't remember the case. I take any crime committed against my constituency seriously—particularly violent crimes against young women—but I don't quite recall that one. I'm sorry."

Ellis supposed it was possible the senator missed the case because he hadn't actually been elected as senator yet when Nayeli was killed. At that time, Lawrence was still an attorney and serving in the House of Representatives and couldn't be expected to know about every murder case in his state.

Still, there was something about Lawrence that rubbed him wrong—or maybe it was just that Ellis felt all politicians, at some level, somewhere, had something to hide.

As they left Lawrence's office, Dakota felt the senator's eyes boring into her back. A warning, or a threat? Or was she seeing what her bias wanted her to see?

She shook off the ominous feeling as Ellis held the door for her. Still, unease lingered in her gut. Men like Lawrence weren't used to being questioned. For now he wore the mask of polite cooperation, but how long until it slipped?

"He's definitely hiding something," Dakota said quietly as they walked down the echoing marble hallway. "If he's involved in Nayeli's case…"

She didn't need to finish the thought. They both knew what

was at stake. A killer escaping justice. And even worse, if Lawrence was involved, now that he knew Zoey was alive, her safety could be at risk.

"Just to be on the safe side, I'll beef up the security at the safe house," Ellis said.

Dakota unconsciously flexed her hands, longing to grab Lawrence by his expensive lapels and shake the truth out of him, not the politically savvy responses that might as well have been crafted by his PR manager.

But they had to move carefully. Lawrence was no petty criminal. His wealth and connections could potentially make him dangerous, capable of burying inconvenient truths.

"Did you buy that?" Dakota asked, still chewing on the conversation. "Are we really supposed to believe that the senator doesn't have a clue what properties and businesses he owns?"

Ellis wasn't sure. "It's possible. He's a wealthy man and definitely enjoys his creature comforts. Priceless art on the walls, luxury furniture, and that suit probably cost an easy couple of Gs. From what I've seen, the super-rich go about business differently than the average person. You and I wouldn't let a group of people handle our big purchases but the super-rich don't think twice about it."

"Yeah and then they cry about it when their investment team or adviser ends up ripping them off for millions," Dakota quipped derisively. "Honestly, I have no sympathy for them when that happens. They're so far removed from reality that it's hard to work up a tear when they get taken advantage of."

"Being rich isn't a crime," he reminded Dakota with a grin.

She shrugged. "Try saying that to a kid who hasn't eaten in a few days. Sorry, but living on the reservation, you get a different view of people with more than most. Maybe I'm wrong for saying it but I'm just not a fan of uncontrolled capitalism."

Dakota didn't often share her particular views on economic issues but people like Lawrence triggered her childhood wounds all over again.

When her mom had sunk deep into her alcoholism, money had become desperately scarce. Amara had lost one of her two jobs for showing up drunk on-site and barely held on to the first.

Dakota had picked up an after-school job to fill in the gaps but it was hard to focus when sheer exhaustion and hunger ate at your ability to function. She nearly dropped out of high school when her failing grades had threatened her graduation status.

Somehow she'd pulled herself together in the nick of time, graduating with good enough grades to get her to college, but she remembered those times like they were yesterday—and she wasn't alone. Lots of kids went without on the reservation and it was a serious problem of varying levels for all First Nations tribes.

"I'm just saying, the guy seems like a rich, entitled asshole and when he smiled at me with those perfectly white teeth, I felt like a crocodile had just grinned my way."

Dakota's unexpected comparison popped a laugh from Ellis. "A crocodile?" he exclaimed.

"Yeah, or something else with big, sharp teeth that'll take a bite out of your leg if you turn your back on him. A Komodo dragon would've worked, too. Those things are scary. I saw one on a nature documentary swallow a whole baby goat without blinking an eye—and then kept walking like it was just enjoying a leisurely stroll through the garden."

"I never realized you felt so strongly about the Komodo dragon."

She smothered the urge to grin. Ellis always had the ability to coax her away from a bad mood but she didn't want to let this go.

The opulent office, expensive suit and rehearsed charm had set her teeth on edge. Men like Lawrence represented everything wrong with the system—and maybe it rubbed her the wrong way that he had zero clue, nor seemed overly distraught, about Nayeli's case. Sure, he said the right things but true empathy had never actually reached his cool blue eyes.

Glancing over at Ellis, she knew he understood her cynicism, even if his own views were more tempered. Even though he'd experienced poverty when his dad was alive, he hadn't grown up watching the cycles of poverty and neglect on the reservation the way she had. Hadn't felt the bitter sting of injustice carved deep into her bones as there seemed to be one set of rules for one set of people and an entirely different set for her people.

"You really think he doesn't know exactly where his money goes?" she said, unable to keep the bite from her tone. "I think guys like him just play dumb when it's convenient."

Ellis shrugged. "Probably. But we can't make accusations without evidence."

Dakota breathed out hard through her nose. She knew he was right. Still, seeing such ostentatious wealth flaunted by men who ignored the suffering around them lit a fire in her gut—especially when that person was in a position of power and did nothing to help those less fortunate.

"I don't trust anything that came out of his mouth," she said bluntly. "You saw how rehearsed his answers were. He's hiding something."

But Ellis didn't fight her on her assessment, saying, "No argument there. We'll figure out his role in all this, I promise."

His calm certainty helped temper Dakota's simmering anger. In spite of their past sitting between them, she was grateful to have a partner who understood her fire for justice wasn't just recklessness.

Until then, she had to be patient, follow where the evidence led. For Nayeli's sake, and all the others failed by men like the senator. Even if it turned out that the senator was only guilty of being an entitled politician more interested in his career trajectory than the health and welfare of his constituency, the truth would come out.

Dakota would make sure of it.

Chapter 19

An unexpected complication popped up with the safe house location and the decision was made to move Zoey to a Billings location, which worked in Ellis and Dakota's favor because it meant they could return to home base for a few days at the very least.

By the time they got back to Billings, each going straight home for some much-needed recharging, Dakota was emotionally and physically exhausted.

After sifting through her mail, tossing the junk and placing the important mail in its own pile to go through later, she stumbled into her bedroom and fell into bed, instantly crashing, even though it was only late afternoon.

She woke several hours later to her apartment door buzzing from a package delivery. Disoriented at first, she stared blearily at the bedside clock, rubbing at her eyes when she couldn't make sense of what she was seeing. Eight o'clock? Had she really slept that long? Good grief, she was going to have a helluva time trying to sleep tonight after that epic nap. She climbed from her bed and walked with an exaggerated yawn to the front door, checking the peephole to see a package wrapped in brown paper.

She opened the door, grabbed the package and brought it inside, frowning when she saw no return address, her name and address handwritten in a hasty scrawl.

Using scissors, she cut the box open and immediately knew something was terribly wrong.

A wretched smell wafted from the open box the minute she cut the tape sealing the box. Decomp. Whatever was in that box was dead.

Rising, she grabbed her kitchen gloves and slid them on before returning to the box. She carefully pushed aside the crumpled newspaper to find the culprit—a long-dead rat, its insides oozing out of its slashed stomach, as it rotted into a pulpy, rancid mulch. Gingerly closing the box, she placed the box in her freezer and then called Ellis.

"Someone just delivered a dead rat to my apartment door," she said. "Seems my keyboard warrior just got a little more brave."

"Are you okay?" Ellis asked.

"Yes, I'm fine. I'm not scared of a dead rat."

"It's the fact that they got your personal cell and now your home address that concerns me. Whoever it is, they're escalating their threats."

Dakota refused to be intimidated. She was more annoyed than anything else. "Like I said, they're going to have to up their game if they think a dead rat is going to send me hiding in my closet. I'm well-armed and I'm trained to kill with my bare hands so they can take their chances and come at me if they're feeling lucky."

"Dakota, I'm serious. I don't like this and you're being too cavalier about it. I'm coming over," Ellis said. "Text me your address."

It was on the tip of her tongue to shut him down but she remained silent and texted him the address. "Bring a forensic kit. I have the box in my freezer."

"Will do. Be there in twenty."

Dakota paced her apartment, adrenaline still pumping through her veins after the disturbing delivery. She was angry more than afraid that this coward thought they could intimidate her with something so juvenile. A dead rat? *C'mon, that's child's play.*

When her buzzer rang, she checked the camera before buzzing Ellis up. He strode in wearing a stern expression, his sharp eyes sweeping the space as if to ensure her safety.

"You okay?" he asked first thing, clasping her shoulder. Dakota nodded curtly.

"I told you, I'm fine. But I want answers about how this piece of shit got my address." Gloved up, she went to the freezer and pulled out the box, handing it to Ellis.

Ellis, also gloved, carefully slid the box into an oversize evidence bag and sealed it quickly. "I'll get this to the lab right away, see if we can pull any prints or trace evidence. In the meantime, you should pack a bag just in case."

Dakota bristled at the suggestion of running. "I'm not going anywhere, I just got home."

Ellis sent her a hard stare that brooked no argument. "Don't be a stubborn ass, Dakota. Your home address has been compromised. It's not safe and you're not staying here."

"I'm sleeping in my bed tonight," she maintained stubbornly.

"The hell you are. Think about it, Dakota. Imagine this happened to a confidential informant. What would your advice be?"

Damn him for using logic against her. Of course, he was right. If the situation were happening to anyone else, she'd insist that they leave for someplace safer.

Ellis sensed her resolve slipping and pushed harder. "They're going to escalate when they realize you're not scared by what they've done so far—and that's how people get killed. I'm not taking that chance with your life. Pack your things."

"And where exactly am I going? I've just spent a week in hotels and I'm not about to spend another when I have a perfectly good bed of my own right here."

"You're not going to a hotel, you're coming home with me."

Dakota started to push back on principle but stopped. She was being childish and immature. Ellis was right—her place was compromised and if she didn't want to go to a hotel, Ellis didn't live far from her place so it made sense to bunk up. "Fine. I'll take the couch," she said, grudgingly accepting his offer.

"I'll take the couch, you can have my bed."

"That doesn't seem right," she said, frowning, but one look

from Ellis and she didn't fight it. If he wanted to give up his bed, fine.

"Did you call your building manager when this came?" he asked. At Dakota's blank look, he sighed. "We should review security footage, see if they got the delivery on camera."

Chagrined that she hadn't thought of that, Dakota dialed the manager. Ellis's presence kept her levelheaded, focusing her adrenaline into constructive action instead of panic or rage. "I would've called, but I called you first," she admitted quickly before the site manager came on the line. She told the manager what happened and why she needed to see the hallway footage but his response wasn't great.

"Sounds like a prank," the manager said, dismissing her concern. "I wouldn't worry too much about it. If you want I can toss the carcass for you."

"It's evidence—and I still need to see the footage."

"Evidence? C'mon now, you're going a little far, don't you think, to bust a couple of bratty kids."

Dakota's patience was wearing thin. "My partner and I will be down in a few minutes to see the footage."

That's when the guy realized she wasn't messing around and wouldn't take no for an answer, causing him to admit sheepishly, "Yeah, about that... The cameras in the hallway don't actually work. They're just there to provide a deterrent. People see a camera and they think twice about vandalizing things but yeah, there's no actual feed."

Dakota was dumbfounded. One of the selling points of this complex was the seemingly robust security systems, and now she finds out it was all a marketing scheme?

"Sorry about that. Did you want me to throw away the carcass?"

"I told you, it's evidence, but I expect those cameras to start working real quick or else I'm reporting this building to the authorities for false advertising." She clicked off and percolated in silent anger. She met Ellis's questioning gaze, shaking her head. "Cameras are just for looks. They don't work."

Ellis nodded and said, "All right, grab your stuff. We need

to get out of here, drop off this evidence at the FBI field office and then we'll head to my place."

Dakota didn't argue. His solid reliability comforted her, even as fury simmered beneath her calm surface at this violation of her home. She refused to be cowed by spineless threats but she felt a certain level of helplessness that rubbed her wrong. She wasn't the girl who needed saving, and yet Ellis was riding in, her white knight to rescue her.

"I don't need rescuing," she blurted out as she shouldered her bag.

Ellis chuckled and said nothing, simply leading out the front door, knowing she was right behind him.

But Ellis was the only person on this planet she'd ever allow even the semblance of rescuing her and that fact was not lost on her.

Ellis and Dakota dropped off the evidence at the FBI field office, filled out the paperwork and then headed to his place. Like Dakota, he'd only just moved to Billings in the last year, which made him the right choice for the task force collaboration, according to his supervisor.

Ellis tidied his sparsely decorated living room, trying not to focus on the reality that Dakota was there with him, in his space. The old, overstuffed couch and recliner were comfortable but shabby compared with Dakota's stylish place. Mismatched thrift store end tables held stacks of car magazines and the TV remote. After a quick tour of the apartment, he grabbed some extra blankets and a pillow for himself and tossed them to the couch. He'd fallen asleep plenty of times on that sofa to know that it was comfortable enough to fall asleep on, but the thought of Dakota sleeping in his bed made his pulse quicken, even as he knew it was the only sensible option.

He sighed, wishing he had art on the walls, fresh flowers or something to make it homier for Dakota. But he could barely keep his tiny kitchen tidy, let alone make a place warm and welcoming. That had always been one of her gifts. Well, she knew his place wasn't a contender for *Better Homes & Gardens* editorial and that hadn't changed.

"It still doesn't seem right to kick you out of your own bed," Dakota protested with a frown. He watched Dakota's throat move as she swallowed, eyes flickering with some interior debate. Ellis tensed, unsure if she would agree. The wire-taut energy between them left no doubt this was intimate territory. Dangerous territory, given their history.

Ellis held her gaze, willing her to accept. "I insist. You need rest—a proper mattress will do you better than my lumpy couch. Besides, you'll be happy to know that bed set is brand-new and the mattress is one of those super-fancy ones that you were always trying to get me to buy."

"You pulled the trigger after we broke up?" she teased. "Nice."

"Yeah, and I'm a big enough person to admit you were right. Best damn purchase of my life. Turns out my aching back wasn't from my misguided childhood but just a really bad bed that wasn't doing my back any favors."

"Even more reason for me to sleep on the sofa," she protested. "I don't need your aching back on my conscience."

"You're taking the bed," he said decisively.

"If you're sure," Dakota finally acquiesced. Ellis let out a slow breath, ignoring the heat flooding his veins at the images her words conjured. Dakota, hair splayed across his pillow. Dakota, wrapped in his sheets. "I'm going to shower real quick, if you don't mind."

"Be my guest," he said, busying himself with making up his bedding, needing the distraction. This was about safety, nothing more. The distant sound of the shower tightened his groin as memories flooded his brain and he realized it would take the strength of a saint to stick to his guns, keep it professional and ignore the very real need to feel Dakota in his arms.

Especially knowing that someone was targeting her. It seemed some misogynistic bullshit that whoever was targeting Dakota hadn't also targeted him. Joke's on them—Dakota didn't scare easily.

One thing he knew for sure, if he got his hands on the person trying to terrorize Dakota—he'd tear that person apart. They didn't know whom they were messing with, or the demons he held at bay.

Thoughts of Dakota's nude body, water sluicing over her curves, made his throat go dry. This was dangerous territory, given their history. But even more perilous was the escalating threat she now faced.

Ellis paced the living room, pausing to peer through the blinds into the dark parking lot. Were they being watched? Followed? Someone knew where she lived—someone with a sick mind.

The shower stopped. Ellis tensed, listening to Dakota's muted movements in the next room. He busied himself arranging blankets on the lumpy couch, trying to ignore his pounding heart.

When she emerged in a haze of steam, Ellis busied himself fluffing a lumpy pillow, avoiding looking at her damp hair and pink cheeks. *Don't go there*, he warned himself.

"Let me know if you need anything," he muttered, catching a trace of her lavender shampoo as she passed. He ached to pull her close, breathe her in, but resisted the urge. *Keep it professional.*

After brushing his teeth to have something to do besides imagine her in his bed, Ellis splashed cold water on his face. Gripping the cheap laminate sink, he drew a deep breath. He wouldn't fail her. This humble place didn't matter, only keeping her close, keeping her safe. He could battle his desire for her sake. For Dakota, he would stay strong.

And that meant going to that sofa, climbing beneath the blankets and pretending that it was just another night—and that the love of his life wasn't in the other room.

Chapter 20

While Ellis debriefed his people, Dakota debriefed hers. It felt like an age since she'd seen her team in person but this case was dragging them all over Montana and back with very little to show for their effort.

Dakota tried not to compare how her case was faring in comparison with how Sayeh and Levi's case closed with an epic capture, but Dakota was naturally competitive and the need to close this case was eating at her.

Of course, it was more than her competitiveness that drove her but it was an aspect of her personality that had always worked in her favor in her field.

They all met in the conference room and Isaac took the lead, wanting to know everything.

Dakota didn't sugarcoat anything, sharing everything they'd discovered so far, and even included the most recent delivery of the rat to her doorstep, but she stretched the truth about where she was staying, saying that she was staying with a friend.

"You can stay with me if you want," Shilah offered. "I've got a spare room that's just collecting dust."

"I'm good, thanks," she said, appreciative of Shilah's offer, but she'd slept better than she had in months last night. She wasn't naive—she knew the reason—but she didn't want to draw attention to it, even within herself. Denial could be useful at times. "So, now with Zoey here in Billings, we're taking a few days to regroup and make sure she's okay before heading back out into the field."

"What's the word on that rat delivery?" Sayeh asked, frowning. "That's some gangster-type shit."

Levi agreed. "I don't think you should dismiss that threat as nothing."

Dakota didn't like admitting that they were right but she also hated that someone had sent her running from her own apartment. She loathed weakness and she definitely hated feeling like the damsel in distress. "Well, the FBI has their forensics on it. The apartment manager thinks it was a kid prank but Ellis doesn't agree."

"I'm with Ellis," Levi said. "Especially after that text message. Someone's toying with you. The question is, why?"

"If it's because of the case, that must mean we're making people uncomfortable," Dakota said, taking that as a good sign that they were on the right track. She turned to Shilah. "What's the progress on getting Deakins's financials?"

"Still working on it. It's taking a little longer than I anticipated but we should have the financial audit in a few days."

Isaac grunted in approval, pleased with their progress. "You here for a few days?"

"Yeah, I need a break from the car."

"Take a few days off, recalibrate."

Ordinarily, having your boss tell you to take a few days off would be a godsend but Dakota didn't feel right resting when Zoey's future lay in the balance. Maybe she'd take a day but then it was back to the case.

But Shilah had news that definitely set her teeth on edge. "The Grojans were released from custody yesterday. There was nothing to really hold them on aside from malicious mischief, which is a weak misdemeanor at best. Their lawyer got the judge to dismiss the charges given their emotional duress. They went back to the compound."

"But we don't know their involvement with Nayeli's murder," Dakota protested. "What if they're guilty of killing Nayeli to get her baby?"

Shilah shrugged, as if she didn't know what to say. "The judge didn't seem to feel they were a threat and let them go."

Dakota swore under her breath. "Well, crap."

Maybe she wouldn't be getting that day off after all.

She knew as soon as Ellis found out that the Grojans were free he'd blow a gasket, too.

"How'd the interview with Senator Lawrence go?" Isaac asked, keeping the flow going. He was a no-nonsense kind of boss, something she appreciated, but she would've liked more discussion about the Grojans. Personally, she didn't feel it was responsible to let them go when a shadow of doubt clung to their potential involvement with a murder.

Dakota shrugged. "Fine. He's as cool as a cucumber and always says the right things but I didn't like him. I mean, he might be innocent but I just didn't like him as a person."

Sayeh commiserated with a chuckle. "I get that. Politicians always rubbed me wrong. It was always hard for me to believe that all of them weren't cut from the same cloth, but as much as I hate to admit it, Lawrence comes off as pretty clean."

"How so?" Dakota asked.

Sayeh pulled her paperwork, sharing, "Well, he donates every year to a nonprofit that helps orphaned children find homes. He and his wife are active in their church, big donors for all of the church-related functions, and they host an annual fundraiser at their home to help feed the homeless on Thanksgiving. I mean, as far as optics go, the guy is squeaky clean and well-liked."

"Ugh, I still hate him," Dakota muttered with a derisive grin.

Isaac didn't find the humor in the situation, though. "Keep your personal feelings under wraps. The last thing this task force needs is the accusation of an unwarranted witch hunt on personal reasons alone. It's already hard enough keeping interest in this task force past the initial honeymoon phase. Keep it professional and by the book."

Dakota didn't like being schooled. She kept her gaze lowered, jaw clenched, as irritation simmered just beneath her calm surface. She was the last person who needed to be reminded to keep things professional, but she was still new to Isaac and she didn't need to make enemies with her boss by mouthing off.

Satisfied, Isaac moved on, looking to Sayeh. "What have you managed to dig up on The Congregation?"

"Hate to disappoint but that field trip was even more boring," Sayeh said, passing copies of her research. "Zachariah Deakins formed The Congregation thirty years ago, started off with a few followers who agreed with his simplistic approach to life, going-back-to-nature kind of thing, and slowly he gained enough followers to purchase the summer camp two years later."

"But he didn't actually purchase the camp. Technically, the senator unknowingly did as an investment through his financial advisers," Dakota said. "Which is still weird to me, but whatever. Why would his advisers feel a bankrupt summer camp was a good investment for the senator? That doesn't make much sense to me."

"If I were you I'd head back to the compound and ask Deakins how he got the investment group to invest in his church," Levi suggested. "I mean, if Lawrence truly had no clue about his investing in The Congregation, then somehow Deakins managed to convince the senator's investment firm that he was a solid bet, and if that's the case, how?"

"Sounds like a bunch of magic beans to me," Sayeh quipped.

Dakota agreed, unless there was more to the deal than met the eye.

"If you're heading back to the compound to question Deakins, be careful. The charges against the Grojans were dropped but that doesn't mean they're not still dangerous, okay?" Isaac warned, gathering up his paperwork. "And I want you to take a few days. You look exhausted, Foster."

It was an order, not a suggestion.

As much as she wanted to decline, she knew it wasn't an option. She shared a look with Shilah but murmured her acquiescence.

Looked like a few days of R&R were on her plate—which meant she and Ellis were going to have to figure out how to share space without falling into old habits that included falling out of their clothes and back into bed together.

She groaned silently. Maybe it was better to get a hotel after all.

* * *

Ellis slid the pizza onto the kitchen counter, the savory aroma filling his small apartment. He'd grabbed Dakota's favorite toppings, hoping she was still fond of them after all this time.

Taking a steadying breath, he called out, "Food's here if you're hungry." He tried to keep his tone light, casual. This was just two colleagues sharing a meal. Nothing more.

Dakota emerged from the bedroom, hair damp, wearing an old academy T-shirt. He remembered plenty of nights like this in their past. Easy domesticity, passion simmering just beneath the surface. Did she have to look so effortlessly sexy?

He busied himself grabbing plates, hyperaware of her moving around the kitchen. Their banter stayed surface level as they dished up slices, but each laugh, each shared glance seemed weighted with history.

Sitting across from Dakota now, Ellis sipped his beer slowly, curbing the urge to reach across and tuck back the strand of hair falling across her cheek. To pull her close, get lost in her familiar warmth...

He cleared his throat, steering the conversation to safer waters—case updates. "My superior is putting a rush on the forensics on your rat," he shared.

She grimaced with a groan. "Don't call it *my* rat. I doubt they're going to find anything. Seems a waste of resources, honestly."

Ellis didn't agree. "You and I both know that even the most careful criminals forget something. With any luck, we'll find a print we can match in the system and I can personally introduce myself."

Dakota chuckled, biting into the pizza. "Mmm, you remembered. Mushrooms, black olives and pepperoni—"

"With the garlic white sauce, not red," he finished with a grin. "Yeah, some things are ingrained in my memory."

"Thank you. Glad to know I left an impression of some kind," she teased with a smile that threatened to reach into his chest and pull his heart out. God, he missed this. Her quick mind and wry humor drew him in like no other. That vibrant connection still sparked between them, if he let it.

"Tell me what you've really been up to since we broke up," he said, reaching over to wipe a smudge of grease from her cheek. For a tidy and organized person, Dakota was the messiest eater. She always ended up with something in her lap, on her shirt or on her cheek. It was adorable.

Dakota hesitated, a moment of vulnerability flashing across her expression, before answering with a small shrug, "Just work. I buried myself in the job. Seemed safer that way. When the task force assignment popped up, I jumped at it. It was exactly what I needed to keep my head on straight and focused. Gave my brain something to chew on instead of the constant over-thinking that usually consumed my thoughts." She drew a halt-ing breath, admitting, "My pride wishes I could say that I went out, dated a lot and easily moved on, but that would be a lie and we've already established I'm a terrible liar."

"You never have to lie to me, Dakota. I know you better than anyone."

"Then you should know that getting over you was the hard-est thing I've ever had to do, and honestly, I can't say that I'm actually out of the woods just yet but I'm doing my best."

"I'm not over you, either."

"I know."

Just as she couldn't lie to him, the road traveled both ways. He wiped his own mouth. "So where does that leave us?"

"Confused."

Ain't that the truth?

She met his stare. "What are we doing, Ellis?"

"Besides torturing ourselves, I don't know," he answered with blunt honesty. "You tell me." He had to stay disciplined, guard his heart, but it was so much harder with her two feet away from him, her lips glistening, close enough to see the gentle beat of her heart beneath her skin.

He could fight this feeling, but he couldn't make it disappear. Not completely. Not ever. She still owned every bruised, bat-tered corner of his heart.

"We both have our reasons for standing by the decision to break up," Dakota said quietly, though something in her tone made Ellis think part of her hoped he would argue. "Even if we could move past the past, I still believe you shouldn't go back to narcotics work and that would cause friction between us."

Ellis took in her words, sensing she spoke out of care, not cruelty. It took a minute to process that truth, but he couldn't find a hole in her reasoning. Further proof that it was best to keep things platonic—except, that decision tasted like cardboard in his mouth.

"You know I'm right."

He resigned himself to the fact with a nod. Her concern was valid. But why couldn't she see how important Narcotics was to him? He wasn't going to give up his desire to return to Narcotics and she didn't want to be with him if he succeeded.

All they could do was see this case through, then go their separate ways once more.

Even if doing so tore the ragged stitches holding his battered heart together.

Chapter 21

Waiting a handful of days as directed was excruciating for Dakota, especially when she and Ellis were tiptoeing around each other, trying not to take up too much of each other's space so when it was finally time to hit the road, Dakota was grateful.

They pulled into the dirt parking lot reserved for Eden's Bounty customers and headed for the main building where Zachariah Deakins kept his office. Unlike their last visit, the compound felt different this time, the air taut with tension.

They looked for Lina Vasquez, the nurse that'd been manning Eden's Bounty booths the last time, but someone different was assisting customers and they weren't as friendly.

"Not even a hello or an offer of a bag of nuts," Ellis joked as they walked into the building.

Zachariah Deakins's smile was cold when he greeted them, lacking its prior evangelical zeal. Dakota exchanged a wary look with Ellis. The chill coming off the man could freeze a penguin's privates.

"More questions, Agents? I'm quite busy today," Deakins said brusquely, his attention drifting. "I thought we clarified everything last time."

"A few follow-up questions as the investigation progresses is common," Dakota said with a professional smile.

Zachariah glanced at the small clock on his desk with a short nod. "What would you like to know?"

"We've recently discovered an odd connection between The Congregation and Senator Mitchell Lawrence that we'd like you to help us understand."

Zachariah's expression didn't change. "Which is?"

"Which is why would Senator Lawrence's investment firm pay for this compound? At first we thought perhaps you and the senator were friends but he claims not to know you, which only confused us further. How did you manage to convince the senator's investment firm that this compound—a bankrupt and defunct summer camp—was a good investment?"

Zachariah's annoyance returned but he answered calmly. "Our flock was growing exponentially each month with significant donations and the promise of more growth. As you know, religious organizations enjoy tax-exempt status so any properties owned by the church would avoid property tax burdens."

"And each congregant liquidates their assets and donates to the church," Ellis said, watching Zachariah's reaction.

Cool as ever, Zachariah didn't flinch or deny, simply nodded. "That's correct. We see to our people's needs, food, shelter, emotional sustenance—something the outside world doesn't care to provide—and in exchange our flock pours into The Congregation as we pour into them. And, in case you're wondering, yes, it's all voluntary and done without coercion. Ask anyone."

"We will, thank you," Dakota said with a thin smile. "Still, that's a significant investment based on a handful of members."

Zachariah shrugged as if the why didn't concern him. "The asking price was low enough to represent a good return on the investment in the event our improvements increased the property value, and if not, it would be a good tax write-off. The financial risk was relatively small but afforded excellent financial growth for the senator's portfolio. However, with that said, it's not my business to defend the firm's decision. I was simply grateful they saw the value and made the purchase."

"Do you pay rent?" Ellis asked.

Zachariah smiled. "No, but we do send a gift basket every

Christmas to the firm address. I'm told it's always very well-received."

Even with that dispassionate and articulate explanation, it didn't make sense to Dakota. Still, Zachariah made an excellent point—one that would be hard to fight. It wasn't illegal for an investment firm to make a seemingly odd purchase.

And it definitely didn't point to murder.

Zachariah claimed to never know Nayeli and the senator couldn't recall her case.

This felt like a giant dead end.

"Was there anything else you needed clarified?" Zachariah asked.

Dakota looked to Ellis, hoping he had a reason to keep Zachariah talking.

And he did.

"We heard the Grojans were released from the Butte County Jail a few days ago. Are they here?"

Zachariah's gaze narrowed, his mouth tightening as he leaned forward, purposefully clasping his hands in front of him as if he needed to collect his patience with them. "The Grojans have been through a terrible ordeal. I won't have you heaping more emotional trauma on good people while you bumble your way through this investigation. The Grojans had nothing to do with the terrible crime that happened to Zoey's birth mother. They are as much victims in this as Zoey and her birth mother. Unless you have a warrant and just cause to drag them back down to the police station, I respectfully ask that you leave them alone while they grieve this situation."

Dakota caught a glimpse of compassion in Zachariah's stern decree. The Grojans were someplace on this property but no one was going to give them up without a fight. Seeing as they had no evidence that pointed to the Grojans' involvement, Dakota and Ellis had no choice but to walk away.

For now.

"You said that according to your sources, Zoey's mother was an addict who OD'd. Where did you get that information?" Ellis asked.

Zachariah stiffened, admitting, "Obviously, my information

turned out to be false but I had no way of knowing that at the time and no reason to question. The private adoption agency supplied the information and I connected the Grojans with the agency. It seemed an answer to a prayer that I was humbled to facilitate."

"We followed up on the agency on the adoption paperwork but it doesn't exist anymore and we can't find any documentation stating it had ever filed for nonprofit status," Dakota said.

Zachariah didn't have an answer for that. He shrugged, as if, once again, they'd bothered him with a problem that wasn't his to solve. "I only worked with that agency once, for the Grojans. Everything seemed professional and organized. Why would I question the procedure?"

Fair point, Dakota realized with frustration. Was it possible she was hoping to find something that would point toward Zachariah's guilt because of her personal bias or was he really good at hiding a truly evil agenda?

Zachariah gestured to the burly men who appeared at the doorway. "James and Theo will escort you out. Good day, Agents."

An escort off the compound when last visit he'd practically given them the run of the place?

The little hairs on the back of her neck prickled as she rose, Ellis right behind her.

How could Zachariah say all the right things and still make her feel as if she'd just stared into the eyes of a shark?

Ellis chewed on Zachariah's distinct change in attitude toward them. One minute he was warm and effusive—the next, chill and curt.

What changed? Either he was offended on behalf of the Grojans for their recent treatment, or he was uncomfortable with Ellis and Dakota continuing to poke around. Maybe he hadn't expected them to keep circling back to him. Or maybe he felt the need to protect his "flock" from a perceived persecution.

They walked across the compound, toward the parking lot, and his gaze snagged on the Eden's Bounty booths. He paused, looking to their burly escorts with an apologetic smile, asking,

"You don't mind if we make a purchase, do you? Lina gave us a gift basket full of goodies last time, and I've never tasted pear jam so good."

The one named James shared an uncertain look with his partner, but Theo grudgingly nodded, giving them permission but not before instructing gruffly, "Stick to the booths."

"Of course," Ellis agreed easily, moving to the first booth featuring an array of jams and jellies. Dakota followed his lead, shooting a look toward their escorts as they waited impatiently for them to finish. When they were out of earshot, Ellis pretended to peruse the wares but said under his breath, "We need to lose Frick and Frack over there so we can talk to people without a shadow."

Dakota nodded, turning to James with an apologetic smile. "Mind if I use the restroom before we hit the road? Long drive, small bladder."

James looked discomfited but relented, pointing toward another building. "Public restroom is over there. Come right back, and then it's time to leave."

"Got it, there and back," she said with a thumbs-up. To Ellis she said, "Pick me up a couple of goodies, too."

"Will do," Ellis said, returning to the person manning the booth, rubbing his hands with relish. "Now, I'd like to sample pretty much every jam and jelly you have on display. I have my credit card ready to spend."

Ellis knew Dakota would detour from the bathroom and wander around a bit, and he needed to buy her time. He made a show of tasting every sample slowly with appropriate enthusiasm, even asking questions as to how they got the flavor profile to explode in his mouth. Just as he expected, they were eager to talk about their work, and that ate up some more time as he pretended to care about soil conditions, fertilizer and crop rotations.

As he hoped, James and Theo soon became restless and, judging them as a nonthreat, drifted farther from their guard post until they were gone entirely.

Ellis paid for his purchases—he wasn't lying about enjoying their wares—and went to find Dakota.

He found her talking with a young couple in the large green-house as they planted young seedlings with their two children.

Ellis smiled in welcome as he joined Dakota. "I love the smell of a greenhouse. Always smells so fresh and clean," he said.

Dakota introduced the couple she'd been talking to, "Ellis, this is Georgina and Ross Wilson and their four-year-old daughters, Hazel and Mabel. Twins."

"Adorable," Ellis murmured, ruffling the jet-black hair of the one closest to him. Then Ellis noticed there was no possible way the twins were biologically related to their parents. More adopted children in The Congregation? Strange coincidence or something else?

Georgina grinned as she saw his bag of goodies. "You have good taste. Eden's Bounty has spoiled us all when it comes to fresh produce and delicious things. Hazel can't get enough of the homemade applesauce."

Ellis checked in his bag. "Seems I missed that one. I'll have to go back and rectify that oversight. I haven't had applesauce since I was a kid," he lied. His dad hadn't given two shits if there was any kind of fruit in the house he grew up in. He was lucky if there was any kind of food in the house, but there was always plenty of beer.

Dakota said, making conversation, "Georgina was just sharing how she and her husband joined The Congregation. What an amazing story. Can you imagine being a defense attorney and an HR administrator in one life and in the next, minimalist churchgoers sharing resources? Amazing."

Georgina bobbed her head, smiling with true joy. "Best decision of our lives. I never realized how burdened I was by modern living. The rat race, as they call it. Before joining The Congregation, Ross's blood pressure was through the roof. He was on three different medications, and he could barely get through the day without crashing before eight o'clock. Now, he has more energy than men half his age, and he's no longer taking any meds. I used to say it was a conspiracy theory that the pharmaceutical companies want you sick, but now I believe it."

"Clean living, huh?" Ellis said, nodding as if impressed. "And here I thought stress was just part of the adult package."

"That's what late-stage capitalism would have you believe, my friend," Ross said solemnly. "I was guilty of it, too. I was in the thick of it, running on an endless treadmill until Father Zachariah showed us a better way. Know better, do better—that's the way to live your life."

"Your daughters are so beautiful," Dakota murmured, appealing to their mother's pride. "Those eyes are dark enough to lose yourself in for days."

It was a deliberate attempt to get either parent to admit they weren't biologically related to their daughters. Both Georgina and Ross had Nordic features with pale blue eyes; both girls were clearly Asian.

"Aren't they, though?" Georgina gushed with love in her gaze. "Sometimes I think they are perfect China dolls. We're so blessed to call them ours. Just another reason meeting Father Zachariah was meant to be."

Dakota smiled, interested. "How so?"

Georgina was only too happy to share. "I'm not ashamed to admit that I had fertility issues. We tried for years to have a baby of our own, but God had different plans." She looked to her husband. "Should I share our testimony?"

"I don't see why not," Ross answered, caressing his wife's cheek in a loving manner. "It's a beautiful story."

Georgina agreed as she launched into their testimony with her husband's blessing. "We were at our darkest moment. We had just left the fertility clinic after learning our last and final round of IVF had failed. We were devastated, but then Father Zachariah happened to see us crying and he approached us in the spirit of kindness. That moment changed our lives. He invited us here, to The Congregation, and we knew we'd found our place."

Ross's smile mirrored his wife's as he shared, "I know it sounds crazy, but we've found bliss."

What was in the water at this place? Ellis held his benign expression, even though on the inside he was starting to question if Father Zachariah was secretly dosing his people with Xanax. No one was this happy without chemical intervention. "So… You gave all your assets to the church and became members?"

"Once we saw what was possible, we didn't even hesitate. It was a relief, actually," Ross said. "No more chasing unattainable goals, running on a treadmill that never slows down so you can catch your breath. But even more important, we finally had our family."

That caught Ellis's interest. "How do you mean?" he asked.

Georgina handed each girl a bright red cherry tomato and directed them to start pouring potting soil in awaiting pots down the lane. Hazel and Mabel skipped away, hand in hand, giggling as they went.

"It's their favorite part of the greenhouse detail," Georgina shared, admitting with a rueful laugh, "But I think they get more potting soil on their clothes than in the actual pot."

"Seems like a small price to pay for those cute giggles," Dakota said.

"I agree," Georgina said. "I'm sure you can see that our daughters are adopted."

"Yes," Ellis said. "Interesting that there are two adopted children as members of The Congregation."

"Oh, there's more than that," Georgina laughed, looking to Ross for confirmation. "How many would you say? Ten or more? I've lost count, honestly. Just more proof that God directs Father Zachariah's hand and guides his mission."

Ten adoptions? "Are you saying Father Zachariah has facilitated all of the adoptions here at The Congregation?"

Georgina's eyes sparkled. "Yes. Isn't he wonderful? God has chosen Father Zachariah as his vessel, and he has humbly taken his role to heart. We owe everything to Father Zachariah."

Ellis's smile never faltered, but his mind was racing. He shared a look with Dakota, and he knew she was thinking the same—how the hell was Zachariah Deakins facilitating all of these adoptions? And why?

Chapter 22

Dakota stared at the corporate documents, adrenaline spiking. Senator Lawrence and Zachariah Deakins, partners in an industrial supply company based in Arizona. On the surface, Western Horizon Solutions appeared utterly mundane—a manufacturer of barrels, piping and containers.

"I'm telling you, these can't all be coincidences," Dakota said, sliding the corporate documents in front of Ellis. "I don't care what the senator says, he and Deakins are connected."

"Interesting that our distinguished senator seems to do a lot of business with a man he said he doesn't know." Ellis rubbed his temple as he read the docs. He frowned. "What's the connection? What are we missing? The land purchase for the compound, okay. But what's the senator want with an industrial supplier?"

"That's the million-dollar question," Dakota admitted with frustration. "I mean, just taking a guess, drug smuggling, human trafficking, selling weapons... The options are endless."

Ellis raised an eyebrow, chuckling darkly. "That's quite a leap. This is a business that sells plastic barrels and PVC piping. All totally legal."

"So they want us to think," Dakota quipped, ticking the facts off on her fingers. "Deakins is facilitating secret adoptions, Lawrence is lying about knowing him, now they own a company together? There's something bigger we're not seeing."

Ellis leaned back in his chair, considering. "I'll give you Deakins seems like a shady character. Zero doubt in my mind about that, but Lawrence? The guy has a squeaky-clean reputation and people seem to genuinely like him. As much as it pains to admit, Lawrence seems the real deal—a politician who is genuine about wanting to help people."

Dakota continued to chew on that bone, reminding Ellis, "Who's made some questionable business deals. Think about it. What if Deakins is moving illegal products under cover of this company? Lawrence provides protection."

"Using the business as a front and a way to launder money?" Ellis supposed, going along for the ride. "But what products? We'd have to find evidence that Western Horizon Solutions was doing shady shit to even try to connect those dots, and you and I both know, right now, what we've got is flimsy. I'm not even sure we'd get a judge to sign off on a warrant."

Yes, but flimsy was a start. "Oh, Shilah can get the warrant. She's magic with her requests. We get the records, we can connect the dots. Whatever they're hiding, it's big. My gut says we're on the right track."

"Look, far be it from me to question a gut instinct—hell, half of the reason I'm still alive is I listened to my gut when it told me things were about to go sidewise—but we're not dealing with some crusty drug dealer. We're talking about a US senator with a lot of connections. Connections that could seriously derail our careers if we bark up the wrong tree."

Dakota knew the stakes were high but she didn't care. She stubbornly held her ground. "When we get the warrant, the company records should give up the dirty laundry."

"If it's there at all," Ellis reminded her.

She thought of the adopted children at the compound, Deakins's slippery charm. Her skin crawled imagining what those supplies could facilitate away from prying eyes. "Either way, this is concrete evidence of a relationship between them—a relationship the senator previously denied," Dakota said.

Ellis couldn't deny that logic, tapping the table lightly with his index finger. "And where there's smoke..."

"There's fire," Dakota finished.

Ellis nodded, his brow furrowed as he sank deeper into thought, sharing, "This case feels a whole lot bigger than Nayeli's case. I don't see how it's all connected. I can see strands of suspicious activity but none that travels back to Nayeli, and that's what our original focus was when Zoey appeared on the radar. What if we end up spending all this time chasing leads that send us further away from solving Nayeli's case? Zoey needs to know what happened to her mom—and her."

"I haven't lost sight of what we're truly chasing. I believe they have to be connected," Dakota insisted, refusing to believe they were wasting their time and energy. "My gut says we just have to keep going. We're on the right track."

Ellis didn't seem as sure. She could sense his frustration and she didn't blame him, but Dakota knew they were pulling on the right threads. She gazed out the front window of her office, jaw tight. Whatever Deakins and Lawrence were up to, this company linked them together in it. She didn't know how yet, but those barrel drums made the hair on the back of her neck stand up.

Speak of the devil, Shilah walked by and Dakota flagged her attention. "Would you mind working your mojo and get a warrant started for Western Horizon Solutions? We need all financials, sales records and inventory logs."

"Yeah, sure. You getting some traction on your case?" Shilah asked hopefully.

"Maybe. It does seem like each time we catch a break, the case splinters into a bunch of new directions."

"Sounds exciting," Shilah said. "How's the kid doing?"

"We talked to her this morning. She's tough, hanging in there. She said she liked the cook at the other safe house better than this one. Apparently, Zoey has a sweet tooth but the new cook doesn't seem interested in doing much baking."

Ellis chuckled. "I say we drop by the safe house and rectify that little problem."

Dakota grinned, shaking her head. Ellis had such a soft spot for the kid. Someday, he'd make a great father. The intrusive thought caused her smile to freeze and her throat to close against the unwelcome grief that followed. The thought of Ellis making a life with someone else was more than she could handle right now and it was the worst time to sink into that way of thinking.

Forcing a chuckle, she acted as if everything was fine and her heart hadn't silently cracked in two.

Sleeping in his bed while he camped out on the sofa was weird. She tried to convince him to let her go back to her own apartment but he wouldn't hear of it—and to be honest, she hadn't tried all that hard to convince him, either.

Even though she'd like him lying beside her, there was an odd comfort in knowing he was in the other room—and she enjoyed having dinner with him each night, too.

That was an added emotional perk that buoyed her in ways that she truly needed right now.

Ellis watched Dakota pore over the files, her determination evident. He admired her tenacity, but privately worried this crusade against Lawrence could backfire. Dakota was letting the case get personal, too clouded by the shadow of her sister's death to realize she was riding the edge.

Usually he was the reckless one, while Dakota played it conservative. Now their roles had reversed. This case had lit a fire in her that was burning so bright they might all get burned.

Ellis understood her thirst for justice. But tangling with a powerful senator was risky without solid proof. He didn't want to see Dakota hurt if her hunch proved wrong.

And there was another fly in the ointment—one he wasn't ready to share just yet.

The lab results on the rat had provided zero usable evidence. Poisoned, mutilated postmortem, no prints or traces left behind. Another dead end.

Ellis was reluctant to tell Dakota, though. She'd insist on going back to her compromised apartment. And as much as he knew he should keep his distance... He wasn't ready to give her up just yet.

Having Dakota here these past nights was a double-edged sword. He treasured their easy camaraderie, her quick wit and laughter filling his small place. Each morning he found fresh excuses to linger over coffee, stretching out their time.

Yeah, talk about playing with fire—he knew he was prolonging the inevitable but he couldn't bring himself to push her out the door. He loved the stubborn woman but they didn't have a future together. Their history was too scarred, but he clung to these last stolen moments. Let himself imagine, just briefly, that she was here to stay.

Ellis swallowed hard, dragging his thoughts back to the case. He had to remain objective, no matter how his heart threatened to steer him off course. For both their sakes.

"We'll get the records," he assured Dakota, but tried to insert some caution into the mix. "But let's be smart. I don't want you hurt over this."

She cracked a grin, calling him out. "What's this? Ellis being the worrywart? Did we just jump timelines or something? C'mon, where's the reckless devil-may-care agent who laughed in the face of danger?" she teased.

But when it came to Dakota's safety, he wasn't laughing. "Maybe I've learned there's some value in being conservative. Not every situation calls for stupid bravery."

Her smile faded when she realized he wasn't playing around. "Are you okay?"

"I'm fine," he answered, but he wasn't really. He was on edge. Dakota didn't have the experience he did stepping into the arena with dangerous people. She didn't consider that tangling with Lawrence could kill her career—a career she loved and used to fill that emptiness left by her sister's death.

"Well, then enough with the sour face. We have a lead and we're going to chase it down." She leaned over with a sassy grin, adding, "And we're going to stop by that bakery and buy a ton of sugar cookies for our little federal hostage because we're part of the kinder, gentler federal government."

He chuckled in spite of the heaviness in his chest. The thought of a sugar cookie did make him smile, though. "All right, but only because Zoey deserves something sweet after everything she's been through in the last couple of weeks."

Dakota smiled, seeing right through his facade but letting him have it. "Any word from the lab about my rat?"

"Nothing yet," he lied. "Probably a few more days. They're backed up."

Dakota shrugged, letting it go. "It's probably going to come up with nothing anyway, but I suppose the sooner we know, the sooner I can get out of your hair. You probably want your apartment back."

Not really, but he smiled and let her believe what she wanted. If he had the balls, he'd admit that he loved having her around, that he selfishly wished he had a reason for her to stay and that he spent half the night wishing he was lying beside her when he was tossing and turning on his old sofa.

But he wouldn't say any of those things. They'd already agreed they had no future together and that the best they could hope for was a good working relationship built on a solid friendship.

Except he didn't want to be friends—he wanted to be the man he used to be to her, but who was that man? Did he even exist anymore?

Ellis didn't know. He was different now, changed in ways he couldn't even put into words but felt in his soul.

He feared he would never lose the thirst for the relentless adrenaline of narcotics work, even though, like Dakota had said, he was good in Missing Persons. But working Narcotics, he'd felt honed to a razor's edge, every nerve alive. Purposeful in a way civilian life had never matched.

Yet at what cost had that razor focus come? Softness eroded, vulnerabilities sharpened into weapons. Dakota used to quip he had ice water in his veins when he was deep undercover. But she'd never feared him—until the day that ice cracked.

Some changes were for the better—his hair-trigger temper now held in check, empathy where rage had once simmered. When he was moved to Missing Persons, he'd felt declawed, defanged. And that longing for the electric urgency of life had kept him on the edge, pushing for that goal to return to where he belonged.

Was Dakota right? Was it impossible to return to Narcotics without sinking back into those familiar dark places? Dakota didn't trust that he could and it wasn't right of him to ask her to try.

Ellis craved the clarity of his old life, before shades of gray blurred every line. Yet when Dakota looked at him now, he glimpsed a flicker of stubborn hope in her eyes that squeezed his heart.

Whoever he had been, whatever he became, some essential truth remained unchanged. She owned every battered, broken shard of his soul. Always.

And that was a problem that he couldn't fix without risking breaking them both.

So keep your ass on that sofa and don't make things worse by thinking you guys can fix what broke—because you can't.

Chapter 23

Realizing they had to rewind to the beginning, Dakota and Ellis made the long drive to Whitefish, to the hotel where Nayeli had worked before her murder, while Shilah chased down the warrant for Western Horizon Solutions financials.

The manager, an immaculately put-together woman with frosted blond hair and fashionable wire-rimmed glasses named Paula Simmons, greeted them politely, if not warmly, but her memories of Nayeli had faded with time. "Hmm, well, from what I remember, she was a strikingly beautiful girl but kept to herself mostly," she recalled. "We were all shocked when she admitted she was pregnant. Hadn't even known she was seeing anyone. Of course, we threw her a lovely baby shower and offered to help in any way we could. We're a family here at the Glacier View Hotel and Resort." Her expression dimmed. "We were devastated when we heard the news about her murder. It was simply awful to think of something like that happening here. Whitefish is such a safe community."

"So Nayeli never shared who the father was?" Dakota asked.

Paula shook her head. "Sorry, no, and it didn't seem appropriate to ask. Whoever it was, was no longer a part of her life so we didn't want to pry. She loved that baby so much. She would've made a wonderful mother."

Dakota's sinuses tingled at the sentiment. Was she emotional over Nayeli's loss or her sister's for never having the chance to have a family of her own? Dakota didn't know and there wasn't time to figure it out. She jotted down the notes but nothing seemed useful yet.

"May I ask why you thought the father was no longer part of Nayeli's life?" Ellis asked, curious.

"Well, I hate to talk about someone else's business, but right before the baby was born, I caught Nayeli looking at a pamphlet for a birthing class and I asked if the father was going to attend with her and she just shook her head with the saddest expression. That's when she shared that she'd be raising the baby by herself. I felt so bad for her."

Dakota imagined Nayeli had been devastated to discover she was alone in the biggest change in her life but she'd been trying to make a go of it. "Did Nayeli say she had plans to return to work after having the baby?"

"Yes, and we supported her decision to do so," Paula said quickly, as if fearing a human resource reprisal all these years later. "But unfortunately, childcare was an issue. She was nearing the end of her six-week maternity leave and still hadn't found an affordable childcare option. Placing an infant is difficult, from what I understand. I don't actually have children of my own."

Dakota wondered if money was tight for the new mom and she'd reached out to the father, hoping for some help. Sometimes that was enough to trigger a desperate person to act out in a murderous rage—especially if they weren't interested in being a part of the child's life.

"I'm sorry I'm not more help," Paula apologized. "Nayeli was such a lovely girl."

"We appreciate your time," Ellis said, handing her a contact card. "If you remember anything else, please don't hesitate to call or email."

"Of course," Paula said, tucking the card into her sharp blazer before moving on to more pressing matters.

The Glacier View was elegant, sophisticated and rustic at the same time, similar to the Ahwahnee in Yosemite National Park, but much larger in scale. Dakota remembered Evelyn sharing how they'd dreamed of going into hospitality together and Nayeli had hoped to manage a hotel like the Glacier. She'd probably looked up to Paula as someone who'd achieved the very goal she was reaching for.

"Damn it," Dakota muttered in disappointment. "Looks like we came all the way here for nothing."

But as they turned to leave, a housekeeper who had been hovering nearby hurried over.

"Wait, wait!" she called after them in a hushed tone, motioning for them to follow her out of the main lobby. "I overheard you talking to Paula about Nayeli Swiftwater and I couldn't believe my ears. No one's talked about Nayeli in forever but I'm glad someone's asking questions again."

Ellis and Dakota shared a look, interested. "How did you know Nayeli?"

"We were hired at the same time, except I never expected to still be here all this time later and Nayeli had her eye on becoming manager someday. Funny how things work out."

"What's your name?" Ellis asked.

"My name's Holly Pickler but I don't want my name in any reports or anything. I mean, Nayeli's killer is still out there. The last thing I need is someone coming after me for talking."

"Do you know something?" Dakota asked.

"Well, I'm pretty sure I know who the father was," Holly said in a low voice.

A rush prickled across Dakota's skin. "You do? Who?"

"Nayeli had a boyfriend named Patrick who worked for that politician, Lawrence Mitchell. He's a senator now but he was just a congressman at the time. I think Patrick was his assistant or something because they were joined at the hip and Patrick got all the perks, like the hotel suite, an executive black card, you know, all the fancy stuff. They used to stay here campaigning, and that's how Nayeli and Patrick met."

Excitement flooded her veins. "Do you have a last name for Patrick?"

"Sorry, I don't remember that, but I remember him being real handsome but in a pretty-boy way, kinda like you." She pointed at Ellis.

Dakota bit back a snort of laughter at Ellis's expression. He was immune to being called handsome but pretty boy?

Ellis recovered, saying, "If he worked that closely with the senator we should be able to find out his last name easily."

Holly nodded. "Yeah, but I'm positive Patrick knocked her up. He was, no offense, too pretty. I mean, the man had more toiletries than any woman I've ever seen—and we know because we're the ones cleaning up after them. The stories we in housekeeping could tell…but we won't because, you know, we're professional."

"Why are you so sure it was him?" Ellis asked, puzzled.

"Because even though she tried to hide it, she always got super excited when the congressman's entourage were scheduled to check in. She'd go to extra lengths to pretty herself up, not that she needed much help in that department. And even though she said it wasn't for no man, the girl was so obvious. You'd have to be dumb and blind to miss that she was head over heels for that man."

"Thank you, Holly," Dakota said, handing her a contact card. "If you think of anything else, please don't hesitate to call."

Finally, a real lead—and one that tied directly to the senator.

Holly pocketed the card. "Well, I just hope it helps. Honestly, I just assumed the police probably already talked to him and I didn't really want to get involved but I think it's time to let that secret out."

"We do, too," Ellis agreed with a short smile.

They left with a solid description of Patrick and the SUV he drove at the time. Dakota's mind raced with the new implications as Ellis drove them back.

"This confirms the senator knew Nayeli, despite claiming not to remember her," she said. "If his aide got Nayeli pregnant, there's no way the senator was unaware."

But Ellis wasn't so sure. "That's a possible theory. Or he really didn't know his aide got Nayeli pregnant because Patrick probably hid that information from his boss."

Dakota liked her theory better. "Maybe," she allowed with a grudging nod. "But we need to find this Patrick guy, like yesterday, and I think we ought to start with the senator."

"On that, we agree," he said, that fierce light returning to Ellis's eyes. The one that made Dakota's pulse skip despite herself. They were close, she could feel it. All the twisted threads were intertwined, but the truth would come loose. She would make certain of it.

Ellis drove steadily back toward Billings, half listening as Dakota breathlessly rehashed the hotel lead. A secret boyfriend, tied to Senator Lawrence... It was certainly the best lead they'd had from the start, but doubts gnawed at the back of Ellis's mind.

The source was hearsay, the story nearly two decades old. Was it enough to justify the risk of antagonizing a powerful politician based on a tenuous connection? He knew Dakota wouldn't appreciate his skepticism, but he had to be the pragmatic one, which was an unfamiliar feeling. Was this how he'd made Dakota feel every time he went off half-cocked on a situation, high on adrenaline and the electric rush of the chase?

He didn't like it. Made him feel anxious and untethered—and not in a good way.

Ellis recalled one night in particular, seeing it from a different angle now. He'd been flush with excitement. A tip from an informant had the team gearing up in the middle of the night for a raid on a warehouse with a suspected huge haul of cocaine. It was the biggest bust of his career and he'd been in charge of the raid. Dakota had been a bundle of nerves, worried, asking him questions like, "Was the informant trustworthy?" (Not really) "Has the informant come through before with good intel?" (Never met the guy before that night) and finally, "Are you sure this is safe? I mean, don't you usually need more time to coordinate these things?" He'd brushed off her fears, ignoring the fact that her questions were valid. He'd been too hopped up on the possibility of getting that haul off the streets to pay attention. He should've listened. The bust had gone down in flames, the intel was bad, it was a trap—and he'd almost gotten his head shot off.

Not his finest moment. Eating crow on that detail had been tough but worse was seeing Dakota nearly throw up when she heard he'd narrowly missed meeting his maker. He'd always been the one to take the chances, without taking into consideration the toll it took on the person waiting for him to come home.

Dakota had always accepted that they both worked dangerous jobs, he more so than her, but he took unnecessary risks because it felt good—hell, he could see now that it wasn't fair.

Glancing over, Ellis took in Dakota's flushed cheeks and bright eyes, alive with renewed hope. She was lit up from within, her passion for justice radiating off her. It resonated deeply with his own determination, calling to him like a siren song.

Could this scrap of information finally break the case open? Or was it just one more severed thread leading nowhere? There was no way to know unless they ran it down. Dakota's hope was contagious—he wanted to believe they'd caught a real break but that hope was tempered by the possibility that it was another wild-goose chase.

Let her have this, a voice said. This case wasn't the same as her sister's but he sensed that Dakota was shadowed by a ghost. He didn't have any siblings—the one thing his son of a bitch father did right was get a vasectomy after knocking up Ellis's mom—but he saw how losing Mikaya had affected Dakota and he hurt for her.

So, yeah, for now, he was going to let her enjoy this reinvigorated lead before he brought pragmatism back into play.

"Secrets never stay buried forever," Dakota chirped, munching on her potato chips from the gas station. "No matter how much money, how many connections, eventually secrets surface, and when they do, there's always someone there to scoop 'em up like fishing in a barrel."

He chuckled. "I wouldn't go that far. Just because we've got a good lead doesn't mean the case is closed," he reminded her, watching her devour those chips like it was her last meal. "You still going to be hungry for dinner?"

"That's a stupid question, this is a snack," she said. "I've been thinking about that little sushi place. Spicy tuna roll, get in my belly."

"Sounds good to me," Ellis said with a nod, steering them closer to home as the sun dipped low on the horizon. They still had a long road ahead, but suddenly the shadows didn't seem quite so deep. If this lead panned out, maybe, just maybe, the long-silenced ghosts would finally rest. A stubborn bud of hope bloomed in his heart. He could only pray it wasn't misplaced.

Chapter 24

The next morning, Dakota and Ellis were back on the road to Lawrence's in-state office, determined to confront Senator Lawrence about his aide Patrick O'Malley before he left for Washington. Despite coming in late, Dakota and Ellis had stayed up late researching what they could find on the senator's entourage seventeen years ago. It wasn't hard to find the one aide named Patrick and even easier to track down his current whereabouts.

The slick former lobbyist had joined Lawrence's team early on, but left politics for the more lucrative finance sector several years prior.

The senator was visibly annoyed to see them again so soon. "Agents, I fear you've made a trip for nothing. I've already told you everything I can," he said as they walked into his office. "And my schedule is booked with prior appointments."

"We apologize for the short notice but we have another lead that you can help us with," Dakota said.

At that the senator's brow rose in a subtle question. "What kind of lead?"

"We received information that you had an aide named Patrick O'Malley seventeen years ago when you were still a congressman. You and your entourage stayed frequently at the Glacier View Hotel in Whitefish and a housekeeper remembered you and Patrick being close."

The senator leaned back in his chair, narrowing his gaze with deeper annoyance. "Pardon me, Agents, but how is this a lead? I try to have good relationships with those who work for me. It's just being a good employer, wouldn't you agree?"

"I work for the FBI, I wouldn't know anything about that," Ellis deadpanned. "Can you tell us more about your relationship with Patrick?"

Senator Lawrence checked his watch and blew out a short breath. "I think you're playing fast and loose with the term *relationship*. We weren't golfing buddies or even friends. I was his boss and we had a typical employee/employer relationship. He served in his position well enough, he switched gears in his career and I gave him an excellent reference. That was the extent of our 'relationship,' as you call it. Just as I've done with countless other employees."

Dakota watched the senator's expression for any hint of subterfuge but Lawrence was cool as a cucumber—an annoyed one, that is.

"Senator—"

Lawrence held up a hand. "I appreciate your dedication, but this is fruitless," he said. "Patrick left long ago and we didn't keep in touch. I'm sorry I can't be more helpful but please, I must be going."

But Dakota wasn't ready to let him go just yet. "Was Patrick dating Nayeli Swiftwater?"

"Who?" the senator asked, but quickly realized his mistake and apologized. "Right, the young murdered Native girl. Sorry, my mind is full of appointments and commitments right now." He took a minute to search his memory but ultimately came up empty. "I really couldn't say. I try to stay out of my employees' personal lives. Keeps expectations manageable. I'm sure you can appreciate how getting too close to an employee can look on the outside."

Ellis caught Dakota's gaze, signaling that they weren't getting anywhere with the senator. Frustrated that the senator hadn't even blinked weird, betraying nothing, Dakota grudgingly agreed to end the interview.

"Good luck, Agents," the senator said with a perfunctory

smile as he grabbed his briefcase and began packing his paperwork, signaling that it was time for them to leave.

Back outside, Dakota fumed at the stonewalling. "I want to say he's hiding something but he didn't really give anything away. The man might as well have been talking about the valet. Of course he doesn't remember someone as inconsequential as an aide that's no longer with him."

Ellis agreed, but said, "We're here. Patrick O'Malley works in the area, so let's pay him a visit."

The Risen Financial Partners office tower gleamed like a pillar of polished granite and glass amid Helena's lower-slung buildings. Inside, Dakota's boots sank into plush carpeting as soft as a cloud. Behind the sleek walnut reception desk, an athletic blonde manned the phones with crisp efficiency.

"Good afternoon, how can I help you today?"

Both Dakota and Ellis flashed their credentials. "We're here to speak with Patrick O'Malley," Dakota said, glancing around the cathedral-like lobby, taking in the pervasive displays of wealth—massive floral arrangements, abstract sculptures, a trickling stone waterfall along one wall. *Fancy place.* Seemed Patrick gravitated to places that liked to show off their wealth, much like the senator.

This place was a temple to privilege, catering to the rich and powerful. Senators, CEOs, heirs and heiresses...the 1 percent who shaped worlds with the stroke of a pen. Men accustomed to doing as they pleased, without consequence. Dakota hated it instantly.

"Do you have an appointment?" the receptionist asked, adjusting her headset with a small, precise movement. "Mr. O'Malley has a very tight schedule and doesn't take walk-ins."

"He will for us," Ellis said, finished with this elitist bullshit.

The receptionist's indulgent smile was almost smug. "I'm sorry, there really isn't any wiggle room. Maybe you'd like to leave a business card—"

"How about this... Either he can talk to us now or we can make a big show of it and have him arrested in front of all of your fancy clientele. How's that sound? Think he can make time for us now?" Ellis said.

The receptionist's smile faded and she visibly swallowed as she quietly called Patrick's office. "Mr. O'Malley, you have federal agents Vaughn and Foster here to see you. They say it's... um, important." She listened and nodded. "Yes, sir. I'll send them right up." She hung up and smiled. "Fifteenth floor. He'll see you now."

"Well, look at that, there was some wiggle room after all," Dakota quipped, pushing off the marble counter to step into the elevator. "Amazing how that works."

In the elevator, Ellis said, "Remember, stay on your toes. Patrick might be wearing Italian leather but if he's guilty of Nayeli's murder, as soon as he realizes we're onto him, things could get dangerous."

Dakota grinned. "How cute, you're worried about me."

Ellis rolled his eyes, adjusting his holster behind his back. "Smart-ass. Just don't do anything stupid, okay?"

That was the pot calling the kettle black but he was so damn adorable in that moment that Dakota shocked him by sneaking a quick kiss on his cheek and said, "I'll leave the stupid up to you," before the elevator dinged at their floor.

She smothered a laugh at his expression. *Worth it.*

Goddamn it, Dakota. What'd you do that for? Now his head needed a reset. The elevator doors slid open, but Ellis still felt the warm imprint of Dakota's lips on his cheek. What did it mean? A playful gesture or something more? Ellis's pulse quickened at the possibilities, but he tamped it down. He had to stay focused. He growled for her ears only, "We'll revisit *that* later," as he stepped out of the elevator into a marble-floored suite with floor-to-ceiling views of the city.

Even though he cautioned Dakota about putting the cart before the horse, he was guilty of his own bias. Men like O'Malley and Lawrence lived by different rules, expecting to evade consequences. He'd seen it too many times during his time in Narcotics. Big money had a tendency to play fast and loose in ways that ordinary citizens didn't have the luxury.

Ellis resolved to be direct but professional with Patrick. Apply pressure if needed, but don't let emotions take the reins. He had to be ready for anything—or nothing. The decades-old lead might crumble to dust in their hands.

A sharp rap on the office door was answered by a crisp "Come in." Patrick O'Malley rose from behind a heavy oak desk, extending a manicured hand and polished smile. Ellis noted the smooth features, perfectly white teeth and nary a wrinkle betraying his age.

"How can I help you?" Patrick said, clasping his hands in front of him with an air of helpful concern. "It's not often federal agents show up to chat."

"Really? Considering how much money flows through this firm, I'm surprised it's not an everyday occurrence," Dakota quipped.

Patrick chuckled. "We run a clean ship. We don't take risks with our clientele's assets and we don't have clientele that aren't thoroughly vetted. Our firm is one of the oldest in the capital and most trusted," he shared with pride.

"You used to work as Senator Lawrence's aide. What made you go from politics to finance?"

"To be frank, more money," Patrick admitted. "When I started as an aide, I was fresh out of college, a little naive and I idealized what it would be like to be a politician. In reality, it's less about making meaningful change and more about doing favors and it just didn't sit well with me."

"Careful, Mr. O'Malley, I might start changing my opinion about you," Dakota said with a mild smile. "When you left the senator, you came to work here?"

Patrick nodded. "With help from the senator. He wrote a very nice referral letter that got me in the door and then my qualifications got me the rest of the way. Been here ever since. Best decision of my life. This is definitely where I'm supposed to be. I probably would've made a mediocre politician but as it turns out, I'm a damn good financial adviser."

Enough chitchat. Ellis tossed the bait. "Do you recall a woman named Nayeli Swiftwater?"

"Nayeli...sounds vaguely familiar but I can't place it. Who is she?"

"Well, for one, she's dead," Ellis said, scrutinizing Patrick's reaction. But O'Malley's wide-eyed surprise seemed genuine.

"Dead? That's terrible. What happened?"

"She was killed in her Whitefish apartment seventeen years ago and her six-week-old infant was kidnapped," Dakota shared.

Patrick swallowed, looking horrified. "That's awful."

"It was," Dakota agreed. "We received information that you and Nayeli might've been dating while she was a housekeep at the Glacier View Hotel. Do you remember her now?"

Ellis regarded Patrick with keen interest. Even a cool liar could crack with the right leverage but Patrick looked more stricken than scared or guilty. "I... I don't remember her but that's just terrible."

A flicker of something passed over Patrick's gaze but it was gone in an instant. Ellis narrowed his gaze. "Are you sure, Mr. O'Malley, that you don't remember her?"

"I would tell you if I did. I'm trying to remember who she might be... It was so long ago, though. At the time, Senator Lawrence was on the campaign trail for his first shot at his current seat and we saw so many different people, they all started to blend at some point, but it feels terrible to admit that about someone who's dead. I mean, I would never want to imply that her life wasn't worth remembering."

"Of course, we understand," Ellis said. "But seeing as you were specifically remembered as a potential love interest... Would you mind submitting to a DNA test?"

"Why?" Patrick shook his head, lips sealed stubbornly even as a panicked sweat beaded his brow. His wide-eyed alarm seemed at odds with his claims of ignorance.

Ellis shared a tense look with Dakota. If Patrick knew nothing, why was stark fear rolling off him in waves? Whatever secret he harbored had him terrified right now. Enough to make an innocent man seem guilty.

"We'd like to test your DNA to see if you're a genetic match for Nayeli's daughter," Ellis explained. "And see if your DNA shows up from the samples taken at the crime scene."

"What? Am I a suspect?" Patrick gasped, truly horrified.

"You can't think that I had anything to do with that poor girl's death."

"We'd like to rule you out," Dakota returned calmly.

"And if you have nothing to hide, the DNA will help exonerate you," Ellis said.

Ellis leaned forward, holding the man's frightened gaze. "If you're innocent, why are you so scared? Who are you protecting?"

"I'm not protecting anyone." Patrick wiped at his forehead. "Don't you need a warrant for that?"

"We can get one if you prefer but I thought you'd want to do this quickly and *quietly*," Ellis said.

Patrick flinched, his neck cording with strain. "I already told you everything I know," he insisted hollowly.

But the pallor of his skin, the pleading eyes of a cornered animal, told Ellis they were circling something dangerous. Patrick was in the crosshairs of powerful men who could make problems disappear.

They were running out of time to break through his fear. Ellis slid his chair closer, the threat implicit. "I don't think you have," he said grimly. "Now tell us about Nayeli."

He could almost hear Dakota's thudding pulse matching his own. They had stumbled into deep waters here. And he feared Patrick might not survive what came next if he refused to talk.

Patrick swore fervently, "I am not the father of that girl's baby. I swear to you, it's not possible."

"And why is that?" Dakota asked.

"Because I'm gay!"

And the plot thickens. Ellis shared a look with Dakota, shrugging, "Gay men can father babies. Were you openly gay seventeen years ago?" he asked.

Shame colored Patrick's cheek as he admitted, "No, I wasn't. I didn't come out until I'd been with this firm for seven years. I was afraid of losing clients but everyone was quite accepting. Made me realize I'd lost a lot of years of potential happiness for no reason. But I swear to you, I wasn't sleeping with that girl."

Ellis believed Patrick wasn't Zoey's father but Ellis was willing to bet his eyeteeth the man was hiding something.

Something that scared him.

He leaned forward, pinning Patrick with a hard stare. "We're going to try this again—do you remember Nayeli Swiftwater?"

"Yes," he finally admitted in a horrified whisper, shaking his head. "But I swear I didn't know she was dead until you told me."

"If you weren't dating her...do you know who was?" Dakota asked.

Patrick lifted his gaze, fear in his eyes. "I can't—"

"Who was she dating?" Ellis cut in, not playing around.

"You have to understand, I was just following instructions," he pleaded, shaking his head. "I didn't like it but it seemed harmless enough. We would switch rooms so that when Nayeli came to see him, it looked like she was coming to see me. He was newly married and the scandal would've tanked his career and mine."

"Who was she actually seeing?" Ellis pressed, needing him to say the name, his nerves drawn taut. "Just tell us."

Patrick swore under his breath, realizing he was in a corner. "It was the senator. She was seeing Mitchell Lawrence."

We got him! Ellis wanted to crow but now things were about to move real fast and by the numbers.

They couldn't afford to miss a single step if they were planning to arrest a US senator.

Chapter 25

Euphoria coursed through Dakota's veins as they left Patrick's office. Finally, they had the break in the case they'd been chasing, and she was practically dancing on thin air.

"I told you he was dirty," Dakota crowed to Ellis as they climbed into the car. "Family values, my ass. If Patrick's lead pans out, it means the senator was sleeping with Nayeli months after marrying his wife. If the DNA comes back as positive paternity for Zoey, it gives the senator motive for killing Nayeli." She ticked off the reasons. "He was newly married and messing around with a young impressionable teen while peddling a family values ticket to the voters. If the news had gotten a hold of the fact that he'd knocked up the girl, his career would've been over. That's the oldest motive in the book—the inconvenience of a pregnant mistress."

"It's a damn good motive and a solid lead," Ellis agreed. "But we have to do this by the book or else that slimy bastard will find a way to wriggle out of our hold."

"The hell he will," Dakota growled, determined to bring the corrupt bastard down. She quickly called Shilah. "We got him," she said with excitement. "We need a DNA warrant for Senator Lawrence Mitchell, ASAP, and while you're at it, file the arrest paperwork for Zachariah Deakins."

"On what grounds for Deakins?" Shilah asked.

"For the kidnapping of Cheyenne Swiftwater," she answered boldly, earning a warning look from Ellis. True, they didn't have concrete proof yet that Deakins was guilty but there were too many threads that led back to those two being connected to be coincidence.

"You got it," Shilah said, clicking off.

Dakota drew a deep breath, blowing it slowly. This was the biggest case of her career and it was either going to be an epic win or a devastating failure. Poking the bear could get her bit in the ass but she couldn't back down when victory was so close.

But Ellis, of all people, was the quiet voice of reason as he said, "If the senator's DNA turns out to be a match for Zoey, it's a fantastic break in our case but I feel bad for Zoey. She deserves better than Mitchell Lawrence for a father."

"He has two other kids, too," Dakota shared, frowning. "Two sons. Just like that Zoey would inherit two half brothers that will probably want nothing to do with her. She'll be looked at as the enemy."

"They could create problems for her later on down the road," Ellis warned. "From their point of view, Zoey would be looked at as the downfall of their family."

They weren't supposed to make it personal but there was no way Dakota would let that happen. "We'll find a way to protect her."

Ellis nodded, silently agreeing to break that rule with her if need be.

"I know it'll take at least twenty-four hours to get the warrants but I wish we could just hit the road now. I have all this adrenaline and nowhere to put it," she said.

Ellis chuckled. "I know that feeling all too well. When we get back to town, we could hit the gym, use up some of that energy so it doesn't drive you crazy."

Dakota knew it was a good option but she was riding a high and feeling reckless. "I know of a different way we could use up this energy," she said coyly.

"Dakota," Ellis warned, shooting her a quick look. "What are you doing?"

Something out of line. She unbuckled her seat belt and moved closer to Ellis, nuzzling his neck, inhaling his scent. "What does it look like I'm doing?" she purred against his skin, her tongue darting to taste him, tasting faintly of sweat and masculinity.

"Dakota, I'm driving," he said with a strained chuckle. "Knock it off and put your seat belt back on. This is dangerous."

"I thought you liked dangerous," she teased, going to unbuckle his belt. "I seem to recall you being addicted to dangerous."

Sweat started to pop along his forehead. "Yeah, well, I've since learned that maybe I was an idiot," he said, sucking in a tight breath as she popped his top button, reaching into his pants to grip his quickly thickening member. He tried to focus on the road but she was purposefully making it difficult. "Dakota," he half pleaded, half-sternly tried to get her to stop. "There are a million different reasons why this is a bad idea—and I can't believe I'm going to say this but... Get your hands out of my pants."

Was he serious? She paused, meeting his gaze questioningly. When he didn't back down, she realized he meant it. Swallowing what felt like a boulder in her throat, she gently withdrew her hand and quietly buttoned his pants, leaving him to deal with his belt.

Tears burned behind her eyelids as rejection burned a hole into her feminine pride.

"Actually, I think I should probably sleep in my own bed tonight," she said, her voice strangled.

There was no way in hell she could handle sleeping in his bed now—or ever.

Ellis wanted to swear, yell and pull the car over to have the conversation that needed to happen but he could tell Dakota had completely shut down and now he had to try and talk some sense into that stubborn head when she was likely to tell him to piss off.

He knew he'd hurt her feelings but did she really expect him to forget everything they'd already talked about just to get wild in the car?

The car was silent save for the hum of tires on asphalt. Ellis kept sneaking glances at Dakota, but she stared fixedly out the window. What a way to crap on an otherwise exhilarating win for the case. They ought to be celebrating the break, splurging on expensive takeout and taking a breather because they'd earned it.

But no—instead they were stuck in a bubble without enough space to breathe, the tension thick enough to knock over a buffalo.

Way to go, jackass.

He shouldn't have been so blunt rejecting her advances. And could he get a little recognition for how much strength it'd taken to make her stop? The memories of what Dakota could do with her mouth made him sweat, but as thrilling as it'd felt, he knew they were playing with fire. Nothing had changed between them—not really.

They'd already seen how this story ended the last time they ignored their better judgment and ended up in bed together and they'd both agreed—never again.

So what gives? Now she wants to play around, ignoring the consequences? Wasn't that his role in their little dynamic? Being the reasonable one sucked.

After an interminably long, excruciating car ride, they arrived at his place and immediately Dakota exited the car, heading straight for his apartment. She waited for him to catch up, avoiding his gaze. He sighed, opening the front door and pushing it open for her. "Dakota…"

But she wasn't going to talk. She grabbed her things without a word, shouldering her bag with her keys in hand. "Thanks for letting me crash," she mumbled, heading for the door.

Ellis tried to catch her arm. "Hey, can we talk?"

She avoided his eyes. "I'm pretty tired. I should get home."

Frustration rose in his throat. Why was she being stubborn about this? "C'mon, Dakota, please. I didn't mean to hurt you. But you know this thing between us is complicated and we need to focus on the case."

At that, Dakota looked up sharply, her gaze bright. "Forget it, Ellis. I don't know what I was thinking in the car. We're partners, let's leave it at that."

Dakota's aloof tone felt like a slap in the face. But as she turned away, Ellis caught the sheen of tears in her eyes before she could hide them. His chest squeezed at the glimpse of vulnerability she quickly shielded behind cool indifference. Dakota would rather chew her own leg off than admit when she was hurt.

Ellis ran an agitated hand through his hair. "Why does everything have to be so black-and-white with you? Just talk to me, help me understand—"

"Understand what? That once again I'm the stupid one acting on feelings you don't share?" Dakota choked out a bitter laugh. "Message received, trust me."

Before Ellis could respond, she slipped out the door, head held high despite the tears he knew she was fighting back.

That's not at all how he felt. How could such a smart woman be so clueless? He opened his mouth to clarify but Dakota wasn't in the mood to listen. The urge to go after her warred with giving Dakota space. He stepped toward the door, then forced himself back. She needed time to cool down and process. Didn't she?

Damn it, Dakota!

Should he chase after her? Or let her go? Was her place even safe? What if it was Lawrence sending people after Dakota to shut down the investigation? It wasn't that Dakota wasn't capable of handling herself, it was that he didn't like the idea of needlessly putting her in harm's way at all.

Raking his hands through his hair, Ellis swore under his breath. He should have handled that better instead of blurting the first frustrated thought. But the walls Dakota threw up infuriated him even as he understood their cause.

Ellis sank onto the couch they'd shared such a short time ago. The ghost of her still lingered as the scent of her perfume clung to the cushions. The idea of returning to his empty bed after she'd been in it for days made him angry all over.

He'd have to strip the sheets. There was no way he could sleep with the smell of her shampoo teasing his nose, torturing his senses. Rising, he stalked to his bedroom and started pulling the bedding, pushing thoughts of Dakota far from his mind so he could get through the night without chasing after her and forcibly putting her in the car, whether she liked it or not.

That was something the old Ellis would've done—the one with the heart full of rage and soul full of bitterness.

Hell, the old Ellis would've happily let her give him a blow job on the road, relishing in the carnal adventure, and screw the consequences but people had to evolve, right? In this moment, being an evolved man felt like a giant crap sandwich.

But that was just a remnant of who he used to be.

The kinder, more sensitive Ellis cautioned that he needed to let Dakota choose what she wanted to do and when she wanted to talk it out—if at all.

The ball was in Dakota's court now.

And he'd just have to be okay with that.

He lifted the balled-up sheets in his hands to his nose and deeply inhaled, groaning as her particular scent enveloped him like a sensual blanket. Why did she smell like heaven and hell at the same time?

He dropped the sheets to the floor.

Forget sleep, buddy, just take the couch again.

He knew a lost cause when he saw one.

... between ... ...

Chapter 26

Dakota spent an uncomfortable night in her own bed, tossing and turning, alternately burning with rage and crumpling in on herself with embarrassment. By the time her alarm went off, she gratefully climbed out of bed and walked like a zombie to her coffeepot.

Shake it off, there are bigger issues than your messed-up relationship with Ellis Vaughn, she reminded herself sternly.

They were poised on the precipice of a major win in the case. *Cling to that, not how epically you fell on your face in the seduction department.*

Both she and Ellis had their issues but returning to the case as professionals wasn't one of them. Gulping down her coffee, burning her tongue in the process, she jumped into the shower and washed off yesterday. By the time she left her place to meet up with Ellis at the office, she was back on solid ground.

Ellis took one look at her and knew her mind was razor-focused with a healthy distance between her feelings for him, which was the best way to handle the post-seduction fail of yesterday.

If she lived to be a hundred, she never wanted to think of yesterday's car ride again.

Shilah was close to getting their warrant for both Western

Horizon Solutions and the senator. All that remained was going to the compound and picking up Zachariah Deakins.

Sayeh rounded the corner before they hit the road, concern in her expression. "Are you sure you don't need backup? We can all go or we can call local PD to provide assistance."

But Dakota felt confident they could handle one fruit loop cult leader. "Even if Deakins decides to put up a fuss, I think between the two of us, we can handle him."

"What about the rest of his cult?" Sayeh said, worried. "One ant isn't dangerous but a whole colony coming at you will mess your shit up."

"They're a bunch of pacifists who don't like confrontation. We'll be fine," Dakota said, knowing Sayeh was reliving her own experience when her partner, Levi, almost died because they didn't call for backup. "The worst that might happen is someone throwing a cucumber at us as we handcuff their fearless leader. It'll be fine. Right, Ellis?"

Ellis jerked a short nod, agreeing, but his eyes were hard. She tried not to take it personal. Ellis went into a different zone when he was going to arrest someone. She'd seen it before. It was only because of what'd happened yesterday that she was even remotely twinged by it.

"You ready?" Ellis asked, grabbing the keys, taking the lead. She adjusted her vest, nodding.

They exited the building and climbed into the car, tingles of excitement overriding the lingering awkwardness between them, and she was fully prepared to pretend that yesterday didn't happen but Ellis had different plans.

"We need to talk about—"

"No we don't," she cut in more sharply than she intended. Her heart rate kicked up a notch at the thought of touching that hot stove between them. She forced a brittle smile even as her heart thundered in her chest. "Let's just focus on the case, okay? We need to stay on target. The stakes are too high to mess around with anything that might get in the way. We can't afford any screwups."

It was good, solid advice but Ellis wasn't happy about it.

"Fine," he muttered, shaking his head, clearly irritated at her unilateral refusal.

But she'd prepared this time. Pulling her headphones from her bag, she hooked into her phone and closed her eyes to listen to her favorite true-crime podcast, eliminating the need to fill any silence between them.

Soon enough, they pulled into Stevensville and went straight to the compound. Immediately Dakota's intuition prickled at the energy difference on the compound.

There was a heavy tension, a seeming dark cloud that hovered over their heads that wasn't there before. Even Eden's Bounty was closed, which given how that was their bread and butter— or so they said—it seemed odd to have the booths empty and unmanned.

"Well, this is creepy," Dakota murmured. "Where is everybody and why does it feel like we interrupted a funeral?"

"I don't know. Let's go find out," Ellis said, his sharp gaze taking in everything.

They headed straight to the main building where Deakins's office was located, shocked at the general disarray. It looked like a bomb had gone off in the building. Loose paperwork fluttered along the hardwood floor like broken planes run aground and the sound of crying children was a jarring change from the usual laughter that rang across the campus.

"What happened here?" Dakota asked, getting a bad feeling. They weren't stopped by anyone, which felt distinctly different from the last time they were escorted everywhere. Stepping into Deakins's office, they were alarmed at how everything was trashed. File cabinet drawers were left open, the guts ripped open and emptied of anything of value, as well as Deakins's desk. "Someone left in a hurry," he murmured, taking in the scene.

Dakota grimly agreed, a sinking feeling in her gut. "How much you want to bet Deakins is gone?"

Ellis didn't have time to answer. The Grojans appeared in the doorway, their eyes red and gritty as if they hadn't slept since returning to the compound.

Tensing, Dakota readied for anything. The last time they

had any interaction with the harried couple, they'd been openly hostile.

But this time, they seemed desperate.

Dakota didn't know which was worse—or more dangerous.

Ellis moved into a better position to protect Dakota if need be. He didn't trust the Grojans, but also the general vibe of the compound was unstable. "What happened here?" he asked.

Barbara-Jean's eyes were raw and swollen, her face pale and tightened by grief. Ned's hands trembled though his jaw was set—whether from rage or shame, Ellis couldn't tell. Their despair was palpable. Ned spoke first. "He's gone," he said, unable to meet Ellis's gaze. "Took every last cent and left us with nothing."

"What do you mean?"

Barbara-Jean said bitterly, "Zachariah… He left in the middle of the night, liquidated all of The Congregation's accounts and left us to rot. At first we didn't want to jump to conclusions— he was always doing something for the good of The Congregation and didn't always explain his actions. But when he didn't return after a few days, then a week…we checked the accounts and they were empty."

Ellis bit down on his frustration that Deakins had managed to escape. "I'm sorry. I know you believed in him."

"You don't understand what he's done to us," Barbara-Jean insisted, tears spilling from her eyes. "It was more than just believing in him. We put our lives in his hands, thinking he would protect us, but he was no better than the world we were trying to escape. He took everything we had…and we still lost Zoey."

Ned swallowed, looking as if his pride was in tatters and he didn't know which way to turn. "Please, can you help us? We don't know what to do."

It was an earnest plea. He'd have to be a stone-cold asshole to be immune to the devastation in the man's voice but Ellis knew this was their one chance at getting them to talk when they'd been buttoned up before.

"We'll do what we can but we need your help to bring this

con man to justice," he said gravely. "Tell us everything about how you came to adopt Zoey."

In the stark meeting room, the morning light cast unflattering shadows across the Grojans' haggard faces. The lingering scent of stale coffee did nothing to warm the Spartan space. This had been Deakins's inner sanctum, Ellis realized. The nerve center of his power.

"If we tell you, do we get to see Zoey?" Barbara-Jean asked, the hope in her voice almost heartbreaking.

Dakota, less moved by the woman who'd been a royal pain in the ass, was noncommittal. "We can't make promises but if your information turns out to be truthful... We can try."

It was the best they could—or would—offer and the Grojans knew it. Ned jerked a nod, looking to his wife, who was wiping at stray tears. "We'll tell you everything."

Dakota leaned over to murmur in his ear, "I'm going to step out and let Shilah know what's going on. Be right back. You good here?"

Ellis nodded and returned his attention to the Grojans, recording the conversation on his phone. "Go ahead, whenever you're ready."

"We just wanted a baby," Ned said gruffly, his mouth trembling. "We'd been to countless adoption agencies but the waiting list was years long and IVF wasn't an option any longer. We were desperate and when Zachariah Deakins showed up, right when we were at our lowest... We thought it was a sign from God. Then he brought us here to the compound and we fell in love with the ideology, the possibilities and the wholesome way of life that seemed lacking where we were coming from. Then, he said he had a baby available for adoption, a newborn baby girl, and he could facilitate the adoption if we were ready to commit to The Congregation."

"And by commit...?" Ellis asking leadingly, needing them to state the financial scheme for the record. "Please be specific."

"We had to liquidate our assets and turn them over to The Congregation. If we did that, we'd have our baby girl within the week," Ned said. "We prayed about it and decided by morning it was ordained by God to have this baby. We did as he asked, and Zachariah delivered Zoey into our arms a week later, just as he promised."

"You paid that monster for a stolen child?" Ellis said, trying to keep his voice devoid of the instant rage and disgust coursing through his veins, but when Ned flinched, he knew he had to try harder.

"We were fools," Ned admitted in a choked voice. "Blind, stupid fools."

"We were so happy," Barbara-Jean cried with a hysterical hiccup. "Why did this happen to us? I don't understand how he could do something so horrible to good people."

Ned wrapped his arm around his grieving wife in comfort, saying gruffly, "We were being selfish. We only cared about getting our happy ending, no matter the cost, and this is our punishment. We should've asked more questions, should've realized that no infant came that easily unless there was something shady going on."

Ellis shook his head, drawing a deep breath. These people weren't criminal masterminds, just a desperate couple willing to believe whatever they had to, to see a dream come true. Ellis's anger dissolved, leaving only pity in its wake. He tried to imagine the pain of wanting a child so badly that moral lines blurred. What lengths would any of them go to? "Our belief structures may be different but it seems unlikely that God put Deakins in your life as punishment for wanting a baby. Deakins conned a whole bunch of you from what I understand by preying on that desire. How many adoptions did Deakins make happen?"

"Fifteen," Barbara-Jean admitted in a shamed whisper, fear and longing mingling in her eyes. "We thought he was a miracle worker."

"And we were desperate enough to believe it," Ned said heavily. "Even when my gut said something wasn't right. But holding Zoey for the first time..." His voice cracked. "Nothing else mattered."

"He preyed on your hopes and dreams," Ellis said, shaking his head. "Tell me about where he said the baby came from."

"He explained about the substance-addicted mother, the overdose," Barbara-Jean said. "How the baby needed a good Christian home. It seemed meant to be."

"What'd he tell you about the money?"

Their shame was palpable. "That the adoption fees were high. Worth it for a miracle. We paid every cent, no questions asked." Barbara-Jean's face crumpled. "I should've known we'd bought a stolen child. How will God forgive us?"

Ellis had to turn away, breathing hard. The enormity of Deakins's deception was staggering. How many lives were destroyed chasing his twisted vision?

"We realize now he trafficked those children," Ned said heavily. "Every family here paid Deakins for their sons and daughters, believing his lies." He met Ellis's gaze, eyes shining with tears. "We just wanted to be parents. To love her. I swear to you, we had nothing to do with the murder of Zoey's mother."

Maybe he was getting soft but he believed them.

"We know we can't atone for our mistakes," Barbara-Jean said, swiping tears away. "But please, if there's any way…"

Ellis held up a hand, emotions churning as Dakota quietly returned to the room. "I'll do what I can. But you may face charges," he said, not willing to sugarcoat the truth of their situation, harsh as it may be.

They nodded, faces pale but resolute. "As long as Zoey is all right, nothing else matters now," Ned said.

But the general energy of the compound was unstable. They needed some semblance of order returned for everyone's mental health. What would come next was likely to rattle everyone. They were going to have to do an audit of every child here at the compound to find their original parents. That news was likely to go down like a turd in a punchbowl but they'd deal with that after Deakins was in custody.

"We need you to help rally your community here," Ellis directed. "They need someone to look to now that Deakins is in the wind. Keep everyone calm. Can you do that?"

Ned wiped at his eyes, eager to find some purpose. "Yes, we'll do that. Anything to help."

He watched the Grojans hustle from the office, heading out to talk to their people. He turned to Dakota, shaking his head.

"How far could any soul be pushed by desperation? Makes you wonder what really separates the guilty from the victims in all this."

"Well, as soon as we get Deakins and the senator into custody, I'll be sure to ask," Dakota said grimly. "Shilah has the warrant and a BOLO's been sent out for Deakins. We'll catch him."

They stepped out of the main building, preparing to head back to Billings, when a shot rang out and screams followed.

And then the agony of something burning hot like a sizzling poker taken straight from the fire rammed into his shoulder and sent him to the ground as screams erupted all around him.

Ah, hell... He'd just been shot.

Chapter 27

Everything slowed. The crack of gunfire. Ellis crumpling. Dakota's vision tunneled, the edges going dark.

Then rage exploded through her veins, white-hot, obliterating all else. She became a vessel of raw fury, honed by years of ruthless training.

With a feral scream, she launched herself at the shooter, channeling every ounce of strength into her tackle. They crashed to the ground and Dakota became a vicious, single-minded machine, determined to disarm the threat. The woman landed a few weak strikes in return before Dakota pinned her down, wrenching away the weapon with a snarl, "Stay down, you crazy bitch!"

The red haze receded as Dakota zip-tied the woman, extra tight. As she scrambled to Ellis, she hollered to Ned Grojan, "Call 911, now!" Her breaths came in ragged gulps, the copper tang of blood thick in her mouth.

"The righteous will—" the woman tried spouting but Dakota roared over the top of her as she tried to find something to stanch the bleeding.

"Shut it before I stuff a sock in your mouth!"

Ellis swore loudly as she applied pressure. "Talk to me, Ellis. What's the damage?"

"Right shoulder, through and through," Ellis ground out. "But it hurts like a son of a bitch."

She released a shaky breath. A through-and-through on the shoulder. Nonlethal. He was alive, but it could've been so much worse if the woman had been a better shot.

Within minutes, sirens split the air and ambulance and local police flooded the compound. The local cops hauled the weeping woman to her feet. "Gun's over there," Dakota directed, refusing to leave Ellis's side, giving room for EMS to stanch the bleeding.

"Always looking for the glory, aren't you?" she teased, though tears tingled behind her sinuses.

Their eyes locked through the chaos. Wordlessly, promises and confessions passed between them, Ellis's pain reflecting her own. She couldn't fathom losing Ellis. She kept replaying that awful moment over and over in her head until she thought she might break down and sob in front of everyone.

But Ellis seemed to know she was privately falling apart, and he grasped her hand with his good side. "This is nothing. A few stitches and I'm right as rain," he told her, trying to soothe her growing anxiety.

Dakota chuckled ruefully, rubbing the moisture from her eyes. "Only you would call a bullet wound 'nothing.'"

The EMS loaded Ellis into the ambulance and Dakota followed behind to the local hospital.

As the compound faded into the distance, Dakota faced the truth—her feelings for Ellis had never gone away and likely never would. He was burrowed into her soul like a burr tangled in a woolen blanket.

And she would do anything to protect what they had together. Anything to keep him with her.

The ghosts of the past could wait. Right now, she just needed Ellis to be okay. They would figure the rest out later.

Dakota paced the hospital lobby, emotions seesawing between relief and dread. Even though the bullet didn't hit any major arteries or nerves, going under the knife, even to repair damage from a bullet, could go sidewise.

She used the time waiting to quickly update her team.

"How's Ellis?" Shilah asked, concerned.

"I don't know. He's still in surgery."

"He's going to come through. He's tough," Shilah assured her.

Dakota's shaken nerves appreciated Shilah's confidence. "I hope so," she murmured, drawing a deep breath to ask, "Any news on Deakins or Senator Lawrence?"

"An arrest warrant was issued for Senator Lawrence just a few minutes ago. Let me tell you, it was pulling teeth to get the judge to sign off. You need to stay with Ellis. Sayeh and Levi will serve the warrant with local backup. You just focus on Ellis."

Before Ellis was shot, the idea of letting someone else put that politician in handcuffs made her teeth hurt, but now all she cared about was hearing that he was going to come through.

"Thank you," Dakota said, "keep me in the loop."

"Will do."

Shilah clicked off, leaving Dakota with her anxiety, chewing on her fingernails as she awaited news from surgery. *It's just shoulder surgery*, she told herself when her nerves threatened to drown her good sense. *Almost routine. Except for the part where a bullet shredded his musculature.*

It seemed like an eternity before the doctor walked through the doors to deliver the news. "Agent Foster, I'm pleased to tell you your partner is going to make a full recovery." The fatigue etched on the doctor's face told Dakota the damage must've been extensive to repair. "Although the bullet missed the major nerves and arteries, it really did make a mess in there. He's stable, sleeping off the anesthesia. If you want to go home and get some rest, we'll let you know when he's awake."

Leave Ellis? No way. She shook her head vehemently. "I'd like to stay. I want to be there when he wakes up."

The doctor understood. "I had a feeling you'd say that. Follow me. You can wait in his room. There's no sense in sitting in the lobby when you can just as well sit by his bedside."

Dakota was thankful for the doctor's compassion and followed him to Ellis's private room.

She should feel calmer knowing the worst had passed. Instead, an anxious pit gnawed in her stomach. Ellis was going to be okay physically, but where did that leave them?

This brush with tragedy had shaken something loose inside Dakota. Seeing Ellis bleeding, faced with the potential of losing him, stripped away her stubborn defenses. There was no more denying what he meant to her. No more wasted time.

But doubt crept in as she stalled outside his door. Did he feel the same? Were they ready to confront the past? So much still felt unresolved. Sometimes love wasn't enough to get past some of the obstacles in your path. You can love a road, love the scenery, and yet love wasn't going to move the boulder blocking you from traveling down the road. If love were enough, she and her mom's relationship would be repaired by now, but it remained awkward and strained on both sides. Was that the future she and Ellis faced?

Quietly entering the room, Dakota studied Ellis's sleeping face. Dark lashes fanned against his cheek. Her fingers twitched, aching to touch him. To assure herself this wasn't a dream.

Settling into the bedside chair, she twined her fingers together tightly, fighting against the tears that sprang to her eyes as a wave of emotion crashed over her. Why'd she have to fall in love with a man like Ellis? Why was it only him that made her heart beat like a wild thing inside her chest? Why couldn't she have fallen for Tom, the engineer who'd been calm, stable, a little on the serious side and drove a sensible car? Probably because he kissed like a middle schooler afraid of sneaking a peck from his girlfriend between classes for fear of getting caught by a teacher. Also, he'd been too fussy about table manners, gently chiding her when she didn't immediately place her napkin in her lap at the restaurant.

Ellis lived life with a joy that seemed to fill the empty spots in her soul. He grinned in the face of danger, and laughed at situations that could likely get him killed.

Except with this case. He'd been subdued, reserved and more cautious because he'd been working with her. Ironic that the one time he started playing by the rules he was the one who got shot.

She brushed a lock of stubborn hair away from his brows, releasing a small exhale as the questions crowded her brain, demanding answers she didn't have.

Somehow, she fell asleep in that awkward chair, but the second Ellis started to stir, she was instantly awake and alert. Their eyes met, and the breath caught in Dakota's throat.

"Hey, you," Ellis said hoarsely, fighting against the pull of a drugged sleep. He started to sluggishly shift, then grimaced and stopped. "That hurts like a mother," he said.

She laughed softly. "Yeah, well, your little 'through-and-through' made a big mess, according to your surgeon. You should get him a fruit basket or something."

"You think Eden's Bounty will deliver?" Ellis joked weakly, ending on a short cough as his lungs readjusted after being under anesthesia. "What's the w-word?" The stutter in his words showed the lingering hold of the powerful drugs in his system.

"Don't worry about that. You focus on healing." Dakota hovered anxiously until the pain meds kicked in. He was hooked to a high-tech, state-of-the-art automatic drip that would start as soon as he woke. When he relaxed back against the pillow, she reached for his hand and held it tightly. "You scared the crap out of me," she said quietly.

Ellis's mouth quirked with loopy sass. "Going to take more than one zealot to finish me off."

Dakota tried to acknowledge the joke with a smile but she couldn't get her mouth to cooperate. Tears welled in her eyes. "Ellis… All I could think about was, 'What would I do if I lost you?' And I couldn't think straight. Pure panic turned me stupid and all I wanted to do was cry. We've both been so damn stubborn about everything and I don't have all the answers but I know I don't want to live without you."

Ellis focused bleary eyes on her and with complete tenderness said, "Dakota… I'm…s-s——" and then he was out.

Ellis drifted in a drugged sleep for an indeterminate amount of time but he sensed rather than saw Dakota by his side. When he finally truly woke up, he saw Dakota sacked out in an uncomfortable chair beside his bed, curled up like a cat, resting her head on her knees. The poor woman was going to need magic to unkink her spine from sleeping like that.

He blinked against the pain that sucker punched him and as his blood pressure spiked, a calming influx of medication kicked in, soothing the ragged pain within minutes. *That's handy*, he thought as he relaxed.

But his mind was no longer dulled by the anesthesia hangover and he wondered if he'd dreamt Dakota saying she didn't want to live without him.

Something about both of them being stubborn and something-something-something and then, did she say she wanted to buy a broom? That had to be the anesthesia. God, he loved that woman. What he didn't say was he'd gladly take a bullet if that meant shielding her from harm. It'd been pure luck that that deranged zealot had gotten him instead of Dakota and it could've ended a lot differently.

He couldn't stomach the thought of losing Dakota like that. Or at all.

Was it possible to find a way back to each other? To push past all of the obstacles that seemed stacked in their way?

Was he willing to try? To brave the possibility and the heartache of a fresh breakup if it all fell to crap again?

And he knew his answer—almost immediately.

Being with Dakota was worth any potential heartache down the road.

She was the missing component in his life, the solid stability that kept him grounded when he was about ready to spin off into the distance.

He loved that she fell asleep halfway through a movie, hated brussels sprouts but insisted on trying them because they were full of "good vitamins" even knowing that every time she put one in her mouth, she spit it right back out. For all of her serious nature, there was a sweetness to Dakota that she only let a few people see—and that sweetness was something he craved unlike any other.

So, how did they move forward? What happened next?

Should he wait until this case was done or put his personal life first and let the case follow?

The pain meds started doing their job and his eyelids grew heavy. Time to sleep again.

But as his eyes drifted shut, knowing Dakota wouldn't leave his side was more powerful than any pain med to lull him into a healing sleep.

Chapter 28

Several days later, as Ellis was released from the hospital, Shilah called to let them know that both Deakins and the senator were finally in custody and Dakota was willing to bet Deakins was ready to squeal to save his own ass.

"Are you sure you're okay to do this?" Dakota asked as they drove to the local police station where the two were being held without bond. Deakins was apprehended at the airport trying to leave the country under an assumed name and the senator tried to use his lawyers to stonewall but eventually turned himself in to avoid the embarrassment of press.

"Even if my arm was hanging by a tendon, I wouldn't miss this," he said with a steely look. "I want to watch these two jackasses turn on each other and enjoy the carnage."

"So bloodthirsty," she teased. "But yeah, me, too."

They arrived at the station, their credentials allowing them immediate access. Deakins and the senator were held in different rooms for questioning. They chose Deakins first. Dakota was willing to bet a kidney the slimy con artist would flip the fastest and they needed his testimony to nail the senator.

Dakota and Ellis walked into the holding room, both taking great satisfaction in seeing him handcuffed to the metal table.

They seated themselves opposite Deakins as he regarded them with wary expectation. He was a smart man. He knew he was busted but he seemed content to wait and see what they knew first.

"Hello, Mr. Deakins," Dakota started, clicking the recorder, purposefully using "Mister" instead of his fake cult personification. "Seems you weren't entirely honest about a few things."

Deakins smiled but said nothing.

Ellis wasn't in the mood to play. "Let's cut to the chase. You're busted. We know you and Senator Lawrence are connected and you're responsible for the death of Nayeli Swiftwater and the subsequent kidnapping of Cheyenne Swiftwater, so why don't you help yourself and connect the dots for us."

"And why would I do that?" Deakins returned calmly.

"Because it all comes down to who's going to give up the most information. Right now, the senator is pinning it all on you. He's a US senator with a lot of clout and influence. Who do you think is going to get hit the hardest for this without conflicting testimony? You or him?" Ellis said. A silent thrill chased Dakota's spine as she watched Ellis play hardball. "If you don't want to end up taking all of the blame, you'd better start offering something of value."

Deakins's smug smile faltered, as if realizing he might actually be in trouble, but he stalled. "What happened to your arm?"

"One of your loony tunes followers shot me. You've got those poor people hopped up on a dream that doesn't exist and now they're in a tail-spin—and armed, apparently," Ellis answered bluntly, returning to the topic. "Did you kill Nayeli Swiftwater?"

"I didn't have anything to do with that," Deakins said. "And you have nothing proving that I did."

"Just the senator's testimony saying otherwise," Dakota lied coolly with a shrug. "Are you saying that's not true?"

Deakins's gaze narrowed. "He would never say that."

"Why not? Are you close? As I recall, you hardly know the man," Ellis said.

Deakins seamed his mouth shut as if realizing he was in a bad position, but his friend wasn't going to save him. At this point, it was every man for himself. He exhaled a long breath before admitting, "Mitch and I go way back. We met at a Montana State frat party freshman year. He was a prelaw and I was a political science major with a minor in theology."

"So you've always been interested in religion at some level," Ellis said.

"More of a fascination in belief structures and how easily people are led when faith is involved," he answered without a hint of shame.

"I imagine with your background it was easy to start your own group," Dakota said.

Deakins shrugged. "Broken people are eager for a way to rebuild themselves. Patch those broken pieces with 'faith' and they'll do anything."

"Even kill?" Ellis interjected.

"Yes. But again, I didn't have anything to do with Nayeli's death. That was all Mitch."

Excitement built under her collar. This was it. Deakins was about to roll on his partner—and Dakota was ready for it.

Ellis shared Dakota's excitement. This was the moment everything had the chance to blow up or fizzle to nothing. They were holding both men on circumstantial evidence that loosely connected them to Nayeli's case but neither seemed to realize this yet.

They needed one of the men to roll on the other to make this case stick. "All right, so tell us what really happened the night Nayeli died," Ellis said.

Deakins shook his head. "You have to understand where it all started, not just that night," he said. "You have to understand it wasn't exactly planned out what happened. It just sort of evolved."

"Go on," Dakota said.

"Mitch liked my talent for...creative money management," Zachariah continued. "In the early days I helped fill his campaign coffers, no questions asked. We made a good team, but for obvious reasons, we kept our friendship private."

"Until the pregnancy complicated things," Ellis said.

"I warned him about messing with that girl," Deakins said. "She was too young and she idealized what was happening between them. It was a red flag from the start but Mitch was addicted to how that girl adored him, thought the moon rose and set in his eyes, definitely believing that he was going to leave his *new* wife and be with her."

Ellis caught Dakota's wince, feeling her pain for a girl she'd never known. Nayeli had been sheltered, naive and ripe pickings for a sophisticated predator like Mitchell Lawrence.

"Then she got pregnant and the senator felt threatened," Dakota surmised.

"Mitch offered to help the girl get a termination. Offered to pay for it and everything. She would've had the best, private care at the senator's expense but she refused and Mitch panicked, cutting off all ties to the girl. She promised she wouldn't come after him for child support but I didn't believe her and told him as much. Six weeks after the kid was born, she called him looking for money—just like I figured she would."

"She couldn't find affordable childcare," Ellis said, unable to hide the contempt in his voice. "She was a kid with a kid, trying to hold on to a dream."

Deakins shrugged as if that wasn't his problem but more of a headache. "I told Mitch to ignore her calls but he went against my advice and tried talking some sense into her in person."

"And when that failed?"

Deakins spread his hands, limited as they were by the handcuffs, with a fatalistic expression. "And you know what happened that night."

"The senator killed Nayeli," Dakota supplied.

"He panicked. Strangled the girl, then realizing what he'd done, called me. He couldn't stomach killing his own daughter so he left it to me. He told me to 'handle' the situation and left. But I'm not going to kill a baby, either. Besides, babies are big business. All I had to do was scope out the fertility clinics, look for the couple reeking of desperation and lure them in with the promise of a newborn. It was really too easy but before you pin the badge of villain on my chest, I gave that child a beautiful life with wonderful parents. I watched that little girl grow into a smart, kind and capable young adult. How is that a bad thing? Would you rather I snuffed out her life that night instead?"

"I would rather that she grew up with her *actual* mother who loved her more than life itself," Dakota returned with a cold stare. "Don't bother trying to rewrite your part in this story. Make no mistake. You are a villain."

"A matter of perspective, I suppose," Deakins said. "Life is about seeing when one door closes, another opens."

"When did the larger child trafficking operation begin?" Ellis asked tightly.

"After we realized how easily we could expand on the private adoption idea," Zachariah answered, holding back nothing. "Desperate people will throw money at you to get what they want most. We were giving them a gift, really. Tell me, did any of those children look unhappy? No. They were raised in loving homes, with traditional values, eating fresh food they helped grow. They had a better life than any of their biological mothers could provide."

"How did you get access to so many newborns?" Ellis asked, narrowing his gaze. "Do you have an unmarked grave full of dead biological mothers?"

"That's pretty macabre, Agent," Deakins said with an amused smirk. "But to answer your question, no. You'd be surprised how easy it is to source infants from third-world countries. They practically toss unwanted babies in the trash and walk away. Trust me, those children were better off with me than where I found them."

"That's not your right to decide," Dakota said. "You might have played at being a messiah but you're not God."

Revulsion roiled through Ellis. This man didn't care about the lives he had ruined, only the money he made exploiting them. He never wanted this case to end more than he did right now.

He looked to Dakota with a short nod. "I think we have what we need. Is there anything else you'd like to add?"

Deakins leaned forward. "I'll hand over every document, every bit of evidence linking Mitchell to our scheme, including the firm that does our books for the adoptions, if you can promise me I'll be sent to a minimum security prison. I want Club Fed, you hear me?"

Dakota snorted. "And why would we do that? You've already given us what we need."

"It'll take you months to ferret out our financials—we were very diligent in hiding our tracks—and if you don't move fast enough, Mitch's lawyers will eat you for lunch, sending this case straight to the toilet and your careers with it."

Ellis knew Deakins was right. The senator had far more influential contacts and their case had to be airtight. A DNA draw would prove paternity to Zoey but was that enough to push the case to trial for murder? Even with Deakins's testimony?

Ellis hesitated, then gave a curt nod. "We'll see what we can do."

Dakota shot him an incredulous look, but didn't contradict him in front of Deakins. They'd debate this later.

"In that case, let's talk paperwork," Deakins said, visibly relaxing. "I can have my lawyer draw up an immunity agreement in exchange for everything I've got on the operation."

"You'll remain in custody until it's all verified," Ellis countered.

Deakins waved a hand. "Of course, of course. But we have a deal?"

Saving his own ass, just as Ellis figured he would. Ellis stood, signaling the end of the interview. "We'll be in touch."

In the hall, Dakota rounded on Ellis. "You can't seriously be considering a deal with that man."

"I don't like it, either," Ellis admitted. "But we need leverage on the senator, fast, and he's got it."

Dakota crossed her arms. "There has to be another way. That monster doesn't deserve immunity after profiting off innocent lives."

"You're right," Ellis said heavily. "But the justice system doesn't always serve the righteous. Sometimes you have to get dirty so the truly dangerous face punishment." It was a valuable lesson he'd learned in Narcotics. Compromise wasn't something Dakota was familiar with in her line of work but she was a fast learner.

"Look, I hate it, too. But it could be our only shot at victory. We have to do it."

After a tense silence, Dakota swore under her breath. "Fine. Draw up the damn deal if we have to. But that piece of garbage better deliver everything as promised."

Ellis let out a breath. They could loathe Deakins and still use him—distasteful as it was. The ends had to justify the means this time, for Zoey's and Nayeli's sakes.

With Deakins flipped, Senator Lawrence's house of cards would soon come crashing down. The ghosts were so close to resting in peace at last.

Chapter 29

Dakota's heart was heavy as they drove to the safe house. Telling Zoey the truth about her parents would change the girl's life forever but there was hope to be found in the closure—something she and her mother never received with the murder of Mikaya.

"You think she's ready to hear the truth?" Dakota asked quietly.

"She's a strong kid. She'll be able to handle the news." Ellis was confident but Dakota worried how it might scar the girl. Ellis seemed to read the private thoughts running through her brain and he reached over to squeeze her hand. "She won't be doing it alone. We'll help her get through this."

It was breaking the "Don't get personal" rule but neither cared. Zoey had managed to wriggle into their hearts and she wasn't going anywhere. Damn the rules.

The safe house was located on a sprawling ranch property, far from any major roads. As Dakota and Ellis pulled up the long gravel driveway, a quaint cabin came into view, smoke curling from the stone chimney.

They walked up the short sidewalk to the front door, used their key cards to open the door and walked inside. At the chirp of the front door opening, an agent appeared and they identified themselves. "We're here to talk to Zoey," Ellis said.

"She's in the living room, playing with the Xbox. For never playing video games before, the kid has beaten me more times than I can count."

Dakota chuckled as they went to the living room.

The cabin was cozy and a bit rustic, designed more for function than aesthetics. The main living area contained a stone fireplace surrounded by a couple of dated yet sturdy couches and armchairs. Braided rugs covered the hardwood floors.

It was comfortable yet secure lodging. The cabin's remoteness and solid construction ensured it could safely house endangered witnesses like Zoey until the trial concluded. A perfect temporary haven from the threats of the outside world.

Zoey heard them walk in and turned, controller in hand, smiling broadly at the unexpected visit. Then her gaze fell on Ellis's sling and she gasped. "Oh my goodness, are you okay?"

Ellis grinned, playing it off. "This? Just a flesh wound. Besides, scars make me look cool." They both picked a place to sit and prepared to give Zoey the news. Zoey sensed something big was coming and put her controller down. "Zoey, we have news to tell you about your mom's case," he said.

Zoey swallowed, preparing herself. "You caught who killed my mom?" she asked.

"Yes, we did, but there's a lot to this case that might be hard to hear," Dakota said gently. "Some of the truth is...difficult."

She summarized the sordid tale as best she could. Zoey listened silently, eyes downcast, absorbing everything with a maturity that stunned Dakota. Finished, she asked, "It's a lot to take in but do you have any questions?"

"So my dad is this senator guy? And he... He killed my biological mom?" Her voice wavered uncertainly.

Ellis leaned forward, compassion in his eyes. "Yes, but he's going to answer for his crimes. We're going to make sure of that."

Zoey blinked back tears. "Does he...have any other kids?"

"Yes," Dakota answered, hating this part. "He has two sons."

"So, I have two half brothers," she said.

Dakota nodded, but wanted Zoey to know that it might not be a happy reunion for them. "They might not want anything to do with you and I don't want you to take that on as your burden. However, your mom's sister, your aunt, very much wants to have you in her life. You have a grandmother, too. They're very excited to meet you."

Tremulous hope brightened Zoey's eyes. "Really?"

"Really. They're just waiting for the green light. It's all up to you. They'll go as fast or slow as you need. You're the last piece of their sister and daughter that they have, which makes you very precious to them."

Zoey absorbed that, looking small and lost. "What happens to me now?"

"You get to decide where you belong," Ellis said. "We can arrange visits with your mother's family, if you'd like."

Hope flickered in Zoey's eyes. "Really? I'd like that." She bit her lip. "And, I know it's a lot to ask, but..."

"You want to see the Grojans," Dakota finished gently, understanding. At Zoey's nod, she squeezed the girl's hand. "Now that we know they didn't have anything to do with the murder of your mother, of course. They love you so much, Zoey."

Ellis asked, "One thing that's been lost in the shuffle of all this happening... Why'd you run away in the first place, Zoey?"

Zoey drew a deep breath before answering. "I know it sounds selfish but I'd been struggling with the rules at The Congregation. Don't get me wrong, I loved my family and I had a good life, but I wanted to do more. I wanted to go to college and my parents were adamantly opposed to the idea of me leaving the compound. They said the world was an ugly place and I was safer with them. I was angry and felt suffocated. Then I found the adoption paperwork and I lost my temper and bailed. Looking back, I realize how childish it all was but I couldn't get my parents to hear what I was saying. I honestly didn't even have a plan aside from getting out to make my own life choices. Then I took that turn too fast and rolled the car, putting me here in this situation."

"It's not selfish or immature to have your own needs and wants, Zoey," Dakota said. "And everything happening like it did... Well, I think it was meant to happen that way."

"You think so?"

Dakota shared a look with Ellis considering everything that'd happened between them as well, answering, "Yeah, I do," and realized she was ready to see where the road might take them.

Ellis sat lost in thought as they drove back from the safe house. Dakota's words about things happening for a reason echoed in his mind. Could this be their second chance? After all the pain, did he dare reach for happiness again? His heart ached to bridge the distance still between them. But the old wounds they'd inflicted on each other made him cautious.

After all they'd endured, was a second chance possible? He'd been scared of the violence that potentially lurked inside him but getting shot had changed his perspective. Living in fear was robbing him of a future with the woman he couldn't stop loving.

That was the downside to having the kind of connection they shared—there were scars and hurts to navigate but he'd wasted too much time letting fear stand in his way of what he really wanted.

Glancing at her profile, Ellis swelled with gratitude that she was there beside him. He'd been given a gift—the gift of time to make things right. He refused to waste it. Time to take that chance or spend the rest of his life wondering "What if?"

Taking a bracing breath, he reached to caress her cheek. Dakota startled briefly before softening into his touch. The feel of her skin under his fingers was electric. Ellis pushed down the surge of hope rising within. He had to be sure Dakota felt the same way before he risked his heart again.

"It's not often our cases get a happy ending," she said. "But I'm so glad it was this one that did."

Ellis hesitated, struggling to keep his voice steady. "I've been thinking… What about our happy ending?"

"I didn't think we had one," she murmured, her gaze shining with vulnerability. "Do we?"

The question hung between them, weighted with past hurts and the promise of a fresh start. Ellis searched Dakota's face, looking for a sign that they shared the same hope.

Everything hinged on this moment. He had to place faith in the knowledge that he wasn't his father and that he'd worked hard to heal what his father had broken inside him. If she was willing to walk the road ahead together, no matter how long and winding, he was, too. He held his breath, scarcely daring to hope for the words that would make him whole again. He grasped her hand. "I was afraid of being unable to control my demons but I realize running from the one thing in my life that was ever beautiful and pure was a cowardly way to avoid facing my fear."

Dakota risked a look his way, her gaze cautiously optimistic. "Watching you get shot… It made me realize I don't want to live without you any longer. I'm willing to try if you are but I'm scared of your need to return to Narcotics. You're right—Narcotics will always need an investigator like you in the field because you do make a difference, but I don't know if I can stomach the toll it takes on you."

She was willing to brave the darkness that may lurk inside him but his driving ambition to return to Narcotics was the thing that scared her most. Getting shot must've knocked some sense into him. That hot need to return to the streets was gone. For the first time since transferring to Missing Persons, he saw how fulfilling the work was—and bringing families back together was a true way to make a difference out there in the world. A difference he could see with immediate effect.

He didn't need the adrenaline high of a chase to tell him that he was doing a good job. In Missing Persons, he had a chance to heal wounds within families that would reverberate for a lifetime. He couldn't say the same thing with Narcotics. It wasn't that he didn't believe in the importance of the work—no, it was still a vital component—but it wasn't his reason for getting up in the morning anymore.

Letting go of that need felt like he'd finally shucked off his father's phantom grip on his soul.

But he hadn't told Dakota that yet. Now was a good time to come clean. Ellis rubbed the sweaty palm of his uninjured hand on his pants as nerves took hold. This was his chance to show Dakota he'd changed—that she was more important than the thrill of the chase.

He took a shaky breath. "I've been thinking…" His voice cracked and he paused to steady himself. Dakota glanced over, surprise flickering in her eyes. He tried again. "I don't think Narcotics is where I belong anymore."

The words hung between them as Dakota processed their meaning. Ellis held himself tense, pulse racing. Everything hinged on this moment.

Finally Dakota risked a longer look his way. Her eyes shone with tentative relief and something that looked like fragile hope. "You don't?" she asked.

Ellis let out a breath he hadn't realized he was holding. "No. I think I was chasing something that had nothing to do with the job. Getting shot cured me of whatever it was." He gave a small, apologetic smile. "I know I've been stubborn about going back. But none of that matters now and I'm sorry it took getting shot to realize where I belong."

He reached over to brush a stray hair from her cheek, heart swelling when she leaned into his touch instead of pulling away. There were tears in her eyes when she met his gaze again. "Oh, Ellis," she whispered. "Are you sure? I know I've been vocal against your desire to return to Narcotics but it's not right of me to keep you from where you truly want to be. I want to be supportive even if it scares me."

The crack in her voice pierced him to the core. Ellis had vowed not to hurt her again—to be the man she deserved. As joy surged through him, he knew he was finally on the right road.

"That's just it, I don't want to return to Narcotics anymore. I want to stay with Missing Persons. The work matters and I'm embarrassed to say that it took me this long to see past my own bullshit to what was right in front of my face."

"You really mean that? You're not just saying that to make me happy?"

"As much as I would do anything to make you happy, no, I'm being honest about my own feelings. Going forward, I always want us to be honest with each other. Even when it's easier to bend the truth to prevent an argument."

Tears leaked from Dakota's eyes as she chided with fake frustration, "Damn you, Ellis. Why'd you have to tell me this while I'm driving? Now I'm crying and I can barely see the road."

"So, pull over," he said, grinning. "It's hard to kiss you like this, anyway."

The second the car rolled to a stop, Ellis couldn't hold back any longer. He leaned over the console in a rush, his mouth finding Dakota's in a fervent kiss. She made a small sound of surprise before melting into him, her fingers tangling in his hair.

Ellis poured everything he felt into that kiss—all the longing and heartache of their time apart, and the dizzying joy of this reconciliation. With the press of her lips, the stroke of her tongue, Dakota erased any shred of doubt. She was his future.

They came up for air both breathless. Ellis rested his forehead against hers, overcome with emotion. A thousand unspoken words passed between them in the space of a heartbeat.

There would still be uncertain days ahead, obstacles to overcome. But they would face it together. Dakota was his anchor, his guiding light. And he would walk by her side wherever she led.

Ellis brushed his thumb over her cheek, lost in her shining eyes. "No matter what comes, we'll figure it out," he murmured. "Always."

The past could not be changed, but they could shape what came next. Hand in hand, heart to heart, they would build something lasting from the ashes. Something beautiful.

Epilogue

A week later during the debrief session, Isaac Berrigan groused, "What is it about this task force that makes love bubbles pop around my team?" when Dakota revealed her past—and her planned future—with Ellis. "First Sayeh and Levi and now you and the FBI agent. Well, seeing as Agent Vaughn isn't one of my employees and was only a co-op agency thing, at least I don't have to fill out any paperwork." He eyed Dakota, then shifted to Shilah with an arched brow. "How about you? Planning on falling in love on a case?"

Shilah openly balked as if the thought made her instantly nauseous. "Me? Oh hell no, that's definitely not my style." Shilah shuddered dramatically. "I've sworn off dating, probably indefinitely. I'm already looking into a rental that allows lots of cats." She paused, a wry smile touching her lips. "Maybe just one cat, though. I'm not that lonely yet."

Sayeh snorted with laughter while Levi chuckled.

Isaac returned to business quickly, though his eyes shone with pride. "All right, that's two major wins for the task force. I gotta say, I didn't see the senator being dirty, but thankfully I didn't vote for the guy so at least there's that." He smiled, folding his arms across his chest. "However—love bubbles aside— I'm real proud of this team. I don't say this often but this team is probably one of the best I've ever had the privilege of working with. Let's keep up the momentum. Shilah, you're taking point on the next case."

"No pressure," Shilah joked.

With a rare smile, Isaac returned, "No pressure, just bring home another win."

Isaac ended the meeting and everyone filed out, the click of heels and shuffle of feet echoing down the hall. Dakota checked the time and hurried to gather her stuff. Shilah, who knew where Dakota was going next, gave a wink and a thumbs-up.

Outside, the sun was bright, glinting off the rows of cars. Dakota grabbed her purse and shut down her office, anticipation welling inside her. She pictured Ellis waiting, grinning from ear to ear, and quickened her pace.

Ellis waved with his good hand when she emerged, his smile wide. Dakota rushed to meet him, heartbeat quickening. She kissed him deeply, sinking into a deliriously happy place, the stress of the day fading away.

"You ready to do this?" she asked breathlessly.

"I should be asking you that question," he teased. "Because I've been wanting to do this since the day we met."

Dakota smiled up at him, thinking of the hints he'd been dropping all week, the ring she'd caught a glimpse of that he wouldn't let her see until he slipped it on her finger at the courthouse. "Oh, you did not," she shot back, calling him out with laughter in her voice.

They exchanged excited, joyful looks, both ready to start their new life together.

"Okay, maybe not the first day but definitely after you did that thing with your—"

"Ellis!" She gasped in fake outrage but he kissed the fake indication right out of her. He was her other half and always would be. She would happily marry him, today, tomorrow and every day for the rest of their lives, if only to ensure she was never without him again.

They'd lost two years to their stubborn natures and she vowed to never let her ego, pride and rigid need to be right ever get in the way of her heart ever again.

With Ellis she'd learned that it was better to bend with the wind rather than letting it break you. She'd even made the first step to truly work on repairing her relationship with her mother. No more avoiding the past—no matter how painful the healing.

She wanted a family—a real family—and that was hard to do when you were hanging on to a bitter past.

That's what she liked to imagine Mikaya would offer by way of big-sister advice.

Or maybe she just would've smacked her in the arm and said, "Stop being stupid. He's a good man. Marry him before I do," and then told her what the color scheme for the wedding should be because Mikaya looked best in winter shades—and Mikaya had been notoriously bossy.

Either way, Dakota knew Mikaya would approve of the man she was ready to call her husband.

And that felt like sunshine on her happy heart.

This was what a new beginning was supposed to feel like.

And she was ready for whatever the future might bring with Ellis by her side.

* * * * *

Escape To The Bayou
Amber Leigh Williams

MILLS & BOON

Amber Leigh Williams is an author, wife, mother of two and dog mom. She has been writing sexy small-town romance with memorable characters since 2006. Her Harlequin romance miniseries is set in her charming hometown of Fairhope, Alabama. She lives on the Alabama Gulf Coast, where she loves being outdoors with her family and a good book. Visit her on the web at amberleighwilliams.com!

Books by Amber Leigh Williams

Harlequin Romantic Suspense

Southern Justice

Escape to the Bayou

Fuego, New Mexico

Coldero Ridge Cowboy
Ollero Creek Conspiracy
Close Range Cattleman

Hunted on the Bay

Visit the Author Profile page at millsandboon.com.au for more titles.

Dear Reader,

Once upon a time, a mother took her daughter to New Orleans and they were never quite the same.

During our first venture to the Crescent City, she snapped a photograph of pint-size me at the foot of the Monument to the Immigrant. I still keep the Polaroid tucked inside a book.

Our second trip was encapsulated by another photograph of her on a rainy corner of Bourbon Street. It's completely candid, but she looks effortlessly chic in her T-shirt and shorts with an umbrella angled just so against the wet banquette.

During our most recent girls' trip, we started the day at Café du Monde, then wove through voodoo shops, dive bars and apothecaries before attempting to find the Angel of Grief in Metairie Cemetery. We never did. Instead, we wandered the labyrinth of tombs until the keeper locked us inside the cemetery and we had to find creative ways to escape.

If not for this very New Orleans adventure and all the others, *Escape to the Bayou* would not have been written. I hope you enjoy this first book in the Southern Justice trilogy.

Happy reading, *cher*!

Amber

For Mama

Prologue

Sneaking away to Mexico before the first week of college had been Sloane's idea. It was a bad one. But as with most bad ideas born out of teenage desperation, this one was especially enticing.

One last "free girls" weekend, Sloane had beckoned.

Grace offered a fast yes. Pia, hesitant, echoed it.

Free girls, Grace thought three long weeks later, dejected.

She hadn't seen Sloane or Pia in seventeen days. Where had they been taken? They had been abducted from the same house—the little waterfront villa Sloane had rented on the sly. Her well-to-do parents would have flipped if they had known what she was up to. The senator and his wife would never have allowed it. So Sloane had paid for everything on the spot in cash.

Cash had been the problem. Throwing cash around had been their undoing.

If they had been more discreet, would they have been taken? Would the men have even known they were there?

And Alejandro. If Grace hadn't met Alejandro, would she, Pia and Sloane still be free girls? Had she doomed them all?

"I want to see my friends," she told him.

Alejandro didn't look up from the television. Fútbol was on. He leaned forward on the couch, inches away from the screen, his dark eyes magnetized to the ball. "Bad girls don't get visits," he said in a flat voice accented heavily in Spanish.

She'd tried escaping again. Could he blame her? She only left the house he and the other men had dropped her off at two weeks before to "work," as they called it.

Work. She was from the hard streets of New Orleans. She knew what it was to work. This? What he made her do—it wasn't work.

It was criminal, exploitation... It would take her soul if she let it continue.

She'd made it farther this time. Through the little window of the bathroom into the alley. He'd caught her before she could hit the street.

He'd beaten her. She'd thought someone...*anyone*...would hear her screams.

No one came. No one stopped Alejandro from locking her back inside the house. This time he had tied her up.

The rope around her wrists burned. She'd stopped tugging at the bind. Her face hurt. There was something wrong with her right arm, her ribs. Every inhale was agony.

At least he'd been generous enough not to traffic her in this condition. He hadn't driven her to some strange man's apartment in the city and thrown her at his mercy.

She lay awake at night worrying about disease—about pregnancy. About her friends. Where were they? What were the men doing to Sloane and Pia? Were they even alive at this point?

"Please," she said through lips that had long gone dry. She felt the bite of tears, but she had none. He hadn't given her anything to drink in the last twenty-four hours. Her one meal a day was down to rations of aging bread and cheese. "Just tell me if they're alive. That's all I need to know."

At long last, Alejandro turned his face away from the television. The box's light flickered across one half of his profile. It shrouded the other in darkness. He was a handsome man. It was how he'd drawn her in. Handsome and charming with a smile quick as lightning and just as white.

Was his name even Alejandro? Or was that part of his scheme? How many other women had he drawn into his web—into this life that wasn't a life—simply by smiling?

Now his smile came slowly. Her heart galloped in fear. She

knew him well enough to know what that smile meant for her... for Sloane and Pia.

"Your friends have gone to a better place, carne fresca," he informed her. Then he turned back to the television, leaning back into the cushions of the couch as he scooped his beer off the side table and drank, satisfied.

He wasn't looking, but she turned to face the wall. Her lip split as she grimaced, her shame and grief big enough to bite. She was afraid it would eat her up.

There'd be nothing left for him then. Nothing left for him or the rest of them to take.

The sound of glass shattering made Grace instinctively duck—her nerves were on a hair trigger. She'd gotten quick under his "care."

She peered over the edge of the table. Alejandro slumped forward. He moved gradually, limply, to the floor.

Her lips trembled as his arm flopped toward her, the beer bottle rolling across the bare planks. His sleeve crept up his biceps, revealing the brand—the burned, black Aztec skull she'd noticed he and his men all wore like harbingers of death.

The door burst open, kicked off its hinges.

She ducked farther under the table. The rope cinched tight against her raw wrists.

A pair of boots crept across the threshold. She watched them cross the floor to Alejandro's prone form. They looked like cowboy boots—snakeskin. She didn't dare breathe or think or move as she watched a large hand remove the pistol from the small of Alejandro's back where it was wedged between his beltline and his skin.

"Grace?"

It had been so long since anyone had called her anything but carne fresca, "fresh meat." She blinked, coming awake on a startled inhale. Still, she didn't raise her head above the table-top. Instead, she peered at the boots.

She watched the jean-clad legs bend. Knees appeared. Then thighs. A leather belt, silver buckle, plaid shirt...

A bronze face. Long, dark hair fell from hairline to jaw. Eyes glittered at her, black as night.

"You," she said, recognizing him at once. She backed away.

He held up his hands. One held a pistol. He tipped it to the floor. "No, no. I'm not here to hurt you," he blurted.

His English was better than Alejandro's. And his eyes were kind. But he'd been at the house the night of the abduction. She'd seen him...with the men who'd taken Pia. "Where is she?" she hissed. Emboldened, she tried to grab him...his gun... The rope held her back. "Where's Pia?" she demanded.

He put his finger to his lips. "You mustn't yell. I'm here to get you out."

"Where is she?" she shouted.

His hand fit tightly over her mouth. His face was close to hers under the table, nose to nose.

"Listen," he told her. "I don't want to leave that rope around your wrists. But if you fight me, I won't have a choice. Do you understand, bonita?"

His hand was warm and dry. He'd just shot a man. Shouldn't it be cold or wet with sweat? She could feel the rough texture, calluses. There was strength there, and she trembled despite the endearment—despite the fact that his grip didn't hurt. Over the last few weeks, they had conditioned her for pain. She waited for it.

He reached for his belt. She heard the slide of steel. Her eyes widened when he raised the knife.

"I'm going to cut your binds," he said, his gaze holding fast to hers. "You must be very still."

She closed her eyes and breathed hard through her nose as the knife lowered to her wrists. She felt the cool steel against the sore skin of her wrists and whimpered.

One pull and her hands fell away from each other. Something in both of her shoulders ached with gratitude. "Ah..."

His hand loosened from her mouth. She gaped at him as he tossed the rope aside. "We must go now," he explained. "They'll be coming. Tell me you understand."

She nodded faintly. He retreated, motioning her to do the same. After a moment's hesitation, she crawled out from under the table.

"Back door," he said when she veered for the open one splintered around the locking mechanisms Alejandro had kept firmly in place when she was inside.

She turned to follow him through the house and nearly tripped over Alejandro's form. Covering her own mouth, she stared at the blood pooling on the floor. "You... You just killed him."

"What would you have me do instead?" He didn't raise his voice. He kept it even-tempered as he walked around the body. "Knock on the door and let him use you as a hostage?"

They made it halfway down the hall before she stopped. "Tell me about Pia. What happened to her and Sloane?"

"I'll tell you everything. But first we—"

"I'm not going anywhere with you," she said stubbornly. "Not until I know they're okay."

Frustration ticked across his face. "They're alive. And they know we're coming back for them."

"Alive?" She could hardly grasp the possibility. Hadn't Alejandro just told her the opposite? "Sloane and Pia are...alive?"

"Si. They're alive."

It seemed too good to be true. She resisted when he tried to move her toward the back door again. "I don't believe you."

He made a noise in his throat. The trembling strengthened. His eyes reminded her vividly of Alejandro's—dark, practically liquid.

Where Alejandro's had been hard and cold, like smooth volcanic rock, this man's sparked with heat. They contained firestorms. She didn't know what to make of that.

Stepping closer, he lowered his face toward hers. "'Free girls code.' Does that mean anything to you?"

Free girls. Her heart leaped. "Oh...oh my God." The bite of tears was back. A sob worked at her throat, and she gasped.

"Now you believe me?"

"Take me to them. Please."

He took her hand. "This way."

"I need your name," she insisted as she followed.

"Javier," he whispered before sticking his head out into the alley behind the house. It bisected others surrounding the tight-knit neighborhood where there were no yards, no gardens, no trees...just stone and walls and pavement. "Javier Rivera."

She dropped her voice to a whisper. "Why are you doing this, Javier?" she asked as she trailed him into the alley. "Why are you helping us?"

He stopped long enough to check around the corner. "Because it's the right thing to do, Grace. Stay close. Entiende?"

She nodded fervently. "Si."

Pressing his finger to his lips for quiet, he lifted his gun hand before coaxing her around the first in a series of blind corners.

Chapter 1

On any given Sunday, the commute in New Orleans was intense.

During Mardi Gras, it was downright hellish.

Normally, it took Dr. Grace Lacroix twenty minutes to traverse the city from her loft above the pizzeria on Saint Peter to the hospital uptown.

Today, it took her forty minutes. By the end of her shift, the gray-bottomed clouds had opened up and a deluge fell on the Quarter. The hardy festival crowd didn't have the sense to dissipate. Grace dodged revelers in party hats, tutus, and bright T-shirts that boasted THING 1, or BITCH 2 or DRUNK 3. Some carried tall hurricane glasses or potent "hand grenades." Others drank Abita out of to-go cups. Drinking in New Orleans was legal anytime, anywhere.

The tourists were out in force, which meant the performers were, too—tap dancers, singers, musicians who catered not just to their mistress, jazz, but also to rock and roll, blues, R&B and zydeco.

Grace swerved around two police motorcycles as she attempted to cross Bourbon Street. She dodged a man with a thick Jamaican boa constrictor draped across his shoulders like a feather boa. Reaching into her purse, she pulled out a five-dollar bill and dropped it into the sidewalk tip jar in front of a small girl with braids who tapped a cadence on upturned buckets.

Grace tried not to think about the boy she'd lost on her operating table hours before—the one with the gunshot wounds who hadn't been much older.

Tree roots knuckled the pavement, catching the toes of her wet sneakers. Ambient light from bars, restaurants and souvenir shops played across plastic Mardi Gras beads tangled in the fingers of oak trees and their cloaks of Spanish moss. She caught snatches of scent—everything from cigarettes, marijuana, sage, Cajun cuisine, ripening garbage and the ever-present bouquet of the Mississippi.

The Crescent City was her birthplace. She knew better than anybody how it mimicked Old Man River. Both were tough, twisted and tricked out in their own mythology. The city had changed hands so many times, its architectural origins often confused people—even the locals.

Her parents had brought her up in the Ninth Ward, not the pizzeria on Saint Peter where she presently lived in the Vieux Carré. Still, she almost took the Creole-style architecture and jewel-toned houses for granted now. She'd grown numb to the city's flagrancy and, to a degree, the blatant indicators of poverty. The unchaperoned child drummer on Bourbon, the barkers, addicts, transients and hustlers who were never discouraged by rain or the immense summer heat when it arrived.

New Orleans may have been the infamous confluence of cultures and history that lured visitors from all corners of the globe. But Grace had become immune to it. There wasn't much along the route home that startled her.

A tiny mew reached her ears over the endless cacophony of raindrops. She stopped and backtracked to an open, abandoned cardboard container.

The face was as black as night. In the center was the tiniest, pinkest nose she was sure she'd ever seen. The kitten shivered, wet. Its eyes were bright and blue. It curled in on itself, trying to keep warm.

Those sad eyes cleaved her.

She dropped to one knee in a puddle. On the side of the box, the words KITTENS FOR SALE drooped, the rain chasing them in teardrops to the banquette.

The kitten opened its mouth to mew again, but nothing escaped. The cold had stolen its voice.

Look away, Grace cautioned herself. *Walk away.* She did it every day, didn't she? She, too, routinely walked by the people who slept clustered around monuments, the ones warmed by little more than worn coats and newspapers. Sometimes, she stopped and asked someone if they needed anything. If it was food or clothing, she brought it. If it was a place to stay, she called her friend at the nearby shelter. But none of those poor souls ever came home with her.

Still, she found her hands reaching into the box. She felt the wet fur, the ribs underneath. Unfurling the pathetic creature from its corner, she raised him into the dim light of the voodoo shop. Grace glanced around. No one was watching. New Orleans ignored her, too—a wet, bedraggled woman leaning over a sagging box in a woolen coat and scrubs.

The little paws curled inward as the kitten's front legs splayed. It closed its eyes and opened its mouth, showing fine white teeth in a silent scream.

Tucking the animal against her chest, she opened her coat and offered it the last dry place she had against the scrub shirt underneath. Flipping the coat collar so that it served as an umbrella, she wrapped both arms across her front to keep the cat in place and walked on.

The pizzeria was family-owned and -operated. It had been around for thirty years—not as old as the corner store. Still, the familiar faces of the Sicilian Russo brothers were a comfort, even with their voices raised in spirited debate.

As Grace escaped the rain, she breathed a sigh. The floor of the dining area was black-and-white and sticky in places, but the smells of fresh dough and authentic red sauce beckoned. As she pried back her coat collar to check on the kitten, she caught the shouts from the back of the kitchen where the restaurant's famous brick pizza oven lived.

Marco and Giovanni's row had no effect on the patrons that packed the tables, chatting over large pie slices or nursing clear plastic steins of beer.

Grace caught the eye of Marco's daughter, Gina, who carried a round silver pizza tray skillfully over her head. "Everything okay?" she asked.

Gina, coming around fast to eighteen, rolled her eyes. "Shipping costs went up again."

"Ah," Grace said knowingly. The brothers had most of their ingredients shipped from the Old Country. It was what set them apart. She stepped aside so Gina's cousin Angelo could set up a fold-out for the tray next to the table to her left.

"Somebody came in looking for you," Gina told her, lowering the tray to the fold-out.

"Who?" Grace asked.

"Dunno," Gina replied. She helped Angelo pass out shell-white plates to those seated before stacking their empty salad bowls. "Never seen him before."

"A guy?" Grace said with a frown. "Is he still around?"

"Dunno," Gina said again. Her hands were full, so she walked with Grace to the door to the kitchen, scanning the patrons. "I don't see him."

Grace hugged the kitten through her coat. Its desperate shivering had finally ceased. She felt the soothing vibrations of purring through the cup of her bra. She was dripping on Marco's and Giovanni's tiles. Before either of them could see her, she dropped her chin to her chest and barreled through the kitchen's heat to the back door.

The courtyard was private, its sun-blanched bricks lost to vines that grew green and thick even in the cold season. She avoided the center open to the moody sky, winding around to the spiral staircase.

Her footsteps were loud on the metal steps. The building's designer had been wise enough to leave them grated, so that they weren't slippery when wet. The landing was open, a 360-degree balcony boasting wrought iron railings hammered, bent and worked by hand. They predated her—predated the Russo brothers' pizzeria, too. It had endured as much as the corner store, the streetcar on Saint Charles, and Café du Monde. It would outlast the Russo brothers and Grace, too.

She dug her keys from the bottom of her purse while balancing the kitten's slight weight on her forearm. She didn't see the shadow until it was too late.

Rolling to her heels in defense, her heart hitched into her throat. Her fingers clutched her keys. The longest one tightened between her first and middle knuckles. She thrust it in front of her, shouting, "Don't move!"

Through the corkscrew curls that had fallen into her eyes, she saw the shadow lengthen into a man's form. She blew at the hair, but it was limp and wet. Flicking her gaze to his feet, she froze.

Snakeskin boots.

Cowboy.

Jean-clad legs.

She followed their ranks up sun-bleached knees to a silver buckle and leather belt, a black outdoor jacket that looked as worn as it was hardy...

She lost her breath at the sight of his face. Her molars ground, and her shock and fear persisted. "Javier."

His dark eyes swam. They were liquid, like all those years before.

Dark water. Hadn't her father always told her not to swim in dark water? *The dark water'll get you, minnow. Swallows young 'uns like you whole.*

As Javier stared, she felt swallowed. Under the shade of his cocoa-colored felt hat, his eyes reached—they grabbed.

She felt the kitten stir against her breast, unsettled by her tension. Forgetting the makeshift weapon in her hand, she crossed both arms over that warm spot against her chest. "Wh-what are you doing here?"

He blinked once, twice, his lashes long and spiked together by rain. "You're still afraid of me. Why?"

"Why?" A helpless laugh escaped her. She was trembling down deep in her bones just like she had twelve years ago, damn it. It had been over a decade, but Mexico felt close. Too close.

Shouldn't she at least have been able to put some of it in her rearview? "The last time I saw you," she said, "you were being taken away in handcuffs."

"At the embassy," he said and nodded. "I remember."

She remembered, too, the way he'd looked at her, Sloane and Pia as he was being led away by the Feds. "I thought I'd never see you again."

"You were happy about that," he seemed to realize, dimming.

She felt a lick of shame, then stopped and shook her head. Her feelings were valid. Yes, Javier had saved them. He'd gotten them out of the hellholes the traffickers had been hiding each of them in. He'd saved them from an awful fate. But his role in it at the beginning… She still didn't know enough.

How could she trust a man when he and the others had taken Pia and Sloane away?

Whatever his role—whichever way he was tied to Alejandro and the Solaro crime family responsible for ruining their lives and the lives of countless other women—Javier was a physical reminder of the summer holiday neither she nor her friends had ever wholly recovered from.

She eyed the door to her apartment on the other side of him.

He glanced at it, too. Under the shadow of his hat, she saw his mouth tighten and the long muscle in his tan cheek twitch. He stepped away from her escape route, leaving her plenty of room to pass.

She didn't waste time. Juggling the squirming kitten, she fit the key in the lock. Cranking it, she stepped inside as the door swung back.

"Grace," he said before she could close the door. "Please. I just want to talk."

She gripped the knob and made herself pivot back to him. "I'm not sure we have anything to talk about, Javier. It's been twelve years."

"It has," he said with knowing eyes. "But neither of us has forgotten."

"I've put it behind me," she said. It wasn't entirely a lie. Right? She'd pushed through college, med school, a grueling inner-city residency… She couldn't have done all that if some part of her hadn't moved on.

"I have news," he said.

"What about?" she asked, apprehensive. "Not about...your family. Right?"

He was connected to Alejandro and the Solaros by blood. The details had been too confusing when the Feds had broken it down for her. Information didn't process correctly when trauma was taking its toll on your body and mind. She'd learned that, along with a lot of other hard truths she hadn't wanted. She remembered only snatches from the FBI's debrief.

Man on the inside.

The Solaros' reign over human trafficking in Mexico ended thanks, apparently, to Javier Rivera. Most of the Solaros had gone to prison, including the head of the family, Alejandro's father, Pablo, and Alejandro's older brother, Jaime—Pia and Sloane's handler. Only a few minor players inside the operation had made deals to avoid a lifetime behind bars. Alejandro was dead. Grace had seen him die, even if he still came for her in her sleep.

Javier nodded. "It's about the Solaros. Si."

She flinched, then closed her eyes and gripped the jamb. *Get a grip, Grace. These people don't have a hold on you anymore. You're a free girl.* "Have you spoken to Pia or Sloane?"

He shook his head. "I just found out yesterday."

Her brows gathered. "And the first person you thought about was me?"

He didn't offer an explanation, but in the smattering of light from her apartment, she saw those dark waters stir. His gaze swept across her face, from her prominent forehead to her wide mouth. They dived lower, over her throat, to the opening of her coat. His expression changed, softening into surprise. "How did that get there?"

Grace looked down and saw the kitten's small, wet head peering out of her shirt. She stroked his ears. "Someone left him on the street. He was cold..."

"Do you bring home stray cats all the time?" he asked, amused.

"No," she answered. "But today was..." *Hard.* The kid on the operating table...

Grace realized she'd needed something...someone...as much as the kitten had. "I don't think I can talk right now, Javier. I'm sorry."

He nodded. "Can we talk later?"

"How long are you in town?" she asked.

"As long as you need."

"Not here," she decided.

He nodded understanding. "At a restaurant. Do you like the one downstairs?"

"I do," she said, "but not there, either. There's a place in the Marigny. I know the owner. He never lets it get too crowded, even with the festival. We should be able to talk there. I'll call ahead and see if we can't get a table for eight o'clock. Is that all right—or are you staying further uptown?"

"No. Perfecto." He hesitated, darting looks between her and the kitten. "I'll see you there."

"Yeah." She waited until he walked away and the rain pounding on the slate roof drowned his footsteps. Then she shut the door and locked it.

Setting her keys on the kitchen counter, she set aside her purse, too. "You can come out now," she told the kitten, scooping him out of his nesting place.

He mewed as she cradled him in the crook of her arm. She picked up the phone from its cradle and, using one hand to dial, inputted the number for the kitchen downstairs. The ringtone droned eight times before Giovanni picked up with a brusque greeting. "Russo's Pizzeria."

"Gio, it's Grace," she said. She could hear Marco shouting in the background, the sounds of plates and cutlery clacking together. "Sorry to bother you—"

"Gracie," Giovanni said, his tone warming. "Sweetheart. How are ya?"

"I'm...okay," she decided. The truth was too complex. "I won't keep you. I was just wondering. Do you and Marco still have some of that kitten food you were using for those strays you found at the back door?"

"Sure do," he said.

"Could I come down and get it?" she asked, bouncing the

kitten lightly when he mewed again. "I found a hungry one out in the rain on Bourbon."

"Ah, Gracie. You're a softie."

"I'm not keeping him," she claimed. "I just thought he'd like a warm place until I can find him something permanent."

"What you need's a companion," Giovanni lectured. "A cat's perfect for you. They're self-sufficient, which works with your hours at the hospital. You don't have to take it for a walk when you get home. And it'll keep you company. Me and Marco... We worry about you living up there on your own. Especially since your ma passed."

She stopped bouncing, realizing she was doing it more to soothe herself than to distract the kitten. "I just need the cat food. I'll come down and get it."

"Stay where you are," Giovanni ordered. "I'm sending Angelo up with it and a little something to whet your appetite. Girl's gotta eat."

She thought to refuse but couldn't manage it. "Thank you, Gio."

"Sure thing, doll. You need anything else, you let us know."

"You, too," she said, then placed the phone back in the cradle. She found the kitten's eyes on her. One paw extended.

She reached out to take the tiny offering, expecting claws. There was nothing but fur and fragility beneath. With a sigh, she shrank all the way to the floor to sit with him as she dialed the number for Hugo's. As she listened to the ringing again, she watched the door and stroked the cat until they both relaxed.

Chapter 2

Javier kept his head low to keep the rain off his face as he walked past a nighttime art bazaar where artisans and craftspeople sat under strings of golden lights with their wares in spite of the weather...or maybe *to* spite it. A corner brass band piped cheerful tones into the air.

Javier followed the wrought iron gate of Washington Square. The carnival crowd had thinned in the Marigny District, likely thanks to the night's parade. NOLA never closed, from the looks of it. The dancing, drinking, eating, partying hadn't stopped.

Mardi Gras in New Orleans was something else. The sheer number of people...the sights, sounds and smells... It overloaded the senses. It surprised him. There was so little that surprised Javier anymore.

Servers in black vests and white button-down shirts leaned against the walls of restaurants, smoking through a break. On Chartres, Javier found the restaurant Grace had spoken about with warm brick walls and French doors. Pulling his hands from his pockets, he ducked inside and rubbed them together as the coziness of the place enveloped him.

Grace was right. It wasn't as crowded as the bars, clubs, restaurants and bistros he'd snatched glimpses of through windows and open doors. Pleased, Javier took off his hat and scanned the two-bladed ceiling fans looping like large, lazy flies.

The maître d' approached. "How can I help you?"

"I'm here for someone," Javier claimed, unable to find Grace among those knotted together around the small tables.

"Mais oui?"

Javier noted where the man's gaze had gone. He looked down at the bottom of his jacket. The rain dripped liberally from it, marking a puddle around his boots. "Permiso," he said. "It's really coming down out there."

"Do you see your party?" the maître d' asked.

"Not yet," he said.

"Then perhaps you should wait outside."

Javier frowned. "I'll get wetter out there."

"I'm sorry, sir. As you can see, our tables are booked."

The door opened at Javier's back. The sound and smell of rain filled the entry as Grace entered, wearing a long wool coat and black leather calf boots. "It's all right, Hugo. He's with me."

Hugo's smile seemed ill-fitted as it stretched the bounds of his bony face. Still, the sight of Grace made him light up like a tarnished lamp. "Dr. Lacroix, how good to see you!"

She placed her hand gently on his wrist. "Hugo. How's Fleurine?"

"She's well! Thank you! Erm..." He darted a glance to Javier. "You're sure this is who you're meeting?"

Grace stared down the blade of her nose.

Hugo quickened. "May I take your coat?"

"And his," she said, juggling a large black leather purse that matched the boots as Hugo helped her out of the coat, uncovering the sleek, understated turtleneck sweater dress underneath. When he disappeared briefly into a small room off the entrance with the coat and her umbrella, she took off her gloves and lowered her voice. "Sorry for that. His family's owned the place for almost a century. He can be a little stuffy about it."

"It's all right," Javier said, still dripping. He pressed his tongue to the roof of his mouth as she looked elsewhere. She'd fixed herself up—for him. Or was it routine? he wondered, letting his gaze linger on the way the lights complimented her skin, the long slope of her neck...

When he'd met her, she'd had bruises everywhere, a bloodied lip. He'd never seen her polished. He'd never seen her whole.

She had haunted him. Through the last twelve years, she'd followed him everywhere—the flash of her quick, dark eyes. The dogged way she'd protected her friends.

She'd been the leader. The strongest of the three. She was the one who had galvanized a hysterical Pia and an injured Sloane for the arduous trip from the seaside town where they were held by the Solaro family to the embassy, where they'd finally found safety and reprieve.

Pia and Sloane had trusted Javier to get them there because Grace had told them he could do it—that he was worthy of their trust. He wondered if she'd believed it. They had believed her.

He had, too. Her faith had given him the wherewithal to dodge the men his family sent to kill them all.

The Solaro men had turned the girls into property. That did things to people. But Grace...

The low thrum of her voice broke into his head as her gaze swung back to his and caught him admiring.

We can't go back, she'd told him years ago as the two others slept in the back of his car. They'd avoided capture, dodging bullets as they did. She'd whispered to him in the dark, *I'll die before they go back to those houses. And I'm taking as many of your family members with me as I can...*

Hugo swooped in, breaking the contact. Javier shifted so that Hugo could remove his coat and ignored the way the man pinched the collar with discerning fingers.

"Ann Marie will show you to your table," Hugo told them.

"Thank you," Grace said, taking the lead. They followed a leggy server in a black shirt and matching skirt to the back. Their table had two chairs on opposite sides. It hugged an exposed brick wall. Javier felt the chill off it as Grace took her seat and he lowered to the other.

"What can I get you two to drink?" Ann Marie asked.

"Bloody Mary for me, please," Grace said, setting her purse carefully on the table. She looked at Javier.

"I'll have the same," he said.

"I'll be right out with those and some waters."

As the girl swept away, Grace peered at him. "Are you sure about the Bloody Mary? Hugo makes them strong."

He unrolled his utensils and shook the white linen napkin loose before placing it in his lap. "I can handle it."

"Don't say I didn't warn you," Grace said cautiously.

"You look nice," he said, noting the long curls that framed her face.

She fiddled with her fork, knife and spoon. "Thanks." The points of her shoulders met the back of her chair, her spine long and straight as she scanned the shoulders of his plaid shirt. "I thought the cowboy thing was just a getup. Something to help you blend in with the Solaros."

He looked down his front. "My mother brought me up on her rancho. We bred horses. It was what I did before…"

She lifted her chin slightly. "Oh. Did you enjoy it?"

"It was a good life."

"Why did you leave it, then?" she asked, perplexed.

There wasn't enough time to explain. Not near enough. And yet, he owed her so much more than a simple explanation. "My mother left my father to get me away from the Solaros. She didn't want me to become like the others, so she kept me away. When she died, the authorities took the rancho. They took everything."

"Why?"

"Because her married name was Solaro."

"Yes, but the ranch was your birthright," she said. "Wasn't it?"

"It doesn't work like that," he said. "Not when you're connected to one of the most notorious crime families in Mexico."

"Did the police leave you with anything?" she asked.

"Some money," he admitted. "But only if I worked for them."

She looked at the table without seeing the crystal votive with its flickering candle and the curved vase with a single red rose. "That's how you became an informant."

"I was more than their informant," he said. He heard the bitterness in his voice. *Still*, he thought. *After all this time?* She wasn't the only one who thought she'd moved on. "I had to become a Solaro—do everything I was told. But I saw things…

My mother was right. I wasn't built for that life. She was right to keep me out of it…"

She still didn't meet his eyes.

Ann Marie came with the drinks and Grace stitched together a smile. "Thank you."

"Are you ready to order?"

"Not yet," Grace said, unfolding her menu.

"I'll give you a few more minutes."

"Gracias." Javier waited until she was gone. "I didn't want to do what the Solaros asked me to do. But it was the only way to clear my name and my mother's."

"And get your inheritance back," Grace murmured. She picked up the Bloody Mary. A large stick of celery jutted out of it, which she used to stir the drink.

"Once I saw what Jaime was doing to Pia…after what he did to Sloane… I made a move," Javier admitted. "My police handlers wanted me to stay in deep cover, gather more intelligence and wait for the opportune moment. But I couldn't."

Grace lifted the Bloody Mary for a long drink. "I'm glad you decided to go against their orders. Pia, Sloane and I couldn't have gone through one more day. I haven't forgotten what you did for us, Javier. It's just… Seeing you… It's hard."

It brings it all back. Seeing her had brought more back for him than he had thought imaginable. "I wouldn't have come unless it was important."

"I'm going to need more to drink before you tell me," she warned him.

He reached for his Bloody Mary and raised it to her before taking a sip.

Her eyes rounded. "You didn't even flinch," she said in wonder.

He ran his tongue over his teeth. Sniffing, he decided, "It's memorable."

She pressed her lips together but couldn't quite hide a smile. "That's putting it mildly," she said, taking another sip and watching him do the same over the rim.

It occurred to Javier that he'd never seen Grace smile before. The warming of her mouth, the curve of her cheekbones…the way her eyes flared... The effect was heart-stopping. "What's in it?"

"I asked Hugo once for the recipe. He acted like I insulted his bourgeois ancestors."

"He acted like my coat insulted his ancestors," Javier considered, looking around to make sure the man wasn't lurking.

"Why do you still dress like a cowboy if you left that life behind?"

"It's what I do now, too," he said. "I think Sloane's family called in some favors, as a thank-you. I became a US citizen. There's a cattle ranch in north New Mexico. The owner took me on and I've been working there since."

"Did you ever receive your mother's inheritance?"

"What was left of it."

She shook her head. "I don't think they should've taken any of it, much less used you to get inside the Solaro family. It went against everything your mother protected you from or wanted for you."

"Life rarely gives someone a fair deal," he noted. "And if it had given me one, you and I never would have met."

She stirred the Bloody Mary some more. "I can't believe you're a genuine cowboy."

"Vaquero," he corrected.

"Vaquero," she repeated.

He smiled, hoping to coax the fragments of hers out once more. "You left your little friend at home?"

"I couldn't."

"What do you mean?" His eyes took a dip over her front. He couldn't detect any kitten-shaped lumps. "He's here?"

She looked around for Hugo, then gestured to her purse.

His chair scraped across the floor as he gripped the edge of the table and leaned forward far enough to see inside the open bag. It was roomy enough for her phone, wallet...and a small, folded T-shirt. The little black kitten had his nose to his tail and was sleeping soundly on top.

He chuckled, then stopped when he glanced at Grace and saw a true smile building on her lips. He ran his eyes over her mouth.

The smile froze. She turned her gaze away.

Regrettably, he lowered back to the chair, feeling the punch her smile had brought. It had come and gone in a flash, but her eyes had danced.

Javier confronted the sharp, unexpected edge of need.

She didn't need him, much less want him. What was he doing getting wrapped up in her?

Ann Marie returned. "Did you decide what you want?"

Javier frowned at the question. What he wanted? Suddenly, that was a dangerous proposition. He opened the menu he had yet to read and saw a long list of drinks and appetizers. He looked to Grace for help.

"Let's try the special," she decided, folding her menu and handing it to Ann Marie. "Is that all right with you?"

"What is the special?" he asked, unable to find it on the menu.

"It changes from day to day," Grace informed him.

"Chef Andre never cooks the same thing twice," Ann Marie reported. "You just have to put your faith in his hands."

"He rarely disappoints," Grace added.

Javier nodded. He handed the menu to Ann Marie, measuring the amount of liquid left in Grace's Bloody Mary glass. The reason for his visit weighed on him. Was she ready now? "You asked me why I came to you first—not the others."

"I did."

"I couldn't find any trace of Pia," he admitted. "It's as if she's disappeared off the map."

"Good," Grace said. When he frowned, she added, "I didn't mean it like that." She pursed her lips. "Or, maybe I did. You showing up on her doorstep wouldn't be good for her. She's the one who's had the hardest time moving on."

"There was a child," Javier knew.

Her expression closed off. She smoothed the napkin on her lap. "She's doing better now. Sloane and I... We do everything we can to make sure she stays that way. You can't contact her, Javier. It'll ruin everything. Whatever information you have for all of us, I can pass on to her. And Sloane, if need be. She's busy."

"Si," he said. "I hear she works for the FBI."

"She does," Grace said, "in the Crimes Against Children unit.

She's taking down human traffickers, fighting the same system that hurt her, me and Pia on US soil."

"If she's a federal agent, I assume her leg healed."

"It took far longer for our minds to heal than our bodies."

Javier swallowed. He'd known it would be a tough conversation. He'd imagined what she and the others had gone through after coming home. But the truth was harder than anything he had conceived. "Grace."

Her gaze crawled back to his. He saw the pain swimming in her eyes—and a waver of fear that made his lungs clutch.

He pushed out a breath. "I'm sorry. I'm sorry that I went along with it. I'm sorry I heard what I did and saw things and did nothing."

"You got us out, Javier," she whispered. "If not for you resisting orders to remain inside the Solaros' operation, none of us would've gotten out with our lives. Sloane certainly would have died. Pia would have lost her mind. She nearly did, even after we were safe. I'm grateful to you. I really am. None of us had it easy when we came home. But we've lived our lives because of you. I'm sorry none of us have ever flipped the script and tried to locate you—to thank you."

"You don't have to thank me," he said with a quick shake of his head. "You never have to thank me." He ran his eyes over her again and relief elated him. "I'm just happy to see you doing so well...*looking* so well."

He saw her soften. Her lips curved. She blinked, and he saw the wet sheen over her eyes before she turned them away again. "Our meal's here."

He leaned against the back of the chair as Ann Marie swept in to deliver their entrées. It was a good thing she'd interrupted. As he ran his hand over the buttons of his shirt, Javier wondered at himself. Relief had morphed into something else. Something that reached for the woman across the table in a plea he was afraid to name.

As he picked up his fork, he studied the collection of wares on his plate. "What is this?"

Grace had already dug in. She lifted a shoulder. "Where Chef Andre's concerned, you don't ask questions. You just eat."

"I thought we ordered the same thing," he commented, squinting at her plate where a different collection of ingredients sat atop one another.

"We did," she said with something of a laugh as she went in for another bite. "You heard Ann Marie. Chef never makes the same thing twice."

"Está bien," he said hesitantly, forking something that looked like fish up to his mouth. He chewed, swallowed, made a thoughtful noise.

Grace watched him closely. "Impressions?"

Javier took another bite. It wasn't fish. "It's good." He chewed and swallowed again. "It's great. *What is this?*"

She laughed her low laugh again, enchanting him through and through. "Magic."

Chapter 3

The rain had let up by the time they finished their meal and thanked Chef Andre personally. After Hugo returned their jackets and Grace's umbrella and she had carefully hung the purse from her shoulder, they waved goodbye to the waitstaff and ventured out to sip the cool night air.

"That was surprising," Javier said, as they set off down the long stretch of Chartres.

"New Orleans is one big culinary adventure," Grace explained. "If not for the crowds, I would've taken you to Felix's for oysters. Or fried chicken at Dooky Chase. Or we could've split a muffuletta from Central Grocery. Each is life-altering in its own right. It's a shame my father's restaurant closed after he died. You could have had the finest BBQ you've ever put in your mouth."

"Your father was a chef?"

"One of the greats," she told him. "By the time he met my mother, she'd joined a civil rights law practice downtown. She liked the idea of someone cooking dinner for her every night. They bought a house in the Lower Ninth and raised me there."

"You were brought up in the city," he realized. "Is it always like this, then?"

"Things get more baffling than usual when Mardi Gras rolls around," she replied. "And there's no shortage of other festivals throughout the year. Not that anyone in New Orleans needs an excuse to party."

"How do you live at the center of it?" he asked. "It's chaos."

She shrugged. "It's home. I didn't always feel that way. Going to college at Tulane, Loyola or the University of New Orleans wasn't an option for me, like others with college aspirations. I planned to go somewhere quieter, smaller... But when the three of us came back from Mexico... I wanted nothing else but this. The crowds, the noise, the music... They were familiar distractions I needed. With them, I couldn't always hear what was going on in my head. And that helped—at least for a time. When they offered me a residency in the city after med school, I didn't even think about it. My mother and I bought the apartment above Russo's, and I've been there ever since."

"Does your mother still live there, too?"

Grace shook her head. "She died. A little over a year ago."

"Tu pérdida me da mucha pena."

She caught her breath. She'd heard condolences spoken a thousand different ways. But to hear him say *Your loss gives me great sadness*...and mean it... Her heart did something funny in response. "You don't have to be sad," she replied. "It came like a friend, as they say. She was sick and, unfortunately, suffered for a while. My father passed before I finished high school. She wanted to go like he did—while he was sleeping. In the end, she got her wish."

"It must've been hard for you," he surmised. "I lost my mother when I was eighteen. Then I lost everything that reminded me of her, down to her Chanel perfume and the nail file she liked to keep tucked behind her ear. She kept it sharp enough to cut a man."

"How did she die, if you don't mind me asking?" Grace asked cautiously.

"It's all right," he told her, keeping his head low as they crossed Frenchmen Street. A nearby car alarm went off, but no one gave it any mind. "No one knows what happened, exactly. I was away—in America. She wanted to move here, eventually, and fought all my life for both of us to be granted asylum. We thought we were close. But she died."

Grace bit her lip. "You don't think the Solaros did something to her?"

"I thought about it," he said. "Everybody thought about it. But there was never enough evidence." He shrugged in a restless motion that spoke to Grace of his discomfort.

She let it go. She knew they had never gotten around to his news about the Solaros and his real reason for being here. The food at Hugo's had been phenomenal, but not so much that he'd forgotten his mission, she was sure.

He was being patient with her. And she was stalling. She stopped, letting people mill around them. In the lantern light, the shadows cut across his face as he stopped, too, drawing close so that those around them could pass on the narrow banquette. He raised his hand to her elbow. "What is it, Grace?"

She could see his chiseled cheekbones clearly. His hair had been long twelve years ago. Not anymore. When he'd taken off his hat in the restaurant, she'd been able to study every aspect of his face.

She'd studied…and she'd admired. Since Mexico, she'd decidedly put men and relationships on the back burner. There had been dates, the occasional rendezvous, a dalliance when med school wrapped up and there was cause to celebrate… To her mother's distress, there had been nothing permanent. She'd never told her mother she intended to keep it that way. It would have broken Matilde Lacroix's old-fashioned, well-meaning heart.

A relationship meant admitting to things she'd worked to forget. Grace liked work. She was accustomed to it. It had been her chief coping mechanism for so long. And just like the crowds and the noise of the Big Easy, it had distracted her from the hole her mother had warned her not finding a mate would incur.

None of it meant she didn't know how to stop and smell the roses—or pause and drink a man with her eyes. Javier's face was more than drinkable. Thirsty, she admired how it was wide at the brow and narrow at the chin. Everything in between tapered from high to low in a tantalizing triangle, with a thin nose, narrow lips and eyes that shined when he smiled. When he smiled, the ever-present lines in his brow that hadn't been there twelve years ago tapered off.

There was kindness there. She'd thought the same thing the day he'd come to rescue her. He had kind eyes...so kind they sheared off the knee-jerk urge to push him away in the low light of the street. They made her want to flatten her hand against his. Would it be warm or cold?

Warm, she remembered from all those years before. *Warm and sure.* Grace felt her tongue pass over her lips and watched his gaze travel from her eyes to her mouth.

Her heart did a deft enough ditty to make a street musician join in. She was glad it wasn't audible. "Tell me," she said.

He shook his head. Then he stopped as understanding struck. "Here?"

A taxi whooshed by, tires spraying cold mist in its wake. "Once we reach Jackson Square, there won't be quiet. The crowd's getting thicker. You've come all this way to talk to me. Just tell me, please."

He didn't let go of her as he looked around. "I wish you could sit down. You should probably be sitting."

"Please," she said again, bouncing on her toes. Her heart was pounding for different reasons now.

He took her other arm so that he had a steadying hold of her. He dropped his voice and said, "My uncle Pablo? The head of the Solaro family—he died."

Her lips fumbled briefly before she recovered herself. "When?"

"About a week ago," he said.

"Oh." She sucked in a breath. She'd forgotten to breathe for a minute. "Well... That's not so bad. Right?"

He hesitated long enough for her to panic.

"Right?" she said again, down to a whisper.

Someone bumped into him from behind, making his torso knock against hers. He gripped her as their feet rearranged, re-balanced. He looked around. When the clumsy person stumbled, laughed and kept going, he turned his attention back to Grace. "If that was all, no, it wouldn't be so bad."

"But there's more." She'd known there would be. Somehow, she'd known.

"You know my cousin Jaime, Pablo's son? Alejandro's brother."

"Pia's handler," she said.

"That's the one. A few days after his father's passing, they found his prison cell empty."

She tried to take it in. It wasn't an easy cocktail to swallow. "Empty?"

"Si."

She shook her head. "What does that mean, Javier?"

"It means that he escaped, Grace," he said gently. "The authorities in Mexico haven't been able to recover him."

Her lips had numbed. She rubbed them together before she asked, "What does that mean for us? He wouldn't... They won't let him cross into the US. He'd never get across the border..."

Javier said nothing. A dull light entered his eyes.

It made her teeth chatter. *Dark water.* An involuntary exhale swept through her as denial turned to awareness and awareness tripped into distress. "He's already here."

"Nobody's sure where he is," Javier assured her. His hands passed up and down her arms, soothing when an involuntary tremor went through her, from head to toe. "There may have been a sighting in Corpus Christi. The witness wasn't one hundred percent certain."

"Why would he come here?" she asked. "It's been over a decade. And we weren't the only women he and his cartel kidnapped..."

"No," Javier said. "No, but you were the only ones who ever escaped."

She looked around at the people milling...their faces in shadow. New Orleans might have been the epicenter of gluttony and sin for others, but for her, it was her sanctuary city. Yet in this moment, it felt treacherous. Grace felt exposed, unsure, unsafe. "I—have to get back to my apartment. I have to call Sloane. And Pia. She'll be devastated."

"*You're* devastated," he observed. He stepped closer and lowered his head so that his brow nearly flattened against hers. "Grace, I'm sorry. I'm so sorry I had to be the one to bring you this—after all this time. After everything you've done to move on."

"We need to get off the street," she said faintly.

He nodded. "I'll walk you home."

She didn't know how, but as they set off side by side again, his hand found hers—or hers found his—and held firmly as they ventured into the epicenter of bon temps.

The roar of the crowd at Jackson Square was audible a block away. The banquette became clogged, so Grace and Javier took to the street, avoiding knots of like-minded tourists, living statues in gold and silver paint, small dogs with sparkling collars that barked at the commotion, honking cars that navigated the cluster, and mule-drawn carriages.

Grace saw nothing and everything at once as she searched the passersby. She heard drums and her own heartbeat, and she tried to pick them apart from each other. Faces were a blur—moms and pops from Iowa, drunken frat boys on a bender, clairvoyants hawking mystic talents and protesters projecting diatribes through portable amps.

They were all Jaime Solaro. Her hometown—this baffling, uninhibited city that was her safety net—was suddenly rife with Solaros, and she felt vulnerable. She jumped at the sound of Snap Dragons hitting the ground, sidestepping into Javier.

"It's okay," he murmured. Lights bathed the white facade of Saint Louis Cathedral, making it glow like a great white ghost. They veered around the church, his footsteps mimicking the urgency of hers. Around the back of the church stood the statue of Jesus with hands upraised in Saint Anthony's Garden. Lights cast Jesus's looming specter against the building's posterior. The effect was unsettling.

Once that long shadow was well behind them, Grace breathed a little easier. The air stank of spilled beer and sulfur. Still, she could taste the rain on her tongue and feel the cool, clarifying mist on her face.

It could have been that Javier hadn't let go of her hand and the friction of hard-earned calluses on the pads of his fingers and palm reassured her.

His thumb stroked the soft skin between her thumb and forefinger in fast repetitions that brought her back to the present. She loosened her hold because the familiar sight and smells coming off Pat O'Brien's on Saint Peter dragged her frenzied mind the rest of the way back. She didn't sprint the rest of the way to Russo's, but it was a near thing.

The restaurant had closed so she used her key. "Russo's is more of a family place," she told Javier as she held the door open for him. Her hands fumbled as she snicked the lock back into place and took a wide gander at the street on the other side of the glass. "They close at ten most nights. Eight on Christmas."

Javier's hand grazed her shoulder. "You're safe."

She hadn't thought twice about letting him in. A few hours ago, he wouldn't have made it this far again. Without much thought, she led him through the dining area and kitchen, through the door into the courtyard. His boots clattered after hers up the iron steps.

"Which hotel are you staying at?" she asked as she steadied her hands enough to unlock her door, too. "I can call a cab for you so you don't have to walk."

Javier was quiet at her back. She glanced over her shoulder. At his frown, she asked, "You booked a hotel, right?"

He shook his head. "I didn't think about it before I left New Mexico. There wasn't time. I hopped on a plane and—"

"Here you are." Grace leaned back against the door. "It's the last Mardi Gras weekend. If there were any openings yesterday, they've all been booked."

"It's all right," he assured her. "I'll come up with something."

"What're you going to do—sleep at the airport?" she asked incredulously. "You realize that's your only option?" She shook her head. "I won't be able to sleep knowing you're stuck in that place till morning, maybe even the afternoon or tomorrow." She thought about it, the rooms beyond the door—her private sanctuary and what inviting a man into it meant.

Switching on the light, she motioned him forward. "You might as well come in."

Javier watched through the open door as Grace set her large purse on the kitchen counter and pulled the mewing kitten from its depths. He hovered as she tutted to him, bowing her head to whisper close at his ear. She cupped his soft, round shape in her palm before lowering him to the decorative tiles where he could stretch his legs.

When she stood back up, she looked at Javier. Shedding her wool coat, she asked, "You're not going to come in?"

"Are you sure you want me to?" he asked. *Are you sure you want me to spend the night with you?*

His heart missed a beat when he heard *with you* echoing in his head. His hands felt damp. He seated them in his pockets.

"You can't sleep outside," she told him, taking matches from a drawer. Striking one, she tilted the wick of the voodoo candle on the counter to its glow. "You won't wake up in that jacket. And Giovanni and Marco won't take as kindly to you as they do the strays they find on the doorstep."

"Grace," he said and waited until her eyes snatched back to his. "I want you to be sure."

She watched him over the little match flame burning toward extinction between her fingers. "I'm sure, Javier."

She looked a little glassy still, as she had after he'd dropped the news about Jaime. But her spine was straight, her shoulders high and back, and her voice didn't bobble any more than the match did.

"Come inside," she added softly. "Please. I'm renovating my mother's old room, but I can make up the couch."

He watched his boots cross the threshold, as if they were leading him. Not the other way around. "I don't want you to go to any trouble." Moving to her and the kitten twining around her ankles, he held her gaze over the match. He cupped his hand around hers and lowered his head, blowing out the flame.

He saw her throat move on a swallow before she turned to the sink to run tap water over the matchstick. She tossed it into the disposal, then filled a small bowl with water. Lowering it to the floor, she kneeled as the kitten tottered to it for a drink.

Javier watched her drag her fingers through the kitten's fur, gripping the counter's edge with his fist. "Have you named him?"

She shook her head. "Why would I—when I don't plan on keeping him?"

Javier lifted a brow. She seemed too attached to be the kitten's foster parent. "You don't like cats?"

"I don't have a problem with them," she admitted, keeping her head low. "I'm just not prepared for one. He'll need medication, vaccinations, boosters, food, litter..."

"Luis," Javier said.

She raised her eyes to his, questions bleeding to the forefront. "What?"

"That's what you should call him," Javier told her. "Luis."

It caught her off guard enough. A thin smile bloomed on her lips. "Why Luis?"

"After the famous jazz musician," Javier explained. "You know, Storyville? Satchmo?"

"Oh," Grace said. The smile widened. "You mean Louis Armstrong."

"Si." Javier crossed his arms over his chest. "Luis."

A soft chuckle brimmed from the base of her throat as she shook her head. Then she stopped and thought about it. "He does look like a Luis." Glancing up at Javier, she asked, "What about you?"

"Me?"

"Are you always Javier?" she questioned. "Or do your friends call you Javy?"

He didn't know how to tell her he'd made few friends. His mother had taught him that there were a select number of people he could trust in this life. Childhood hadn't been an ample environment for friendships. His mother's voice had followed him into adulthood. *Trust no one, mijo. Only yourself.*

"You can call me Javy," he told her. "If it pleases you." When her hand stopped roving over the cat's fur and her eyes seized on him again, he nearly lost his breath. "*Does* it please you, Grace?"

She stilled. Then, she flattened her hands against her thighs and pushed herself up to standing. "I'm going to check the locks and find you some blankets and a pillow. Giovanni sent up tiramisu earlier. We didn't eat dessert at Hugo's. Would you like some?"

He shook his head as she switched on the lamp in the living room. There was a single sofa, long enough for him to stretch out on. Tribal art and wooden masks crowded the yellow-bright walls. Two doors with shutters shut tight over them barred access to a balcony. "I'm not hungry."

"I probably have a spare toothbrush," she said, plumping cushions. Absently, she brushed imaginary dust off the surface of a side table. "I could go check."

He pulled the backpack off his shoulder. "I packed a few things before I left."

She nodded, then went to the door. She opened the slats to peer out.

"Would you like me to check the perimeter?" he asked when she lingered for several seconds, searching.

"I'll warn you. Morning's the only quiet time in the Quarter, and we're a long way from that." She closed the slats. "Do you think you'll need to use the shower? Just the one's working, off my bedroom."

"I can wait until tomorrow," he decided.

"Okay." She veered toward the door to what he assumed was her bedroom. "Make yourself at home." Then she disappeared, closing it behind her.

The kitten tapped against the jamb. Javier shrugged off his jacket, leaving it on the counter, before he scooped up the creature. "Ven aquí, pequeño," he murmured. As he straightened, he saw a framed photograph of Grace and an older couple on the wall. The woman had a quiet smile that marked her for Grace's mother. The man's arms spanned both women's shoulders. There was pride in his eyes. Grace looked young—fresh-faced and hopeful. *Pre-Mexico.* Her cheek rested on her father's arm.

There was another photo on a shelf. He lifted it, tilting it toward the light.

The faces of the girls struck him. He had to swallow the knot in his throat as he recognized Grace, Pia and Sloane. They were wearing caps and gowns and broad smiles for the camera, their arms linked around each other's waists. It must've been their graduation from the Catholic school they had all attended. That was how they had met.

It was one story Grace had told Javier over the days and nights it had taken to reach the embassy.

Sloane's the Amazon and the athlete, Grace had murmured to him in the dark. *Pia's the beauty with the brains.*

And you? he had asked.

Grace had thought about the question for a long while before answering. *I'm going to be the one who makes sure they get home.*

The kidnapping must've happened a month or less after this picture was taken.

The kitten mewed, insistent.

Javier moved to the balcony doors. "Si, gatito. We'll go check, won't we?"

Grace couldn't bring herself to shower.

She'd been in the shower when the men had broken into the villa in Mexico. She hadn't heard Pia's calls for help until it was too late. The men had broken down the door to the bathroom and grabbed Grace from under the spray. She'd barely had time to snatch a towel off the rack and wrap it haphazardly around her before one of them had paraded her through the house in front of a dozen whooping men, shouting "Carne fresca!"

Javier hadn't been one of the men who had leered and shouted gross obscenities or tugged at her towel. But she still couldn't bring herself to turn on the spray in her bathroom with him two doors away.

She bound her hair in a high pony after changing into a blue cami, matching wide-leg pajama pants and a thin robe in the same hue. She took down linens and a pillow from the closet. When she opened the door, Javier was nowhere to be seen.

A cold draft wisped across her face. Setting the pillow and blankets on the back of the couch, she followed it to the balcony door. It was parted from the jamb. Peering out, she found the man, the cat against his sternum, frowning through her wild jasmine vines at the street below.

Javier wasn't tall. He was maybe an inch taller than her. But he had a boxer's build and a ready look—as if someone had accustomed him to responding to trouble at a moment's notice. His stillness spoke more of wariness than calm, more lupine than human.

With the light dappling through leaves onto his face, he looked dark and dangerous. She shivered.

His head snatched sideways. He found her, and her bare toes curled under in reaction. "You didn't have to check."

"Luis thought it was a good idea," he said, walking to her. The cat made a noise, and he held him out to Grace.

She gathered the cat under her chin. He knocked his head against her cheek, stretching into her warmth. Scratching his ear, she kissed him on the back of the head, then subsided when she found Javier watching.

"You should keep him," he said. "I'll feel better knowing he's with you when I'm gone."

When I'm gone. She frowned. The juxtaposition of the nameless man who'd taken Pia away and the Javier she saw in front of her clashed. It frustrated her, too, as did the ready attraction she'd felt from the moment he'd locked eyes with her in Hugo's over the shared secret of the kitten hidden inside her purse.

Moving away, she escaped into the safety of the apartment. She set the cat down on the floor and began unfolding the linens.

The balcony door rapped closed, making her jump. The hand Javier placed on her shoulder was meant to soothe. It only made her more restless.

"Are you sure you want me here?" he asked uncertainly.

She nodded quickly. "It's fine." Hadn't they taken turns sleeping in the front seat of his car as warm air whistled past bullet holes in the windshield? She had watched the street when it was his turn...when she wasn't watching him, wondering why he had betrayed his own family to save her and her friends.

"Let me help," he offered, taking one end of the sheet.

Together, they wrapped the couch cushions in a fitted sheet before she tucked a coverlet on one end, leaving the other open for his pillow. "Do you think you'll need another blanket?" she asked.

"This is more than enough," he assured her.

"You can use my bathroom if you need to," she offered.

"Gracias," he acknowledged. "I won't be long."

"It's through there," she said, gesturing through the door to her room. He'd taken off his hat, she realized when he closed the door behind him. Looking around, she saw it on the table next to the couch.

She could smell him here—in her apartment. He smelled of blue agave—citrusy and woodsy—like those stolen nights in Mexico before everything went to hell.

She caught her fingers trailing across the brim of the hat. Her fingertips skimmed the soft, weathered felt. It belonged to a working man.

The kitten's playful motions drew her gaze. He batted a small snaggle of thread between his paws under the potted banana tree she had brought in from the cold.

When watching the tiny thing play didn't settle her nerves, Grace veered into the kitchen and opened the fridge. She took out her trusty bottle of rosé and poured herself a large glass. If she was going to sleep with Javier in the next room and the Solaros on her mind, she was going to need it.

She thought of the kid again—the one who'd died in the OR today—and felt her eyes sting. "Damn it," she muttered. She drank.

Thank goodness she wasn't due at the hospital until tomorrow afternoon. She'd need the early hours to sort through her feelings. She'd need to call Pia and Sloane and tell them the news.

Sloane would be angry. She'd go on the offensive, as she always did. Pia... Pia was another story. Grace could only hope that her longtime boyfriend, Sam, wasn't overseas again. He would help her. And if Pia needed someone, Grace could be at her beach house in a matter of hours. Sloane might come, too.

They'd circle the wagons. They'd weather the storm. The three of them had done it before—they would do it again.

This time the threat wasn't memories, however—or trauma. It was the man who was free to hunt them again.

He wouldn't succeed, she thought. Things were different here, now. She, Sloane and Pia were different. They were free, and they would remain that way.

They had to.

Chapter 4

Javier found sleep difficult. About thirty minutes after his and Grace's awkward good-nights, Javier drifted from a half dream to the sound of creaking. He jerked upright, frowning at the door to Grace's room as it parted from the jamb.

The woman didn't appear. In her place, he heard the distinctive pitter-patter of paws. He relaxed and tutted, reaching down until he felt the kitten bump against his knuckles. Grabbing Luis around his slender middle, he lifted him onto the couch. "It's past your bedtime, niño," he whispered.

The cat paced the length and breadth of Javier's chest. Finally, he settled on his stomach, nose to tail.

Javier petted him. He felt the purring start faint, then increase, the sound reaching his ears and the vibrations soothing his abdominal muscles. It put a moratorium on Javier's restless thoughts, like breakers washing onshore in gentle laps. Raising one arm above his head, he closed his eyes, trying not to think about the cat's mamacita in the next room.

She would need more than a kitten for protection. How was he supposed to leave her here with no one to watch out for her?

He considered the idea of taking her back to New Mexico with him until Jaime was captured. There, she would be safe. His boss was a gentleman, a fair one, and he knew what it meant to look after his own. If Javier came to him asking for protection for someone he feared for…someone he cared about…the boss would accept unquestioningly.

Javier had seen her in her city, though, hadn't he? Remembering how stricken she'd looked when she found him on her doorstep, he frowned at the ready ache inside him.

She didn't need or want him here…in New Orleans or her rooms. In her sphere at all.

She belonged here. He belonged out west—with her out of reach.

Javier made himself stop listening for sounds of her. He rubbed the lines on his brow, frowning at the guttering light from the voodoo candle she'd left burning on the kitchen counter nearby. He draped a hand over his eyes, forcing himself to close them. It was true, he thought grimly. There was no rest for the wicked.

A knock rapped against the apartment door.

Javier tensed, frowning across the length of the kitchen to the entry.

The knock came again, harder this time.

He tossed the blankets off his legs, lifting a protesting Luis from his lap. He was on his feet, shoving them into his boots, when Grace emerged from her room. She reached for the light switch.

He held up a hand to stop her.

She froze, eyes cavernous in the dark.

He moved to her, lifting his finger to her lips.

She nodded, taking Luis from him.

He pressed a hand to her shoulder, making sure she would stay against the wall, out of sight of the door. Shirt open down the front, Javier slowly crossed the tiles to the door.

The knocking was more insistent now. On the other side, he could hear a voice.

"Doctor! I need a doctor!"

He heard Grace come forward, but he waved her back.

"Javy, it sounds like someone needs my help," she hissed.

"Get *back*, Grace," he hissed back.

She hesitated before pressing her back against the wall again.

Stay there, he willed. He had no weapon. From the butcher

block on the counter's edge, he pulled a long boning knife. Wedging the handle in his fist, he shuffled the rest of the way to the door and peered through the peephole.

The face that greeted him on the other side wasn't friendly. The gun in his hand with the silencer attached looked even less so.

Javier cursed, backtracking. "Is there another way out?" he whispered.

"Who is it?"

"Grace, is there another way out?" he persisted.

"There used to be," she said. "The fire ladder attached to the balcony. But I've never used it. I wouldn't count on it supporting either of us."

"This way," he said, pulling her to the balcony.

"Javier, who's at the door?" she asked. When he opened the balcony door, peering out furtively, she sucked in a breath at the cold. *"Answer me!"*

He gauged the dark space beyond. "Keep your head low," he ordered, ducking down and tugging her along.

Fog had arrived, crawling across rooftops and funneling down to choke the streets and alleyways with its mixed bouquet of fish and millworks. Grateful for the vines that snaked in leafy, thick contortions from the planters lining the railing to the roofline, he stayed low and willed her to do so, too, as they crossed to the far side.

He leaned over, checking that the metal steps of the fire ladder were clear.

"Javy," Grace muttered at his back. "This isn't wise. When I bought the place, the Russos warned me not to use the ladder."

Luis's head peered out from between the parting of the lapels of her thin robe. It was too cold for her to be wearing anything less than her wool coat. He felt the wind penetrating the material of his undershirt. Going back inside was not an option, though. Through the window of Grace's bedroom, he could hear the entry door splinter. "We need to move quickly," he told her. At the shake of her head, he leveled with her. "You trusted me once. I need you to do it again."

The sound of glass breaking made her jump, her head whipping toward the door.

He tightened his grip on her hand to bring her back to him. "Can you do that?"

She flinched at the sound of a chair being turned over. She closed her eyes and nodded swiftly. "Yes. Bon Dieu."

"Duck," Javier said quickly when he heard the bedroom door splinter against the wall of her room. He covered her head with his hand. The intruders were tearing apart her room. "Quickly, go."

With one hand on hers and the other wrapped around the metal rail, Javier walked out onto the metal fire escape platform. While her soft-bottomed slippers didn't make a sound, his boots clattered noisily. He scanned the street below before the fire ladder took a sharp left into the dark alley between Russo's and the next building. Javier probed the shadows, looking for threats in the smog-tinged darkness.

A window shattered. Grace shrieked, her footsteps picking up pace. She froze when a tread gave way under her foot.

Javier grabbed her around the waist, jerking her back. They watched the tread fall to the pavement below. Its clatter echoed against the alley walls.

"I told you," she breathed, trying to back up a step. "I told you they weren't safe…"

"No, no," Javier said, refusing to let go. "You can't go back. The man had a gun!"

"A *gun*?" She glanced back the way they had come.

They wouldn't reach the ground fast enough. Javier urged her forward, hooking one arm around her waist. He drew her close. With her one tread higher than him, his eyes were level with her chin. He could hear her breath scraping against her throat and felt the shaking in her hands. He tightened his grip on her. "Nothing's going to happen to you, bonita. I'm not going to let anything happen. Do you believe me?"

After a second's pause, she nodded in a fervent motion.

Javier kept his arm around her waist as they both stepped over the space where the tread had been. The stairs creaked, but they reached the second platform. Javier tried to find the release that would lower the second set of stairs to the ground. There wasn't a single light in the alley. He glanced over the rail to gauge the distance to the ground. "We're going to have to jump."

She groaned but followed his lead, clambering over the rail as she kept one hand on the kitten-shaped lump under the neckline of her shirt. Her hand fumbled for his as they both eyed the drop.

Her slippers were soft-soled. They wouldn't absorb the impact, and there was no soft place to land. If she twisted or broke an ankle, he'd have to carry her. "Bend your knees," he instructed. "Try not to tense."

Grace gave a startled laugh. She had a death grip on him.

Javier didn't have time to count, so he just said, "Go" and they fell through the dark.

The landing jarred him. He felt the impact singing up his knees but stayed upright. Grace fell sideways. He righted her quickly. "Are you all right?" he asked.

Grace's mouth fell open in a scream.

Javier turned. The blow from the butt of a gun fell on his shoulder instead of his head. He pushed Grace toward the opening of the alley. "Run!" he shouted as he struck out, knocking the gun out of the attacker's hand.

Bent over double, the man tackled Javier headlong, and the boning knife went flying.

The uneven asphalt was no cushion. Shock forked up the length of Javier's spine. He gritted his teeth, trying to use the momentum of the tackle to flip the man over his head.

"Traitor," the man spat, driving a fist into Javier's middle.

Javier groaned, unable to stop himself from curling onto his side. The man's hand was like iron, his voice familiar. "Carlos," he said. "Primo."

"I'd kill you," Carlos said, his face inches away from Javier's. His breath stank of tobacco. Javier felt Carlos's hands close around his throat. They dug in, cutting off his air supply. "I've thought about killing you. We all have."

Javier groped the asphalt, searching for the knife. He tried to tip his chin up so that he could see the mouth of the alley. He'd heard Grace's soft footsteps retreat. How far had she gone? Could he give her more time?

Carlos's grip tightened, making Javier go blind for a split second. "Jaime wants you for himself."

"Jaime—"

Carlos cut off Javier's choked reply with a fist to the mouth. "You'll come quietly. And you'll help us track down the woman and her friends…"

"No—"

Carlos's hammer of a fist connected again, this time with his nose. Javier felt the bone give way. White-hot pain split his skull, familiar in its extremes. Pain and the taste of his own blood had marked his brief time under Pablo Solaro's tutelage.

"Then you'll watch," Carlos went on. "You'll watch Jaime finish what he and Alejandro started twelve years ago."

A cry split the alley's quiet, and Carlos snatched his chin up. Something heavy smashed against his face. His head arced back, taking his body with it in a sound slump.

Javier coughed, reaching for his throat. He stared up at the curvy figure and the heavy metal plaque in her hands. "Grace?"

She dropped the plaque and grabbed him beneath the shoulders, helping him to his feet.

His face was on fire, and he could feel blood pooling from his nose. He tasted it. "I told you to run."

"Are you all right?" she asked, panting.

He wanted to take a second to admire the woman she was. She'd come back for him just as she'd gone back into hell with him to rescue Pia and Sloane. The pain throbbed alongside his need for her—the incredible, undeniable force that was Grace.

The second set of fire stairs he'd struggled to release from the up position creaked, the hinges squealing as the ladder arced toward them.

"Move!" Grace yelled even as their feet flew toward the mouth of the alley.

Javier doubled back. He saw the sheen of Carlos's gun barrel. He picked it up and dived out of the way as the ladder hit the ground with a thunderous clatter.

Chapter 5

Javier wanted to run toward the river. Grace redirected him.

She veered onto Bourbon where Mardi Gras clambered on. The music screamed. The crowd writhed. Neon lights clashed, spotlights blinded. As Grace led Javier by the hand through the throng, she passed a woman lifting her shirt to the sound of hooting and hollering from the surrounding balconies, towering drag queens, two men engaged in a V-J Day-style kiss, a young man doubled over, retching, a middle-aged woman curled up asleep on the banquette...

Grace looked back, searching for their pursuers. She'd heard shouts from her balcony as she and Javier fled into the night. She'd heard running feet behind them before the music drowned them out.

It would help if she knew what their attackers looked like. "Do you see them?"

"Keep moving," Javier instructed.

She glimpsed his face. "You're bleeding!"

"We can't stop."

Neither her pajamas nor his cowboy getup had drawn attention from the partygoers, but Grace saw a bouncer outside a club narrow his eyes on Javier's bloodied face as they raced past. "We need to get you cleaned up."

"There's no time, Grace."

"In here," she said quickly, detouring through the open doors of an apparel store.

The woman at the counter stared at Javier as Grace sprinted to the counter. "Sabine, we need help."

"Dr. Lacroix," she said in surprise. Her gaze bounced from her to Javier in an intrigued dance. Her insouciant mouth puckered. "Coucou, cher. What hammer did you run into?" she murmured, leaning on the counter so that the vee of her sweater opened over generous cleavage and the gris-gris that hung from her neck swayed like a pendulum.

"We need a changing room," Grace said, glancing toward the back of the store. It went deep into the building. There was an alternate exit, too, if she remembered correctly.

"Together?" Sabine asked, raising a penciled brow. To Javier, she said, "I bet you're right pretty under all that carnage."

"And merchandise," Grace rattled off, trying to think through the miasma of terror and adrenaline. "I don't have my wallet..."

Sabine looked her over. "The store doesn't offer credit."

"It's an emergency," Grace said, "otherwise you know I wouldn't ask."

Sabine considered. Then she lifted her chin. "Go all the way to the back and hang a left. Pick a room. I'll bring you what you need."

"You're a lifesaver," Grace declared, covering Sabine's tattooed hand briefly with her own. She took Javier's elbow. "This way." She grimaced, seeing the damage on his face for what it really was. "Do you have a first aid kit?" she asked Sabine as she steered Javier toward the changing rooms.

"You going to play doctor after you get him undressed?" Sabine asked as she closed the doors to the street and flipped the placard to Closed. She flipped a switch and the front of the store darkened. "Can I watch?"

Grace took that as a yes and kept going. The middle of the store fell dark, too, as they passed racks of clothes, feather boas, postcards and assorted knickknacks featuring grinning men, women and alligators in assorted compromising positions. Across from an Out of Order bathroom, she found the first changing room. Shoving aside the curtain, she ushered Javier in before snatching it back in place. "Sit down."

"It's not as bad as it looks," he mused.

"Javy, your nose is broken," she informed him, refusing to soften the delivery. Pressing a hand into his shoulder, she snapped, "Sit. Or I'll make Sabine sit on you." Gingerly, she tugged Luis from her shirt. The cat mewed loudly. "It's your turn," she said, offering him to Javier.

He lifted his hands and accepted the kitten, passing his palm over Luis's head to flatten his ears and calm him. "Va a estar bien, michi."

Grace tried not to think about what her insides did when she saw the little kitten in Javier's wide, working hands or how the rough tumble of sweet words spoken as he brought the cat up to his lowered chin made her stomach flip like pancakes. She scrubbed her hands over her face, bringing herself around to the reality they had only momentarily escaped. "They destroyed my apartment."

Javier's gaze swept up to hers. "Si."

At least he told no lies. "You knew the man in the alley," she stated.

Javier's fingers stilled on Luis's arched spine. Before he could answer, Sabine snatched the curtain back without warning. "Aw," she muttered after her eerie white contact lenses took a dive over Javier's folded form. "He's not naked." She frowned at Grace. "You're slow."

Grace took the clothes from Sabine's arms and draped them over the top of the changing room wall. She then took the first aid kit. It was small, but it would have to do. "I need wet towels."

"Sure," Sabine said. She leaned toward Grace and murmured, "At least have his nipples exposed before I get back."

When the curtain snatched back into place, Javier gave a soft laugh. It didn't quite ring true. Pain webbed across his features. "How do you know her?" he asked.

"It's a small town," Grace muttered. She scooped up Luis and placed him in a small wicker basket in the corner that served as a trash can. It was empty, and it kept the animal in place so she didn't have to worry about him wandering through Sabine's store. "You'll have to take off the shirt. It's a mess."

Javier unsnapped the first two buttons with one hand. He gathered the material around the shoulders, then pulled the shirt over his head.

Underneath, he wore a plain white T-shirt. There was blood on the collar, but not much. As the plaid shirt fell to the floor, she said, "Tip your head back against the wall."

Javier looked at the light overhead, the back of his head meeting the mirror behind him. He kept his hands on his knees as she leaned over him, tilting her head left, then right. "Is there obstruction?" she asked. "Does it feel blocked?"

He nodded slightly.

"There's swelling," she confirmed. And bruising already coloring faintly around his eyes. "Did you black out when he hit you—even for a moment?"

"I saw stars," Javier muttered. "But I didn't black out."

"How's your neck? Does it hurt?"

"No."

"Okay," she said, still examining. "It looks like the bleeding's slowed. I'll need to clean you up, regardless."

"There's no time for that."

The curtain opened again. Sabine thrust wet paper towels at her. Grace took them, then paused when Sabine offered her a half-drunk bottle of moonshine.

Sabine shrugged at Grace's ready skepticism. "Man needs *something* for the pain." She unscrewed the cap, then thrust the bottle in Javier's direction. Shaking it so the liquid sloshed, she said, "Go on, cowboy. Have a nip."

Javier hesitated before wrapping his fingers around the bottle's neck. He placed it on his knee.

"I'll go watch the front," Sabine offered, skimming one last look over Javier's form before the curtain closed again.

Grace started mopping up the bloody mess. She went through the paper towels quickly. "You can drink. It's probably better that you do."

"I don't want to get sloppy."

"Pain'll do that, anyway."

"Sometimes pain makes you sharp."

Her brows came together. Had he learned that from working inside the Solaro cartel? "Sabine was an addict. During my residency, she OD'd and was brought to the ER. Her brother's her only living relative. He thinks I saved her life. And he makes the moonshine. Every couple months, a package arrives on my doorstep with anonymous contraband."

"Is it any good?" he asked.

"If you like that sort of thing," she said. "Moonshining's illegal, so I normally toss it."

"She's giving us free merchandise because you saved her life," he surmised.

Grace wadded the last of the paper towels and wiped a small bloodstained water droplet from his cheek with her thumb, lowering her voice. "She was just nineteen, my first OD. I was new to the ER. My hands shook the entire time. It's a wonder I was able to do anything for her."

"Doesn't make you any less a hero."

She could feel the glide of his dark eyes and trained her attention on his nose again. She placed her thumbs on either side of it, trying not to hurt him. His inhalations elongated sharply when she probed the bridge. "I don't think you're at risk for hematoma. You may, however, have a deviated septum. You're very lucky the bleeding's stopped. I'll keep the first aid kit in case it starts again. Here." She took one shirt down from the top of the stall. "Put this on."

Javier spread the black T-shirt between his hands and read the front. He glanced up at her in question.

"Sabine doesn't carry plaid." She took down the second shirt and unfolded it for his view. "Or anything that won't make your nana blush."

His mouth quirked as he read the pirate pickup lines on the front. He fed his arms through his shirt, which Sabine had brought in a fitted medium instead of a large. He widened the neck so that it didn't get hung up on his nose and stretched the front over his torso.

Grace did feel hot around the collar, seeing the words "Suck Me Dry" underneath a trio of crawfish. She loosened her thin robe from her shoulders. Turning halfway away, she discarded it with his shirt on the floor. She really didn't have time to dwell on how the heat culled around her center when he didn't look away. *We're running for our lives and I'm thinking with my glands*, she thought. She blamed Sabine's incense, fitting the T-shirt over her camisole.

She took down the jeans Sabine had found for her.

"I'll wait outside," he said, pushing up from the bench. He lifted Luis from the basket and squeezed by her. The curtain swished open, then closed at his back.

She quickly discarded the pajama pants, then wiggled the jeans over her hips and discarded the slippers for a pair of socks with jalapenos wearing sunglasses and the label "Hot Stuff." The go-go boots Sabine had chosen for her were black with platform heels. She hoped she and Javier had lost their tail. Running would be a triumph in these.

Knowing Sabine didn't have any other options, Grace stuffed the first aid kit into an enormous canvas bag with Mr. T's face on it and wrapped a black feather boa around her neck. The tourist wear would help them blend in long enough to reach the end of Bourbon Street.

Trying to figure out where to go from there, Grace opened the curtain and froze.

Javier tilted his chin in her direction, but Sabine hissed at him. "She sat on me," he said needlessly. Luis, smooshed between Sabine's breasts and Javier's sternum, let out a slightly strangled cry, eyes as wide as marbles.

Grace crossed her arms. "Sabine, you're scaring the boys."

Sabine tutted. She'd pinned Javier into a chair and splayed her wide thighs across his lap. Tongue caught between her teeth, she dabbed concealer over the starter bruises around his eyes. "The pretty one didn't want a hat, so…"

Grace saw a pile of discarded hats on the floor. She toed aside a purple fedora and placed a hand under Sabine's arm. "You're suffocating the kitten."

"I'll pet his kitten," Sabine crooned, closing the compact with a grin as she wiggled off Javier's lap. "All he need do is ask."

As Javier stood, rumpled and abashed, he moved from the

corner quickly. "Thank you for…" He trailed off, charmingly at a loss.

"Not a problem, baby," Sabine said. "You going to tell me who did that to your face? My brother's got a pet gator he can feed the bastard to."

When Javier only stared at her, Grace quickly said, "It's his first Mardi Gras."

"Oh," Sabine said knowingly. "Well, in that case…" Grabbing Javier by the neckline of his T-shirt, she yanked him to her. Grace quickly grabbed the kitten before he became flattened again. Sabine yanked Javier's mouth down to hers and gave him a suckling kiss. He groaned as her nose nudged against his and swiftly retreated.

Taking pity on him, Grace said quickly, "We really have to be going. Thank you for everything, Sabine. The back exit isn't blocked, is it?"

"Nope," Sabine said, thoroughly satisfied with herself. She pointed down a tight hallway. "It's that-away. I'll turn off the alarm." She grinned at Javier, wagging her fingers. "You come back now, cher."

Javier made a noise before taking the lead. He and Grace moved to the back door. They opened it, and the alarm chirped. The red security light over the door chirped and washed the alley behind Sabine's shop in sinister scarlet. The sounds of Mardi Gras pulsed from the street on the other side of the building.

After several seconds, the chirping stopped. Javier looked furtively around, making sure the coast was clear. He palmed something at the small of his back.

Grace saw the handle of a gun and tried not to balk. "Where'd you get that?"

He paused. "From the alley outside your place."

She lifted her chin in understanding. The kid on the operating table yesterday came back to her. She'd seen far too many gunshot wounds throughout her tenure at the hospital. Guns on the streets of New Orleans were as common as cocktails.

He'd carried a gun in Mexico, too, she remembered. He'd shot Alejandro through a dark window, leaving Grace with little doubt he knew how to use it. Determined not to think about how deadly he could be, she opened the canvas bag. Taking out a rolled-up hoodie, she tossed it to him. "Throw this on. It's warm."

Javier did as he was told. She knew he'd experienced enough of New Orleans when the sugar skull with its middle fingers raised to the sky on the front didn't give him pause. "I don't know how she did it."

"What?" she asked, taking out the moonshine. She set it on the ground, hoping Sabine wouldn't find it out here. She hated knowing the girl was using again and made a mental note to tell her brother.

"Sabine," he explained. "One minute we were standing at arm's length, the next she was—"

Grace heard herself laugh as she tugged a matching hoodie down over her front. She kissed Luis and placed him carefully inside the canvas bag where he would be safe, leaving it open to the night air. "Everybody has a gift. Sabine's is bedding a man in thirty seconds flat."

"She bit me."

"I've seen her do worse." She inched toward the corner that would take them into a courtyard that led back out onto Bourbon. A sound reached her ears.

Javier's hand clamped over her shoulder. He edged forward. She saw his hand fit around the handle of the gun again at the small of his back and closed her eyes, nudging the bag and Luis with it on the other side of her hip.

She stayed so close to Javier, she felt the moment his tension drained and opened her eyes. "It's okay," he said. "Sabine isn't the only one practicing the art of seduction tonight."

Curious, Grace peered around the corner. The noise she had heard was the sound of a couple's deep-throated moans. Her chin dropped, and she closed her mouth carefully as Javier led her toward the street and the pair continued, unceasing, against the smudged alley wall.

Javier stopped before they could blend back into the carousel of drunken spectators. A brass band leader with a feathered umbrella was leading anyone who cared to join in a second line. "Where to now?" he asked.

"Farther that way," she said, pointing. "We can flag down a cab on Canal."

"We left our wallets at your place."

She reached into the canvas bag and retrieved the roll of cash Sabine had deposited there. At his arched brow, she said, "I'm lucky you're so pretty. Otherwise, she might not have been this generous."

The beginnings of a grin were born in his eyes. He looked good in neon, she thought. Her center keened. She supposed running for your life must awaken things inside a person. Seeing the way his eyes caressed her didn't help.

A gunshot ripped through the uproar. At first, no one reacted. Then a second shot, closer now, cleaved the party atmosphere in two. People screamed and scattered. Javier pushed Grace back against the wall, covering her.

She saw the two cops in motorcycle helmets surge in the opposite direction. Grabbing Javier by a handful of his hoodie, she shouted, "Follow the crowd!"

Chapter 6

The panicked mass swelled around Javier. People thinned, then condensed when more gunshots cracked like whips. The herd quickened. He tried to keep a grip on Grace's hand, but the crowd jostled him, making it difficult.

The girl in front of her in high heels and a minidress stumbled. Grace went down with her, made clumsy by the boots Sabine had loaned her. Javier halted. The brass band's tuba player nearly trampled him. He swerved to keep the instrument's mouth from swallowing his head. From the open door of a club, upbeat disco music surged in a cheerful, discordant backdrop.

"Grace!" Javier called. The faces passing were masked in terror. They blurred as he searched, growing frantic. "Grace!"

The girl's bubblegum pink minidress flashed between runners. As Javier fought his way toward the pop of color, he saw Grace supporting her with an arm around her waist. Javier shouldered people out of his path and reached for her. "Grace—" She lurched on her right leg. "You're hurt!" he exclaimed.

"I smacked my knee on the ground." She waved it off. "This is June. She's twisted her ankle."

The girl sobbed, quaking with terror. He lifted her with an arm under her shoulders and another under her knees. "This way!"

He fought his way forward. The girl whimpered against his

throat. He felt Grace take hold of his belt and was happy for the link. He couldn't lose her.

The throng came to the end of Bourbon and spilled helter-skelter onto Canal Street. Police whistled and directed foot traffic, holding off a torrent of honking vehicles.

"June!" someone cried.

A group of college-age girls in short skirts and cowgirl boots descended on Javier, cooing over the girl in his arms. He set her delicately on her feet. She fell, weeping, into the arms of her companions.

"Javy!"

Grace pointed into the crowd pouring off Bourbon Street.

He tensed. The man he had seen through the peephole of Grace's apartment door was coming. Javier didn't recognize him as he had Carlos. Javier did, however, recognize the gun firmly clasped in his hand. The man's scanning eyes narrowed on Javier and Grace. He leveled the gun, took aim.

"Get down!" Javier yelled, folding himself over Grace's form.

The report of gunshots deafened. Everyone around them hit the ground.

Grace called, "Hurry!"

Javier followed her into the major thoroughfare. Horns bellowed. Whistles screamed. Gunshots bounced off the pavement. Someone to his right fell, shrieking. They crossed the center, then fled in front of traffic going in the opposite direction. The street was littered with beads.

Clang!

Javier spotted the red-and-yellow streetcar moving swiftly across their path. "Grace?"

"Open the doors!" she called to the driver.

The doors opened. She ran straight at the doors and leaped onto the streetcar.

Javier jumped. His boots slid across the opening. He grabbed the bar over his head to stop from skidding.

"Close them!" she cried.

"Y'all all right?" the driver asked even as the doors whished closed and the trolley continued to clang down the line, leaving the chaos on Bourbon and Canal behind.

Grace shrugged in answer, unable to speak. She fumbled over the hoodie and the pockets of her jeans, then remembered they weren't hers. "Damn. I don't have change or a ticket. I'm sorry." She reached into the bag and pulled out the cash roll. She peeled off a ten-dollar bill and handed it to the driver over his shoulder. "Will this do?"

He studied Hamilton's face before taking it between the tip of his first and middle finger. "I got you, chère."

"Thank you," she said. She slumped onto the closest bench.

"What's happening on Bourbon?" the driver asked curiously.

Grace exchanged a look with Javier, who collapsed to a seat as well, struggling for breath. "Shooting."

The driver made a disapproving noise. "That's no way to end Mardi Gras. Anybody hurt bad?"

Javier thought of the person he'd seen fall to his left. He looked back through the night but saw nothing but police lights. "Si."

"Shame, that."

Javier felt the wriggling inside the bag. He opened it. Luis's claws had torn the inside lining. He tried crawling to the opening.

Grace's hip nudged Javier's as she slid onto his bench. "Is he okay?" she asked, reaching in to extract Luis.

The driver cleared his throat when he saw the kitten. "Service animals only."

"How 'bout a service animal in training?" Grace suggested, tucking Luis against her cheek.

The driver thought about it. He shrugged and let it be.

Grace let out a sigh. She tipped her head to Javier's shoulder. He'd draped his arm across the back of the bench. Lowering it to her shoulders, he pulled her close. His heart still rapped a hard cadence against his sternum. He turned his cheek against her hair as they rode through several stops in silence.

"It wasn't Jaime," she murmured.

He barely caught the words and shook his head. "No."

"Who was the man in the alley?" she wanted to know. "I heard him talking to you. He was speaking Spanish."

...you'll watch. You'll watch Jaime finish what he and Ale-

jandro started twelve years ago... Carlos's warning was loud in Javier's ears. He probed the tender skin around his nose and tried not to grimace. "Millions of people speak Spanish," he heard himself saying and frowned at the dismissal he heard in his own voice. Why shouldn't he tell her about Carlos?

She was scared enough. He knew how much the Solaros had hurt her. He'd seen her face when she learned Jaime was free again.

They'd lost the shooter from Bourbon. For now, they were safe. Once they reached a secure location, he'd tell her.

"How's your face?" she asked.

"I can live with it."

"You didn't drink the moonshine."

"No."

"You're stubborn, Javier."

"So I've been told."

"I'll need to check the first aid kit for aspirin. The pain's only going to get worse."

"I'll manage it."

She straightened, peering through the windows. "We should get off here."

"Why?" Javier asked as the streetcar slowed. "Are you sure?"

"Trust me," she said.

They bid the Canal Street streetcar driver farewell and got off on a corner lit by a single streetlamp. She hustled Javier to another streetcar—this one green with red trim—and they rode it until any chance of a tail had been lost.

"Not much farther," she assured him after they disembarked again, and she set off down the sidewalk.

"Where are we?" he asked, trying to get his bearings. It was impossible. There were no stars in the city to guide them.

"Garden District," she replied.

The fog was still thick. He could barely make out the top of the live oaks that lined the street or the long faces of buildings leering out of the haze.

They walked for a few blocks before she asked, "How good are you at scaling fences?"

Seeing the apprehensive look on her face, he asked, "Why?"

She tipped her chin toward the wrought iron gate across the street.

Javier narrowed his eyes. "You want to go in there?"

She lifted her hand. "I'm out of ideas. I have friends in the city. But if these men are looking for me specifically, they'll be able to trace my associations. I'm not going to endanger an innocent person simply by showing up on their doorstep. This is the only place I can think to hide until daytime."

Javier considered. They couldn't stay out in the open. They couldn't go back to her apartment. He looked around and saw no cabs or buses. The streetcar was long gone. It had clanged off into the night, looking every bit the ghost of a bygone era. Steeling himself, he nodded and followed her across Washington Avenue.

The wrought iron gates were held together by chain and lock. There was a large sign on the gate that read: CLOSED FOR RESTORATION. APPOINTMENT ONLY VISITATION. The arch pronounced it Lafayette Cemetery No. 1.

"Are you sure about this?" he asked.

Tension limned her jawline. "Let's walk the perimeter. The fence is easier to climb on the other side."

"You sound like you've done this before," Javier observed. It did well to mask the uncertainty and discomfort he felt about breaking into a cemetery.

"Sloane lived in the Garden District," she revealed, lengthening her strides. "Walking the tombs after dark was a rite of passage. At least, that's what she, Pia and I thought. If any of our parents had known..." She shook her head. "We'd have been in for it."

"Is it not safe?" Javier asked, gauging the area. It was difficult with the fog.

"The cemetery's been closed for restoration for a while. Something about a water main. When it's open to the public, there are people who try to take advantage of the tourists. Pickpockets, beggars... This being the Garden District, though, it tends to be safer than other cemeteries in the city, like Saint Louis No. 1 where the old voodoo queen, Marie Laveau, is buried. This looks like a decent spot."

The pale brick wall did look more accommodating than the wrought iron spikes over the entrance. "I'll go first," he decided and handed her the bag. Planting his hands on top of the wall, he boosted himself up before dropping in on a raised surface. Something loose scattered beneath his feet and pinged across the ground.

Grace's voice floated to him from the far side of the wall. "Coins. Either to ensure passage to the next world or to acknowledge a visit from a living soldier to a deceased one."

Javier made a note to right the coins back in place. He reached over the wall for her.

Grace's hand latched onto his. It tightened as he leveraged her over the wall. "Thank you," she said when she stood eye to eye to him in the shadow of the tombs. Her breath feathered his cheek and her hand remained in his. He could smell Sabine's incense on her, a hint of spilled liquor from the debacle on Bourbon. But overall, he smelled the radiance that was Grace. He'd smelled it in her rooms, hints of lemongrass and cedarwood. He'd need to hang on to that—the living essence of her in this city of the dead.

Her words lowered to a hum. "I wish we had a light."

Javier dug something from his pocket. He'd all but forgotten it was there. A crack spidered over the screen of his phone when he toggled it and the battery level warned that it was at only 20 percent, but it illuminated the fine points of Grace's features as he held it between them.

She smiled. "If all else fails, we can call for a pickup."

He nodded. "And anybody else we need."

"If the police didn't catch the shooter on Bourbon," Grace said, her smile tapering off in thought, "they'll be looking for information." She scrutinized him. "Are you sure you didn't recognize him?"

"No," Javier said, with a shake of his head. It wasn't a lie. The gunman hadn't been part of the Solaro operation when Javier had left. He *could*, however, give police Carlos's description.

"I wonder if anyone called in the trouble at my place," she wondered, her brow furrowing. "Or if the police have the time to investigate. They likely only have the personnel to handle emergencies, like the shooting." She paused. "Javy, did you really see someone hurt badly on Bourbon?"

"Canal," he replied.

"I wish I'd seen. I could've done something." Her hand was still in his. It flexed, then released and flexed again in convulsions of agitation.

"The gunman had spotted us," Javier told her. "If you had stopped, he would have shot you."

She shuddered. The air was so eerily quiet he swore he could hear her heart knocking inside her breast. "It's my responsibility to help those who're sick and injured, no matter the danger."

He could hear it in her voice—the guilt of leaving the trouble on Bourbon and Canal. He drew her close.

She was tense from stress, from cold. For a moment, she stood stiffly in the circle of his arms. Then her chin flattened against the plateau of his shoulder. He traced her spine through the hoodie. "Todo estará bien. Lo prometo, mi sol."

She leaned, giving way to the weight she carried. "What does that mean?" she wanted to know in a hushed tone.

"It's going to be all right," he translated. "Lo prometo."

"I know that part," she told him. "I spent a lot of time with Sloane and her family, the Escarras. But what does 'mi sol' mean? I don't think I've ever heard that before."

He heard the precariousness behind the query. He hesitated, unsure whether she'd welcome how far his feelings had tunneled at this point. When she pulled back, he could not meet her eye. "Ask me later." Before she could argue, he asked, "How's Luis?"

She looked down at the kitten clutched in her free hand. "Restless. He's either cold or hungry. Or he's sick of being handled."

"We can fix part of that," he assured her. On the street, a car sloughed by, fanning a wall of runoff that had gathered in the gutter. The sound of far-off shouting, sirens and the deep barrage of a large dog's warning bay set him on edge. "I feel like we're standing on someone's grave."

"That's because we are," she said matter-of-factly. "It's a coping wall."

"A what?"

"It's where an unembalmed body was buried under dirt brought in from outside the city—likely from the person's home country. That was the custom. As most of the graves in this cemetery are from the eighteen hundreds, it's likely the person succumbed to yellow fever."

He guided her down to the ground. "Sometimes a simple answer will suffice."

As he retrieved coins from the ground and transferred them back on top of the coping wall, she asked, "You're not superstitious, are you?"

"I'm Latino," he stated in answer.

"So it's fair to say you're not comfortable with this?"

"You say it's safe. I believe you. But if I scream…"

Her voice warmed in amusement. "I won't think you're any less a man. Follow me. I'll show you around."

Chapter 7

"Lightning struck this wall in the nineties," Grace explained, running her hand along the vaults that lined the riverside wall of the cemetery. "It blew off the stones, exposing those inside."

"If you're trying to make me feel better," Javier said beside her, "you're doing a fantastic job."

Grace almost smiled as she let the beam of the flashlight on Javier's phone guide them. She was still jittery, still unsettled, so she kept talking. "Sloane dared Pia once to crawl inside the Koenig Tomb. It was never occupied. The family moved away from New Orleans before they had need of it."

"Did she do it?" Javier asked.

"She got halfway in before Sloane shouted something and scared her so bad, I swear her soul left her body," Grace said. "That was Pia's last visit to the cemetery." She frowned, pausing at the statue of a weeping angel. "We didn't have much respect for those at rest here. I feel bad for that now."

"You were kids," Javier pointed out.

"The definition of." It seemed so long ago now, but she, Pia and Sloane had once been a trio of foolish, carefree girls.

Mexico had changed that. Mexico had changed everything. It was fair to say the girls that had left Louisiana for adventure had never come home again.

Javier's light swept across cracked crypts and closure walls.

Vegetation crept between graves, some fronds fanning onto the broken path. Vines engraved a tomb wall as much as the names etched there. Grave markers were split in places. The soil had been turned over, exposing the earthen underbelly of the cemetery. Machinery crowded the main vein, forcing Javier and Grace to detour farther into the heart of the graveyard. "I wonder how many graves they've dug up by accident. That's common of construction in the city. Contractors break ground with the new and expose the old world underneath."

Javier stopped. "Did you feel that?"

"What?" she asked, feet faltering.

Javier backtracked, his light swinging. Then he retraced his steps. After several contemplative seconds, he shook his head and rejoined her.

"What was it?" she wondered.

He glanced over his shoulder. "It felt like a warm pocket of air. Maybe a vent pushing gases up from underground?"

She shook her head. "We're three feet above sea level. There aren't any vents."

He made a noise as he fell back into step with her.

They heard it at the same moment. A voice drifted through the tombs, low at first, then stronger, bouncing off brick and masonry.

Javier pushed Grace toward a waist-high gate buried in a tangled hedge. They clambered over. She went to her knees, relieved he'd already switched the light off his phone. Shrinking to her side so she was cheek to ground, she felt something dig into her hip. She glanced up. A fractured cross jutted over her. Javier's torso wedged against her back. His arm stilled across the flat of her belly. He didn't vibrate as she did with fear. He didn't even breathe, his lungs still.

She fought for that kind of control. Any kind of control.

The voices closed in. Two men, one speaking in a fervent mutter, the other in the terse notes of authority.

"I got your blow. Now where's my money?"

"I'm good for it. I told you. Here."

There was a snatch of movement, the sound of notes being fanned. "You tell anybody where we're meetin'?"

"I ain't no snitch."

"Cops're everywhere. You get caught—"

"I told you, I'm your boy."

There was a pregnant pause. "A'right, then."

Luis strained against Grace's hold. He attempted to climb to freedom, breaking free. She caught him. Before he could yowl, she placed the pad of her forefinger to his lips.

The kitten struggled once before latching. He suckled furiously, the rough spines of his tongue scratching. His paws milled, churning against her sleeve as he made biscuits in contented motions.

"Man, let's split. Place gives me the creeps. Your ancestors buried here or somethin'?"

A curse split the night. "My ancestors never touched this place. Cost you two hundred Gs to be buried here."

"*Dayum.* What, they think this is holy ground?"

"It's reserved for that one percent, you know..."

The voices faded into obscurity. Still, Grace's heart lodged in her throat. Neither she nor Javier moved for a minute...two... then three. He lifted his head, looking long in the direction the dealer and the buyer had gone. "They walked toward the gate."

She couldn't speak. She couldn't make a sound.

"We'll stay here," he said. "Just in case." When she didn't speak again, he asked, "Are you all right?"

Furtively, she shook her head. She hated this fear. She hated how it sank its teeth in and didn't let go. For twelve years, it had been an all-too-frequent habit of hers not to fight or flee but to freeze and it terrified her—maybe more than the threat itself.

The flat of his palm touched her cheek. "Grace?"

She fumbled for speech. Bringing the suckling kitten into her chest, she curled around him. "I thought they found us."

"No one knows where we are."

"It happened on the fire escape," she blurted. "I froze, remember? And then again in the alley. I found the plaque and ran back to help you, but when I saw you on the ground underneath the other guy... I could hear you choking, and I couldn't move."

"You bashed his head in," he reminded her.

"I'm going to get us both killed."

"You were the one who got us out of the alley," he insisted, his voice strengthening after the sounds of the gate rattling in the distance echoed back to their hiding place. "You saved the girl, June, from being trampled. You jumped onto a moving streetcar." He turned her face to his with the gentle urging of his hand. "It was you who got Sloane and Pia out of Jaime's grasp."

She blinked at the assertion. She shook her head. "You were the one with the gun."

"They wouldn't have gotten into the getaway car with me," he told her. "Neither one of them would have made it to the embassy. Without you, Grace, there would only be one free girl left."

She still couldn't fight the shaking that had taken over. She focused on the kitten, reaching for the present. "Luis almost got away."

Javier reached for the cat. He murmured things in Spanish from the back of his throat.

The sound climbed the wall of her fear. It rolled itself into a smug ball somewhere below her navel. The friction set off heat. It cindered like coal, chasing terror with something tantalizingly physical.

She wanted to turn into the warmth of him—wanted to burrow there—and understood better now how disaster could bring bodies together for distraction, validation… To ground each other.

Lightning rods were dangerous. But they were also necessary.

Javier was her lightning rod. The understanding hit her with a thunderclap of trepidation.

"I should check and make sure the dealer left, too," he said. When she remained silent, he grazed his lips across her cheek. "I'll come back."

She watched him climb back over the little fence that had kept them hidden. Something glinted in his hand. The gun he'd taken off the man in the alley. As he moved off without a sound, she raised her head enough to look around. Seeing and hearing no one, she sat up cautiously.

Luis meowed as she took her finger from his mouth.

She hastened to give it back, humming the first tune that

came to mind—"Eh La Bas," something she'd heard her father croon a hundred or more times over the stove at the BBQ joint where he'd reigned as chef until his dying day. His smile and his voice had been infectious. He'd led his staff in a music round at least once a day. "Eh la bas, cheri," he'd sung to them over the heat of the kitchen, his scratchy tenor threading cheerfully through the busy clatter of cookware. The others had come right back at him with the same verse.

"Komon sa va," she sang softly to Luis, but the repetition didn't ring back to her like it had for her father. Lowering her head into Luis's fur, she let the next line drift off unsung.

Sabine's bag could do more tricks, Javier discovered, as Grace pulled out two bottles of water and a couple of protein bars. She frowned at the joint she found there. When she looked at him over the tip, he shook his head in refusal. She tossed it away. In the small gap between two white, time-stained crypts, they sat opposite one another. His knees overlapped hers and Luis wound around their ankles, complaining in yowls.

The space was cramped, but they were well hidden in the event the dealer returned or anyone else ventured inside the walls.

Grace had been reticent since the near encounter with the dealer and the buyer. There had been no more history lessons or teasing comments regarding his superstitious nature.

He wished she'd poke fun at him, just so he'd know she was okay.

"You have a missed call," she said, turning the screen of his phone around to face him.

He tilted his head, studying the unknown number. There was no notification for a voice mail. "It's lucky I put it on silent."

She filled the cap of her water bottle and offered it to Luis. The cat lapped it with his tongue, tucking his tail around his haunches. "I need to call Sloane."

Javier nodded. He had expected she would. "She can get you somewhere safe."

Grace glanced at him. In the light of the phone, he saw her lashes waver. "You, too. Until we know more about who broke into my apartment and chased us down Bourbon, we can only assume you're no safer than I am."

He thought of Carlos again and frowned. He pinched off a corner of his protein bar and stuffed it in his mouth. "You should call Pia as well—just to check."

"You're right." When she held her hand out for his phone, he gave it to her. "How much battery is left?"

"Ten percent," he said and winced. "The flashlight used more than I thought it would."

"Should be enough," Grace said and started dialing. After a moment, her frown deepened. "Pia's not answering."

"It is four hours before sunrise," he pointed out.

"Yes, but she always answers." Grace shook her head, dialing again. She leaned her head back against the crypt behind her as she held the phone to her ear. She closed her eyes in relief when someone picked up. "Sloane. It's me. You heard? No, I'm fine. Really. Do they know who broke in?" She listened to Sloane's reply, her eyes scanning the darkness. "But there was someone in the alley outside. One of the men who attacked us... Me and Javier." Grace's focus sharpened on him. "Yes, Javier Rivera. He arrived yesterday. He came to tell me about Jaime's escape." She scoffed. "You knew about Jaime? Why didn't you *tell me*?"

Of course Sloane would know about Jaime. As a federal agent, she probably knew more about it than Javier did. Watching Grace, he saw her grimace. "It's not your job to protect me and Pia," she said. "The three of us... We protect each other. Always." She shook her head, bracing one arm across her middle. "No, I think Javy and I are okay for now. We should meet, though—at Casaluna. Have you spoken to Pia? I can't reach her." She cursed. "Well, keep trying. What about Sam? Is he still overseas?" Swiping her hand across her brow, she brushed hair aside. "I wish he were back, too. I feel better when he's with her and Babette. We should be at Casaluna late tonight or early tomorrow. The two of them could already be there. I hope so, too. You be careful, too. I mean it. Bye, chère."

She lowered the phone and passed it to him. "Thanks."

"She knew about the break-in," he assumed.

Grace nodded. "Police were called to the scene. The place is torn apart." At that, she released an unsteady breath. "There'll be a lot of damage to deal with when all this is over. *If* it's ever over."

"You won't have to live like this."

Her eyes softened on him. "*We* won't have to live like this."

"What did she say about the attacker in the alley?"

"There was blood at the scene, but that was all," Grace explained. "She asked about Bourbon—if we were mixed up in that. She knew we would be. She's great at what she does."

"There's a meeting place?" he asked.

She nodded. "Casaluna. It won't be easy to get to. But I know where we need to go from here at first light."

"Then we have a plan." He finished off the protein bar and balled up the wrapper. He cracked the seal on his water bottle.

"Your face is killing you."

He lifted his shoulder, tipping the bottle for a drink. "Don't know what you mean."

"And here I thought we'd established that I'm a doctor."

"We have," he acknowledged. "But I'm fine."

She scowled at him, then shifted onto her knees, lifting the phone for light. "Hold still."

Leaning over him, she probed the swelling around his nose. She made noises but said nothing until she settled back on her heels again and he instantly missed her warmth and the close, heady wave of her scent. "It doesn't look great. But there's no sign of bleeding. No hematoma. Is it still blocked on one or both sides?"

"It's better now," he tried to tell her.

"You may need surgery, Javy."

"Not here, I hope."

That startled her into smiling, and it was a welcome sight. "No. Not here." She reached for the bag and took out the first aid kit. Inside, she found a small envelope. "You'll take this now that you've had a bite to eat." Ripping the package, she shook out a dose of aspirin.

He took it, knowing not to argue. After popping the pills into his mouth, he washed them down with water.

She picked up Luis. "It's been a long night," she told him.

"Aren't you tired?" When the cat rooted around her collar, she happily obliged him by lifting the hoodie's hem. He sank in snug across her middle.

Despite the thrumming around his nose and eyes, Javier smiled at them both. "And a few hours ago, you didn't want him."

"It's not that I didn't want him," she said, hesitant. Her eyes avoided his as her arms cradled the Luis-shaped lump. "We can't always have what we want."

Javier thought about that. Her curls had gone tight and springy, teased and tossed by the night air. She no longer looked together or polished as she had at Hugo's. Crescents of fatigue underscored her eyes. The hoodie and jeans hid her inviting shape.

And something inside him still reached even if he knew all too well how right she was. He couldn't have what he wanted, however much she made him ache.

"I'm sorry about earlier," she murmured.

She said it so low he almost didn't hear. "What?"

"When I froze," she reminded him. "In the alley, it nearly got you killed."

Javier shook his head. "You don't need to apologize."

"I wish that part of me was different," she said. "I wish I was more like Sloane. What happened in Mexico had the opposite effect on her. She swore she'd never be helpless again, and she hasn't been. She doesn't hesitate to save herself or others. It galvanizes her. Over the last few hours, I've felt as helpless as I did at Alejandro's hands. At least then I had the gumption to fight back."

"You're much stronger than you give yourself credit for, Grace," he told her. "*Confía en mí.*" *Trust me*.

She dropped into a discontented silence.

Javier didn't know what to say to make her believe him. He fought for something to comfort her. Between the chill in the air that refused to let up, the slow milling tendrils of fog and the company of the catacombs, he didn't have much to draw on. Finally, he said, "I'm no good in a fight."

Her brows came together. "What do you mean?"

"I've lost every hand-to-hand fight I've gotten myself into," he explained.

"Surely not every…" She trailed off when he nodded. "But you're…"

When the words drifted off, unfinished, he heard what she didn't want to say out loud. She knew in some part he was a Solaro. Pablo's brutality fed into his DNA. "When I was forced to join the trafficking business, Pablo tried to train me. He put me in the fighting ring against every man he had, thinking if I got beat up enough, it'd make me less soft. He thought I'd get sick enough of being beaten or I'd rise to the task and come out on top. Maybe it was because I knew it was never about survival— it was about hierarchy. I never wanted to rise through the ranks. He eventually wanted me to be his lieutenant. I didn't want that. Impressing him wasn't part of my agenda. He assumed I lacked 'the killing edge.'"

"You killed Alejandro," Grace pointed out, grim around the mouth. "You shot him—through the window, and you didn't miss."

"A gun's different," Javier said.

"Is it?" she asked. "It wasn't your intention—to end his life?"

"It was," Javier admitted. "It's easier to pull a trigger than to kill someone with your bare hands. My mother taught me to shoot when I was a boy. For my protection. And I knew if I forced my way inside the house, Alejandro would've done one of two things. He would've either used you as a hostage or he'd have fought me. I faced him inside Pablo's ring. I knew I couldn't beat him. If he'd beaten me, who knows how much longer you and the others would've been under the Solaros' control."

Grace released an almost imperceptible shiver. For a while, she was quiet. Then she said, "I don't think being bad at fighting is anything to be ashamed of."

"It is when it's a matter of life and death," Javier pointed out. "It is when the life of someone you care about hangs in the balance."

She gazed at him, and he felt curls of heat beneath his navel. "Lacking 'the killing edge,' as your uncle called it, doesn't make you weak. It makes you human. I like that about you."

His pulse hitched. It cantered. She could look at him knowing who he was and the part of his blood he could hardly face
and see someone worth admiring? He hadn't thought he could
ever be worthy in her eyes. Not after she, Pia and Sloane had
watched him being led away in handcuffs at the embassy. Sloane
had looked relieved. Pia, wrecked. Grace's expression of exhausted disenchantment had lived inside his head for too long.

He'd spent that decade wondering if he'd succeeded, if he'd
saved them at all…or if he'd been too late.

He saw Grace blink several times and watched weariness
grow heavy on her. He reached for the light to switch it off.
"You should sleep."

"I don't know if I can."

"I'll keep watch."

"You can't shoot ghosts, no matter how good your aim is."

He, too, looked around. "I don't think spirits are capable of
harm the way the living are."

She was subdued for a while but seemed to relax gradually,
the points of her shoulders lowering. Still, she didn't close her
eyes. "It's hard going to sleep. Pia and I still have that in common. She has the crash of the sea to soothe her."

"Does anything help you?" he asked.

She frowned. "My mom's voice. She never slept well after my
father died. She said she still reached for him under the covers
at night and when she couldn't find him, her heart would break
all over again. After I started school, I'd call her. It didn't matter what time it was. She would answer and talk to me until I
felt sleep take hold. After she moved in with me, I would get
up in the middle of the night and find her on the couch. I can't
count the number of nights I'd fall asleep listening to her read
or telling her own stories."

She drew her shoulders up tight. "How pathetic is that? I'm
over thirty and I can't go to sleep without the sound of my
mother's voice."

He saw her bottom lip quiver—from fear or cold…it didn't
matter. He shifted toward her.

She went still as he turned so they sat beside one another between the tombs. Lifting an arm, he kept his movements slow as he lowered it over her shoulders.

Relief broke loose inside him when she eased forward, accepting the link and letting him cushion her back from the masonry. As she settled back, he heard her small sigh. Rubbing his hand over her arm for friction and heat, he said, "You want to hear one of my stories?"

"A vaquero story?"

The faint trace of mirth in her voice enlivened him. "Whatever you like."

She thought about it. Then she tipped her head to his shoulder, settling in. "Tell me more about your mother."

His mother. The thought of her made his chest tight. "What would you like to know about her?"

"You could start with her name. If that makes it easier."

It did, he found. Grief didn't respect the laws of the land. It didn't obey the limits of time. It had long outlived the lease he'd given it after riding the tide of anger and bitterness her loss had incurred. And even if he'd learned to live with it, it still didn't pull punches when it crept up on him in the quiet. Alone under the stars in New Mexico with cattle alone for company, he swore he could hear her speak. It had made the boy he thought he'd left in Mexico reach.

"Her name was Valentina Rivera," he said. "But no one called her that. Everyone I knew called her 'señora' or 'jefa.' Boss."

She made a noise. "Doesn't sound like a woman to be trifled with."

"She wasn't," Javier noted.

"So how does someone like that get mixed up with the Solaros?" she asked.

"When she was fifteen, her father gave her away in marriage," he explained.

Grace lifted her head. She surveyed his profile. "Gave her?"

"Sí," he said. "She didn't have any say in the matter, or anything, until she got out."

"How did she become a free girl?" she asked.

"Money," Javier told her. "Lots of it. Her father had given her a horse as a wedding gift. It won several races, so she built her first stable with the money from sponsors and started a breeding program. It eventually made her enough money that she could buy her way out of the Solaro family. She hadn't been able to give my father a child, either. That helped him let her go without complications."

"So how did she have you?" Grace asked.

"She was pregnant when she left," Javier explained. "That's why she did it. She had to do it quickly—before the Solaros found out there was a child."

"What happened when they found out?"

"They tried kidnapping me," he pointed out. "But my mother learned many things in the Solaro family. She learned how to kill a man. She learned how to protect her assets. And she learned how to make her enemies afraid."

"The Solaros were afraid of *her*?" Grace's voice held a trace of awe.

"Si. She was…" He groped for a description that was worthy enough to match the woman who had molded him. "Untouchable. That's a word. Si?"

"Si." Grace nodded. "How did it feel…to be raised by someone untouchable?"

"She made it clear I should never let my guard down," Javier replied. "She arranged for me to have bodyguards. I never went to school with other children. She trusted no one and taught me the same. When we weren't working or grooming horses, she educated me herself. It was her who taught me to work the land, not the men she hired. She knew as much as they did, if not more. She taught me to love it, respect it, how to protect it and the people I love."

The fog and the dead seemed to absorb Grace's silence until he thought she must have slipped into repose.

Javier waited. Then he spoke again, mutedly. He spoke in secrets. "Sometimes when I work late or I'm camping out, I hear her. I feel, wherever I go, as long as I remain close to the land, she's with me."

She lifted her head slightly. "Maybe that's why you're superstitious." Her hand found the bend in his elbow. It stayed there as she yawned. "I'd give anything to hear my mother tell stories again. Or hear my father sing. What does she say to you? What do you hear?"

He frowned, turning his attention to the tomb wall in front of them. "Warnings."

"About?"

Javier thought of Jaime's escape—and how he'd stood on the mountain on the boundary of his boss's cattle ranch just days before the news broke and known. If he told Grace what he'd heard on the wind slicing through the canyon, would she believe him?

Grace had gone still and heavy at his side. He let the quiet envelop them and lowered his head, listening to the long pulls of inhales and the slow exhalations. Turning his head to hers, he kissed the space at the peak of her brow. "Que duermas bien, mi sol," he whispered. "Sleep well."

Chapter 8

The fog played tricks on his mind. Or Javier had reached the point where exhaustion had firmly taken the wheel and imagination chased him. The no-man's-land between night and day brought a strange wind that teased the fog. It danced in wisps above the tombs, contorting into ever-changing shapes until Javier closed his eyes to clear them.

He heard Luis meow. When the cat's head popped out of the pocket of Grace's hoodie, Javier held out his hand. Grace stirred as the animal attempted to escape. "Shh," Javier soothed. "I've got him." He closed his hand around the kitten's form, balling him against his sternum.

Stuffing his phone in his pocket, he edged toward the opening. Looking long down the corridor toward the front gate, he could find nothing in the darkness.

The kitten yowled softly. He pressed his paws against Javier's restraining hand. Javier set him on the ground and stayed close on his heels as he picked his way over loose stones and tree roots. The cat stilled finally and crouched to relieve himself.

Javier eyed the space between the tombs where Grace rested, marking them and the distance. He wouldn't let Luis roam too far from mamacita.

He cranked his head to the side and groaned. Stiffness had

taken over the muscles of his neck after the fight with Carlos and reclining for hours against stone.

The soft sound of sobbing made him still. His body went rigid. The sound wafted on the wind. It raced through the catacombs. The cold thickened.

Luis's back arched. He danced back so that he poised between Javier's boots. Then he hissed, fur standing along his spine.

Javier scooped him up. He itched to back up but stood his ground even as the skin on the back of his neck and head prickled warning.

The wind slowed, lifting the teeth-knocking cold slightly. The wailing ceased, and the fog tore like a shroud. Javier could see glimpses of the sky in the gaps. It was strange seeing that normal cloudless blue after the bone-chilling events of the night. Then again, day often turned a blind eye to night's devilry.

Regardless, the timid hue of coming day made him blink in relief. He could hear the whoosh of a car passing on a distant street, then another as the neighborhood around the cemetery woke.

Javier shuffled back to the place he'd left Grace. He stopped when he felt the phone in his pocket vibrate.

He dug it out and studied the screen. The name of the incoming call flashed as Unknown.

Javier felt that prickle at the base of his neck again. He toyed with letting it roll over to voice mail. Then he swiped and raised the phone to his ear. "Aló?"

"Hermano."

Javier retreated from the place where Grace rested. His feet shuffled backward until stones snagged the heels of his boots and he nearly upended. Speaking in low tones, he dropped his chin and replied, "Jaime."

"You shouldn't have gone to the girl's apartment."

Javier forced himself to remain calm. "How long have you been following me?"

"Carlos was with you on the flight from Taos."

Javier shook his head. How could that be? "He let me get on the plane?"

"I heard you were boarding a flight to New Orleans. I knew you were coming for her."

Grace. Panic blipped, bright as a streetlight. "Are you here?"

"I've been here for days. Watching Grace. Waiting for her to lead me to Pia."

This was about Pia? Jaime's pointed interest in Pia twelve years ago was sick...obsessive. "You've been watching Grace," Javier said, unable to stomach the fact.

"I thought once Sloane told her of my escape, she'd run to Pia. Then who do I see wandering into her place above Russo's? My long-lost brother."

"We're not," Javier snapped. He heard the words slice through the air, decisive. "We're not brothers."

"Is that what you tell yourself when you're singing the cows to sleep?"

"It's the truth," Javier gnashed through his teeth.

"Is that what you've told the chica?"

Javier ignored that. "If you've been watching her, it means you don't know where Pia is. You have no clue. And you're too afraid to go after Sloane."

"Would you like to know what I have planned for the three of them?"

Javier wouldn't. He opened his mouth to say so.

Jaime interfered, his cool voice serving the words slowly. "I'll kill Grace quickly, but only if you bring her to me. I'll give Sloane the same courtesy if you help me catch her. When I find Pia, she's coming with me. I have a plane on standby for her and me. You do this for me, hermano, I'll let you fly off with us into the sunset. Like John Wayne. Si?"

It was a lie. Javier had killed Alejandro to get Grace out of his clutches. Others when he went for Pia and Sloane. There was no possibility Jaime would let him live. Not when there was blood to be repaid. The phone beeped and the sound of Jaime's voice dropped. Javier looked at the screen. It was blank. The phone had died.

"Javy?"

He turned. There was enough light to spot the concerned

gleam in Grace's eyes as she poked her head out from between the tombs. "Who were you talking to?"

He felt the automatic shake of his head. "Nothing. No one."

"You were on the phone," she pointed out.

He glanced at the dead screen. His mouth worked fast, expelling lies. "I was trying to call a cab. It died." He held it up for her to see.

"Oh." Looking around, she adjusted her hoodie. "The Commander's Palace is just around the corner. There's a museum, too. We might catch a cab there. How's Luis?"

Javier looked down at the cat in his hand. Luis's luminous gaze fixed on his face. He might have been mistaken, but the kitten looked not a little accusing. "He went to the bathroom."

"Good," she said. "We'll both need a place to do that, too. Maybe snatch a bite to eat somewhere if we end up having to wait. Are you ready?"

Javier glanced around the cemetery. The last thing he wanted to do was linger. But knowing Jaime was out there waiting for him to make a mistake... "We should stay off the street."

She nodded. "You're right." Shouldering the bag, she held out her hand for his.

Javier hesitated for a split second before wrapping his fingers around hers. He walked with her.

Why had the lies come so naturally? His half-truths were mounting by the second.

What would happen when Grace found out it was Jaime who was looking for them—who'd been watching her for days?

Javier burned at the thought. Jaime could've snatched her off the street. It would have been easy in the city, even in broad daylight. What would have become of her if Javier had been too late?

They would meet Sloane before sunup the next day. Javier had to tell Grace everything before that.

Javier had to tell her Pablo Solaro wasn't his uncle. He was the man Javier's mother had been forced to marry at fifteen. He was Javier's biological father, which made Jaime and Alejandro Javier's half brothers. And if Grace knew that, Javier wasn't sure she'd ever look at him the same again.

* * *

Grace prayed it wasn't a mistake as she stood at the pay phone. Javier's back nudged close against hers as he watched the passing cars under the hood of his jacket.

She closed her eyes, waiting for someone to pick up on the other end of the line. His body heat had been more than comforting through the night. It had been a ballast. It still was, she found. Fighting the urge to lean her head back against the rock of his shoulder, she bounced at the knees, swaying to entertain Luis, who was becoming increasingly agitated. His patience with the hunger and cold was ebbing and Grace couldn't blame him.

Would he have been better off if she had left him in the box outside the voodoo shop?

The thought made her sad. She shucked him underneath the chin.

The line clicked. A woman answered. "Yes?"

"Tante Lalie?"

"Gracie Boo Lacroix? Is that you, chile?"

"Yes," Grace said, beaming. "Oh, it's so good to hear your voice."

"I've missed hearin' yours. Where y'at, chère? Not working too hard, are ya? Your mama worried you would after she was gone."

Grace felt her eyes sting at the combined memories of her parents and Eulalie Breaux. She blinked against the white morning sun that had conquered the fog. "Would you mind if I brought a friend 'round to your place?"

"A friend?" Eulalie's tone peaked with apprehension. "You finally pick a man? Talk about! You needin' ole Lalie to pass judgment on him? Bring him over. We'll see how he handles my witherin' stare."

Grace thought of the way Javier had kissed her in the cemetery to break the spell of her deep freeze. "It is a man I'm bringing, but not for scrutiny. The two of us... We're in a bit of a bind. Is Dante home?"

Eulalie clicked her tongue. "Dante's never home no more."

"Could you make sure he's there?" Grace asked. "I'd like to speak with him. About his boat."

"You and your man friend wantin' to go up the bayou?"

"Yes, ma'am," Grace said quickly. "And seeing as your nephew's the best guide in Louisiana…"

"I'll make some calls, see if I can't bring him 'round before y'all get here. Probably have to flush him out of whichever floozy's bed he's talked his way into this week."

"Thank you, Lalie," Grace replied, clutching the receiver. "We'll be there shortly." Replacing it in the cradle, she whirled toward Javier. "She said yes!"

"Good," he said. "Let's hail a cab. How long will it take to get to Eulalie's house?"

"Not long at all."

"And you're sure whoever's chasing us can't trace her to you?"

The question made her nibble the inside of her lip as she had done from the second the plan formed in her mind. "We're not related. Lalie worked with my father in the early years. Our families remained close until he passed. My mother and I saw her around Christmastime to exchange gifts and good wishes and phone calls, and she took care of me for a time after Mama died…" She peered at him. "Do you think it's a risk? Should we leave her alone?"

"We need a boat," he reminded her.

"And Dante," she added. "Dante will get us to Casaluna, no question. From there, we're in Sloane's hands."

A question lurked behind his eyes.

"What is it?" she asked. He'd been quiet since the cemetery and since they'd freshened themselves in the National WWII museum's bathrooms and grabbed a quick coffee at the corner café. "If you think this is the wrong plan, just say something."

"I think it's a good plan," he told her.

"Not because it's our *only* plan," she ventured, "right?"

His mouth tipped up at one corner. "Right. Do you want me to take Luis?"

"I've got him," Grace assured him. "Let me call the hospital and tell them I won't be back today or tomorrow. Then let's hope the cab driver doesn't turn his nose up at pets. And that Tante Lalie has some cat food handy. If we don't get this guy some breakfast soon, we're looking at a full-scale toddler meltdown."

The Tiffany blue shotgun house in the Lower Ninth Ward boasted lime green shutters and a chain-link fence around its beds of hydrangeas that burst with blue crowns in the summertime. It had flooded during Katrina. The National Guard had rescued Eulalie and her nephew, Dante, whom she was raising at the time, from the roof...along with a rack's worth of copper-bottomed pots and pans she'd insisted coming along with her. When the guardsmen balked at the request, she famously remarked, *You can bring my copper pots or I'll see you in hell!*

The storm door opened with a creak as Grace opened the gate on the fence. She held up a hand before Eulalie could come down the cement steps to meet her. "No, no," she called. "You stay there. We're coming up."

Eulalie's hair was bound in a silk handkerchief. She wore thick glasses and a sweater over her caftan. In the kitchen with Grace's father, she'd been pretty to his plain, big to his small. She was still pretty, but the only thing that remained of her heavy figure was a pouch of skin beneath her neck and the sweater slipping from her shoulders. "What you wearin', Gracie Boo?"

Grace looked down at the sugar skull on the front of her hoodie and its crude middle-fingered salute. "Mardi Gras," she said in excuse. Luis keened from the crook of her arm.

"Who's this little one?" Eulalie asked curiously.

"Tante Lalie, I'd like you to meet Luis," Grace said, gesturing to the cat. She stepped aside carefully as Javier squeezed onto the porch. "And this is the friend I was telling you about. Javier, this is Ms. Eulalie Breaux."

"Señora," he greeted, dipping his chin.

Eulalie leaned into Grace. "This your new man friend?"

"Yes," Grace explained. She saw Javier scanning the street and urgency got the best of her. "May we come in?"

"Sure," Eulalie said, turning and opening the door. "Just be careful. We don't want to let the mister out. Last week, I had to chase his ass all the way down the canal 'fore he slowed down enough for me to catch him. Nearly had a heart attack. The Rhodes boy had to carry the both of us back."

"Who's 'the mister'?" Javier asked Grace as they followed Eulalie inside.

If Grace was going to have to explain everything about him to Eulalie and everything about Eulalie back to him, it was going to be a long visit. "If you see something small and quick coming at you, just slide to the right and hope for the best."

The long post-Katrina recovery led to the eventual redesign of Eulalie's house. Grace's father had helped knock walls down, opening one room to the next. The cottage was no longer a testament to the historic shotgun design. A den yawned into the open space of a kitchen, and two bedroom doors and a bathroom were visible toward the back. The house smelled of red beans and rice. Grace's stomach lurched in longing. Eulalie shuffled into the kitchen and rattled the lid off a pot. "That little one had anything to eat yet?"

"Not since last night," Grace admitted. "We were hoping you had some food for him."

"Let me see here now…" Eulalie opened the cupboard doors, banged them shut, opened others, took items down before turning to the fridge and opening it. Muttering, she pulled out ingredients before coming back to the stove. "How many weeks?"

Grace looked at Luis and Luis looked at her. "I… I don't know. I haven't had a chance to take him to the vet. Eight? Nine maybe."

"Don't matter none. This here'll fix him up."

"Can I help you?" Grace asked, edging toward the stove.

"You can stand there and look pretty," Eulalie suggested. "Like your papa always asked you to."

Being with Eulalie brought back the smells and sounds of his kitchen. Grace waited for Eulalie to scoop, measure and mix while Javier surveyed the large sign that had once hung over the BBQ restaurant Eulalie and Grace's father had made famous together. The words HEAD TO HIGHER GROUND were printed above an arrow. On the next sign, HIGHER GROUND was stacked in large type over the smaller words, BBQ. CRAWFISH. GUMBO. COLD DRINKS.

Higher Ground had been in business since the early '80s. Then Eulalie had taken over Dante's custody and had left the busy restaurant life to care for the young boy. After Grace's father died, Higher Ground had cycled through a few other chefs before finally closing, no longer able to live up to the hype it once had. People still spoke of Higher Ground in reverent tones before the regretful murmur of "Ain't dere no more" capped the conversation.

"Where'd you find yourself a Latin lover?" Eulalie asked philosophically as she poured the homemade cat food into a small dish.

"He's not my lover," Grace muttered, pitching her voice to a discreet level. "He's a friend."

"Friend?"

As Eulalie's gaze swung back to her, Grace tried not to swallow. "Yes, ma'am."

"Humph. He don't look at you like no friend." Taking Luis from Grace's hands, Eulalie plopped him right on top of the kitchen counter next to the dish. "There you are, tiny. Have yourself some supper."

Grace didn't need to think about how Javier looked at her. "Have you heard from Dante?"

"He's got a set of nice dark eyes, him," Eulalie noted.

"Dante?"

"No. Pedro Pascal in there."

Grace opened her mouth, then closed it. Then she asked cautiously, "You know Pedro Pascal?"

"Dante's got that TV streamin' service hooked up here now. We watch *The Last of Us*. I like that Joel Miller. Wouldn't mind callin' him 'daddy,' if you know what I'm sayin'."

The suggestion gave Grace a mild headache. "His name isn't Pedro. It's Javier."

"Nice eyes lie, too."

Grace shook her head. "Javy wouldn't lie to me."

"You sure 'bout that?"

Grace noted how Eulalie's eyes had grown peaked, the skin of her eyelids pinched so that they pitched like gables. "He wouldn't lie," Grace said stubbornly.

Eulalie lifted her chin. It wagged a bit as she swung back to her copper pot. "You hungry?"

Again, Grace felt a pang in her stomach. "Yes, ma'am."

"Sit down at the table and I'll bring you somethin'. You're skin and bones. I told them Russo boys to feed you. 'Bout time I came for a visit. Maybe they'll take me seriously when they see a marble rolling pin in my hand."

Grace looked down at the curves underneath her borrowed hoodie and jeans. She was hardly skin and bones. "Giovanni and Marco have been more than generous. They send up more food than anybody could handle." After picking up Luis and balancing his dish on her other hand, she walked to the small round table clad in a clean white tablecloth. Catching Javier's eye, she motioned for him to follow.

"Has she said anything about her nephew?" Javier asked as they took their seats. He lifted the dish from her hand and set it in the center of the table.

Grace released Luis, who surged back to the edge of the dish and lapped again with abandon. "No. She's hung up on you right now. She thinks I need protecting."

"From me?"

"My parents aren't around to do it anymore, so…" Grace canted her head to the side. "She thinks you look like Pedro Pascal."

"From *Narcos*?"

"Yes."

"He's Chilean American, not Mexican."

"Would you like me to explain that to her?" Grace asked.

Javier looked in Eulalie's direction, then shook his head decidedly.

"She also thinks you're a liar."

His eyes widened. "A liar?"

Grace watched the cat eat. She was almost hungry enough to lean over the dish and do the same. The power bar she'd eaten in the cemetery had burned off long ago. But the sight of trouble folding Javier's mouth into a thin line distracted her. "I wouldn't let it get to you."

Eulalie swooped in, setting a plate under Grace's nose, another under his. "Don't shove it down too fast, Dark Eyes. It's as hot as the seat of your pants. Y'all want some corn bread?"

"We're fine," Grace assured her. "Please sit and eat with us, Lalie."

"Don't mind if I do," Eulalie said with a good-natured chuckle, rounding the table again with a plate of her own. She waved a hand at the kitten when he sniffed the entrées. "Don't go stickin' your nose where it don't belong, tiny."

"Luis," Javier muttered at him, pulling him back from Eulalie's plate. He set the cat in his lap, petting him from head to tail before digging into Eulalie's cooking again. "This is delicious. Gracias, señora."

Eulalie peered at him. "You're not from 'round here, are you, cher?"

Grace cleared her throat, but Javier extended a good-natured smile. "Is it that obvious?"

Eulalie cackled shortly, shook her head and went back to her food. "This here's nothin' special. Just enough to get you by."

"That's not true," Grace murmured. When Javier glanced at her, she added, "After my father died, Lalie made sure my mother and I didn't have to cook for weeks. Every night without fail, she brought us a home-cooked meal. After my mother died, she did it all over again."

"Couldn't let you go hungry now, could I?" Eulalie asked. "The grievin' forget to cook for themselves for the sake of nourishment. They need others to do it for them."

Eulalie's food and company had saved Grace from the brink of despair. She draped her hand over the knotted one Eulalie had braced against the table's edge. A pair of Band-Aids crisscrossed over her knuckles. Still, it reminded Grace of her father's hand. For a split second, she wanted to weep. "I should come to visit more."

"Why would you," Eulalie asked, eyes shining with understanding and truth, "when it hurts still?" Brushing her fingers over Grace's cheek, she tutted. "It'll get easier with time, Gracie Boo. Then you can come visit me and the mister once a week."

"Who's 'the mister' again?" Javier asked once more, trying

to prevent the paw that had risen over the edge of the table from swiping beans off the edge of his plate.

"What'd you say, Dark Eyes?" Eulalie asked, raising her voice and squinting through her glasses.

Grace took pity on him. "'The mister' is Mr. Monty. Lalie's…" She trailed off, wondering how to explain. "…companion?"

Javier cast a glance down at Luis, whose wide eyes were now level with the edge of her table. The kitten shifted from side to side, as if to pounce. Javier cupped his hand over the cat's ears and lowered him back to his lap. "Is it a dog?"

Eulalie dropped her fork. "My mister's no canine and he sure ain't no 'it.' He *is* sensitive." She thrust her finger in Javier's face. "And you *better* not let him hear you comparin' him to no dog. Not if you want to remain a guest in this house!"

Javier held up his hands. "Permiso, señora. I didn't mean to upset anyone."

"He's just worried about Luis, is all," Grace added. "Right, Javy?"

He nodded rapidly. "Si. Yes. I'm sorry."

Eulalie raised her chin, her lips pressed together, measuring Javier across the blade of her nose. Finally, she groped for her fork and picked it up. "You better not give my Gracie any grief, either," she muttered. "You do, you best believe me and Mr. Monty be comin' after you. You may see an old lady with your eyes. But, underneath, I am one hundred percent Cajun."

"I hear you," Javier assured her. "I would never hurt Grace. Créeme. Believe me."

Eulalie pursed her lips before shoving a forkful of rice into her mouth and chewing slowly, watchful. After a moment, she cut her eyes to Grace. "Take your hand off the man. I'm not goin' to take a knife to him. Not yet."

Grace realized she had placed her hand on Javier's knee under the table. She lifted it fast and avoided looking at either him or Eulalie in the eye. Her face filled with unwelcome heat, and she worried about the stain it would leave on her cheeks. Lifting her fork, she took a calming breath before taking another bite. After a moment, she tried to broach the subject of Eulalie's nephew again. "Did Dante say when he would be here?"

"Mm." Eulalie shook her head unsatisfactorily. "Boy never says when he's comin' or goin'. These days, he just shows up."

"But he is coming," Grace said cautiously. "Right?"

"He'll be here," Eulalie pointed out. "He may not live here no more. But he knows better not to push his ole Lalie."

Grace bit her lip, then lifted the glass of sweet tea Eulalie had served her at the beginning of the meal and drank, hoping she was right. If she and Javier were to get to Casaluna before the break of day tomorrow, they badly needed Dante to show within the next few hours.

Luis complained loudly from Javier's lap, no longer content with batting the cords of his coat's hood.

"Tiny needs to go outside," Eulalie noted. "You take him out back. Just mind Mr. Monty, like I told you. Don't let him talk you into lettin' him take another constitutional."

Javier lifted his napkin to wipe his mouth and pushed his chair back. "Thank you again for the meal," he said before escorting Luis to the back door beyond the kitchen.

Grace waited until she heard the storm door slap shut behind him. "There's no need to give Javy a hard time, Lalie. He's a good man."

"How long have you known him?" Eulalie asked, stacking Javier's plate and utensil on top of her own.

Grace decided the truth was better than a lie. "We met in Mexico." When Eulalie's head snatched back on her neck in surprise, Grace made herself continue. "Twelve years ago."

Eulalie's wise eyes looked owlish behind her lenses. She planted her hands on the tabletop. "He the one you always talked 'bout—the one who got you and the other girls out?"

"He's the one," Grace confirmed.

"Well, if I'd known that, I'd have given him a hero's welcome," Eulalie informed her, "not the third degree. I expect it's me who owes him the apology. Not the other way 'round."

A smile feathered across Grace's lips. It took a lot to contain it and the amusement behind it. "When you hollered at him for Mr. Monty…"

Guilty mirth spilled across Eulalie's stern features. "He had every faith I'd come after him."

A laugh broke the surface. Grace clamped a hand over her mouth. Once she was sure she had a hold of herself, she dropped her forehead into it, shook her head. "Oh, Lalie. When he broke his nose last night, he didn't turn as white as he did when you put your finger in his face."

Eulalie's shoulders shook and the sound of her chuckle rang throughout the room. "Maybe he knows I'm the one your papa trusted to run a man off if he wasn't worthy of you."

Grace stilled. "Daddy asked you…?"

"He'd have done the same for me and mine. If the Le Bon Dieu had seen fit, he'd have had his hands tied with my sister's boy." Eulalie examined Grace carefully. "What's really troublin' you?"

Grace looked toward the back door. "You don't really think he's lying, do you?"

Eulalie thought about it. "He don't just look at you like the cat eyes the cream. The need's there. A heapin' bucket of it. Think you can handle that?"

Something inside Grace keened. She ran her hand up and down the line of her throat before pressing it to the ache behind her breastbone. It was sweeter than honey and just as thick. "I've never been very good at answering that look in a man's eye," she admitted dully.

"But you see it, don't you?"

Grace gave a small nod. "Yes. But there's a lot still that Javy and I don't know about each other. I won't lie and say it's not thrilling, either."

"If it excites you, then why're you so afraid of it?" Eulalie wondered.

She released a breath, feeling transparent. "Because I shut down that part of me a long time ago. It was the part that led me to Mexico to begin with. Straight into a relationship with another man I scarcely knew—the one who tried to take everything from me."

Eulalie clicked her tongue. "You a long way from Mexico, Gracie Boo. You a long way from that girl that got taken advantage of."

"I know," Grace said. "I know that. That's why I… I need

to know. Are you giving Javy a hard time because that's what Daddy would do—or because you sense something about him you don't like?"

"You say he's a good man," Eulalie reminded her. "Is that your own instinct about him?"

"Yes," Grace answered. "But..."

Eulalie let the unspoken sink in before she elaborated. "It's easy not to trust your gut when it's led you wrong before."

Her gut had nearly destroyed her. Grace swallowed the lump that had grown in her throat and waited.

"I feel the good, too," Eulalie told her. "'Specially when he shines those dark eyes in your direction. But I see shame there. Guilt, too, maybe. What you see in him is truth. But there's something underneath—something he hides from the light."

"From me?" Grace wondered and heard her voice drop to a whisper.

"That I can't see," Eulalie claimed, picking up the plates again. She stood and leaned across the table to take Grace's plate, too. "I read eyes. Not minds."

Grace took the three glasses left on the table and walked them to the kitchen sink, contemplative. "If I had your gift, I'd have saved myself a lifetime of regret."

"Regrets are for fools who don't live their lives," Eulalie stated, cranking the tap so that water flowed. She waited for steam to rise before rinsing. "You never struck me as a fool, chère."

Grace smiled, pouring what remained of the sweet tea down the drain. Eulalie's sound advice never came softly. She turned into the woman, laying her head low on the bony shoulder of her rough-knit sweater.

Eulalie shut off the tap and folded Grace in a warm embrace. She patted her shoulders and hair. "You always were a good girl. You made your mama and papa proud. Responsible. Hardworking. And cautious. *Too* cautious. Don't let caution steal anything you might want. 'Fore you know it, life slips away and you haven't lived it. Your folks were responsible and hardworking, too. But they lived. Ain't you proof of that?"

Grace didn't lift her head or open her eyes. Eulalie's embrace reminded Grace of how very much she missed her mother's arms. Tears burned against their ducts, forcing her to breathe carefully in order to push them away. "I suppose I am."

"You take Dark Eyes up the bayou with you," Eulalie advised. "You take the both of you on a holiday. And if you find there's only one bed, you remember what I said about livin'."

Laughter burst free now from Grace's chest. She shook with it and felt Eulalie do the same. The lightheartedness of the moment wrung out the grief and worry.

The storm door slapped. A startled shout sliced through the cheer. Grace looked around quickly at the distinct sound of pitter-pattering. A large duck waddled across the floor, webbed feet slapping the linoleum.

Javier appeared behind it, his dark eyes perplexed as he watched the creature disappear into Eulalie's bedroom. The door shut slowly behind it. When he swung his gaze inquisitively back to the women at the sink, he said, "Mr. Monty?"

Grace grinned at Eulalie's answer. "The one and only."

Chapter 9

Javier took to pacing the small rooms of Eulalie's house. The light was low at the windows, the sun in freefall near the horizon somewhere beyond them. He roamed the floors enough to know which boards softened under his boots, which ones creaked and which ones moaned.

Grace was curled up on the rug with Luis in the crescent shape of her body. She dragged her feather boa across the floor. The cat stumbled over his feet to chase it. Nearby, Mr. Monty lounged, watching the game with ennui. Eulalie had fallen asleep in the recliner after several episodes of *Grey's Anatomy*.

Javier eyed the phone charging on the kitchen counter. His gut tightened. It would be fully charged at this point. He didn't want to check for missed calls. If he checked his voice mail, he would hear his brother's voice.

He raised his gaze to the ceiling. Careful to keep his voice to a whisper, he said, "He's not coming."

"He could still show," Grace considered. Her tone said something different. She cast a glance over the curtains on the door. "We are running out of time, though."

"If we had a car," Javier said slowly, trying to think out loud, "could we drive to Casaluna?"

"It would be safer by boat," Grace noted. "We would slide

completely off the radar that way. But yes—a car could get us there."

"Maybe that's what we should do," Javier weighed.

"Whose car would we borrow?" Grace asked. Her eyes touched on the sleeping woman. "I'm not leaving Lalie without hers, and I can't think of anyone who would loan us one so easily."

"We could call another cab," he pointed out.

"Casaluna is an hour north," Grace said. "We may not have enough cash left over from Sabine to pay for another fare. I won't ask Lalie for money, either."

"I'll check the bag," he told her before she could get up. She'd set it down in the kitchen. He flipped on the stove light, lifting the bag to the counter. From its depths, he pulled several more protein bars, three water bottles, several twenty-dollar bills, their edges curled around each other, and…condoms?

Javier stared at the square packets, still attached by their perforated tear strips. They looked as out of place in his hand as the duck had seemed wandering Eulalie's spick-and-span floors.

"Is that what I think it is?"

He jerked, upsetting the packets. He caught them, but not before they unfurled like a long guilty ribbon from fingers to floor. Grimacing, he saw Grace's lips caught in a perfect O.

Something surged up her throat, a breathy laugh she stopped by touching the back of her hand to her mouth. Her cheeks colored beautifully. The humor shined from her eyes. "Bon Dieu. What did Sabine think we'd be doing once we outran the trouble on Bourbon Street?"

"Is it not obvious?" Javier wondered out loud.

A giggle broke the seal of her hand. She doubled over, fighting to keep herself quiet by weaving her arms across her ribs.

Javier liked to see her laugh. He wished Eulalie weren't asleep so Grace could let loose. So he could hear her laughter ringing off everything.

His phone chirped with the sound of an incoming call, and Javier felt the foolish grin melt from his face.

Grace reached for it. He dived to pick it up before she could.

Her laughter died in a clutch of surprise. "Who is it?" she wanted to know.

"No one," he said, shaking his head in a lie to match the one on his tongue. "It's no one." Swiping, he declined the call, then stuffed the phone in his back pocket.

Realization and horror sprang to her face. "You are hiding something," she said in a whispered rush.

"I'm not." He wanted to kick himself. Cursing, he turned away, stuffing the condoms back into the bag with everything else.

Her hand flattened against the sleeve of his hoodie. "Javy."

No reprimand accompanied his name. The plea there, however, split him in two. Unable to face her, he tried to flatten out the twenties. "Your friend gave us more money than I thought. It looks like enough for cab fare."

Grace's fingers curled into his sleeve. "You *were* talking to someone in the cemetery. You *were* on the phone. Who were you talking to?"

He sucked in a long breath. "Grace…"

"Javy," she said again. "Please."

His pulse hammered. Still, he made himself turn. Meeting her eyes, he felt singed by shame. "I didn't want you to be afraid."

She shook her head slightly and said nothing, eyes pinging from his right to his left in fast repetitions, searching wildly for the truth.

Guilt had turned to acid in his throat. He tried swallowing. It didn't work correctly. His voice roughened. "The man outside your apartment…"

Her eyes widened. "You knew him?"

"It was Carlos," Javier explained, "a cousin of mine."

Her lungs rose in a sharp breath. She waited for more.

"And the phone calls," Javier went on, knowing she would settle for nothing but the whole truth. "They're from Jaime."

She closed her eyes. Folding her arms around herself, she turned from him and took several slow steps away.

He traced the line of her back through her hoodie with his gaze and felt the cord of trust she felt for him fray.

She stopped to scrub her hands over her face. "Lalie said

you were lying," she mumbled. "Why? Why would you keep the truth from me?"

"The same reason Sloane did," he said.

She spun back to him, her brows drawn together. "What did you say?"

"Sloane kept the truth from you, too," he reminded her. "She knew about Jaime's prison break. She protected you. I wanted to protect you. I'd do anything to protect you."

"I don't need *or* want that kind of protection," she informed him carefully. He could see the anger and betrayal in her tight jaw and posture. She was skilled at tucking it behind the veil of her eyes, but he saw it there, too, all the same.

He felt her slipping away fast. "I never meant to hurt you, Grace. Bonita."

"Don't," she said sharply. "Don't call me nice names. It won't fix it."

"What will?" he asked. Her eyes had gone stern, foreboding—possibly to hide the wet he saw behind them, too.

"I don't know," she said scarcely.

The sound of a throaty engine rumbled through the walls of the house. They heard the thumping of bass speakers. It rattled the plates on the walls.

"It's Dante," she murmured, knowing without seeing. "Looks like we'll get that ferry ride, after all."

"Where'd you say your boyfriend was from?" Dante asked from the driver's seat of the brawny black pickup truck with the Breaux Bayou Tours decal spread officially across the back window.

Grace frowned at the stripes in the road between the headlights. "Watch the road. You're drifting. And I didn't say."

Dante whistled as he peered at Javier in the back seat through the rearview mirror. "He in the doghouse?"

"Eyes on the road!" she shrieked as the headlights of an oncoming car nearly overtook them.

Dante swerved into his lane just in time, laying on his horn. He squinted out his driver's side mirror at the taillights fading and the boat trailer he was hauling behind them. "You see that? People forget how to drive 'round here. Talk about."

She scowled. But Dante picked up a whistling tune, and she remembered how hard it was to stay mad at him. Eulalie knew that, too, which was the reason she'd forgiven him for his transgressions through the years. He had a boyish face well into his twenties, making it easy to remember the little boy he'd been when Eulalie took him in. The sad, angry-eyed boy who never cried, despite the pain of losing his mother. Grace had wanted to ask him why he never shed a tear. Now that she'd lost her own mother, she'd rather know *how*. "He isn't my boyfriend," she pointed out.

Dante grinned a knowing grin and looked again at Javier in the rearview mirror. "You need some advice, amigo?"

"Not from you," Grace cut in. "Lalie says you've got a new girl every Tuesday."

Dante belted a laugh. "Sure 'nuff."

She shook her head. "You really think that's healthy?"

"Laissez le bon temps rouler."

She rolled her eyes but subsided. A black cat skittered across the road in front of the truck. Tensing, she wondered why it was always a black cat, never a ginger or albino one. She kept her hands in her lap instead of lifting them to the windshield to sketch an invisible X on the glass as her superstitious mother wouldn't have hesitated to do.

"You're one to talk," he said, giving her a playful punch on the arm.

She whipped her head back. "What about me?"

"Ain't no ring on your finger," he noted. "If you thinkin' like Lalie, where's your second-line wedding parade?"

"Touché," she decided after a momentary sulk. "How much farther?"

"'Bout five minutes," he said, checking the clock on the dash. He slowed for a turn and still took it too fast.

She gripped the bar over her head and heard Luis yowl as Javier slid all the way across the back seat. "Lalie warned me."

"What?"

"That you drive like the devil himself."

He laughed again. "She won't let me drive her to the store no more."

"You are looking after her," Grace asserted, "right?"

"She doesn't like being looked after."

"But you're still checking in regularly?" Grace pressed. "She needs you."

"We have dinner twice a week," Dante explained, taking his hands off the wheel to talk with them. "And not just cuz I can't cook for myself. We watch TV. Me and Mr. Monty fix whatever needs fixin' 'round the house. She hollers at me not to get a girl pregnant, describes every STD she knows and sends me away with the leftovers."

Grace breathed a little easier. "I worry about her."

"She worries 'bout you, too," Dante warned. He jerked his thumb toward Javier. "She didn't mention whether I should worry 'bout your beau back there. Too busy chastisin' me for being late."

"You don't need to worry about Javy," she explained, though she frowned deeply.

"You ever heard of a disease that turns a man's thing green as swamp moss?" he asked experimentally.

She wrinkled her nose. "No."

He swatted the steering wheel with the heel of his hand. "I *knew* she made that mess up. Couldn't get my thing up for a week after she told me 'bout that one."

Grace flinched at the sound of ringing from the back seat. Closing her eyes, she told her nerves to settle.

The phone rang again and Javier answered, "Bueno?" Then he cursed and ended the call.

"Why would you answer?" Grace asked quietly.

"He used a different number," Javier explained. "I thought it might be Sloane trying to contact you."

It made sense. Still, Grace said nothing in return.

He'd been lying to her since the moment trouble had come to her door. Jaime had come to New Orleans. To do what? Kidnap her again? Kill her? Were Pia and Sloane safe? Had he sent men after them, too?

Why had Javier lied? She felt bruised by his untruthfulness.

Didn't he know how much she had trusted him? Did he know the walls she'd had to chip away to do that?

She'd thought about kissing him in Eulalie's kitchen. He'd looked so sweet with a blush crawling up his neck and a rueful smile taking hold of his face. He'd looked at her with those dark eyes shining and she'd wanted nothing more than to back him up into the still-warm stove and take the reins.

She rubbed her temples where they hurt. Hadn't she heard her father's warning when she found Javier on her doorstep? *Stay away from the dark water, minnow...swallows young 'uns like you whole...* She thought back to her apartment. She hadn't slept. Restless, she'd contemplated the morning. Waking up with Javier. Taking him to Café du Monde for beignets and chicory coffee, if he was interested. Maybe even inviting him to promenade the Moonwalk or the French Market if the weather cooperated...

She'd tried to think of some excuse to stay in touch with him. *Don't be a stranger, vaquero. Call me next time you're in town.* Or, *Let's stay in touch. You can come back to Mardi Gras next year. My treat.*

If she had had time before her afternoon shift at the hospital, she would have gone with him to the airport. She'd wondered what goodbye would be like. Would he have hugged her? Would a kiss on the cheek be too much to expect?

Grace cursed under her breath. New Orleans hadn't desensitized her as much as she thought it had. The last twenty-four hours were all the proof she needed. She'd picked up a kitten on the street instead of walking away as dozens of others had done. For years, she'd ignored the freezing she'd experienced when confronted with physical danger, consoling herself with the fact that it never happened in the ER or her OR. The only place it reared its ugly head was on the streets when shots rang out in the distance or police cars screamed around a corner, chasing someone else.

And Javier. These feelings for him were mixed up in her weakness, too.

New Orleans wasn't her chosen home because it was familiar, she realized. She'd chosen it, hoping it would make her as hard as it was. That person she'd been on the road between the Solaros' hell and the embassy in Mexico…she'd *needed* to be that person. She'd needed to believe her friends had lived because of her fortitude. That was the strength she had carried into her life after Mexico.

Had it all been a lie? An illusion? She felt frayed, not strong.

Grace didn't get Sloane and Pia out of Mexico. Javier did. It had been him alone—all along. He'd carried Pia and Sloane… and he'd carried her.

On some level, had she always known that? Was that why she felt what she did for him? Were her feelings for him wrapped up in her own weakness?

Deep down, had she thought she still needed him because she knew she was weak and he was strong?

She pressed her fingers into her temples where her headache strengthened. Her thoughts spun wildly, as they often did when the gaps between decent nights of sleep yawned too widely. She needed daylight and clarity. Night had fallen on the parish, and it was going to be a long trip upstream riding shotgun with Javier. And once they got to Casaluna… What then?

Sloane would need to question them about the break-in and the Bourbon Street shooting.

But after? Would she go back to her apartment, or would Sloane hide her away? Would that mean goodbye again for her and Javier? Was she better off that way—no contact? No visits. No breakfasts for two. No walks along the river. No phone calls between her and New Mexico. Just silence, like the kind she'd come home to every night since her mother had slipped away from this world in her sleep.

Dante made the turn for the marina. The parking lot was empty. Dante cranked the wheel as he swung the truck around. He ground the shifter into Reverse and rolled down his window. Leaning out slightly, he backed down to the water. "Hope y'all bundled up. Gone be a cold one."

"Lalie sent blankets," she said, thinking of the additional bag Eulalie had insisted they bring with blankets and a cooler full of food, drinks and more servings of homemade cat food. She'd sent blessings as she held Grace tight on the porch, the flat of her brow pressed to hers. To Javier she'd said, *You take care of my Gracie Boo, Dark Eyes, you hear me?*

Dante braked suddenly, forcing Grace to brace her hands against the dash. He winked at her, putting the truck in Park. "She's wet now."

As he opened his door to disembark, she did the same. The night breeze funneled beneath the collapsed hood of her jacket. The smell of the river sank in, tinged heavily in moss and fish.

The truck's back passenger door closed. She looked around and found Javier with the bags and Luis.

Keeping her eyes low, she took the kitten. "Give me the bags."

Javier shrugged them off his shoulder and helped her take the weight of both. She didn't want to think about the way his scent teased her over the river's.

She made the mistake of raising her gaze. His eyes swallowed her as the river had swallowed a good many secrets.

"Forgive me," Javier said softly. "Lo siento, Grace. Forgive me, por favor."

She heard the cranking of the winch. Stepping out of his warmth, she lowered her eyes again. "See if Dante needs a hand."

Javier paused only a moment before passing slowly around her. He followed the ramp to the water.

Grace breathed a little easier. Toting the cat and the goods, she headed for the dock.

Javier and Dante worked in tandem, one holding the bow rope while the other released the boat from the trailer. It drifted free of its moorings, slender and silent with its center captain's console and rows of seats for passengers. The current tugged. Javier pulled on the rope, bringing her about. As the starboard side bumped against the pilings of the dock, Grace tossed in one bag, then the other. "I hope you're not prone to seasickness," she murmured to Luis as she lowered to the edge of the dock, hooking her toes over the gunwale to steady the boat enough to board.

Tires squealed against the pavement. She looked around as several dark Suburbans careened into the parking lot.

Dante was almost back to the driver's door of the truck. He gripped the open window, assessing the situation. When one of the vehicles swung around and stopped, he turned, waving his hands. "Get low, Gracie!"

Grace felt herself freeze as the windows of the SUVs rolled down and rapid fire exploded into the quiet.

Javier crouched, raising one arm. "In the boat, Grace!" he shouted.

"Dante!" she cried, holding Luis to her tight as she watched the man dive into the driver's seat of his truck. The door closed behind him.

"Grace!" Tossing the bow rope into the boat, Javier hunkered over her. "Get in the boat!"

Feeling his hands low on her hips, pushing, she made herself fall. Her feet hit the deck.

"Get down!" Javier told her and lifted his gun from its sheath at his waist.

The glass over the captain's console shattered. Grace screamed. She flattened herself to the deck.

The sound of more tires and the crunch of metal and honking brought a break in the gunfire. She peeked over the bow.

Dante had rammed his truck's grille into one of the Suburbans. The vehicle had skirted sideways into the one beside it. Gunfire resumed, chasing Dante out of the parking lot. When his taillights disappeared, several men poured out of the vehicles.

Grace spotted the man in the center—the long, slender one. He had wide shoulders and a buzz cut. The way he held himself—shoulders high and back—distinguished him from the others.

She remembered Jaime. His hair had been long and sleek, and he had preferred to tuck his silk shirts into pressed slacks, the picture of sophistication.

His face echoed none of that now. It had been bitten by incarceration—cheeks tucked in like his shirtwaist. Eyes like arrows notching hers in the dark. They left her cold. He lifted his gun and pointed it directly at her face.

She ducked again. Bullets winged across the bow and console. She could hear them hitting the water. Enough shots had discharged she was sure he must have emptied the gun.

A splash reached her ears. She looked around. "Javy?" she called. He wasn't on the dock. *"Javy!"*

One hand clapped over the edge of the boat railing. Then another.

Grace placed Luis safely between the seats. She kept her head low as she rounded the console. The key was in the ignition. She cranked it. The engine fired at the stern. "Hold on!" she called before throwing it in Reverse. She hit the throttle.

The boat shrank quickly back from the ramp. She waited until the bow cleared the dock before whipping the wheel around. As gunfire clattered after them, she lunged for the side of the boat. She grabbed Javier's wrists and yanked.

He hooked his elbows over the side. Grace latched onto his belt and pulled again.

He fell to the deck, water pooling beneath him.

"Are you all right?" she asked, helping him up.

"Can you drive this thing?" he asked, pushing the hair back from his eyes.

"Yes!"

"Do it now!"

She dived behind the console again. Out of the corner of her eye, she could see the men running across the dock. The current pulled the boat away. She switched gears and gunned it.

The engine roared. The smell of exhaust filled the air, and the bow pointed into the wind.

Grace looked back to see the lone man standing at the end of the dock. Jaime watched them motor away. Even as he grew smaller in the distance, she felt the target on her back.

Chapter 10

"How did they find us?" Grace asked frantically. The freezing wind stole her voice. She hadn't slowed the boat since leaving the launch. She could still see Jaime staring after them. He was a sunspot on the back of her eyes.

Pablo Solaro's role in human trafficking had been strictly business. He'd looked at Grace, Pia and Sloane as property. It had been the family patriarch that set the rules of the cartel. That was why nobody ever called the girls by name. Dehumanizing them made the Solaro men disassociate, disconnect. Alejandro had gone from murmuring endearments in Grace's ear as they danced close underneath the stars to calling her names like carne fresca and not taking the trouble to look her in the eye as he forced her into the possession of hungry clients. The only time he touched her after she found out the truth of who he was and what he wanted from her was when she tried to run, and he beat her.

Pia had experienced something worse. Jaime had chosen her. He'd kept her not in one of the Solaro trafficking hideouts as Sloane and Grace had been, but in his own home. He hadn't sold her to other men. He wanted her as his own.

Pia had been a virgin before Mexico—before disappearing behind the wide double doors of Jaime's Spanish-style abode. She'd spoken of what had happened there to Grace and Sloane

in whispers years later, after they'd drained a bottle of wine. It
had been enough to make Sloane cry—and Sloane never cried.

That was when the three of them had made plans to meet at
Casaluna. As long as Jaime was alive, Pia would never be free
of her nightmares. She could learn to live in the present. Being
a mother to her daughter, Babette, helped tie her there. Her relationship with Sam did, too, though she'd hid from the subject of marriage and making things permanent with him like a
thief in the night.

Casaluna was the safety net they'd all devised should their
demons cross into the refuge of their chosen lives.

Behind Grace, Javier braced one hand on the console and
the other between her shoulder blades. "I might know how they
found us," he said.

She felt him shift over his feet. Looking around, she watched
him take his phone out of his pocket. He swiped to unlock the
screen. Several missed calls waited for him.

In the blue lights of the console, he looked white under the
black slashes of his wet hair and brows. The corners of his
mouth tipped down, grim. The bruising around his eyes made
them look sunken and pained. He must have been freezing in
his wet clothes, she thought.

"Could they have traced the call?" he wondered.

She considered. "I'll have to ask Sloane."

But Sloane wasn't there. Javier held the phone in his palm,
not wrapping his fingers around the edges.

"You want to toss it," she realized.

"We can't take the risk of them following us to the safe
house," Javier pointed out. "Do you know the way by water?
Have you ever gone this way before?"

"Yes," she said. "My father had a boat. The safe house is Pia's
mother's old plantation home."

"Your father took you," Javier repeated. "That was before
Mexico."

She saw where he was going with this. It had been over twelve
years since the last time she had made this trip by boat. Twelve
years of change for the bayou. Twelve years for her to forget the
way entirely. She, Pia and Sloane had driven to Casaluna sev-

eral times by car—once after Pia's mother, Luna, passed away to clean out the house and grieve, again for the birth of Babette and a few other times to get away and reconnect with each other. Grace would have no problem driving there, even in the dark.

But she didn't know if she could find the way by water. And without light to illuminate the old guidance markers, the bayou was a watery labyrinth walled by thirsty cypresses, guarded by gators and patrolled by mosquitoes.

The alligators would be in brumation, she thought, trying to think beyond the fear of the dark mass of trees growing thicker on either bank as the boat cruised farther upriver. They didn't feed in winter. Not usually. The cold weather would have chased them out of the water into sunny spots where they'd be lying with their long mouths open.

And while the mosquitoes colonized in water and the bayou must be like Disneyland for them with its wide wet footprint mushed into the earth, they didn't breed in cold weather.

That left the silent winding alleys of the bayou itself to contend with.

Grace studied the console. She flipped on the screen. "There's navigation on this thing," she found.

Javier leaned close over her shoulder. "Do you know how to use it?"

"I think so," she said. She knew the main channels of water they would pass through and the towns they would skirt. Keeping one hand on the wheel, she traced the water chambers with her finger. "This is the way. The hardest part will be up here when we get into these little rivulets." She tapped the capillaries that weaved every which way—tiny unnamed passageways on a big green leaf. She pressed a button. A bright white light on top of the console switched on. It cast a spotlight across the water. "This should help me find the markers to Casaluna…if they're still there."

Javier said nothing. Grace turned her head to him. Why did he look so pale? "Are you all right?" she asked.

He nodded and shifted out of the lights.

She grabbed the wet front of his hoodie to force him back to her. She throttled down a bit with her other hand, watching him blink slowly, his lashes long and spiked. "Look at me," she instructed.

He raised his eyes to hers with some effort. She heard his teeth chatter behind tightly woven lips. His hand loosened around the phone, and it dropped to the deck. He wavered over his feet.

She powered the engine down to idle and let go of the controls. Placing both hands under his arms, she buffered her front against his. She spoke in clipped tones, maneuvering him back to the bench behind the console where Luis had burrowed into a pile of blankets, out of the wind. Taking Javier's phone, she toggled the flashlight and shined it over him.

He winced away.

Cupping her hand around the side of his face, she brought it back to hers. *"Where?"* she asked. He shook his head. She gave him a small rap on the cheek. "Tell me!" she demanded.

Wearily, he lifted a hand and motioned blindly toward his left shoulder.

She grabbed his right sleeve and pulled it free from his arm. Then, carefully, she nudged the open neck over his head. Dampness glued the two shirts to each other. As she peeled them off, they unveiled well-defined muscles. He grimaced and she wished bitterly for scissors. As his clothes plopped heavily on deck, a kettle-whistle of distress flooded her ears. "Dammit!" she shouted as he turned his head away from the nasty smear of blood.

She scrambled back to the console. Yanking open compartments, she fumbled her hands over a flare gun, a whistle, a handheld radio and a vial of Dramamine pills. She swept aside a bag of marshmallows Dante and his crewmate used to lure gators to the boat for the tourists to feed them and found the first aid kit underneath.

When she kneeled in front of Javier again, she caught the way he was breathing. Shallow gulps against the pain and cold. Cursing again, she opened the kit. "Hold still," she told him after tearing open a pack of gauze. Sweeping away blood from the bullet's entry site, she examined it under the phone's flashlight.

The wound was still seeping blood. She pressed the gauze

against it. "Hold this here," she instructed. When he obeyed, she pressed her hand over the back of his. "Tight, okay?"

He gave a slight nod. He tremored.

Hurry, Grace thought. *Hurry, hurry*. She sat on the bench, probing the back of his shoulder. "There's an exit wound," she announced. "The bullet went through clean."

"I f-feel that."

She heard his attempt at levity and wondered at him. "There's a lot of blood." She dabbed, cleaned, cursed, dabbed, cleaned, repeat. "I don't know if I have enough here to..." Her voice broke, and she gritted her teeth. Tearing off her hoodie, she turned it inside out and swiped more blood with it. She addressed the wound, desperately trying to stanch the flow. "You need sutures."

"I t-take it you don't have those in your k-kit," Javier muttered.

"We need to get you to emergency care."

"A h-hospital?" He shook his head. "Not possible."

"Javy, this is serious," she tried to tell him. She didn't stop working, not even to argue. "Both wounds need to be closed. You're losing blood. You may go into shock——"

"You n-need to get to the safe house," he argued. "Jaime c-could be close behind us. I can't let him take you."

"I can't let you stay in this condition," she said heatedly. "You *need* to get to an emergency room."

"You're a good doctor, Grace." His eyes were soft on hers. "You can take care of me."

"You're not listening, Javy!" she yelled and heard the quaver in her voice. She choked down the weakness. His gaze looked unfocused, despite her raised voice. "I don't have what I need and I'm not going to let you go into shock or pass out or..." She couldn't say the rest. They were running out of time. She wadded more gauze together and replaced the blood-soaked gauze pad, biting back the urge to yell. "I'm not going to let you," she finished, shaking her head. "I'll get you bandaged and warm. There's a town on the water not far from here. The medical center will be closed, but I know someone who works there..."

"It's too r-risky," he insisted.

"We'll take our chances." He wouldn't make it all the way to Casaluna.

It was a risk, but Grace would gamble if it meant saving this man's life.

"What is this place?" Javier asked, watching houses on pilings creep out of the swamp like skeletons. It sent a chill down his spine. Or was that the cold? It sank into his bones, refusing to let up. He and Luis hunkered beneath a pile of blankets Grace had wound around them.

"Bayou Saint Christopher," she explained as she worked the wheel to bring them about. The boat bumped against the dock. When he sat up, she pointed at him. "Don't you dare."

He'd have gone against her steely warning and helped her tie up at the dock if the pain hadn't clamped down on his shoulder. Trying not to think about how bad it was or the fact that he had grown light-headed, he gathered Luis against his bare belly, drawing the warmest blanket close around his shoulders.

He saw Grace's silhouette in the moonlight as she bent over, knotting the stern dock line around a second cleat. She was wearing the T-shirt Sabine had given her. Her hoodie was with his on the floor, coated in his blood.

She hadn't let him fall asleep. She'd kept talking to him on the journey, nudging him if he was slow to respond, stopping the boat only to check the gauze and replace it with clean pads.

Someone tapped his cheek, bringing him around. He heard himself moan. When he opened his eyes, she was in front of him. Her hands were cool as she turned them underneath his jaw, bringing his face close to hers. "Stay awake, Javy," she said firmly. "I need you awake."

"Grace," he groaned. "Mi sol…"

"Goddamn it," she whispered before slipping away.

Don't go. He heard dialing. The incessant shivering he'd endured on the ride was slowly slinking away, replaced by a numbness that was distressing but lulling. He heard Grace speaking, giving their location, talking medical jargon in urgent tones.

He took her voice with him as he floated away from her and Luis and the pain and the boat entirely.

Chapter 11

"He needs a transfusion."

Grace nodded. She'd suspected as much. "Do you have the resources for that here?" she asked.

Dr. Salim Ibrahim raised a brow. "There isn't a hospital within forty miles of here. We have to keep the resources on hand."

She shook her head. "Right. You're right. I don't know what I was thinking."

Salim's voice grew gentle. "It's different when the patient's someone you care about."

"I know that. You know I know that." Salim had been at her mother's funeral. He had comforted her and offered to stay with her for a time. They'd gone to medical school together. He'd been the one she'd turned to through the years whenever she'd needed something more to get her through the night.

He was taller than any man she knew. His skin was as dark as the far side of the moon. Built like a steam train, he looked like he belonged on the New Orleans Saints' starting line instead of here in a backwoods medical center where he'd taken the only doctor's position in the community after marrying a woman from Bayou Saint Christopher.

Grace wondered if Salim's wife knew he'd offered to stay with her in New Orleans after her mother's death, then shook the thought loose. Her mind scattered, her thoughts a downpour. She had no cover, no umbrella.

It was why she had insisted that Salim see to Javier's care, why instead of joining them in the OR she'd wandered through the rooms and offices until she found the laundry room and searched the scrubs stacked in cubbies for something of Javier's size. He needed dry clothes. And he would need energy, something to eat and drink. She'd gone to the cafeteria as well, grabbed things blindly from the pantry.

Now she stood with the things in her hands, which weren't steady. Luis mewed. She opened her mouth, hating that she was at a loss. "I don't know his blood type."

"I'll figure it out," Salim assured her. "Sit down, Gracie."

"I'm fine," she began.

He stopped her with, "You're exhausted. Sit."

After lowering to the chair in the nurses' station, she piled the things she had found on the desk and reached for Luis.

Salim's hand draped over her shoulder. "Later, you'll tell me what this is about. Who shot him. Why you arrived in Bayou Saint Christopher by boat in the middle of the night. Who this man is to you."

"Later," she agreed, keeping her head down as she pet the cat. The silky fur beneath her fingertips helped quiet a section of her mind. "Thank you, Salim. I'm sure Alicia wasn't thrilled about you leaving so late."

"Alicia knows she married a doctor. That means I get called out of bed sometimes." He squeezed her shoulder. "I'll test your man's blood and get him what he needs. You sit with your friend and rest."

As his hand slipped away, she eyed the doors to the OR. "Is he awake?"

"He came to for a time while I closed the entry site, then drifted off again before I left. You can go in and see him, if you like, but the cat needs to stay here."

Grace glanced down at Luis. Contorted, he hiked one leg in the air and the other straight out to groom his unmentionables.

When she didn't respond, Salim asked solemnly, "Should I call the police? Do they know about the shooting?"

"We're meeting Sloane. She'll know what to do." But the transfusion. Javier would need to rest. It was routine for a patient who received blood to stay overnight under a doctor's care. She'd left Javier's phone on the boat, along with the bags. The phone on the nurses' desk caught her eye. "What time is it?"

"Just after one in the morning."

She frowned, studying her hands, and willing them to be steady. She'd always been able to count on them in the OR. "I can't sit here and do nothing," she decided. "Give me something. I need something to do or I'll go…"

Salim's smile didn't quite reach his eyes, but he offered it just the same. "I thought you might say that. Scrub up, Dr. Lacroix. Let's get you back in the OR."

When Javier came to again, Grace sat at his bedside. His eyelids twitched several times before he came awake, like a man breaching the surface after drowning. Placing her hand on his wrist, she stood up, touching his good shoulder to keep him from sitting up suddenly. "Easy," she cautioned.

He blinked at her, breathing fast. "Where's Luis?"

"In the next room," she told him. "Animals aren't allowed in the operating room."

"Operating room? Where are we?"

"Bayou Saint Christopher Medical Center," she explained.

He closed his eyes and spouted something in Spanish she was certain was a curse. "Grace. I told you not to bring me here."

"Javy," she said, level. "You passed out before Salim could get you in the ambulance. You lost so much blood you needed a transfusion. Coming here was the right thing and don't you dare try to tell me otherwise."

He reached for his shoulder where a large white bandage winged from arm to neck.

"Are you in pain?" she asked, watching his face. He had good color again—like copper pennies. If not for the bruising, he'd look almost normal.

"Not like before," he said after a moment's thought.

"If it gets to be too much, tell me or Salim," she advised.

"The other doctor."

"Yes," she said. "Dr. Salim Ibrahim. He and his wife, Alicia, live just down the road. This is the closest medical facility for forty miles. He cares for the people of this parish."

"How do you know him?" Javier asked. "Do you trust him?"

"I do," she replied. "We went to medical school together."

Javier surveyed her. "What is he to you now?"

Noting how rapidly his breathing was still, she used her grip on his wrist to check his pulse. It was strong again, if fast. "He's married to a really great person who I happen to both respect and like. Trust me, there's nothing there anymore."

"Anymore," Javier repeated.

She tilted her head. "He may have saved your life."

"I'm grateful," Javier told him. "But I heard him speaking to you."

"And?" she said pointedly.

"He calls you Gracie," Javier noted. "Like Eulalie and Dante."

She looked away, rearranging the sheet. He was naked underneath, and she tried not to think about that as she drew the starch-white fabric from his waist to his sternum. He was still without a shirt. She pulled the blanket up, too. The room was warm, but she didn't want him to feel cold again. "Because he knew my mother, and she called me that, too."

"Things must have been serious for your mother to get involved."

She shook her head. "Salim and I had an on-again, off-again kind of relationship. My mother liked him a great deal, and it disappointed her when she realized I didn't have it in me to give him everything I am. Living with that has been harder than letting him go. He now has someone, though, who loves him without compromise." When Javier only looked at her, she arched a brow. "Does that make you feel better?"

He considered. "I don't know."

"You're hurt," she told him, "and you're tired. Your body's telling you to rest."

"I'm too uncomfortable to rest, and it's not safe for you here."

"We're here and I'm not leaving until you are ready and able to travel again and there's nothing you can say or do, Javier, to make me change my mind."

He dropped his head back to the pillows.

She studied the line of his throat. The muscles were taut. She stroked his wrist. "Are you hungry? I can bring you something."

His hand latched onto her wrist and held. He pulled.

She sat down on the edge of the bed. When the circle of his hand clasped her elbow, she leaned forward, planting her hand against the bedrail.

His head turned on the pillow so that his face was beneath hers. His gaze stroked her. The hand on her arm lifted to frame her jaw. "Are you hurt?"

She shook her head, trying to think through the pull of attraction. "Hurt?"

"At the dock… Jaime and his men… They didn't hurt you, too, did they?"

"No," she assured him.

"I didn't ask," he said, his thumb skimming her cheekbone.

"You were bleeding," she reminded him.

"I'm glad you're all right," he murmured. "Bonita."

She knew the nickname was his testing the waters. She fought a smile. "Vaquero."

His dark eyes flooded with relief and need so substantial it made her gasp.

His fingers spread through her hair to the curve of her neck, urging her closer. He angled his chin.

She let herself be led, knowing what he wanted—and wanting the same thing.

His lips were softer than she'd imagined. Had she imagined? *Yes*, she thought truthfully. His fingers kneaded the space above her hip. Angling her head, she increased the pressure of her mouth to his, drawing a sharp breath in through her nose.

She'd wanted this. And it might scare her, but was her weakness for him really a weakness when it flooded her with light?

She dropped her chin, shying. Like a camera flash, what she felt for him was too bright. She had to blink or back away or…

A satisfactory rumble sounded deep in his chest. "That's worth living for," he said huskily. When his nose nudged against hers, inviting her in again, she remained still. The hand on the back of her neck feathered, caressed. It passed from her hair-line to her shoulder blades and back before he spoke again. "What's wrong?"

She thought about lying to him. *No more lies*, she decided instead. They would both be clear about their knowledge and intentions from this moment forward. "I'm afraid I want this too much."

He eased back against the pillows to gauge her. His touch dappled lightly over the point of her chin. "I've heard you say you've never given all of yourself to a man," he said. "I don't expect you to give all of yourself to me."

"I was incapable of giving all of me before," she pointed out. "Not unwilling. But since you showed up again, you've helped me build bridges. It's not that I feel remote anymore. I feel seen. I feel...touched. And I'm afraid."

"Because you may no longer be incapable," he surmised.

She nodded. "I guess I'm realizing why not every bird wants to fly away once the window opens. The last time I did this, I lost a big part of myself. You're not Alejandro. You'd never hurt me—not like he did. But that doesn't make the leap any less terrifying."

His expression had changed when she'd said Alejandro's name. Threads of tension wove across his brow again.

She frowned. "I shouldn't be laying this on you now."

"Grace, I'm crazy about you," he said in a burst.

Her lips pressed together because his soul was in his eyes, and it hurt to look.

"But I'll wait," he added, "until you're ready."

"You'd...wait for me?"

"Of course I'd wait for you," he murmured.

That part of her that was ready...the one that had already crossed the bridge to the other side, toggled. Grace eyed his soft lips, feeling torn between the past and the present and wish-ing she were free to take what she wanted. She hadn't survived all she had, lived through everything, to back away from what she wanted.

She heard her father's voice—that low warning about the

dangers of swimming in dark waters. But she also could hear her mother's silent entreaty and Eulalie's verbal one that she live her life…that she give *and* take, for once.

He released a breath. She loosened the hand gripping his arm. "I'm sorry," she blurted. "I'm hurting you."

The skin on his biceps didn't feel like the rest. It was satiny in texture. She angled her head, examined it. "What happened here?"

He didn't reply. She traced the round, slightly discolored section, then leaned into what she had seen pass in and out of the ER through the years. It wasn't a cut or burn. She'd seen laser treatments do things like this, but…

Her hand lowered from the spot. Tattoo removal could look like this after a long period of healing. And the space was just wide enough to match the tattoo the rest of the Solaros had worn on their upper arms. She remembered the burned-black Aztec skull on Alejandro.

"They branded you," she realized. "They made you get the Solaro skull."

"I didn't have a choice," he told her.

"When did you get it removed?"

"As soon as I could afford the procedure," he explained. "I had to travel to Taos to have it done, and it took several trips, but it's no longer part of me."

She traced the skin again, this time more slowly. "I hear removal is as painful as getting the tattoo."

"It was worth it," he said. "I wasn't going to carry Pablo's mark any longer than I had to. I'm not one of his."

"You were never," she stated, knowing now how much Pablo and the others had tried to turn him into a cold-blooded monster—like Jaime. "Your mother would be proud of this…proud of you."

He blinked several times, then sat up, her name like a prayer on his lips.

"No," she refused, pushing him back to the pillows. "It's my turn."

She kissed him decidedly. She kissed him until she felt both his hands knot in her baggy shirt, until they both sank into it.

Grace kissed Javier until she felt another piece of herself let go.

"I can move," Javier insisted. Grace and Salim had been debating whether to keep him at the medical center or let him go on to the safe house upstream. He tried appealing to Salim. "The men who shot me most likely know I'm injured. They know we went upriver. The first place they'll look for us is hospitals and medical centers. I need to get Grace out of here before they get to Bayou Saint Christopher."

"I can have the sheriff here in ten minutes," Salim explained. "He'll put guards in place."

"I know these men," Javier warned him. "They're not afraid of a badge."

Grace braced her hands on her hips. "Javier's right." She paced. "I've tried contacting Sloane again by phone. It's not working. Maybe they got to her. Pia, too. What if the reason Jaime's still chasing me is that I'm the last one? What if he's caught the others?"

Javier shook his head. "You can't think like that. But without Sloane to supply transportation for us, I think the best place for us to go would be the safe house. Is there phone service there? If she or Pia or both are already there waiting for us, that could be why we haven't heard from them."

"They turned the phone off after Miss Luna died," Grace answered. "Pia never turned it back on. And there's no cell service."

Salim nodded agreement. "I can take you to the safe house. We can transport Javier in the ambulance if that eases your mind about moving him after the transfusion."

"It would," Grace considered. "However, I'm afraid of the road. Jaime and his men were out there. We know that for certain. They found us at the launch. I turned off Javier's phone. If they're tracking it, maybe that'll throw them off."

"I don't believe they can track it unless I answer," Javier

pointed out. "Wouldn't they have found us at the cemetery if they could trace me through it without making contact?"

Salim appealed to Grace. "If it makes you feel better, we can dispose of Javier's phone and I can provide you with another so you can contact me, Sloane, Pia or the authorities—who I still think should be involved in this."

"They are," Grace said. "We have Sloane."

"If she isn't at the safe house and she still doesn't answer your calls after daybreak, I would advise you to seek help elsewhere," Salim insisted. "I'm acquainted with several of the sheriffs and deputies in this parish. You say the word and they'll be at your door."

"Thank you, Salim," she said. "Do you think I should move Javier?"

Javier felt the probe of both sets of doctor's eyes and tried not to fidget. Salim answered, "His vitals are strong. He's thinking clearly."

"He hasn't been out of the bed since the transfusion," she noted.

Javier tried not to roll his eyes. "Because you won't let me out of bed."

"Let's get him up," Salim said. "Let's get him moving. If he stumbles once or shows any sign of weakness, it's transport by ambulance only. If he can get around with no issues, the boat shouldn't be a problem as long as he's kept warm."

Grace nodded. She approached the bed. "Let's get you upright. If you have any dizziness, say so. If you can sit up with no problem, I'll let you stand."

She reached for the sheet at his waist. He flattened her hand across his stomach. "I don't think…"

She closed her eyes as realization struck. "Bon Dieu. You're still naked under the sheet, aren't you?"

"If you'd like to step out, Dr. Lacroix," Salim said, "I can help the patient dress."

Grace nodded quickly, sliding her hand away from Javier's. "I'll try Sloane again on her cell, then make sure Luis hasn't made any messes in the hall."

Salim waited until she left the room and the door clicked shut.

He lifted the folded scrubs she had found for Javier and handed them over. Javier reached for them, muttering, "Gracias."

The muscles of Salim's face grew rigid. "I don't know who you are. I don't know how you and Gracie know each other or where you come from. All I know is I care about her deeply, and whatever you're involved in, she shouldn't be."

Javier opened his mouth to reply, but Salim held up a large hand to stop him. "I'm sure you've got a story. From the sounds of it, the two of you have a history. Which means you know her well enough to know that she doesn't deserve to be mixed up in whatever mess you got her into. The Gracie I know doesn't like guns, much less the man *with* the gun. She may somehow have learned to trust you. But I don't. And the only thing stopping me from calling Sheriff Beaumont is my word to her. You understand?"

Javier frowned. "You care for her a great deal for a man who's married to someone else."

Salim tilted his head dangerously. "Oh, we're doing this now?"

"Apparently." Though Javier wished Salim had let him dress first.

"Gracie is my friend," Salim explained. "Foremost, we were always friends. Things might've progressed over the years. That part of our relationship ended, and I'm fine with that."

"I can see that," Javier threw in, earning a threatening flex from the area around Salim's jaw. "I can see a lot of things."

"She knows she can count on me," Salim pointed out. "Can she say the same for you?"

"I'm going to get her out of this," Javier told him.

"How're you going to manage that when you're flat on your back?" Salim wondered. "You're lucky to be alive right now."

"I promised her I'd get her to Sloane," Javier explained. "And I'd die before I let anything happen to her. I don't expect you to believe that. As you say, I'm just the guy with the gun. But it's the truth."

Salim crossed his arms over his chest in a slow motion, shifting his weight to his heels. "The truth." Shaking his head, he looked at the closed door. "She has feelings for you. So, from one old friend of Gracie's to another, you better succeed. And you better not break her heart in the process. Like her, I'm a highly trained medical professional. I know how to take pain away. And I know how to give it. Now let's get you ready."

Javier tensed. "You think, after that, I'm going to let you dress me?"

"I do," Salim asserted. "And you're going to let me because if she comes back in here and you're not on your feet, she'll have you back in bed before you can say 'Allons.'"

Chapter 12

"Feels solitario," Javier mumbled.

"What's that?" Grace questioned from the captain's chair. She pried her focus off the beam of the spotlight, illuminating the winding corridors of the bayou. The pile of blankets at the boat's stern didn't stir. The man was doing as instructed and staying put, at least.

"This place," he spoke again. "It feels lonesome."

She spun the wheel hand over hand when a fallen tree's branches leered into sight. She had cut the engine almost to an idle to avoid running adrift onto the close-wedged banks or veering into obstructions in the murky water.

It felt wrong, too, to disturb the bayou's thick sounds with the motor's roar.

The crickets and katydids were eerily silent, their loud cries replaced by a winter-breeding frog song. Even with that backdrop, the bayou did feel lonely. Its haunting mysticism gave her the impression of a lost world. Or a forbidden one. They were well past Bayou Saint Christopher. According to the navigation radar, the boat was traveling along one of the unnamed rivulets into what Grace would've thought was no-man's-land had she not spotted the markers her father had taught her to look for as a child—an old plantation house crumbling into ruin on the west bank...an ancient cypress whose pregnant trunk was distinctive amid its counterparts with the words SWAMP COUNTRY carved from its bark…a large sign with painted letters warning that this was breeding ground for gators…

The familiar sights had banked Grace's anxiety about finding the right way upstream to a murmur. The bayou might have been a strange, solemn land where water and wild lived cheek to jowl. But it was also home.

She'd spread her father's ashes in these waters. Pia's mother had died in the old white house her brothers had bought her after her mental breakdown, drowned in a bottle of her own regret. Babette was bayou-born. She had come into the world during a torrential flood—by accident, of course. Pia hadn't wanted her daughter to be born in the same house Luna Russo had died in. But life, earth, space, time… They all worked in circles, Grace thought. She eyed Javier once more. He'd borrowed a ski cap from Salim to help keep him warm enough for the journey. Five-o'clock shadow sprawled across his trim jaw. It matched the dark shadows under his eyes, present even in repose.

She hoped he was sleeping, not unconscious again. She thought of nudging him to be sure but decided not to disturb his rest if he was indeed snatching a few winks of healing sleep.

Grace checked the radar again. The house should be just ahead. She should see it in the spotlight. The sagging dock… then the splintered boards of the boardwalk up to the sprawling front porch.

Spanish moss hung along the shoulders of the bank, masking everything. Grace panicked again…

A guttural cry caught her attention. Her head spun to port. Her mouth dropped at the sight of a lone pelican gliding alongside the boat, wings fanned wide. It flapped them once before gliding on an air current, inches from the water.

She'd seen no other birds, no other creature at all since waving goodbye to Salim at the boat launch at Bayou Saint Christopher. The sight of the pelican sent dread into her bones. What was it doing this far upstream? Why didn't the sight of the boat and the noise of the engine spook it?

Its hoarse cry whisked from the deep pouch underneath its bill before it lifted on the wind and flew across the bow.

Grace watched, transfixed, as it crossed into the spotlight, before its gray wings fluttered, lifting it higher into the canopy.

The boat slowed and the motor complained as silt on the bayou floor rose up to grab it. Grace cursed, tightening her hands on the wheel to turn it before the bow could become wedged.

Then she saw it—like a dried floral bouquet long after the wedding's end. The white facade of Luna's grand bayou house glowed at the attention of the boat's searchlight.

"Javy," she said. She cut the engine and turned to kneel by the bench. Reaching into the blankets piled on top of him, she found Luis, who mewed irritably at being snatched from sleep. "Wake up, Javy! Wake up!"

"Mmph," he groaned, eyelids flickering. "Did we run aground?"

"No," she said, beaming. "We're here."

Grace splashed into the shallow water to tug the bowline, guiding the boat the rest of the way to the dock. She secured it before switching off the searchlight. She turned on the flashlight she'd found among Dante's supplies. "Uh-uh," she called to Javier, who had stooped to pick up Eulalie's and Sabine's bags. "Let's get you and Luis up to the house. I'll come back for those."

"You jumped in the water," Javier said, not resisting when she braced herself under his arm and boosted him to the dock.

"It's knee-deep," she dismissed. "And the boat was hung up."

"You could have landed on an alligator."

"The gators are in brumation right now," she explained. When he narrowed his eyes in misunderstanding, she went on. "Mammals hibernate. Reptiles brumate."

"They sleep through winter?"

"Not completely. They wake up to drink to stop dehydration, but they don't feed. When it's cold, the gators either burrow into the mud or they'll lie still in the water with their noses showing like a snorkel. On warmer days, you'll see them basking on the bank. The scutes on their backs distribute heat through their bodies. You know when they're warm enough because they'll leave their mouths open to relieve some of it."

"They do this for how long?"

"Depending on how cold it gets...anywhere from four to five months. They start around Thanksgiving."

He cursed after a moment. "It's nearly March."

"So?" The boardwalk to the porch groaned under their feet. She kept the flashlight beam in front of them, watching for holes in the worn planks. The go-go boots had been waterproof. However, the chill of the night air seeped in around her knees, thanks to her wet jeans.

"They'll be waking up soon," he said. "And they'll be hungry."

"Most likely."

"If we let Luis out for a bathroom break, we'll need to keep an eye on him."

"I won't argue that."

"This is where Pia grew up?" Javier asked as the boardwalk inclined to the steps and the screen door beyond.

Grace strained to hear voices from inside the house. It was still nighttime, but wouldn't Pia and Sloane have heard the boat? She needed to know her friends were here. If they weren't... "Yes and no," Grace considered. She wrapped her fingers around those of the hand he'd thrown over her shoulders. "Her mother wasn't what you'd call stable. She had a series of mental breakdowns after the death of Pia's father. Her brothers, the Russos, bought her this house so she would have a place to recover—far away from the city's vices."

"The same Russos who own the pizzeria below your apartment?"

Grace watched the windows closely. There was no light anywhere inside the house. Maybe the drapes were closed. Luna Russo had commissioned blackout curtains for each room . When she was on a bender, she'd pulled all the drapes, closing the eyes of the house and her own to the world. "Yes. When Pia started Catholic school in New Orleans, she lived with Giovanni, his wife and kids. During summer and school breaks, she lived here. She's gifted. Did you know that? Eidetic memory. Her IQ's off the charts. She's high-functioning and was summa cum laude, valedictorian... Not that that stopped any of our well-todo classmates from calling her 'swamp rat.' She would have had a free academic ride to the college of her choice."

"I take it that didn't happen," he said solemnly.

"No, it didn't," she replied. They'd reached the porch steps. She wished Sloane's sharp-angled face would appear at the windows. Grace realized she wouldn't feel entirely safe. Not until Sloane made her presence known. She searched with the flashlight, revealing empty garden pots and the glider that, like the boardwalk, needed repair.

"Because of the baby?"

Grace slid her gaze to Javier's. His mouth was grim around the edges. And his eyes looked sad. She swallowed the lump in her throat. Then she nodded silently. "Nothing good came out of Mexico *except* Babette. She was born in this house. Several weeks early. We never would have coaxed Pia to come here for a babymoon if we'd known Babette would come early. There came a flood that washed out the roads, so when Pia started having contractions, we couldn't get out and emergency personnel couldn't get in. So Babette was born in the bed in the upstairs suite."

"You were by yourselves?"

Grace widened her eyes for emphasis. "I don't know who panicked more, me or Sloane. Pia just wanted the baby out. Babette came fast into the world. By the time Sloane and I got Pia up the staircase, the bayou was creeping up the porch steps and she was crowning."

"Who delivered her?"

From the knowing look in his eyes, he already knew, but Grace said it anyway. "I did. Sloane took one look at the top of Babette's head when we got Pia undressed and nearly sank to the floor, so I thought she'd be better in a support position behind Pia's back. The first thing Babette heard or saw was the three of us screaming, crying…and then laughing because in spite of the fact that none of us had a clue what we were doing beyond the Lamaze classes we sat through together in varying states of denial and horror, that sweet little babe opened her mouth, took her first breath and started to scream and cry, too." Grace felt the urge to sink to the porch step and lay her cheek to the foundation. Instead, she unwound Javier's arm from around her shoulders and tried the door. "It's locked." She shook her head, unable to take it in. "They're... They're not here."

"No one's been here for a long time," he said. His hand touched the space above her hip. "It's okay, Grace. I'm sure they're all right."

She didn't know what to believe anymore. "Sit here a minute. I need to find the key."

She made sure he sat on the stoop before she rounded the building. She kept her footsteps light and quiet, peering through windows and venturing a look at the long drive. There were no cars. No lights. No signs of life. The only footsteps in the damp earth around the house were her own. She found the key under the designated coffee can in the garden and went back to the porch.

"Was that when you knew?" he asked as she worked the key in the lock.

"Knew what?"

"Did you know you wanted to be a doctor when you delivered Pia's baby?"

She blinked in surprise. "Yes," she heard herself saying. The lock released. "After the initial panic, something came over me. This calm. It'd been so long since I'd felt calm after coming home. I could hear the clear-cut voice inside my head again—the one that helped you get Pia and Sloane to safety. It knew what to do. And, for the first time since we reached the embassy, so did I."

"You do know you've always been that person? You've always had that inside you. I saw it...that first night at the villa. I think that's when I knew that I couldn't stay inside the Solaros' cartel. No matter the cost to my mother's name. I knew I'd find some way to get you out."

She licked her lips, swinging the door open wide. They'd suddenly gone dry. He had one arm braced against the wall of the house. He was tired and bedraggled—he'd brushed by the graveyard tonight. And yet he shined at her out of the grim night like another one of those clear-cut markers, pointing her in the right direction. Before, it had happened here, too—ten

years and ten months ago, almost to the day. Her heart picked
up pace. For once, she didn't try to control the knocking. She
listened. "I would have asked you to breakfast," she gave away,
leading him inside.

He seemed to know not to say anything. Even as the lines
in his brow eased, he stilled to listen as she shut the door behind them.

"Café du Monde," she continued. "Beignets. Café au lait. A
table for two with a view of Jackson Square. Would you have
come?"

He didn't hesitate. "Si."

She took a steadying breath and rushed on. "I would've asked
you to walk the Quarter with me after. Moonwalk. Market. Dai-
quiris before lunch."

"Yes, yes and yes," he replied.

She sighed and closed her eyes. "Lunch to follow because one
drink makes me tipsy. Oysters Rockefeller to make you change
your religion. To make you come back."

He shook his head quickly. "I had other reasons to come
back."

"Mmm." She rubbed her lips together. The urgency to kiss
him built behind them. She smiled and hugged herself. "We
could've walked some more. Caught a streetcar. Hit the Pryta-
nia for an afternoon showing of that new Tom Cruise thriller."

"The Disney one," he offered as an alternative. "With the
dog. I'm a sucker for a good tearjerker."

Her teeth flashed as joy eclipsed the need to contain whatever this was inside her—this lightning storm. Every bolt in-
vigorated.

"Where could I have taken you for dinner, after?" he asked,
his easy grin flying in the face of his exhaustion.

It looked good on him. "You would have missed your flight."

"And you would have missed your shift," he added, pushing
away from the wall of the door. He crossed to her.

"Yes," she admitted. "We wouldn't have talked about Jaime.
Though you wouldn't have stopped looking over our shoulders."

"No," he said with a shake of his head. "I'd have wanted another night at your place, watching over you and Luis."

His hand had risen to her temple. The pad of his thumb caressed the centerline of her brow. Hearing his labored breathing, she pulled him down with her to the dust cloth draped over the couch. "At what point in the day would you have kissed me, Javy?"

He considered. "I'd have thought about it at breakfast, probably tried to hold your hand on the walk…"

"Mmm-hmm." She was close enough to him now she didn't feel the chill anymore.

"I would have put my arm around you during the movie, invited you to put your head on my shoulder."

"I'd have eaten most of the popcorn while you worked your way up to it," she warned.

A chuckle whisked through him. "I like that about you. I like everything about you."

His brow flattened against hers, and she lost her train of thought. They shared a breath. Two. She trembled. His hands passed over her arms. "It's cold in here," he said.

She shook her head. "I'm still waiting for you to kiss me. Who knew vaqueros moved so slowly?"

"We're slow when it matters."

"Twelve years slow?" she teased.

He sobered. "If I'd have kissed you in Mexico, it would have scared you."

She thought about it. "I wouldn't have been afraid—not of you. Conflicted, yes. But not afraid."

"The doorstep," he decided after a moment. "I'd have pulled you close on your doorstep after dinner."

His hands crossed over the small of her back, bringing her navel snug against his, as if showing her.

His cheek grazed hers, rough with stubble, and his lips were at her ear. "Would you have asked me to come in?"

She nuzzled a kiss against his jaw. "I would have pulled you across the threshold. And we wouldn't have spent the next few hours talking."

He made a noise in his throat. Fingers spread through her hair, cupping the back of her head. His mouth fit to hers.

She liked that he wasn't too tall. She didn't have to lift herself onto her toes to increase the pressure of her mouth. He trembled just as she did, and she enjoyed the long, covetous noise that escaped him as he opened his mouth to hers and she responded in kind. *More*, she thought, quickening.

A small mew sounded from the wide pocket of his hoodie.

She wouldn't have stopped for anything else. "We—we're crushing Luis."

"He's okay," Javier murmured. "Just hungry."

"He eats like a teenage boy." And she was still trying to catch her breath. "I don't know if it makes it better."

"What?" he asked, brushing the curls from her cheek with a sweep of his palm.

"Knowing," she replied. "What could have been." When he caressed her cheek and frowned, she sighed. "You need to lie down."

"Lie with me?"

She arched a brow. "You just had a transfusion."

The corner of his mouth lifted. "I meant to sleep."

"I'll build a fire in the fireplace, get us all something to eat from Lalie's bag…then we rest and wait for the others."

"They are coming," he assured her as she trailed off.

That voice inside her had its doubts. "I'm not sure I could live with the alternative."

Chapter 13

The house had a strong musty tinge from disuse. It was clear no one had lived at Casaluna in some time. Grace located the power box and turned on the breakers. Lights flickered on in the outdated kitchen and den, golden and homey. A cloud of dust flew into the air as she yanked covers off the couches. Luis chased the motes, going up on his hind legs before sneezing repetitively and backing out of the room, back arched, tail high.

Javier helped Grace turn on the water main. The pipes complained when she turned on the kitchen tap. She let it run for a minute before filling a glass and lifting it to the light to test the quality. Deeming it safe, she filled a crystal bowl with water and set about making a very early breakfast.

As she reheated the leftover red beans and rice and the boudin Eulalie had packed for them in pots and pans on the stove, Javier walked through the house. There was no sign of forced entry. No broken windows. He stepped out onto the front porch, trying to pick apart one form from another. Trees tangled over the narrow, shell-lined drive. There was no protective screen. The porch was columned with a second-floor balcony sagging over it.

Finding nothing threatening outside, he went back in. Floral wallpaper, framed photographs of bayou life and oil-painted seascapes covered the walls. There was one small portrait of a woman sitting by the sea in a straw hat, her knees drawn up, shins long, toes bare. She wore a sundress, and her straight, dark hair fell long and thick over her shoulders.

Pia, Javier realized with a start. It took a moment to recognize her because she was smiling. Squinting into the corner of the painting, he tried to read the looping signature.

Babette.

Javier raised a brow. A child had painted this? He glanced over the seascapes and found the style and brush strokes were similar.

Halfway up the staircase, he found the thermostat. The wind fluted down the fireplace, whistling. It had chilled the rooms at large. Hoping to coax some heat into them, he switched it on.

A roar from the subfloor made him stare at the floorboards.

Grace hurried into the room. "You turned on the heater?"

"Si," he said, eyeing the floor above them when it moaned, too.

"You woke the beast," she said apprehensively.

"Turn it off?" he asked and jerked at the sound of knocking at the side of the house.

She laid a hand on his arm when he moved toward the door again to investigate. "It's the unit. Smell it?"

The vent over their heads emitted lukewarm air. It curled, charred, up Javier's nostrils. "That's not good."

"Leave it on for a minute," she suggested after some consideration. "If the smell doesn't burn away, we'll turn it back off."

"How old is the wiring in this place?" he asked. "Has there ever been a fire?"

"No, to the second. As to the first, I have no idea. The plantation seemed ancient when Luna took it over. Floodwaters and time have done work on the place." Her lips turned down as she reached up to touch her hand to his brow. "You're clammy. Come sit. Your plate's ready."

He followed her into the dining room. His feet felt heavier than they should, and his pulse was up. Fatigue pressed in from all sides. He didn't so much sit at the table as slump. The sight of warm food made him perk up somewhat. He circled his hand around her arm and passed it over her wrist. "Gracias, mi sol."

She stroked the line of his shoulders before settling into the chair beside him. "Luis ate so quickly, I thought he was going to heave it all back up." Watching Javier eat, she forked the savory leftovers to her mouth and chewed slowly. "There's a bedroom on the first floor and a hall bathroom. We can use those to rest and freshen up. I'll need to make the bed and uncover the furniture, clean out the tub before Pia and Sloane get here. I'd like to get the rooms ready upstairs for their arrival."

Javier studied her profile. She kept her eyes down. He wondered whether the doubt her friends would arrive safely was still there. "I'll help you."

"Your job is rest and recovery," she told him. "I want your feet up."

"I'm not sure I know how to put my feet up," he admitted.

"Vaqueros don't take self-care days?" she asked.

He slanted her a telling glance. "About as many as trauma surgeons, I expect."

She had no rebuttal. "Over the next two days, I'm going to have to insist you develop a decidedly laissez-faire attitude."

"Will our food supplies last that long?" he wondered.

She pointed her fork at him. "Rest first. Then we worry about the practicalities."

He nodded in agreement, then sat back in the chair because he, too, was eating too fast.

"Do you need pain meds?"

Shaking his head, he closed his eyes.

"I'll go get the bed ready."

He caught her hand before she could leave. Tugging, he urged her into his lap. "You need rest, too, Grace. You've been alert too long."

"Are you saying I'm punchy?" she asked, amused.

He smiled. "A little."

She surprised and thrilled him by lowering her face to his and slowly drawing the center of his lower lip into her mouth. She suckled, then nibbled lightly.

His response was visceral and not at all consistent with the weak patient she presumed him to be. "Is this your usual bedside manner?"

She kissed him flat on the mouth—a hot, stinging kiss—then patted him on the cheek a little harder than necessary.

He laughed as she set herself back on her feet, grabbing both plates. "Five minutes, cher," she instructed. "Then I'm tucking you in."

As she took the plates into the kitchen, he stared after her. When the hunger lifted once more, wolfish and enlivening, he forced himself to look away. He tipped his head against the high back of the wooden chair and breathed carefully.

If Sloane didn't show tomorrow, Javier wasn't going to be able to stop Grace from assuming the worst.

Sloane was FBI. She'd known about Pablo's death and Jaime's escape. She studied human traffickers extensively. No doubt, she'd done a thorough analysis on the Solaros.

Which could only mean Sloane knew the truth—that Javier was Pablo's third son. Javier dreaded confronting her again. There wasn't any way she would lie to Grace, too.

His identity would be revealed. And Grace would be lost to him.

But if Jaime had captured Sloane or Pia or both, it would devastate Grace. The free girls weren't whole without one another. That Javier had seen.

The house whispered of history. It spoke of birth and death. Renewal and anguish.

He felt like an intruder. An imposter. The feeling wouldn't let him go, no matter how much Grace trusted him or how far and fast he was falling for her.

Whether the other women arrived at Casaluna, Javier had to tell Grace the truth.

Grace woke to find tender rays of midmorning sunlight reaching toward the bed from the parting of the drapes. She lifted her head, bemused she'd slept so late, and paused at the sight of Luis curled nose to tail on the pillow. His eyes remained closed, and his purring had fallen silent.

About time, she thought, remembering how his burst of energy after the long boat ride had escalated into chasing dust motes across the floor, scampering from one end of the couch to the other and back, and batting the tassels of Luna's old drapes. When she'd tried settling him in bed next to Javier's sprawled form so she could shower, the feline had sat up against the pillow, his pupils large as they followed the restless pendulum motion of his tail.

She'd failed again to shower. She'd gotten only as far as taking off her wet jeans. As soon as she turned on the spray and steam rose, pipes shrieking in protest, her nerve had vanished. Memories of unnamed hands snatching at the edges of her towel and Alejandro's cruel, empty expression made her lower to the closed seat of the commode and drop her face into her hands.

She'd settled for a sponge bath from the sink, chastising herself again for acting like a victim. She'd then changed into the old T-shirt, running shorts and roomy socks of Pia's boyfriend, Sam, that she'd found in the dresser.

She listened for noise from the rest of the house. Branches tapped against the windows. She could hear a squirrel scratching incessantly from somewhere inside the fireplace flue. But other than that…nothing.

Her heart fell. Pia and Sloane still hadn't made it.

She felt a band around her middle and looked down to find Javier's taut forearm pressed against her navel.

Her lungs seized. She could hear his sleepy respirations, feel his exhales fluttering the curls over her shoulder. The heat of his form sank clean through the thin shirt and shorts, launching her awareness of him through the troposphere.

In the night, he had turned to her, and she hadn't pushed him away.

The knowledge brought an unexpected smile. And the longing that swept her body brought her to the peak of wakefulness. Her eyes closed, and she sucked in a long breath, feeling the sweet, devastating arcs sink clean through her. The need was there—to turn to him, into him, return his embrace, validate it so the golden heat could take her away.

She lay still, however. Not frozen. Just still. She'd only taken what she'd wanted with men when she felt safe. Javier made her feel protected. Cherished, even. *Mi sol.* She didn't have a clue what it meant when he said it, but he'd said it at his weakest point...on the brink of unconsciousness... He'd said it when she'd been paralyzed by fear...at her lowest...

She sighed. She *knew* what it meant.

It meant everything.

But Jaime was out there with his mercenaries. Pia hadn't made contact. Sloane was missing in action.

She couldn't give in to her feelings. Not now with everything around them so uncertain.

She lifted his arm from around her and scooted out from under it. Laying it gently on the hand-sewn quilt, her gaze snagged on his face.

He snored lightly. She chalked that up to his broken nose. The five-o'clock shadow wove appealingly across his jaw. She curled her hand into a fist to stop her fingers from dragging across the new texture of his neglected cheeks. His midnight-black lashes lay heavy and closed, the bruising more red than purple now. The lines in his brow were slack and despite the exposure from the New Mexico sun weathering his skin, he looked almost boyish.

Grace turned away from the sight of him, throwing her legs over the side of the bed. Her hair was in tangles. She desperately needed that shower.

Balling her hands into the mattress, she pushed herself up. When Luis lifted his head, peering at her through narrowed crystal eyes, she held out her arms.

He unfurled slowly, stopping to stretch his front legs long out in front of him, then staggered to the edge of the bed.

Together, they ventured through the house to the front door.

As Grace opened it, hope toggled briefly. But when she saw the empty shell-lined drive and yard broken only by puddles, her stomach did a sickening lurch.

Where are they? Why aren't they here?

The early-morning air wasn't as chilled as she anticipated. Rain had brought a small wash of humidity. The birds called from treetops and the frogs answered. Hints of spring, she thought, seeing the daffodils pushing up around the base of an ancient water oak. She set the kitten at the bottom of the wide steps and watched him pick his way slowly across loose shells and wet grass, wondering if last night's pelican was somewhere close by.

Or had she imagined it? Stranger things had happened here.

She ran her fingers along the marks inscribed in the closest column, reminders of how far the bayou had risen with the name and date of the storm responsible—Ida, Laura, Katrina, Camille and over a dozen in between, some with only a date. Pia, Sloane and Grace had labeled one simply as *Babette*. Grace traced the letters lovingly, wishing her friends would come sprinting down the drive.

She blinked rapidly. "I need to know where you are," she said out loud. She strengthened the words. *"I need to know."*

Luis offered a solitary answer, hopping from the ground to the step to rub his cheek against her baggy sock.

She lifted him and took one last look down the long, empty drive, before going back into the house.

Luis followed her eagerly into the kitchen, clawing at her other sock. "All right!" she said and hissed as his claws dug through the fabric. "You're hungrier than a bull gator." Still, she took time to start the coffee she'd found in a plastic baggie in the pantry with the expiration date handily scrawled in Pia's precise handwriting on the label. Everything in the pantry was labeled and arranged alphabetically. As Grace measured out the grinds, she shook her head fondly at her friend's meticulousness.

The kitten didn't have to wait long for his second breakfast. She placed the bowl on the floor, then addressed the food items from Eulalie and Sabine.

There were several power bars left. Some bottles of water. Not many, she considered, pursing her lips. She and Javier had barely made a dent in the red beans and rice container and the boudin would last them through three more meals. Making calculations in her head, she squeezed the sausage mixture from its casing into a sizzling pan on the stove. She found maple syrup, brown sugar, honey and cinnamon among the pantry items, too, and—perhaps best of all—a sealed package of quick grits. "That'll do," she murmured decisively.

By this point, the morning light was white and brisk as it gleamed through the kitchen panes. It shot through the deep green glass bottles hanging from the boughs of the nearest tree, talismans to ward the inhabitants of the house from "haints," or evil spirits. It was said the pretty green bottles caught more haints than clear ones. Grace had always taken that for a fact as she'd never seen a haint around Luna's house, despite its lore.

With her glassy eyes and flowing white nightgown, Luna herself was the closest thing to a ghost Grace, Sloane and Pia had ever seen in the bayou. *Behold, the disappearing woman*, Grace had thought, watching Luna float down the stairs, pale underneath the knotted reams of her dark hair, the liquor bottle sloshing in her hand seemingly more solid than she was. It had driven a chill through her bones more effectively than anything she'd seen in Lafayette Cemetery No. 1.

Grace had learned that the living were far scarier than the dead.

She found enough tea bags and sugar to make tea. If it was warmer, she would have set it out on the porch like her father had taught her. *Sun tea'll heal whatever ails ya*, he'd instructed.

She knew someone who could use some healing.

She thought of the man still abed. Wondering what her daddy would've thought of Javier, she filled one of the Blue Willow dinner plates with the bounty she'd scrounged. She stuffed the medicine bottle Salim had given her before their departure from Bayou Saint Christopher into the pocket of the running shorts and carried the plate and a bottle of water to the open door of the bedroom.

Luis was back in bed, sprawled across Javier's abdomen. The man was awake and petting the kitten in indulgent strokes.

He was devastating and handsome despite the abuse to his face and he smiled at her when he saw her. "Luis tells me I've slept half the morning away."

"Luis should've let you sleep," she rebutted, setting the plate on the bedside table. She cracked the cap on the bottle and thrust it at him. "Hydrate."

"Buenos días to you, too, bonita," he greeted. He took the bottle and tilted his head. "You didn't have to fix me breakfast."

"Doctor's orders are for you to take it easy," she reminded him. "When you're recovered, you can cook for me."

"I look forward to that." He grunted, attempting to sit up. A grimace painted his face.

Grace braced a hand underneath his shoulder. "Go slow. You're running on empty where Salim's morphine is concerned. And pain's always worse the day after."

"You're telling me." He reached for the bandage, muttering in Spanish.

She mussed a hand over his messy hair. The strands were thick between her fingers. "You need food in your belly before you take your medicine."

She handed him the plate and fork and made a grab for Luis when he eyed it eagerly, standing on his hind legs to get a better look. "Down, boy," she muttered into his fur before setting him on the rag rug at the bedside. Lowering to the edge of the bed, she placed her fingers on Javier's wrist. She located his pulse. "It's still higher than I would like, but I bet that will come down once the medicine kicks in and the pain lessens."

He ate quietly. The grooves dug into his brow, a road map of pain.

She pressed the back of her hand to his brow, then his neck. "No fever. I'll need to check your sutures, see if there's any drainage."

"The bandage is dry," he said between bites. "Your friend did a good job."

She wished he wouldn't sound so grudging about it. "You'll have to send him a thank-you. He prefers single malt brandy, by the way."

"He was in love with you once," he reported. "You know this, sí?"

She closed her mouth quickly. "No."

Javier looked down at his plate. "He threatened me if I failed to keep you safe."

"Interesting," she said after a moment's thought. "He doesn't still…"

He shook his head, then dropped the fork to take a sip of water. When he swallowed, he replied, "His wife holds his affections now."

"How do you know he felt that way about me?" she asked curiously.

Again, he didn't meet her gaze. With a shrug, he settled for a nonanswer.

She eased back, trying to read him.

"You look pretty in the morning."

She reached for her hair. "I look like a haint."

"A what?"

"Never mind. It's my hair. It needs a wash."

He wiped his mouth with the paper napkin she'd brought. "Does the shower not work?"

"The shower works fine," she said. "Hot water aplenty. It's me. I'm the dysfunctional one."

"What do you mean?"

She'd already exposed her other failing to him—that she froze when confronted with real danger. Would he think she was pathetic if she told him about another? Particularly this one. Wanting to shrink from his sight, she picked a place on the wall and stared. "I can't—shower."

"Why not?"

She took a bracing breath. "Because I was showering when Jaime, Alejandro, you and the others stormed the villa in Mexico. Since you told me about Jaime's prison break, I haven't been able to bring myself to—"

He dropped his fork with a clatter. "Grace."

She closed her eyes against the sound of pity. "Don't, please. I already feel like a fool."

He reached for her, then stopped. His hand fell to the bed between them. Haltingly, he asked, "Is it me? Am I the reason you can't shower?"

She shook her head. Her fingers captured his wrist at the same time his linked hers. "You've never been the subject of my nightmares. Not once. But if someone else got into the house... I can't hear through the sound of the spray. And when I'm naked, I feel more vulnerable, naturally. In the shower, you're supposed to relax, let down your guard... It's routine. A mindless task and a ritualistic one. And I can't bring myself to do it. I can't lower my guard enough." The breath had backed up in her lungs, or the pressure was building in her chest. She exhaled, trying to release some of it. Training her eyes to the cords of his arm, she followed the rivers of veins underneath the surface, trying to anchor herself to him. When she caught herself tracing them in light strokes, she pulled away. "Finish eating so you can take the medication."

He didn't let her go so easily. He held her wrist, firm. She dragged her stare back to him and he leaned toward her, reaching up with his free hand to tease the curls over her ear. "What if I guarded the door?"

"What?"

"What if I stood outside the door and guarded it?" he asked.

She eyed the bandage peeking out from underneath the neckline of his shirt. "You can't fight anyone right now."

"I still have this."

When he pulled the gun out from under the pillow, she fumbled. "How…"

"Salim returned it to me," Javier told her, "reluctantly. But he said if it would help me protect you, he didn't see a choice."

When he let go of her wrist, leaving her hand limp on the quilt squares, he removed the catch and dropped the heavy magazine to his lap. Brows drawn together, he yanked back the slide and action, unchambering the round. When he saw her flinch, he stilled. "Guns scare you, don't they?"

"A kid died on my table this week after taking two .38 Specials. Before he went under, he begged me to save him, and I assured him he would wake up, good as new, in post-op. I lied, Javy. I knew his odds before I washed my hands and gloved up."

"I'm sorry, mi sol," Javier murmured.

"I'm not scared of guns," she clarified. Her tear ducts burned. She blinked to clear them. "But they do make me angry."

He nodded. "Entiendo."

She eyed the one in his hand. "It went in the water with you last night. Does it even work?"

"It'll need to be cleaned," he acknowledged, closing one eye as he angled the weapon and peered down the length. "I'll need to test it."

"Not anywhere near the house," she requested.

"No," he agreed. "I'll clean it before you shower, then go to the woods and fire a few rounds away from the house."

"After you take your meds. And I check your wounds. And you rest a bit more."

He smiled, wiping the tension from his face. He tipped the gun to the bed and laid the magazine and the single round next to it. "Are those my orders?"

"Si," she replied. Then, because the conversation had taken the brightness out of the morning, she touched her mouth to his.

He dropped his fork again and made a noise as he angled his head, accepting, giving back.

Shooting stars rained down her chest and legs. Her pulse had quickened at his taste. The scrub of the early growth of beard abraded the soft skin of her cheek as she pressed it to his. He breathed against the line of her throat roughly. Closing her eyes, she savored being here with him. Her nerves danced, and for one blessed moment, her mind emptied. She laved the lobe of his ear lightly with her tongue, then whispered so her breath blew hot across the cool, damp surface, "Buenos días, Dark Eyes."

She felt a shiver go through him from head to toe and felt a satisfactory response far below the line of her abdomen. Her body hummed under his hands.

More. The word came to her on a wave of recklessness and heat, just as it had last night. *Always more with this man.*

She had to swim against the current to tug herself away from him. His eyes were half-lidded and as dark as ever. He didn't look like a gunslinger, or even a man capable of violence. He looked adept at passion. The effect went straight to her toes.

As she left the bed, she ran the back of her hand over her mouth, trying to wipe the tingles away—trying to savor them. She made herself go because as much as either of them might believe it, following the impulse to push him back to the bed and cover him like a blanket wouldn't take away his pain.

Javier waited until Grace had gone upstairs to make the extra beds ready for Pia and Sloane's arrival before he slipped out of the house. He'd chosen not to tell her about the gun-cleaning kit he'd found below the kitchen sink. He'd disassembled Carlos's handgun in the bathroom, oiling each piece carefully. There had been no corrosion, no fouling on the inside of the chamber. No moisture. He had one magazine and could only hope the rounds' water-resistant casings had held up. Nowhere in the house had he been able to locate extra ammo.

Javier wove through a maze of towering camellias. They were in full bloom, their perfume heady. Blossoms littered the moss-covered path.

A pain in his shoulder stopped him next to a fallen fig tree. He glanced back at the windows of the house. Grace had warned him to stay relatively close. The pain meds from Salim had worked to dull the bite of the wounds, but the ache was still there. Javier liked that they didn't make him addled. He felt clearheaded and could even appreciate that they didn't take away the pain entirely. Long ago, he'd learned that pain could make him more aware. Better tuned to his surroundings.

The thicket became less mossy and more tangled as he sought the privacy of the trees. He ducked under low-hanging curtains of Spanish moss and high-stepped through kudzu. The sound of lazy, lapping water and the sight of cattails bobbing, top-heavy, told him the land was falling away to the water, so he adjusted his course, pushing through palmettos until he found heaps of red bricks leaned against one another in the shade of an arch-backed tupelo tree.

Former slave quarters, he discerned, seeing a statuette rising from the undergrowth. The bowed head of a young woman seemed to burst from the vines. She cradled a baby in her arms. Someone had placed a rosary around the angel's neck.

The cold season had taken the tree's vegetation, but its thick arms spread east and west, open arms calling people home. Silence here was thick and far more absolute than what Javier had experienced in Lafayette Cemetery. The tupelo stood between the slave quarters and the house, a shield.

He walked on, careful not to disturb what remained. A wooden ladder leaned against a tree trunk, and a well covering crouched between shoots of spider lilies. The stilts of a hunting blind somewhere in midcollapse buckled.

The blind faced a clearing. Javier crouched over the earth and

recognized recent two-toed impressions. *Deer. Doe and fawn.*
Then baby-like handprints. *Raccoon.* The webbed lines of duck
tracks going toward the water were easily discernible. But there
was one more set of tracks he couldn't place. They were similar
to the deer—two-toed, hooved, but rounder. Javier wondered if
there were boars here in the bayou, as he frowned over them.

The glint of metal caught his eye. Across the clearing, someone had nailed a paneling of old roofing to a tree. Painted circles
spread outward like ripples from the center, and bullet holes
pocked the target area. Spent shell casings littered the ground,
some covered with dirt or growth.

Javier looked back in the direction he'd come. The target
faced the house. The shooter had been shooting away from the
people there.

Grace didn't like guns, but someone had set up a gun range
at Casaluna and had regularly practiced their marksmanship.
Was it Sloane? Pia or her boyfriend, Sam?

He reached around his belt and palmed the handgun. He took
the magazine from his pocket and slid it into place with a satis-
fying *chink*. Taking off the safety, he squared off with the target.

His mother's voice came to him. It wavered on a memory.
He hesitated, letting it play out in his mind.

Both eyes open, mijo.

The gun's heavy, Mami. I'm not big enough.

You're big enough. You must be.

My heart's beating too fast.

*Take a deep breath. If you hold it, your heart will beat faster.
Hold the stock in a firm grip. Steady.*

My arm's shaking.

*Hold it like this. See? Now, take one more breath and lay
your finger over the trigger...*

I'm not ready—

*You're ready, mijo. Believe me. Let half the air out of your
lungs. Good. Hold the next breath and squeeze.*

The gun had kicked like a mule. The bullet had winged far
left of the target. Tears had come, the concussion loud in his
ears. The existential crisis of firing a live weapon for the first
time had been inevitable for a child as soft as him.

His first lesson in firing had come after his abduction. Jaime Solaro and his men had snatched him out of the stables while his mother met with sponsors. Jaime had gunned down both of Javier's bodyguards before throwing a bag over his head and tossing him over his shoulder.

The bag had stayed on Javier's head long after the bumpy car ride to whatever hideaway they put him in. Finally, Jaime had snatched it off, presented him with food and called him *hermano* for the first time.

He'd attempted to lure Javier with details of his lavish lifestyle. He'd told him about his cars, his clothing, his women… He'd invited him to meet their father, Pablo Solaro. *It's your birthright*, Jaime had said. *She's hidden it from you. You're free now. Free to take what you want.*

Javier had fallen asleep as day turned to evening. He woke when he heard crashing in the next room. Gunshots. The door had opened. Javier had expected Jaime and put up his small, shaking fists in defiance.

He saw his mother instead. She'd scooped him into her arms. *Close your eyes, mijo. Don't open them until I tell you.*

She hadn't let him open them until they were clear of the house.

Valentina Rivera nearly killed Jaime Solaro that day. She thought she *had* killed him until news had come. After finding out Jaime lived, she'd taken Javier to the shooting range.

I told you, Mami, Javier had cried as she took the gun from his limp fingers. *I'm not like those men. I can't use a gun.*

The first time is always the hardest.

I can't do it.

Look at me, Javier. It is not normal to hold something between your hands, knowing it will explode. Knowing it might take a life. But you must take the next shot, Javier. You have no choice. To them, a gun is power. To you, it is survival.

Javier caught himself holding his injured shoulder. It throbbed in tune with the ache in his chest where memories of his mother—where her words were alive. He planted one foot in front of the other, gripping the weapon's stock. He raised the barrel. A zing of protest from his shoulder smarted as he sighted the target...

...both eyes open, mijo...

He took a breath, let it halfway out, squeezed.

The bullet ate through the middle, a new hole near the center.

You didn't aim for the brain stem.

But I did, Javier had said, well into his teens and years into practicing hitting the target with his mother.

When Jaime comes again, he won't shoot to kill. He'll shoot to disable, then do as he wishes with you and with me. We won't give him the chance. Shoot again, Javier. And this time, don't miss.

The target had had Jaime's face and shoulders pinned to it. Valentina had already put several rounds in his throat. She had taught Javier more than grammar and mathematics in the little schoolroom she'd fashioned for him in their home. She'd taught him about the Solaro family.

We fear what we do not understand.

She taught him that Pablo had three sons, each by a different woman. The first, Jaime. He was Pablo's illegitimate child. *And Pablo never let him forget it. This is one thing that makes Jaime so dangerous—his thirst for legitimacy. He will do anything, Javier, to be seen as Pablo's equal.* The second child, Alejandro, resulted from Pablo's first marriage. Pablo doted on Alejandro and bred him to be the next Solaro crime boss. He also bred competition into him, which he used to pit Alejandro against Jaime in every aspect of life—from the fighting ring to business.

Valentina, Pablo's second wife, grew to fear Jaime more than her ex-husband. More than any of the Solaros. Jaime had made it impossible for her to stay in the Solaro family.

Javier didn't know the details until after her death, when Jaime had taunted him with them in Pablo's fighting ring.

Maybe you're not his *son. Maybe you're mine.*

The resulting rage had nearly been enough to overtake Jaime in a fight for the first time. Jaime had revealed a knife at the last minute and had nearly taken Javier's ear off. Weapons were forbidden in Pablo's ring. Jaime's cheating had gravely displeased Pablo.

You are not a man, Jaime—any more than you are my son.

The declaration had made Jaime seethe.

Javier scowled at the target. He imagined Jaime's face in the center. He had seen his brother at the boat launch after Dante had escaped. Javier had seen the long scar across his face—the one Sloane had put there before Jaime turned his cruelty on her. Javier had seen Jaime's sunken cheeks, his shaved head. Anyone who didn't know Jaime would think prison had eaten away at him.

Javier knew that wasn't so. Prison had honed him. It had reinforced his tendencies. Javier had seen that in his malevolent stare.

He took aim at where the center of Jaime's throat would be. He wasn't protecting himself or his mother now. It was Grace Jaime would shoot to disable. So he could do as he pleased with her.

Knowing what Jaime did with his women, Javier took one breath in. Let half a breath out. Squeezed. Followed through.

The metal opened with a *plink* where the center of Jaime's throat would have been.

The trees stirred, leaves whispering. A voice came to him on the breeze. *Niño?*

He strained to listen, his pulse lifting. *Si?*

Leaves rustled around his feet as the wind strengthened, carrying a faint reply. *Be ready.*

He lost a breath, the wariness sinking into his bones.

Estoy listo, he thought. *I am ready.*

The wind died away slowly until the last of the leaves grew still and the surrounding trees hushed again. He was alone.

The ache inside him had nothing to do with his wound. He rolled his sore shoulder. Then he took the magazine out of the gun and stuffed it into his pocket, saving the spare rounds, trying to ignore the boy inside him reaching, wailing.

When he came face-to-face with Jaime again, he would need the rounds. He would make each one count.

He would finish what his mother had tried.

Javier would finish Jaime for her and the trio of free girls he'd brought home.

Fatigue wove cumbersome webs throughout his body and mind as he trekked back to the house. He caught the flick of a curtain at the upstairs window and stopped, searching for Grace through the glass.

He found Luis instead, pawing at the abandoned cobwebs that had torn from the mosquito screen and were flagging raggedly in the wind. Javier grinned.

The sound of shells crunching under tires made him reach for the gun on his belt instead. He sprinted the rest of the way to the house and pressed his back against the wall as he crept to the front.

Peering around the corner, he spotted the large black SUV coming down the drive.

Javier cursed and ran.

The door slammed behind him as he entered the house by the screen porch. He bolted the locks.

Grace pounded down the stairs. "What's wrong?" She watched him slide the magazine into place. "Javy."

"Black SUV," he told her. Why weren't there windows along the front of the house?

"Jaime?" He heard the unease in her voice as she fell in behind him.

"Go back upstairs," he instructed.

She went into the kitchen instead. He braced his shoulder against the wall next to the door. There wasn't a peephole. Who built houses like this? Javier gritted his teeth, his weapon in a two-handed hold, the safety off.

He glanced back at the sound of Grace's footsteps and eyed the cast-iron skillet in her hand.

She held the handle in two hands like a gunstock. "Sword and shield, cher," she said in answer to his bald stare.

He opened his mouth to tell her she hadn't frozen—that she was stronger, braver than she thought she was. He wished she could see what he saw.

Someone pounded on the door from the other side. Javier

jerked his chin at Grace, motioning for her to get out of range. When the door opened, Jaime's men would open fire.

The knock came again, hard enough to rattle the hinges.

Javier waited, breathing carefully through the thunder drum of his heart. The adrenaline was thinning the medicine in his blood and pain bloomed fresh in his shoulder, blistering enough to make his eyes water.

The door splintered, swinging in a burst of sound and movement.

Javier crossed in front of Grace, weapon high.

Sloane charged, her weapon drawn, too. "Put the gun down!"

Javier raised both his hands.

She took him down anyway, dropping the butt of her gun over his head.

He saw stars.

Her well-aimed kick knocked his legs out from underneath him.

He found himself on the floor, disarmed, with her face over his. "Sloane, it's me! Javier Rivera."

"I *know* who you are," she growled, showing her teeth. A vein pulsed in her temple. Her eyes were red-rimmed. They were snakes, dark, coiled, venomous. "Turn over, you son of a bitch! Put your hands behind your back!"

Chapter 14

"You cuffed him."

"Damn right I did," Sloane replied before biting into the flesh of a large green apple. "He's lucky that's all I did before you yanked me off him. You're a buzzkill, Lacroix."

Grace frowned deeply. Her relief at knowing it was Sloane kicking down the door and not Jaime still rang true. However, it had dulled swiftly when she'd taken Javier out at the knees. "You interrogated him."

"He held up to questioning," Sloane said, sounding disappointed by the fact.

"You played bad cop."

Sloane lifted her hands. "I'm always bad cop."

"It was unnecessary," Grace pointed out, "and cruel."

"I noticed when I swept the place that only one bed was turned down," Sloane noted. She arched one long, thin brow. "Was that his idea or yours?"

"The man's been shot, Sloane," Grace pointed out. "I needed to keep an eye on him. And don't forget. If it wasn't for him, they would've killed me."

"He's the idiot who led Jaime Solaro right to your door."

"Jaime was already there!" Grace volleyed back. "He was watching me, waiting for news of his escape to come down the pipeline so he could follow me to Pia. He wants me and you, but Pia's his primary target. Where *is* she, Sloane? Why isn't she here?"

"I don't know!" Sloane shouted. "Dammit, I have men searching for her in every parish. In every Gulf state. She and Babette have gone into the wind."

"If she's on the run, she would have come here," Grace said. "This was always the place we were supposed to meet. How do we know Jaime doesn't already have her?"

"Because he asked me where she was," Sloane shot back.

Grace faltered. "You've had contact with Jaime Solaro?"

"I ran into him and his men at a gas station thirty miles south of here," Sloane revealed. She untucked her silk shirt and peeled the waistband of her black slacks down to reveal a bandage on her hip. "We had a nice little chat."

Grace crossed the kitchen. *"He shot you, too?"*

"I'm fine," Sloane said, batting Grace's hands away. "The bullet didn't do much more than graze me. That's why I'm late. I called Remy. He lives close by. He was a navy SEAL who specialized as a medic, and he patched me up."

Grace could see the man lingering in the den—all six feet three inches of Cajun good looks and a glowering stare to pin Javier in place on the couch where Grace had forced him to sit after Sloane had nearly ripped his stitches. "Why does he look familiar?" she asked, dropping her voice.

"He was my bodyguard," Sloane admitted, tucking in her shirt in punchy movements. "The one my mother hired to follow me around after we came back from Mexico."

"'Thirst Trap' Remy?" Grace asked, stunned. *"That's* 'Thirst Trap' Remy?"

"Not so loud!" she hissed. Before Grace could get a better look at him, Sloane dragged her into the dining room. "Jaime doesn't know where Pia is because he asked me where *I* was hiding her."

"What about Sam?" Grace asked.

"He's in the Middle East," Sloane reminded her.

"I know that, but maybe she's tried to contact *him*," Grace said. "She can reach him in the event of an emergency. Maybe he knows where she's hiding."

"I spoke to him last night," Sloane pointed out. "He's getting a flight out tomorrow. He's sick with worry. And while he had missed calls from her, there was no voice mail, and the line was dead when he tried calling her back. She's lost her phone, or it's dead and she can't recharge it."

Grace straightened as she thought of something. "We think Jaime was tracing Javier and me through his calls to Javier's cell. That's the most likely reason he found us at the boat launch. Could he have been tracing Pia through hers, as well? Maybe she turned it off or dumped it."

"It's possible," Sloane said, nodding shortly. She was grim around the mouth. "I refuse to accept the other possibility."

"That she and Babette fell into his hands after the standoff with you last night?" Grace asked.

"Or he's killed one or both of them," Sloane said, her voice dropping away fast.

"No," Grace said, shaking her head automatically. "He wants Pia alive. He's probably still under the delusion that she belongs to him."

"And Babette?" Sloane said with a shake of her head. "It won't take an advanced understanding of arithmetic for him to figure out how old she is."

Grace held up her hands. "Stop. Okay? Just stop."

"I can't," Sloane argued. "Not until we find them."

Grace took Sloane's hands in hers. "I have faith he hasn't found them. I have faith they're holed away from him somewhere. Pia's gone off the grid before. She can do it again. Jaime won't get his hands on our baby. Pia won't let him. Her mama bear tendencies engaged the moment I placed Babette in her arms."

Sloane nodded after a moment. She took a breath. "That's true." Her phone rang. Grace jumped, and Sloane stiffened. She pulled it from the pocket of her slacks and checked the screen. Turning the screen around to face Grace, she showed her the display.

Grace deflated. She sighed in disappointment as Sloane answered, "Hey, have you got anything?" She listened, eyes narrowing to slits. "When?" She checked her watch, then shifted her feet. "Where did the call come from?" Glancing at Grace, she frowned. "And where did she say they were?" She cursed. "I figured. The call may be a problem. You need to make it clear she can't call you from that number again. No, Sam. Listen. Solaro may be tracking them both through one or both of their mobile devices. When's your flight out? Okay. Text me that number. I'll put my guys to work on tracing their location. Don't try to contact her again." She rolled her eyes. Placing her hand over the bottom half of the phone, she whispered, "Papa Bear's ready to throw down."

"Yeah, well, Tante Bear isn't far behind him," Grace drawled.

Sloane uncovered the speaker and said to Sam, "Let me know if you hear anything more and call me when your plane touches down tomorrow in Delaware. Yeah, you, too. Bye."

As Sloane ended the call, Grace raised her shoulders. "Well?"

"Babette called him," Sloane revealed. "Apparently, Sam gave her a cell phone for Christmas. She didn't tell him where she and Pia are, but she said that they're safe."

"When was this?" Grace asked anxiously.

"Twenty minutes ago."

Grace closed her eyes and wrapped her arms around herself. "Oh, thank God," she breathed.

"Yeah," Sloane echoed.

"Okay," Grace said, dizzy with relief. She pressed her hand to the wall for balance and bobbed her head in a nod, trying to think everything through. "We need... We need a plan."

"The plan is to put you under heavy guard," Sloane replied.

"And Javy," Grace added.

Sloane cut her eyes toward the den and shook her long black hair back from her face. "He's a witness, so I'm obligated as a federal agent to guarantee his safety, even if I have to separate you two to do it."

"I'm his doctor," Grace reminded her.

"We have other doctors," Sloane said, unmoved.

Grace came right out and said it. "I don't want that."

"You don't want what?"

She balled her hands into fists, the nails digging into her palms. "To be separated from him."

"Hmm," Sloane said knowingly. She held up an informative finger. "That was a test. You failed spectacularly. And that's unlike you."

"Fine," Grace bit off. "You want me to say it? I'll say it." Lowering her voice, she said, "I have feelings for him."

It did not move Sloane. "You've known him, what? Twenty-four hours? Who are you—Sleeping Beauty?"

"I've known Javy twelve years," Grace argued.

"That's debatable."

"He saved our lives."

"Also debatable."

Grace groaned. "Look, I know your mother has her own narrative about what really went down in Mexico."

"Um, I was there," Sloane said. "I *know* what went down in Mexico."

"Your mother," Grace went on, undeterred, "needed to lay the blame at somebody's door for what happened, and she knew you did, too. She made Javier the scapegoat. And so, by extension, did you."

"He was there the night we were abducted, Gracie," Sloane said in a deadly voice. "You saw that."

"If Javier wasn't the one who got us out, then why did your father expedite his citizenship to the US?" Grace asked insistently.

"He...what?" Sloane faltered. "You don't know that."

"Nobody else involved in this has that kind of pull," Grace pointed out. "He was a senator, for God's sake."

Sloane's mouth had dropped. She shut it carefully, pressing her lips inward.

"They told you, too, at the embassy that Javier was working for the police. He was their informant. He wasn't one of the traffickers. You've just chosen to forget that. It helped you work through the trauma, the pain, and that's okay. But now?" Grace placed her hand on Sloane's arm. "You have to let that go. You have to stop blaming him as much as you blame Pablo and Jaime and Alejandro for what happened."

"If he's such a damn hero, why'd it take him three weeks to

get us out of there?" Sloane wanted to know. Before Grace could answer, she threw in, "Exactly."

When Sloane walked toward the front door, Grace asked, "Where are you going?"

"To make some phone calls," Sloane replied. "Signal's better up the road. And I need to walk."

"It's not safe out there," Grace began.

"I'm trained in marksmanship and hand-to-hand combat, and I have a gun. If you're worried about you and your cowboy friend, Remy will stay behind." She looked back, saw Grace's face, and softened. "Please, don't follow me. I need time, okay? It's a lot to process."

"I know," Grace said. "We're in this together, Sloane."

"I'll have a new location for both of you in twenty minutes," Sloane promised before she swung open the broken door. It hung crooked when she shut it.

"Are you okay?"

Javier turned to Grace in the back seat of Sloane's SUV. He didn't like the worry in her eyes. "Estoy bien, bonita."

"I should've checked your stitches again before we left."

He twined her fingers through his. "They're all right. There's nothing to worry about, Grace."

She slid her gaze away, unconvinced. "Sloane was too rough with you."

"She's your friend, and she's protective," Javier reminded her, meeting Sloane's eyes in the rearview mirror. The woman may have been driving, but she was still watching him. "I've been through worse."

"Don't tell her that. She'll take it as a personal challenge."

"I'll keep it quiet."

"At least she doesn't plan to keep us in separate locations."

"No?" he asked, hope lifting.

"Not for the time being," Grace said cautiously. "Though she stipulated we'll need to stay in separate rooms."

Javier tried to think his way around that and the resulting disappointment. He'd enjoyed sleeping with Grace beside him.

He'd loved turning into her warmth in the night, fitting his body against hers. "For your safety?"

"For my virtue," Grace pointed out, "which she conveniently forgets I lost to her cousin, Enrique, when I was sixteen."

Javier raised a brow. "And she let him live?"

"She *says* he's still alive," Grace said thoughtfully. "Though I haven't seen the guy in fourteen years. So, who knows?"

Javier wouldn't be surprised if cousin Enrique's toes were pushing up daisies in a flower bed somewhere in New Orleans's Garden District.

Sad mewing from the seat behind them made Grace look back. "It's okay, Luis. We'll be there soon."

"She didn't have to have her man put him in a cat carrier," Javier muttered.

"Sloane's not a cat person," Grace remarked.

"She's more partial to cobras?" Javier guessed, when Sloane's stare spit venom at him through the mirror.

"Now that you mention it, she isn't much of an animal person at all," she replied. "Her parents never wanted pets in the house, so…"

"I overheard her speaking to Dante," Javier mentioned.

Grace brightened. "Did you?"

He nodded. "He's all right. It sounds like he and Eulalie took Mr. Monty to see some friends in Shreveport until the heat dies down."

"Thank goodness," Grace breathed. "I wondered if Jaime had seen the bayou tour sticker on Dante's back window. It would have led him to Dante and Lalie. It was smart of him to get her out of the house. Though I'm sure she wasn't pleased about leaving."

"Sloane mentioned Eulalie fought him like a wet cat."

Grace tried to hide a smile. He was pleased to see it didn't work. It faded quickly, however, as she said, "She took your gun."

"She did," Javier acknowledged, sobering.

"I could ask her to give it back."

He squeezed her hand, then lifted it to his lips. As hushed as it was, he heard the quick catch of her breath and lingered. Running his thumb over the back of her knuckles, he murmured, "She'll give it back when she's ready."

Grace's eyes were soft as they caressed his face. "You do realize she may never be ready."

"I'll earn her faith and trust," he pledged. "Just as I earned yours. Even if it did take me twelve years."

"Yes," she admitted. Her arm linked through his as she lowered her cheek to his shoulder.

His pulse quickened. He hadn't yet told her the truth about who he was to the Solaros. And he got the impression that Sloane was looking for the most opportune moment to drop that bombshell.

Like New Orleans, the city of Biloxi, Mississippi, was a city on the water. And while Biloxi could boast twenty feet above sea level to New Orleans's two feet, it stood with open arms to the Mississippi Sound, protected only by barrier islands from the whims of the warm Gulf.

Once, the casinos of Biloxi were only allowed dockside or on the water. After Hurricane Katrina, the Mississippi legislature saw fit to allow gambling establishments as far inland as eight hundred feet, which was how Grace found herself in a one-bedroom hotel room in the Beau Rivage.

The casino wasn't what she'd imagined as a hideout, but she had to admit it made sense. Guards were posted outside her door 24/7 and at Javier's, just across the hall. There was an FBI detail downstairs at every entrance. Security footage was scrutinized minute to minute.

Grace frowned as she sat on her bed. The room was pristine. It even had that retail smell. The carpet was soft under her toes. The bed was firm under her hips. Sleeping there hadn't been a problem, though she'd missed Javier and wondered how he was faring across the hall. There was a mini-fridge. Room service was comped. She could order whatever she liked.

Most tempting of all was the white-tiled bathroom, complete with a wide jet tub and rainfall showerhead.

She'd sunk into the tub the first night while Sloane roamed the carpet of her room, making call after call to field agents, protection officers, her superior, even the US marshals involved in the search for Pia, Babette and the Solaros. But Grace had stayed submerged long enough only to shampoo, rinse, soap and rinse again. There had been no lingering—no soaking until the tension in her muscles loosened and fell away, even with Sloane's generous and knowing gift of her favorite shampoo, conditioner and body scrub.

Sloane had grudgingly allowed Luis to stay with Grace in her hotel room and had Remy bring him a litter box and food plus various kitty accessories, including toys, scratching post and collar. *I guess I went overboard*, he had admitted as Grace unboxed the purchases.

Ya think? Sloane had intoned under an arched brow.

Grace knew Sloane had placed Remy in charge of her day-time protection. The man was standing outside the door now. She'd grown comfortable with him. He kept Sloane on her toes and Grace knew that, despite outward appearances, it was one of the few things preventing Sloane from losing her mind.

However safe she felt with Remy on guard, Grace still couldn't bring herself to stand under that lovely rainfall shower and let it wash the wretchedness of the last few days down the drain.

She'd come close yesterday after noticing how badly she needed to shave while trying on the large bag of new clothes Sloane had had one of her fellow agents pick up at the nearby shopping mall. *You can't wear go-go boots forever*, Sloane had said as an excuse as Grace purred over a pair of boots ripe with the smell of fresh leather. The bag had also held a new silk pajama set that didn't feel right with a few days' worth of stubble on her legs.

Grace had waited until Sloane and Remy left the room to strip off her clothes. She'd opened the glass door of the shower and reached for the tap.

Her muscles had gone stiff. No matter what she did, she couldn't bring herself to turn on the water. She'd made herself stand under the showerhead, counting the seconds up to a minute before backing out like the coward she was. She'd shaved at the sink, chastising herself.

Curling her fingers into the thick white duvet, Grace gritted her teeth. If Sloane allowed her to go home to Saint Peter Street, was it still going to be like this? How long? Would she never heal? Is this what her life would be—living in the spaces between episodes of terror?

She flopped back onto the bed. Raking her hands through her hair, she scowled at the ceiling.

The cheerful tinkling of bells announced Luis's landing on top of the bed. She felt the pressure points of his paws on her thighs. They scaled her torso to the space in between her breasts before he chucked his head beneath her chin.

Her lips curved slightly. "I know," she said, lifting her hand to him in response. "I'm pathetic, right?"

His purring started slowly, then revved as he continued to nuzzle her jaw. He curled up over her throat.

"Tired already?" she asked, amused. He'd spent the better part of the morning diligently trying to bite the head off of a felt fish, chasing a laser up the wall, scratching his post with front and hind legs, rolling luxuriantly in the patch of sunlight Grace had revealed by breaking one of Sloane's rules and opening the curtains a scant six inches and chasing the feet of whoever dared walk around his favorite hiding place under the bed.

Grace sighed as the purring vibrated her collarbone. She couldn't lie anymore. She'd accepted this creature as her companion. The Jinx to her Eartha Kitt. The Jiji to her Kiki. Her Thackery Binx.

"What would you do, hmm?" she whispered, tracing the shape of his tail with the tip of her pinky finger. She scoffed. "What am I saying? Cats don't like water."

Luis lifted his head and sneezed.

"Scat." When he stood to do a circle over the bodice of the emerald cashmere blouse she'd chosen from the shopping bag, Grace added, "Maybe one day we'll go home again. Would you like that? Will you live with me...*furever*, as they say?"

Luis licked his lips and blinked sleepily. Then he cleaned the fur on his chest in diligent laps.

"I want that, too," she returned. She had no idea why she was whispering still.

It was the first time she'd said it out loud.

Why hadn't admitting her ridiculous shower fears to Javier been enough to overcome them?

...I'll guard the door for you...

Could Grace have done it then, knowing Javier was outside the door? Not Remy. Not Sloane, even. Javy.

Their protection detail had supervised every interaction she and Javier had had over the last few days. Sloane had a knack for knowing when Grace poked her head out of her room, asking for a word with the sexy, dark-eyed man across the hall. Sloane pointedly watched any wound checks. Any meetings they had as a team were headed by Sloane. Any walks they took down the hall to stretch their legs or to stop cabin fever from setting in were no doubt seen by Sloane in the surveillance footage.

Grace wondered what she had to do to get her friend to lay off the Marmee tendencies.

Plus, Sloane was hiding things from her. Things about Jaime and his cronies. Things about Pia, Grace feared.

Keeping Grace in the dark was no doubt some form of protection. But it had only been a few days since Grace had told Javier off for doing the same.

Grace rolled toward the bedside table, dislodging Luis. His purring rolled into a disgruntled growl. She picked up the hotel phone and dialed the number Sloane had had her memorize. It rang once before her friend answered with the traditional New Orleans greeting, "Where y'at, chère?"

"Meet me in the bar," Grace demanded.

"The bar? I don't have guys down there."

"How long will it take to put them in place?"

"I don't know. Half an hour, minimum."

"Make it happen," Grace persisted. "I'm coming down."

"And you started giving orders when?"

"Since I realized how badly I need a glass of wine."

"I'll have a bottle sent up."

"The bar," Grace said again firmly. "Twenty minutes." And she hung up.

Chapter 15

"You didn't have to make everybody else leave."

Sloane looked satisfactorily around the empty bar and lounge. "It's one o'clock in the afternoon. If anybody needs a drink that badly, they need an intervention."

"I'll try not to take that personally," Grace muttered. She canted her head to take a good hard look at the man who appeared behind the bar. "Bon Dieu. You look an awful lot like my protection officer."

Remy picked up a shot glass and tossed it. It arced through the air before he snatched it. "Sloane tells me you're in need of liquor."

"Remy's one of those handy jack-of-all-trades," Sloane pointed out. "He bartended for a little while before he signed up for BUD/S. Or was it after? I can't keep it straight."

He rolled one large shoulder in response.

Grace squinted at the labels behind him. She pointed. "That rosé looks promising."

"You and the rosé," Sloane chided, seating herself on Grace's right. "Committed to each other, eternally."

Grace eyed Remy again, the sleeves already rolled up his muscled forearms, the ink that flashed on each one as he selected a clean, long-stemmed wineglass from the mirrored shelf. "I don't suppose G.I. Joe knows how to make a Bloody Mary."

He made a face. "You insult me, Dr. Lacroix."

"I've told you," Grace replied, watching him replace the wine-glass on the shelf. He reached for a highball instead. She whimpered at the promise of vodka and tomato juice, that unlikely couple that had cured more woes than the drink's designer could have anticipated. "You don't have to call me that. It's Grace."

Sloane made a disagreeable noise. "He's never called me Agent Escarra."

He arced a knowing brow. "I still remember the lippy senator's daughter, with the fake ID and the mile-wide chip on her shoulder."

Sloane frowned, folding her hands over the top of the bar. Grace knew her little duck feet churned under the surface and blistering words scored her tongue.

Sloane preferred not to speak of the months after her leg had healed from her injury at Jaime's hands. Back stateside, she'd lived like Mexico never happened. She'd chased her PTSD with Bourbon Street hand grenades and dancing till dawn. Instead of facing the cold light of day, she'd slept through most of those hours, resenting anyone who tried to pull her out of her freefall.

It was Luna's death and Pia's subsequent plea for Sloane to stop spiraling down the same path that woke Sloane up at last. Not long after, she'd reenrolled in college courses. She'd finished her associate degree before applying to the FBI, finally finding her calling.

Remy set a mixed Bloody Mary on the bar in front of Grace. "Couldn't find the celery," he confided when she fingered the okra spears sticking out of it.

"That's all right, cher," she assured him. She sniffed, then took a testing sip. "Ooh, he's good," she confided to a surly Sloane. "This here's almost better than Hugo's."

"Don't flatter him," Sloane warned. "He's insufferable enough as it is. And I'll tell Hugo you said that next time I stop in for the special."

"You wouldn't," Grace said, then sipped again and forgot everything with another "Mmm-mmm."

Remy met Sloane stare for stare. "You gonna order or what?"

"I'm on duty, jockstrap," she said, peeling back her vest to reveal the badge and gun strapped to her hip.

"That wouldn't have stopped the Sloane I used to know," he noted.

"Yeah, well, I haven't shimmied up a trellis in a minidress and Manolos in ten years," Sloane informed him, "so you can roll with the times or bend over and kiss my ass."

He set a glass in front of her.

Sloane stared into the fizzy, pink concoction crowned with three cherries. "The hell is this?"

"Shirley Temple." When she hissed at him, a grin cleaved his hard features. It was dark, dangerous. Oddly disarming—a smile that hit a woman in the glands while raising the hairs on the back of her arms at the same time.

The straw Grace was sucking on made a guttering noise, drawing Sloane's narrowed eyes her way. Grace cleared her throat and set the Bloody Mary down. "Wow. That went down quick."

"Don't," Sloane snapped before Remy could wrap his fingers around the highball. "She doesn't need another." She pointed to the corner. "Go sit over there."

As he rolled his shoulders back and obeyed, Grace pouted. "You didn't let me tip him."

"You left your bank roll back in Nawlins," Sloane reminded her. "What isn't tied up in student loans, anyway."

"Mais la." Grace pursed her lips. "This is what he still does for a living—protect people?"

"No," Sloane said. "Officially, he's a bounty hunter."

Grace licked the juice off her lower lip, considering. "Sounds like he'd be much more useful tracking Jaime Solaro than standing at my door."

"I don't trust anyone else with your protection," Sloane pointed out. "Once you're in a safe house, I'll put him on Jaime."

"How much are you paying him?"

Sloane paused, then revealed, "I'm not."

Grace looked long in Remy's direction. "So…you whistle and he does what he's told?"

Sloane chose her words carefully. "When I joined the FBI,

and he was certain I could defend myself, he told me that if ever the Solaros were a problem for me again to call him."

"Why would he do that?"

"He saw me at my worst, Gracie," Sloane admitted. "He was a big reason I could claw my way out of that hole. I'd pay him if he let me. But this is every bit as personal for him as it is for me."

And damned if that didn't make "Thirst Trap" Remy that much more likeable. "I get why you had a thing for him," Grace noted.

Sloane's voice was in her ear. "If you tell him I wanted to bounce on him, I will lock you in the Koenig Tomb and throw away the key."

"Didn't you used to put your panties in his pocket?" Grace widened her eyes for emphasis. "I'm pretty sure he already knows." She took out an okra spear and took a large bite.

"My taste in men is still superior to yours," Sloane told her.

Grace nearly choked. She swallowed carefully. "I'm sorry. How many mama's boy trust fund babies did you trade hickeys with before raising your standards?"

"Hey, at least I raised mine," Sloane pointed out. "Give me that." She took the okra from Grace's hand and bit it clean in half.

"This is about Javy," Grace surmised.

Sloane raised one hand. "Look, I'm Latina. I get it. Dark eyes have an effect on a woman. Add in the accent, some Spanish, and I'm halfway there, too. But Javier Rivera is too close to what went down with us twelve years ago. I don't know how you look at him and see anything else."

"I'm not asking you to understand," Grace stated, stirring the ice in her glass with her straw.

"What are you asking for, Grace?" Sloane asked. "My permission?"

"I didn't think I needed it," Grace said.

Sloane seemed to deflate. She chased the okra with a long sip of the Shirley Temple and winced. "It's so sweet, it makes my eyes water." Pushing it away, she shook her head. "This is neither the time nor the place—"

"Maybe not," Grace granted. "But since we got back from

Mexico, I've stayed on the sidewalk. I've kept my eyes on the ground. I played it safe. I went out with men I knew I couldn't make myself available to or who weren't emotionally available to me. You've taken risks—with men and with your career. Pia, too, took chances with her passions, her work, Sam…"

"Javier Rivera is no Sam Filipek," Sloane reminded her.

"But Javy's my choice. I'm done saying no to what I want because I'm scared. I've been scared for too long. I can't live my whole life ignoring my gut."

"Your gut?" Sloane said cautiously. "Or something bigger?"

Grace thought about it. "At least I'm willing to open myself up."

"Couldn't you have found some golden retriever of a man? Someone with no connection to the past? Wouldn't that have been simpler?"

"Is life simple?" Grace asked. "Would you say that's been your experience?"

Sloane groaned. "No."

Grace saw the weight of everything riding on Sloane's shoulders. "You realize it's not your job to hold our lives together? Somehow, through the years, you've shouldered a responsibility neither Pia nor I ever asked you to."

"Nothing matters more than your well-being," Sloane noted. "Yours, Pia's, Babette's… That's paramount. You still blame yourself for the kidnapping. Neither of us asked you to do that, either."

"If I hadn't fallen under Alejandro's spell…"

"We *all* fell under Alejandro's spell," Sloane countered. "I told you to go for it with him. Daddy Lacroix died six months before we went away. It did Pia and me good to see you smile again. We wanted you to be happy. None of us had a clue it would lead us into sex trafficking."

Grace badly wanted to change the subject. She'd keep blaming herself for Mexico, just as Sloane would still see her and Pia's safety as her responsibility.

Grace cleared her throat. "I noticed Thirst Trap's not wearin' a ring. You want me to talk you up?"

Sloane somehow smiled and winced at the same time. Running her tongue across her top teeth, she slid a long-lidded stare off in Remy's direction. "You'll have to get me tipsy first. Bourbon Street tipsy. Then you'll have to convince him to stop seeing me as the entitled eighteen-year-old who used to scream at him, come on to him, puke on him and cry on him...all within the space of a night, every night—wash and repeat—for the better part of six months."

Grace's eyes had gone round. "That may be a tall order."

"And now you know why I don't believe in getting involved with anyone from the past," Sloane said, raising the Shirley Temple in toast.

"Where's Pia?" Grace asked.

Sloane's mouth tightened unsatisfactorily. "That was sneaky."

"You've been keeping things from me," Grace noted. "Everything, in fact."

"I don't know where Pia is," Sloane admitted, resentful again. Where there was resentment, there was helplessness and worry.

"But..." Grace prompted and waited.

Sloane's jaw clenched. Pushing out a breath, she folded her arms on the bar top. "Authorities found her boat twenty miles from the beach house."

"Empty?" Grace asked, alarmed.

"Empty, burned and on the bottom of the Gulf."

Grace missed a breath. "Burned?" she asked in a scant whisper. "That means..."

"Jaime found her," Sloane finished.

Now Grace understood why Sloane had been so tightly wound over the last few days—why her fuse had been short. "Maybe she and Babette got away," Grace suggested, grasping at straws because it was all she had and she hated the alternative. "Didn't Babette just earn her scuba diving certification?"

"Yes," Sloane said after a moment.

"If the boat was empty..." Grace left the sentence open-ended with the possibilities.

"It's possible," Sloane decided. "But I think it's far more likely that they're in Solaro hands or..."

Grace shook her head quickly, unwilling to accept anything

more final. Despite the fist of despair knotted in her stomach. "They're alive. They have to be. We have to believe it."

"It's my job to consider every angle," Sloane said heavily. "Even the one that says they're adrift or dead."

Grace felt sick. "If you find Jaime, you might find them."

Sloane's gaze sharpened, focused. It burned. "Why do you think I've got every field agent in the Gulf states hunting that jackal? Whether he's holding them or not, when I meet him again, Gracie, he's not walking away. I'll risk my badge to put a bullet between his eyes."

Sloane had scaled so many walls to earn her place in the fight against human trafficking. She'd come so far. But Grace knew if she were in Sloane's shoes…if she ever came face-to-face with Jaime Solaro again… She hoped she'd have the guts to end his life.

And if Pia's and Babette's blood was on his hands—there wasn't much Grace wouldn't risk, either, to avenge them.

Javier wandered, confused, into the bar on the first floor of the casino and stopped when he found Sloane there, alone on a barstool.

"Gracias," he said to the agent who'd summoned him from his room and escorted him down.

Sloane turned her head, one viper eye aimed over her shoulder. "Join me," she said, kicking out the stool next to hers.

Javier heard the doors close at his back. With one look around the room, he realized they were alone. Knowing she was armed, he approached slowly. "I was told you wanted to talk."

"Sure do." When he hesitated, she scoffed. "Have a seat, Rivera. I won't bite."

He wasn't sure about that. Still, he followed instructions, folding himself to the stool. "Is the bar closed?" he asked, looking for the bartender.

"You want a drink?"

She lobbed the question at him. "No," Javier decided.

She jerked her chin in a nod. "Good choice."

"Have you located my cousin?" he probed. He'd been told

nothing since he and Grace arrived at the casino. His questions about Jaime's whereabouts had been ignored.

"Your cousin," she repeated, as if weighing the words. "You're still living under that lie?"

Javier's hands wrapped around the edge of the bar reflexively.

Sloane eyed him, knowing. "Or is that just the line you've been feeding Gracie?"

His lungs wouldn't inflate. She looked more than venomous. She looked perfectly capable of wrapping him in her coils and squeezing.

She picked up the near-empty glass in front of her and tossed it back. An ice cube crunched between her back teeth and she chewed, considering. "What else are you lying to her about?"

"That's all," he said, finding his voice flat.

"You didn't swear on it," she noted. "That's something. In my line of work, I've learned that swearing on the Almighty is all but a confession."

"I'm telling the truth," he said dully.

"The truth is twisted," Sloane replied, "especially for you. Pablo Solaro's third son. Jaime's brother."

"Half brother," Javier argued.

"It's all the same when you get down into it," she told him. "And trust me, I've done extensive background into your family. I know more about the Solaros than you do."

"I don't doubt it," Javier muttered.

"Would you like to know what really happened to your mother?"

Javier's head snapped up. "What?"

Sloane's frown was grim and foreboding. "Your mother. Valentina Rivera. Did you know she was murdered?"

Javier's knuckles whitened on the edge of the bar. "It was never confirmed."

Sloane scrutinized him. "If I tell you more, you and I have to agree on one thing."

Javier measured the silence. "You don't want me to see Grace anymore."

"I'd love that," Sloane admitted. "Would you take that deal?"

His gaze raced across her face. "Isn't that what you're offering?"

She waited a beat. Then she exhaled, the breath winding out of her reluctantly. "I don't know if you've noticed, but there's nothing and no one that means more to me in this world than Gracie and Pia. And I'd love nothing more than to show you the door. But despite what you may think of me, I'm not that underhanded. They've let me make my own choices, even when they disagreed. I'm not their friend—not really—if I don't give them the same grace."

Javier did his best to absorb this. "So, what do you want?"

"If your feelings are anywhere near what hers are," Sloane noted, "I want you to honor her the same way she will you. I want you to love her the way she deserves. She deserves a *man*. Don't make her settle for less. If that's too tall an order for you, I'll ask you to let her down easy. Don't leave her hanging for another twelve years."

Javier couldn't believe what he was hearing. "You're...giving me permission—"

She let out a humorless laugh. "She's made it very clear she doesn't need my permission. And I'm willing to accept that as long as you assure me in no uncertain terms that this cliff I see her heading toward isn't her undoing. After Mexico, Pia and me... We both came undone. But Gracie... She held it together. She was damaged. But she wasn't lost like we were."

"Sloane," he said carefully, "I would protect Grace with my life. Her heart should be protected. If I can't keep it safe, then I don't deserve her."

Sloane's expression hardened. "I need your word."

"You have it."

"Tell her who you really are," Sloane demanded. "Tell her you're Pablo Solaro's biological son. Then we'll see."

He nodded, trying to unwind the knots of apprehension building inside him. "Si."

Sloane's brows came together. Then the truth surged. "Jaime killed your mother."

It felt like a blow to the chest. Javier took the punch. He needed to feel it—all of it. "You have proof of this?"

She nodded. "The original autopsy report was false. Post-mortem photos recovered from Jaime's office after his arrest show ligature marks. His DNA was found under her fingernails."

Javier sensed there was more. As the pause lengthened between words, he felt Sloane hanging back and knew the next part was worse. So much worse.

She licked her lips. "I see it every day. I *face* it every day. But it still sucker punches me."

"You don't have to say it," Javier said in a flat, calm voice that surprised him. There was bile in his throat. "I know what he did to her. He did it before she left Pablo. It's the chief reason she left the Solaro family."

"It's consistent with his behavior," Sloane revealed. "It's what he did to Pia. He took her against her will with his hands around her throat. The only difference is he never exerted enough force to kill her."

"I saw the marks on her," Javier noted. "Pia. I saw the bruising on her throat."

Sloane traced a path through the sweat on her water glass. "Someone needs to put him in the ground. I want that person to be me. Are you okay with that?"

"Why wouldn't I be?"

"Because you've got a score to settle now, too," Sloane said knowingly.

"I've always had one." Because Javier had known on some level Jaime had won. He'd killed Javier's mother.

She clapped her hand over his wrist before he could rise. "One more thing, cowboy." When she raised her eyes again, they were fierce. "These phone calls you received from Jaime... I need to know exactly what he said. Anything he might've told you could lead us to where he is now."

"You're FBI," he said in disbelief. "How could you not have some notion of where he is?"

"Your brother's the rat everybody smells but nobody sees," she growled. "Help me find him so I can find Pia and her daughter."

"He's got them," Javier realized.

"What did Jaime tell you?" Sloane pressed.

Javier settled back in the chair, thinking over his conversations. "He said there was a plane waiting somewhere."

"Where?"

"He didn't say. He told me it was reserved for Pia and him... and me, if I turned Grace over to him and helped bring you in, too."

Sloane's eyes scanned every angle of his face. "What else?"

"I don't have anything else," he admitted. "Other than I heard you talking to Grace at Casaluna. You wondered why it took me three weeks to get you, Grace and Pia out of Solaro hands."

"I did say that," she noted.

"A few days before you were taken from the villa," Javier said slowly, "I faced Jaime in the fighting ring."

"Your father, Pablo, had quite the thing for watching his men one-up each other," Sloane said knowingly. "From what I heard, you never made an impression there."

"I didn't," Javier acknowledged, rubbing his right ear. The scar was still there. "But the last time I had faced Jaime, he cheated. He had a knife on him and would have cut off my ear if it hadn't been for Pablo."

"You wanted another shot," she surmised.

"I knew I could beat him," Javier said. "Pablo sensed it, too. And that made Jaime uneasy. He made a point of breaking my elbow."

She nearly grimaced. Her eyes cleared. "I remember you wearing a sling when you and the others came to the villa," she realized.

He nodded. "I would've gotten you and Pia out sooner. I knew where you were. But not Grace."

He lifted her chin. "Only Pablo knew where all the hideaways were."

"It took some time to heal," he explained. "I used that time to follow Alejandro. I knew he was Grace's handler. I found her the day after you escaped yours and tried to get Pia out of Jaime's house."

She was silent on that point. Idly, she smeared water rings on the countertop as she waited for him to continue.

"He tightened security after that," Javier told her. "Otherwise, I would have been able to get Pia out first."

"You want me to say it was stupid to try?"

"No," he said quickly. "You realize the only person who ever put a mark on Jaime like that before was my mother? He's had to carry yours on his face every day."

"I used to hope the vain prick thought of me every time they let him look in the mirror," she pointed out. "Now I know he did, and maybe it's the reason he couldn't forget Pia, Gracie and me. Maybe that's what made him bide his time for the right moment to escape and come after us again."

"You're not to blame for all this," he said.

She released a weary sigh. "Neither are you." Catching his stunned look, she nodded affirmation. "I realize that now. And I'm sorry for taking you down at Casaluna. Gracie's right. You didn't deserve it."

Javier cleared his throat. "If Jaime ever faced you in the ring, he'd have been hard-pressed to come out on top."

If he wasn't mistaken, a small smile touched her lips. "Now," she weighed, tilting her head, "*that* may help me sleep at night."

Grace heard the knock at the door. Quickly, she knotted the belt of the knee-length hotel robe over her middle.

Glancing through the peephole, she spotted Javier and Remy at his shoulder.

She clutched the lapels of the robe together. Underneath, she was bare. She'd attempted the shower again. She needed a distraction from what Sloane had revealed in the bar downstairs. Pia's fate and Babette's were tied up inside her. She couldn't unknot them until she knew they were safe.

Javier's gaze raced across her face when she snatched the door open. He took a step forward. "Are you all right?"

She frowned in answer. "I could use some company."

Javier was halfway across the threshold when Remy cleared his throat.

Javier froze in midstep. Grace sighed in exasperation. "What's going to happen?" she demanded of her bodyguard.

"I spent two days alone with him. We kept each other alive. What's another hour?"

Remy considered. "Sloane will want to know."

"Sloane knows already," Javier revealed.

"She does?" Grace asked, surprised.

"Si."

His dark eyes reached for her. She spread the door wider, daring Remy to say anything further in protest. "We'll be fine," she assured him.

He gave a slight nod. She knew he would call Sloane as soon as Grace was out of sight.

Grace closed the door and bolted it from the inside before she turned to Javier.

His back was to her as he kneeled to pick up Luis. He didn't murmur as he usually did to the kitten but busied his hands stroking his fur.

She tilted her head. "Are *you* all right?"

His shoulders rose and fell. "Si."

They stood, her with her back to the door, him with Luis across the room.

He read her. "You heard the news about Pia."

"Sloane told you, too?" Grace asked.

He nodded silently. The cat tried to crawl into the front pocket on his button-down shirt. Javier tightened his hold on him, pressing him to the heat of his skin at the opening of his shirt. The cat calmed.

Grace would have purred, too. She focused on that expanse of tan skin, feeling aches spring up everywhere. They were so much better than the helplessness she'd felt before he'd knocked.

He eyed the place where the lapels of her robe parted. "Were you changing?"

She shook her head. "No. I thought I'd try to shower."

His gaze touched the dry curls around her face. "Did you?"

"No."

His lifted his chin, understanding. Carefully, he set Luis on the bed. He walked around her into the bathroom.

She watched through the door as he stepped into the shower stall and turned on the tap.

Something else was wrong, Grace thought. There was anger in him. She'd seen it burning bright like hers. But there was sadness, as well. As he stood with his hand under the spray, waiting for the temperature to warm, she moved across the cool marble floor. "Javy."

He turned to face her. His cheeks stretched down into a frown.

She lifted her hand to one of them, running her thumb across the ridge. "What else did Sloane tell you?"

The drain sipped the puddling water. The spray beat on the tiles. Luis mewed, pleading from the bed's edge. Still, Javier said nothing.

When he veered around her, she braced him in place with a hand on each arm. "It's me, Javy."

"I'll keep watch," he offered. "You don't have to worry about anyone coming in. I won't let them."

"I know you won't," she acknowledged. And she wanted that. But she needed to know what had hurt him. "Tell me," she persisted.

He lifted his chin, flashing a glance at the ceiling as if hoping for interference. Then he settled, his shoulders sagging into a defeated posture. He drilled his gaze into her exposed collarbone. "Sloane told me the truth—about my mother's death."

Grace's fingers tightened reflexively on his sleeves. She flattened her hands over his triceps. "You thought she may have been murdered."

"She was," Javier explained. "She *was* murdered. Sloane found confirmation of it. In Jaime's office. Photos. Lab reports. He bought the coroner's silence, convinced him to give a false report and kept the real one. Like a trophy."

"Jaime..." Grace lost her voice. She shook her head in refusal.

"He killed her," Javier pointed out. "He waited until I went to the States, waited until he could get her alone."

She shook her head again, this time fervently. "You can't blame yourself. He waited for you to get out of the way. That shows he's more afraid of you than you think."

"He *should* be afraid," Javier said tonelessly. "I want him to be afraid. I want to end this, Grace. It's me or him."

She swallowed. "Sloane won't let you go. You can't just leave…" She stepped into the space between them and pressed her brow to his. "Javy, look at me." Raising her hands to his face, she brought his chin up. "Look at me, cariño."

His eyes sprang to hers and he blinked several times.

"Sloane just told you this, didn't she?" At his nod, she added, "Then you need to take a beat. Just take a little while. You can't be practical when you're emotional. You're too angry and sad right now to go running off unarmed into a city you don't know."

She ran her hands over his arms, up his shoulders and back down. "What do I do?" he asked, at a loss. He lowered his voice to a whisper. "What would you have me do?"

She thought about it. The sound of the shower toggled something. A dream, or a wish. She glanced at the rainfall. "Would you like to shower with me?"

Again, he blinked. His gaze raced across her face, as if trying to determine if she was kidding or not.

Grace kept her eyes level. Even as her heart pounded, she refused to waver.

At last, he stopped searching. She saw his throat move. Then he gave a nod.

Her pulse stumbled. She slid her hands off him to wrap them around the belt of her robe. Tugging, she loosened the knot.

Javier didn't move. She wasn't even sure he breathed as she parted the lapels, revealing a line of flesh from her throat to her navel. He wasn't so shy, she found, that he looked elsewhere. He looked, dark eyes growing fathoms that were immeasurable.

Shrugging, she felt the robe slide down her back. It dropped to the floor in a chenille puddle. She shivered, feeling naked in more ways than one. "You… You can't get your stitches wet. Promise."

"Lo prometo," he said quickly, the words tripping over one another. She wondered if he even knew what he was saying.

"Your turn," she told him. Unwilling to let this bravery she felt emboldened by dissipate, she stepped around him to the open shower door.

She ducked her head under the spray. It trickled warmly

through her hair, running in rivulets down her face. She raised her hands, tensing, then stopped.

It felt so good. It felt like glory. Warm, cleansing glory. The tension in her shoulders eased slightly. She gasped, not letting herself move.

The shower door closed with a thud. She jumped slightly.

His hands warmed her shoulders. She felt his face in the back of her hair. One hand lowered to her hip. Then it wound around to her belly, soothing.

She sighed, feeling as if she were about to jump out of her skin but at the same time... Oh, God, at the same time, she knew in her bones there was no other place she'd rather be.

With Javier at her back, she could go anywhere. Do anything.

"Your bandage isn't getting wet, is it?" she asked.

"No."

She didn't know whether to believe him, but still couldn't bring herself to turn. She felt brave, sure, but she was also certain she'd never made herself this vulnerable to anyone.

She took another gasping breath. "The maid came in this morning. She's this sweet Latina lady. I struck up a conversation with her. My Spanish may be better than I thought it was after all these years." *You're rambling, Grace*, she told herself. She got to the point, the confession tumbling out fast. "I asked her what 'mi sol' meant."

"Did she tell you?"

Grace licked the water off her lips and turned.

Javier's shoulders flared wide, like she remembered—burnished copper. The bandage wasn't wet, she saw with relief. She didn't dare touch it with damp hands. His waist was square and trim, neatly packed with firm muscles at the core. Dark hair spanned the length of his torso, gathering low where it thickened.

She took a breath. Two. Then she threaded her hand through the hair on the back of his head, inviting his mouth to hers. Her body flushed high with heat as he took the kiss deep.

Mi sol. My light. My sun.

He broke away. "You do know that I love you?"

She kept her eyes closed. The way he said it…like music… Everything inside her wakened. "Say it."

"I love you."

"No, Javy." She took his face in her hands again, delicate. "Say it."

He understood. And his expression softened. "Ah, mi sol. Te amo."

Her smile bloomed, burrowing into the curves of her cheeks as triumph erupted in twin jets of happiness and radiance. She reveled in all of it, laughing against his mouth as he smiled, too, then kissed her again.

Water rained, pooling at their feet, as Javier's touch swept her away alongside kisses. His calluses grazed the hollows of her throat, collarbone, sternum. Palms teased her ribs, then flattened against the outer curve of her breasts.

"Bonita," he murmured, his mouth against her throat. He suckled. Her chin tilted, giving him plenty of room to work. He traced the shape of her breasts in a barely there caress that sensitized her flesh. By the time he closed the peaks between his fingers, he didn't have to use much pressure to bring her up to her toes. Shudders racked her.

She grabbed his shoulders, then remembered the bandage. Pressing her hand to the center of his chest, she backed him up to the shower wall, away from the spray. Putting her fingers to his lips, she dragged each word out. "Hold very still."

He held up his hands in acquiescence, eyes hooded and watchful. His lips quirked at the corners. "Doctor's orders?"

"Si," she whispered before taking his mouth decisively with her own.

Her hands roamed freely. They ranged across his shoulder blades, making muscles twitch underneath her fingers, low over his hips, over his chest, good shoulder and throat. They trickled down his spine. The hair on his chest was soft. Softer below the waist.

A noise in his throat caught as she took him in hand, not squeezing. Not stroking. She held him, testing the length of him, the weight. She reached lower still.

Javier nearly swallowed his tongue. His hands were still high.

His mouth was open. "You know how to bring a man to his knees," he rasped.

"You're still on your feet, soldier," she observed, then she pushed him one step farther, back to the marble bench. He buckled to it.

His hands came to the backs of her thighs, urging her forward.

She stepped in the space between his parted knees.

His stubble, so new it barely showed on his jaw, raked light across her belly. He drew her toward him until her hands were against the wall above his head.

Playful, venturing, he took his hands up over her rear to her waist, back down, flattening, firm. He planted her foot on the bench beside him. He traced her instep, turning his lips to her inner thigh.

She felt the heat of his mouth, his breath blowing across her center. She froze. Not in fear this time.

He closed his lips over her. Everything inside her pooled, molten, arrowing toward the pull of his mouth.

She hadn't made a noise, she realized, her jaw locked tight. She could see light behind her eyes when she closed them, but her lips pressed taut, white, trapping urgent notes behind the seam.

It had been so long since she'd reached this point. Everything building, clamoring, firing. She'd thought it was as broken as her fight-or-flight reflex, another casualty of captivity.

Her breaths came in pants through her nose. Her teeth clamped. The muscles in her thighs quaked.

A mew escaped. One followed another, unable to be contained. Her nails were digging into the bed of his uninjured shoulder, her other hand clenched in his hair.

She was hurting him, she thought, but she couldn't loosen her grip. He sipped and laved, nibbled and groaned so that the nerves around her labia vibrated and sparked.

Grace got her first glimpse of stars.

If he stopped now, she'd beg.

It was a miracle he hadn't already. How was she still standing? Her joints were pliant, her legs butter.

She clung to the edge as he held her in thrall, one arm under her raised thigh, the other arm over her standing leg so that his hands met behind her, rocking her in waves against his mouth.

Breaking didn't happen all at once. The climax dragged itself out, splitting atom by atom, until she was sated and she sank.

He held her as gingerly as he had held Luis, cradling.

She caught her breath. "We're not done here," she managed.

Javier's smile came freely, knowing. "No, mi amor," he agreed. He turned his mouth to hers, dipping her back in the crook of his arm. "We're not done."

Grace was somewhere between awake and dreaming. The bed hugged her. Her body hummed.

"Are you sleeping, bonita?"

A lazy smile grew from the ball joint of her jaw. It spread to the cheek against the sheet. "Not on your life."

Javier's hands continued to knead the muscles around her spine. She felt his breath across her ear before his lips pressed, soft, to the skin just beneath.

Grace closed her eyes as he nuzzled through curls, working his way around her neck, unhurried. She wasn't sure she'd ever felt so lax.

The shower had just been the beginning, she'd found. The relief that had come with not just conquering her shower fears, but with her enjoyment of what they had done together.

She hadn't abstained from sex, but sex had often come as a disappointment after her experience in trafficking. For a while, sex had been downright confusing. This was normal for survivors. Sloane had told her how it had taken a long time for sex to make sense again and even longer for it to feel right. Pia had explained in halting whispers how long it had taken her to feel comfortable enough in the bedroom with Sam for her to come close to orgasm.

Normally, sex was a frustrating or fruitless enterprise. The buildup was nice. The anticipation sparkled. But the actual deed... How was Grace supposed to come when she was still on that island inside her mind?

It didn't make sense for Javier to be the one to fix it. It didn't make sense that the walls would break now. Somewhere over the last few days, those bridges she had built between herself and him had steeled.

She'd trusted lovers in the past. She'd trusted Salim, implicitly, but to little success. So why now?

You've given all of yourself, some part of her answered.

When had she made that choice? At what point had she given Javier her heart?

In increments, she realized. Slow, steady increments. And she had grown bolder and braver with each piece she gave, so that when it came time to offer herself wholly... She hadn't hesitated. She'd barely even thought about it.

She hadn't told him she loved him in the shower. But it was true. She loved him. And that would be terrifying...so utterly terrifying if they hadn't survived all that they had.

His kisses had spread down her spine. His hand cruised beneath her hip. She shifted, giving him access. She was already wet when his fingers found the juncture of her thighs.

"Am I hurting you?"

She arched her back, humming as sensation reigned again. "No."

"Tell me if I hurt you."

"You won't hurt me."

When she moved with him, cranking the tension, his head bowed to her shoulder and he groaned. "Grace."

Her hand found his. "Farther."

At her urging, he inserted a finger.

She felt his arousal low against her thigh. She felt his body tightening. He nibbled the area between her neck and shoulder. Urgent, she keened and writhed as the kneading quickened. The callus of his thumb dragged across her. Sensation took on the acute edge of exigency. Her need grew sharp. It was white hot. Hotter than stars.

The stars cartwheeled. She groaned, the base of her spine drawing up, then back as her lungs released and her pulse gamboled. The sheet was damp and she realized it was from her own skin. She sighed. "I did it again," she said, the declaration muffled by the bed.

His hand was in her hair, brushing it away to find her. He kissed her temple, then her cheek. "What did you say?"

"Nothing." She rolled into him, chest to chest, so that their legs lay akimbo and she could confront the hot line of his mouth.

His arms ranged across her back. "I'm happy we kept Sabine's bag. It's coming in handy again."

The condoms in Sabine's bag, specifically, Grace thought, amused. She rolled on top of him. "How's the shoulder?"

"What shoulder?"

He knew it had to be hurting him. He'd carried her from shower to bed like a queen. She saw no blood on the bandage but should probably take a moment, check his sutures...

He reached for her. She answered, turning her mouth to his palm when it cupped her jaw. As she lifted her hips, opening for him, she thought fleetingly, *Later.*

She liked to watch, she found, the way their bodies met and meshed. She liked to watch Javier's muscles lock and release. She loved watching ardency and caution fight behind his eyes. Even after what they'd done in the shower, he banked his own needs and let things play out slow.

She didn't mind going slow. She didn't mind the long buildup. When his hips rolled beneath hers in a circular motion, she dropped her head back. She hissed in pleasure, tuning her motions to his in exquisite counterpoint. Panting now, she moaned, "Again."

He met her stroke for stroke, hands seated on the curves of her waist. Vaguely, she wondered who was driving whom. Then the stars bottled themselves again, and she abandoned all thought completely.

Chapter 16

"Room service."

Grace opened eyes languid with sleep. She'd burrowed under the thick, white duvet.

When Javier had heard knocking, it had taken a lot of self-talk to climb out of the nest of blankets and thighs.

She frowned. "Pants."

"What?"

"You're wearing pants."

He looked at his jeans. "I couldn't answer the door without them. Sloane's man would have tossed me out."

"I think Remy knows you and I are tied up in more than the Cajun two-step in here," she drawled, propping her head on her hand as she angled her elbow into the sheets.

Her curls were a dark halo around her head, huge, messy and adorable. There was a small mark where her neck met her shoulder from his mouth.

"What're you grinning at?" she asked.

"A hungry queen," he ventured.

A smug smile pulled at her mouth. It stopped when he handed her a plate. "Wait. Wait. Wait. Slow down."

"What?"

"Before this goes any further," she said soberly, "I have to know one thing."

"Ask," he invited, apprehension tightening his gut.

"Are you a morning person?"

The laughter shook him.

"I'm serious," she said as she balanced the plate on her hand.

"I have no doubt." He snuck a kiss, unable to resist. "Bonita."

She pushed him back with the heel of her hand. "Answer the question," she said, even as her eyes deepened.

He'd seen them plead, go hazy, darken and glaze. The thought made the skin at the small of his back draw up in response.

He'd had her, and she'd most certainly had her way with him. Then they'd poured themselves into bed and, after a short recuperation, they'd done it all again.

One time. He'd thought one time with Grace would be enough to last a lifetime. As he watched her whip the lid off her plate to sniff the quesadillas stacked there, he realized he wasn't done. With Grace, it would never be enough. He'd come back again and again, begging for more.

Turning away, he picked up his own plate before getting back in bed, stacking pillows behind him as she had and setting the plate in his lap. He uncovered the chicken Parm he'd ordered and unwrapped the silverware.

Luis stirred from his throne atop the scratching post. He stood, stretched his back in a long arch before jumping down.

"Incoming," Grace warned a second before four paws met the bed and the kitten wound his way up Javier's legs. "He's going for yours because he knows you're a pushover."

"He likes chicken better than…" He eyed her plate. "Whatever that is."

She gestured to the quesadillas. "This is Mexican."

He frowned, shook his head. "A distant cousin, maybe. Ask them a question. I bet they don't even speak Spanish."

Grace smiled in spite of herself. "You *are* a morning person."

"Si, but there's a bright side," he suggested, cutting the chicken with the edge of his fork. "You get to have breakfast in bed every morning."

Her eyes widened. "You cook?"

"Breakfast," he said. "Just breakfast."

She considered as she took a bite. "What would you have made me—the morning after our date in New Orleans?"

He thought about it. "Assuming you had everything in your fridge…"

She bobbed her head in affirmation.

"Chilaquiles," he told her, "with black coffee and a fruit cocktail."

She licked the sour cream off the end of her thumb, intrigued. "And the next morning?"

The next morning… He grinned. "Huevos rancheros. We'll polish it off with horchata de arroz."

"Mmm," she said with a slight shake of her head. Forking another bite to her mouth, she muttered, "I'm going to be late to work for the rest of my life."

The rest of her life. For a second, Javier didn't think he could breathe. Then he did, in a burst of excitement. Before he could say something foolish, he stuffed chicken Parm into his mouth and tried to chew around the urge to smile like an idiot.

She took his silence to mean something else. "Was it all too much?"

"Was what too much?"

"What we did?" she asked. "All that. Just now."

"No," he murmured, searching her. He cursed. "I did hurt you, didn't I?"

"No," she answered quickly. She smiled. "I intend to talk to Remy and Sloane if I have to. You're staying here tonight."

Longing overwhelmed him. He touched her chin. "Grace, would you consider coming to New Mexico with me?"

She stilled. "New Mexico?"

"I'd like to show you the mesa." He could see it. Grace and the open sky wheeling above her. "I'd like to see you ride a horse."

"That would be a first."

He gawped. "You've never been in the saddle?"

"We both know I have," she said with a sly grin.

"A Western saddle," he clarified.

"No," Grace said. "To tell you the truth… I was always a little afraid of horses."

He shook his head. "The woman who wades into alligator bayous is afraid of horses."

She considered. "You could teach me—to love horses. To ride them. I think I'd like that."

He would, too. "We could camp under the stars. There are more of them in high desert country than you can fathom. We could build a fire, listen to the wind, share a sleeping bag..."

"Will you keep me safe from bears?"

"We don't get many bears in northeast New Mexico," he considered. "Mostly rattlesnakes. And cougars."

"Bon Dieu." She shook her head. "Sounds terrifying. And exciting. I must be crazy. *You're* crazy for wanting to take a city girl out on the range."

"Anyone who could sleep between the tombs of Lafayette Cemetery can handle a night in the wilderness," he wagered. "So will you? You've shown me some of the places that made you who you are. I'd like to return the favor. I'd like to show you mine."

She softened. "Si," she decided. Then, more certainly, she nodded. "It's a date."

He cupped her cheek, kissed the other, then her brow, the tip of her nose before seizing her mouth again. He would unerringly return to this, always.

Kissing Grace was coming home.

He kissed her long enough that Luis snuck a bite of chicken off his plate and retreated under the bed. Grace reached for Javier and their plates nearly upended.

"We can't," he told her.

"Why not?" she asked.

"I don't know if either of us can handle any more," he said, out of breath already.

She grinned. "I love proving a man wrong."

He angled his head, willing to risk it. Risk everything for her.

The phone rang.

She groaned. "If that's Sloane..."

"Tell her to call back," Javier finished.

Grace swung away. She knocked the receiver out of the cradle, then picked it up. "You rang?"

Javier felt more than saw her tense. She pulled the phone away from her ear, stared at it for a second before pushing it toward him. "For you."

Javier frowned as he took the phone. He placed his plate on the nightstand, tossed the duvet off and planted his feet on the floor. "Aló?" he answered.

"Hermano," Jaime responded briskly. "Have you thought anymore about my offer?"

Javier gnashed his teeth. "What offer?"

"Your freedom for the doctor and the she-bitch."

Javier's blood boiled. "What have you done with Pia?"

He heard Grace's sharp intake of air as Jaime paused. "Pia."

"Si," Javier snapped. "Pia Russo. Where are you holding her?"

Jaime's voice treaded lightly. "She's with me."

"You're lying," Javier discerned. He straightened. "You don't know where she is. That's why you need the others. You want to extract the information from them." He felt a lick of relief. "It won't do you any good. They don't know where Pia is, either."

"You're the liar," Jaime lashed. "They know where she is. They know where she's hiding. And so do you. Stop cowering in that casino behind the FBI. Bring me my women."

"I know what you did to my mother," Javier heard himself say. His muscles had gone rigid. His lips were the only thing that moved. "Tell me where to find you. I have a bullet with your name on it."

Jaime chuckled. It might've been a warm sound to anyone else's ears. It made Javier want to reach through the phone and grab him by the throat. "She died in her place—with my name on her lips."

Javier stood up, unfolding himself carefully. "Where are you?"

"Meet me in the parking garage four blocks south and two blocks west," Jaime instructed. "Come alone and unarmed, or the casino comes crashing down."

Grace watched, arms hugging her middle, as Javier slowly walked around the bed to replace the phone in the cradle. "That was him, wasn't it?" she asked, the words muffled against the back of her hand.

He stood for a moment, looking toward the shaft of light between the parting of the curtains. The city was going dark.

Grace sat up on her knees. "Javy." She reached for his hand. "What did he want?"

He shook his head slightly. Fingers circling reassuringly over hers, he lowered back to the bed. "Nothing."

"Don't," she warned. "We're beyond lies. Aren't we?"

The way he looked at her… It was as if she were on the far side of the world. Agony worked across his face before he looked away again.

"Javy?" she said, barely above a whisper now.

"You're right," he said, his chin near his chest. He nodded to himself. "We're past that point…"

She waited with bated breath, watching his shoulders rise and fall.

He spoke by rote, as if sounding out words he'd never wanted to speak. "Pablo Solaro had three sons."

She shook her head. "Pablo what?"

"Jaime was the first," he went on, undeterred. "He was illegitimate."

"Why are you telling me this?" she blurted.

"Alejandro was the second," Javier went on again, "the only child from Pablo's first marriage."

When he paused, she asked, "Why is this relevant?"

Javier seemed to brace himself for whatever came next. "After his first wife died, Pablo married a fifteen-year-old girl from Guanajuato. He thought she wasn't able to give him a child so…when she bartered for her freedom, he let her take it. He let her go."

Grace's eyes widened as the story tugged at ribbons of memory. "Are you…" She stopped, held up her hands as the picture cleared. "Wait. Wait a minute. Are you saying that—"

He nodded warily. "Pablo's second wife was Valentina Rivera. My mother."

She had to close her mouth to form the next question. "And that would make you…"

"Pablo's third son," Javier confirmed.

Her breath stuttered out. "Which would make Jaime your..."

"Half brother," he confirmed.

"And Alejandro?"

The devastation on his face was real, but his voice remained flat. "Also my half brother."

She stared at him in horror.

"I'm not proud of it, Grace."

"You..." She tried to get the words out. Couldn't. Started over, this time raising her hands. "This whole time...from the beginning... You've lied."

He nodded grimly. "I did."

"Why?" she demanded.

"If I had told you," he wondered, "from day one that I was Alejandro's brother? Would you have trusted me? Would you have left that house with me?"

"It's been *twelve years*, Javy," she snapped.

"Si, twelve years," he acknowledged. "And I'm still afraid you'll see me in the same light you see them. And I didn't expect to love you like this. Like it's all I have."

She looked away. He'd made her so happy minutes ago. She choked back the happiness now because incredulity and pain were overriding it. Cursing, she said, "You know, my mother used to say...it's not the lie that makes the man. It's the *act* of lying. You lied, knowing it's one thing I'd have the most difficulty forgiving." When he only looked at her, she threw in, "Alejandro lied, too."

He grimaced. "I am *not* Alejandro. If you can't see that... if Mexico didn't show you that...if the last few days haven't proved that, then what am I doing here? Why are we together? Why are you with me?"

"That anger you're feeling right now," she said knowingly, "that betrayal... It burns. Doesn't it? It hurts like you've hurt me."

"Grace. Do you look at me and see him?"

She folded her arms over her breasts, leaning back against the headboard. Her lip trembled. She bit the inside. "I don't know what to see. Or say. Or feel."

"Do you want me to leave?"

Didn't he hear? She couldn't think. She couldn't feel. His betrayal had numbed her. How was she supposed to know anything anymore?

How could she look at him and not see this?

She looked away as her eyes filled. Her heart guttered and twisted. Why couldn't he have just told her the truth?

It took her a minute to realize he'd left the bed.

He dressed silently. She watched in a faraway daze as he put on his boots.

He stopped, meeting her eyes.

She wanted to look away, couldn't bring herself to, cursed herself again for every weakness she'd ever felt...

His eyes were so dark.

Dark water.

Why hadn't they made her run for the shallows? Why did she feel them pulling her under still?

The undertow was strong with him. It always had been.

"Buenas noches, Grace," he muttered. Then he unbolted the door and left.

If Javier didn't get to the parking garage in the next hour, Jaime might make good on his threat.

He waited until he'd slipped past the guard on his door and Remy. Sloane provided an opportune moment by showing up a half hour after he left Grace's room. They had roped the man at the elevator into the status update. While their heads were together and their voices mumbled, Javier edged out of his room and down the wall of the hallway. He slipped through the door to the stairwell.

He couldn't do anything about the cameras. He just hoped whoever Sloane had manning the security feed looked in the other direction as he passed several of them between his floor and the lobby.

Avoiding more agents by striding onto the casino floor, he immersed himself in the raucous crowd of gamblers. Machines rang out, coins dropped, the roulette wheel ticked, people shouted. Servers breezed by with trays of drinks. Javier saw the agent posted at the door to the pool deck and backtracked.

The kitchen offered another escape route. He passed through steam fragrant with steak and lobster, pushing toward the open door to the street.

A delivery was in progress. Sloane's guard was checking the delivery person's credentials. Javier ventured out of sight before he'd finished.

He found a pay phone two blocks away. Dropping change into the dispenser, he dialed the number.

It rang once before Sloane answered. "Escarra."

"Get out of the building," he told her.

"Rivera?" She stopped, likely to check the caller ID. Her voice dropped. "Where the hell are you and why aren't you upstairs?"

"Did you hear me?" he asked insistently. "You need to get Grace and everyone else out of the casino now."

"Why?" she demanded. "What's happening?"

"Jaime called," he explained. "He knows Grace is there. And you. He doesn't have Pia. But he threatened to bring down the casino if I didn't meet him alone and unarmed."

She shouted something to someone with her. Javier heard other shouts and instructions echoing. Finally, Sloane said, "Where is he meeting you?"

Javier stared at the parking garage. He could see it from his position, a mass of gray, slitted concrete. The lights were on, though the sun wasn't quite beyond the horizon. "He said to meet him alone."

"I need this," she growled. "You *know* I need this. Give me the location. You agreed to let me have him when the time came."

Javier hadn't known he was lying then. But then… *She died in her place—with my name on her lips…*

"You're not a hero, Javier," Sloane chided. "Do you hear me? You are *not* a hero."

Javier agreed. How did the saying go—a rat may run the race, but at the finish line, he was still a rat? "Tell Grace…" He hesitated. "Tell her I love her. Tell her I've always loved her."

"Get back here and tell her yourself, asswipe!"

He hung up as Sloane smoothly switched to creative Spanish expletives. Then he shoved his hands in the pockets of his jacket and crossed the street.

Five stories up, he stepped off the elevator into a sea-salt breeze blowing swiftly off the Gulf.

The lot was empty. But for a few cars, he was alone.

He went to the railing, looking long toward the Gulf.

Jaime should've been here.

Javier fought a wave of uneasiness. He looked toward the Beau Rivage.

Had Sloane gotten Grace out? Was she safe?

Was the reason Jaime was late because Javier had made a mistake telling Sloane he was going to blow up the casino? Would he do it, anyway, when he saw them evacuating?

The shriek of tires made him pivot toward the on-ramp. A black Suburban roared into view.

Javier removed his hands from his pockets. He spread his feet and stood his ground as it accelerated.

The SUV screamed to a halt, the passenger side facing him.

The doors opened. Javier stared, blank, at the battered face before him. "Where's Jaime?"

Carlos sneered. "I have orders to bring you to him. Otherwise, I put this barrel in your mouth."

Javier eyed the gun in Carlos's hand. "He said he'd be here."

"Too much heat in the city," Carlos revealed. "Too many cops with his picture." He used the gun to gesture. "Turn out your pockets."

"I'm not armed," Javier told him.

"Turn out your pockets," Carlos said again firmly.

Warily, Javier looked around. When he was sure it was just him and Carlos, he turned the pockets of his jacket inside out.

"Open it," Carlos demanded.

Javier unzipped the camel-toned garment and parted it wide.

Carlos stepped forward. He patted him down with one hand, the other never losing its grip on his weapon. When he was done, he said, "You're clear."

Before Javier could take a step forward, Carlos's fist whistled forward. The blow snapped Javier's head back. It clamped his tongue between his teeth.

Carlos leaned in as Javier staggered. "You were smart to leave the doctor lady. Jaime wanted her alive, too. But after what she did to me in that alley, I would've thrown her off an overpass."

Javier spat a stream of blood on the concrete. "She's beyond your reach, primo."

Carlos stuck his boot in Javier's back, shoving him toward the open door of the vehicle. "Get in the car. I'm looking forward to watching Jaime rearrange your face. Just like he did all those years ago. There's no walking away this time. You know this, si? You know the only thing waiting for you at the end of this journey is a box."

Javier watched him close the door behind them. The driver took off. Javier grabbed the armrest on the seat as the Suburban careened out of the parking lot. "Si," he said gravely.

Chapter 17

Sirens flashed and screamed. The crowd of evacuees had been pushed a block away from the casino.

Grace searched the milling emergency workers, raising her arm when she saw Remy striding toward the barricade. "Over here!" she called.

He veered straight toward her. Grace was relieved to see the bundle under his arm. When she held out hers, he handed Luis to her. "He was in your room under the bed."

Grace rocked the kitten. "Michi," she murmured. "You must've been so scared." Sloane hadn't given her a chance to hunt for him before snatching her from her hotel room and rushing her out of the building. "You went back in for him?"

"There are still some who aren't accounted for," Remy explained. "I searched a couple of floors…"

Grace searched the people on each side of the barricade again. "Javy?" she asked.

Remy paused. Then he shook his head. "Nobody's seen him."

"If he evacuated, he would have found me by now. He would have checked on me, made sure Luis and I were okay…"

"Sloane accessed security footage remotely," Remy explained. "She'll find him."

"We had a fight. He was upset when he left. He told me a

secret...something from his past. I called him a liar. What if he left...ran away?"

"Rivera doesn't strike me as the type who'd run away when things get hard," Remy said after a moment of thought.

She realized she was holding Luis too tightly. She readjusted him, tucking him inside her jacket when she remembered the way he'd sought the warmth of Javier's skin. "Will you find Sloane—see if she knows anything?"

He shook his head. "She's asked me to stay with you."

She glanced over her shoulder at the agent Sloane had assigned to her. "I have Agent Sapello."

Remy didn't spare the agent a glance. "Sloane wants me on your six."

"Wow," Grace murmured, consoled somewhat by the kitten's little ball of heat across her middle. "She really does trust you."

Remy lifted a shoulder, head swiveling to scan. He was tall enough to see over the bulk of the crowd. "She sees enough in hindsight to appreciate how hard she made my job when she was eighteen. She went looking for trouble—I brought her home."

"You deserve a medal," Grace noted. "I remember that version of her. I wondered how she managed to avoid getting involved in something she couldn't get out of. Addiction. Sex trafficking, again. If you get swept up in it once, you're bound to fall victim to it again. But she had you. You saved her."

"People save themselves," Remy told her. "Some people either choose not to see that or they're so far into the abyss, they don't want to save themselves. For a while, she was the latter. Then one day she decided that wasn't the way she wanted to go."

Grace thought of the conversation at the bar. "She'd rather die with a gun in her hand."

"She's too involved in this," he said. "She's running at a wall and doesn't care what happens when she hits it. She's willing to jeopardize herself and her career to cut this bastard off at the knees."

"I agree," she said. "I'd rather you had her back than mine. You kept her from tipping over the edge before. You can do it again."

"She wants to be the one who puts Solaro down," Remy

added. "She wants it like her next breath. But if he crosses my sights, I won't hesitate to finish it for her. Even if she never forgives me for it."

Remy wanted to avenge the girl he'd pulled away from destruction. "She's lucky she's got you."

His brows rose. "Tell her that."

"I will," Grace decided.

"As to Rivera," Remy said, knotting his arms over his chest, eyes moving across every face, cataloging, "don't think too badly of him. You say he told you something from his past," Remy reminded her. "As someone who's got plenty of ghosts, as long as he didn't hurt or kill anyone who didn't deserve it, I say go easy on him. He came out of your room looking like the world was coming to an end."

"I…"

Before Grace could get the words out, Sloane hailed her. "Where have you been?" Grace asked her. "Why was everyone evacuated? Do you know what happened to Javy?"

Sloane held up her hands. "We need to get you to a secure location. Then we can talk answers."

Grace shrugged Sloane's hand off her arm. "Answer now," she said. "What is going on, Sloane? Why was the hotel evacuated?"

Sloane glanced around. Stepping closer to Grace, she lowered her voice. "There was a credible threat against the structure."

Grace gawped. "Like a bomb?"

"Shh!" Sloane hissed. "You can't toss words like that around without inciting a panic!"

"I'm sorry," Grace said quickly, lowering her voice, too. "Am I right, though?"

"Maybe," Sloane said. "The bomb squad's sweeping the place now."

"Bon Dieu," Grace breathed, reaching inside her jacket to touch Luis's silky back for comfort. "Where did the threat come from?" She sucked in a breath. "Jaime?"

"Yes," Sloane answered. Her jaw tightened, then released. "It was Javier who called it in."

"Javy?" Grace said, stricken.

"He said he had contact with Jaime."

Grace nodded. "There was a call to my room. The man asked for Javy. He confirmed it was Jaime after hanging up."

"Did you overhear any of the exchange?" Sloane asked urgently.

"Stuff about Pia," Grace said numbly. "Jaime said something that made Javy think he didn't have her. It sounded like Jaime wanted you and me. He thinks we have information that'll point to wherever she's hiding."

"You should have brought this to me straightaway," Sloane informed her.

"I was…" Grace's eyes filled. God, Sloane was right. "I didn't know about the bomb threat. I didn't hear any of that."

"Javier went to confront Jaime," Sloane said.

"What?" Grace asked. "Why? How did he get out of the hotel—past his detail? The other agents? Surveillance? He's unarmed. You took his gun. What does he think he's going to do once he gets there—talk Jaime out of killing him? He'll *kill* him, Sloane. Jaime blames Javy for bringing about the Solaros' fall. *He's going to kill him!*"

Sloane grabbed Grace by the arms. "You're no good to me hysterical. Take a breath, Gracie. Take a deep breath and think. Was there anything else from the call you can remember?"

Grace couldn't see anything but Javier's face as he left. "He knew… When he left my room, he knew what he was going to do. He said goodbye."

"You could save his life."

"He's Pablo's son!" Grace said, shaking her head. "He's Jaime's brother!"

"I know," Sloane said impatiently.

Grace faltered. "What do you mean, you know?"

"I've known about Javier's mother and her marriage to Pablo since I joined the FBI eight years ago."

Grace felt like someone had knocked the wind out of her. "You didn't think to tell me? You kept me in the dark, too?"

"I wasn't authorized to tell anyone anything."

"What a load of bull!" Grace shrieked. Heads swiveled in

their direction. "You were protecting me—again! I need everyone to *stop* protecting me!"

Remy grew restless beside her. "Sloane, we need to move."

"I know," Sloane said. "There's a car down the street waiting."

"Hold up!" Grace tried to push them both away. "I'm not going anywhere with you!"

Sloane sighed, defeated. She reached into Grace's jacket.

"What are you doing?" Grace demanded.

Sloane took Luis from her. Holding the cat at arm's length with one hand, she snapped her fingers with the other. "Remy, do your thing."

Remy didn't so much as grunt as he hauled a seething, struggling Grace over his shoulder. He didn't slow when she raked her hands down his back or kicked. The crowd seemed to part for them. Remy and Sloane bundled Grace and Luis into the waiting vehicle. The door closed. A siren chirped. The driver pulled away from the curb.

Grace didn't speak for a while. Not until they were outside the city and Sloane turned to her, her face shrouded in darkness. "I'm sorry."

It sounded sincere, at least. Still… "I called him a liar. I compared him to Alejandro."

"That's not why he left."

"What do you know?" Grace lashed out. "If Jaime has him, he's dead already. Javy asked me before he left if I looked at him and saw Alejandro, and I didn't answer. I let him walk away."

"That's why I need you to think," Sloane said gently. "Is there anything else you can remember from Javier's conversation with Jaime? Anything? It doesn't matter how insignificant it may seem."

Grace closed her eyes, scrubbing her temples. Luis had settled, indignant, on the seat next to her. He wasn't fond of cars. Or Sloane. "They talked about Javier's mother."

"Anything else?"

Grace screwed up her face, trying to bring the fuzzy details to the surface. "There was something about…a parking garage?"

Sloane took out her phone. The screen illuminated her face. "Anything else?"

Grace shook her head. "South? Southwest, maybe?"

Sloane started typing. A map of Biloxi showed up on-screen. She searched the area, zooming in, panning. "There are a dozen parking decks within a five-mile radius of the Beau Rivage."

"Something private," Remy suggested from the front seat. "It's Saturday. Something business related that would be empty near sunset."

Sloane nodded, narrowing her search. "Three possibles."

"Can you pull security footage off of them without a warrant?" Remy wondered.

Sloane tilted her head. "I think the owners will cooperate when I tell them my request is linked to the bomb scare at the Beau Rivage."

"If you find the parking garage…" Grace began.

"We find a plate," Sloane finished. "Add that to the APB on Jaime, and it's only a matter of time before we get eyes on that vehicle."

Chapter 18

They drove for nearly an hour, far from city lights. Far from anything.

The airfield seemed to appear out of thin air. One moment, there were trees everywhere. The next, the dusty, red-dirt expanse stretched beyond the path of the vehicle's headlights.

Another Suburban, this one dented and pitted with bullet holes along its broad side, loomed out of the dark.

The driver slowed. Carlos glanced at Javier. "I hope you've made your peace."

Javier thought of Grace and knew there would be no peace if he couldn't call her his own. He said nothing as the vehicle stopped.

Several men piled out of the other SUV. Carlos opened the door and jumped down to the ground, gesturing with his gun for Javier to do the same.

Javier didn't see that he had any choice.

"He's unarmed," Carlos told the other men when they approached, guns drawn. He pushed Javier forward roughly.

The men parted. Behind them stood a tall figure, his silk shirt the color of oxblood. The material rippled across his chest in the breeze. It was tucked into a pair of nicely pressed black pants.

His hands cupped his mouth and the spark from his lighter wavered bright against his face, highlighting the jagged, thin scar. The lighter's lid clicked smartly as Jaime flicked his hand, closing it and extinguishing the flame. He drew on his glowing cigarette, watching Javier in the crossbeam of the headlights. Exhaling smoke through his teeth, he crossed to him and used the hand with the cigarette to wave an encompassing hand over Javier's front. "I'd be happier to see you, hermano. But you didn't bring my women."

"Because they're not your women," Javier replied. Prison had boiled Jaime down to his essence. Javier felt a waver of fear, and he felt rage. Doing his best to keep it contained, he remained in place. He was unarmed, outnumbered six to one. "They never belonged to you."

Jaime laughed silently, releasing more smoke into Javier's face. His grin was no longer appealing. It was grim. There was a finality to it that was cold and sure. He took a step closer to Javier, the toes of his patent leather shoes inches from Javier's. It forced Javier to look up. Cut down to a lean figure, Jaime seemed even taller.

Javier held his ground. "I came to tell you to stop looking for them. The FBI's onto you. Your face is on the news. There's not a cop or federal agent who isn't looking for you right now. It's only a matter of time before they find you. And you only want Grace and Sloane so they can lead you to Pia. Your obsession with her was your downfall before. It'll be your downfall again."

Jaime's eyes practically glittered in the dark. His lips pursed around the end of the cigarette before he lowered it again. "Would you let that stop you? You and this... Grace. You see her as yours, no?"

Javier didn't like Grace's name in Jaime's mouth. It made the skin on the back of his neck prickle uncomfortably.

Jaime went on, "Would you let anything stop you...from claiming her?"

"She's not my property," Javier informed him. "Nor is Pia yours."

Jaime's brow arched. "A man's wife is his property."

"Wife?" Javier shook his head. "Pia was never your wife."

Jaime ran his tongue over his teeth as he circled Javier. "She's my wife. Just as certainly as Grace is your lover." He leaned in close over Javier's shoulder, smelling. "I can smell her on you, hermano." When Javier flinched, he added experimentally, "Would you like to see her live?" When Javier said nothing, Jaime pulled on the cigarette again. He released a torrent of rich tobacco smoke. "Then tell me where I can find Pia and the girl."

So Jaime knew about Babette. Javier wondered if he knew where the child had come from and if that factored into how badly he wanted to locate Pia. "I don't know where she is. Even if I did, I wouldn't give her to you."

Jaime wound back around to Javier's front. He dropped the cigarette on the ground and crushed it with his heel. "Why are you here, then?"

"You know why I'm here," Javier said darkly, wishing he had a weapon. Any weapon. His fists knotted at his sides. They quaked.

"Ah," Jaime said, and he laughed again, facing Javier fully. "This is about Valentina."

"You're not allowed to say her name," Javier said through gnashed teeth.

"She thought she was untouchable," Jaime noted. "Invincible. The iron woman. That's what they called her. And I crushed her. I crushed her under my boot like a daisy."

A chortle went up through the surrounding men. The bones of Javier's hands vibrated, wanting to strike. "You waited until I was gone."

"You would have just got in my way," Jaime said with a shrug. "My little, insignificant brother."

"If I was so insignificant, why did you wait until my back was turned?" Javier asked in a low, throbbing voice.

Jaime stilled as his men grew quiet.

Javier advanced. "You should have gone through me to get to her. Not waited until I wasn't there. You should have faced me, man-to-man. But you're not a man, are you, Jaime? You're a covarde. A coward."

Jaime's smile had fled. "She wasn't defenseless," he claimed. "I've carried her marks with me. I've carried them and thought of her every day of my life."

"You owe me a debt," Javier informed him. "A fight. You and me."

"That didn't work so well for you in the fighting ring."

"I nearly beat you once," Javier reminded him. He nodded grimly when he saw Jaime remember. "I would've had you had you not cheated."

Jaime lowered his voice. "And I would have killed you had our father not put a stop to it."

"Pablo's not here anymore," Javier reminded him. "It's you and me."

"You made sure of that," Jaime pointed out, "when you betrayed us all."

"It's not a betrayal," Javier explained. "Not when I never believed in the cause to begin with. I joined the Solaro cartel, knowing I would be the one to blow it up from the inside. And I'd enjoy every minute of it."

Javier was quick enough to see the muscle in Jaime's jaw cheek twitch just once. Control, Javier saw. Something Jaime had apparently learned in prison. All that waiting. All that planning.

And now to have all that thwarted—not being able to find the woman he was still under the delusion was his. The old Jaime wouldn't have waited to blow the casino. He would have already lit the world on fire.

"You plan to execute me anyway," Javier pointed out. He spread his arms out to either side. "Fight me, Jaime. Let's fight this out honorably—like Pablo would have wanted us to."

Something changed in Jaime's face. The hard mask of brutality snapped into place. He reached for the small of his back. The glint of steel in the moonlight showed Javier the elegant, long-barreled handgun. The successive *click-click* made him brace.

The gun was Pablo's but the eyes in the hard face were the old Jaime's.

As he closed the distance between them, Jaime's voice simmered. "You talk of *honor*?"

Javier's eyes closed automatically when the barrel pressed to the center of his forehead. He raised his hands slowly, choosing his words carefully. "Jaime…"

He spat a curse in Javier's face. "There was nothing *honorable* about what you did. Nothing."

Javier could feel the watchfulness of the others, their readiness and speculation. They were far too accustomed to watching people bend to Jaime's will. Jaime had brought them to heel with professions that he was Pablo Solaro's sole heir.

If they knew Pablo dismissed him regularly, doubling down on Alejandro's status as second-in-command from the time his favored son could walk... Javier knew how that had eaten at Jaime, how it had nearly broken him—how it had given life to the old Jaime. At his core, Jaime was still that volatile man ruled by his predilections for iniquity and savagery.

Backing down from a challenge wasn't part of his programming, especially in front of men who carried Pablo's brand on their arms like talismans.

"What are you afraid of, *hermano*?" Javier asked, using the term for the first time. Jaime blinked and Javier pushed. "The same thing that kept you from facing me the night you killed my mother?"

Jaime's eyes widened. He glanced around at the men shifting warily around them, sharks scenting blood. He stared holes into Javier's face for several more seconds before lifting the gun. Bending his arm, he pointed it idly at the sky, his lungs lifting and falling.

"Put the gun down," Javier said, trying to sound as calm as he needed to. He opened his jacket and peeled it off, feeling the bandage over his shoulder pull and hoping it was tucked out of sight. If Jaime knew about his injury, he would use it to his advantage. "Let's finish this."

Jaime watched Javier loosen his cuffs and roll them up his forearms. He looked to Carlos. Carlos looked back at him, expectant.

Jaime was the first to look away. He handed the weapon off to Carlos, who muttered encouragement. The other men joined in as Jaime reached for his collar, popping buttons to loosen it. He, too, rolled up his sleeves, watching Javier with predatory aggression.

Javier walked to the place between the vehicles where the

headlights crossed streams. In Pablo's ring, they'd adhered to street fighting rules. The rules were there were no rules...except no weapons. Weapons were allowed on the streets, but Pablo had made an exception, not wanting to lose a man to a knife wound or gunshot.

The fight wasn't over until someone was unconscious or unable to gain his feet.

Jaime had been a master of the ring. For years, he'd allowed Alejandro to come out on top. His love for Alejandro had been as pure and uncompromising as Pablo's. However, too many years of Pablo's chiding and scorn had tipped the scales and Jaime had finally beaten Alejandro, unleashing himself from that last vestige of humanity. Alejandro may have been Pablo's favorite, but Jaime was the strongest and the most brutal of his sons.

As Jaime came into the light, Javier watched his gait carefully for weaknesses. Bad knee, hip? He moved easily for a large man, particularly one who had been confined to a prison cell for twelve years. Javier put up his hands.

His mother had taught him to shoot and, while Javier didn't like to think that Pablo had taught him anything, he had to admit that his father had taught him to fight. Not by instruction. Pablo had thrown him into the ring to fend for himself, interested only in the outcome.

And though Javier was beaten every time, he'd learned things. *Hands up. Chin down. Jaw locked.*

Javier drew on what he remembered of Jaime's beatings. He liked to circle, drawing the anticipation of the spectators, egging them by grin and gesture.

Jaime didn't grin now. Nor did he acknowledge the circle his men formed around the makeshift ring. He did roam around, slowly, forcing Javier to turn to keep him in view. He scanned Javier from head to toe, looking, too, for weaknesses.

Jaime liked his opponent to strike first. Another reason for the circling and jeering, to make his opponent anxious, to draw him forward.

Javier waited him out, staying in the center, counting silently to himself to keep his adrenaline from spiking. He breathed in and out. Careful, controlled draughts, watching Jaime's eyes.

It was watching Jaime fight others that had taught Javier not just to strike at his opponent, but to imagine his strike going through him. That devastating follow-through was the difference between hitting and disabling.

Jaime bounced on the balls of his feet, his hands coming up. He was losing patience.

Good, thought Javier. *Don't flinch*, he schooled himself. *Don't close your eyes.* He waited for the right moment when Jaime's arms opened up, his weight came to the balls of his feet and his fist sang forward. Javier ducked then lunged, following through with a strike to the nose.

The men shouted as Jaime's head snapped back. Javier's knuckles stung, but he didn't waste time. He threw the next strike into Jaime's center mass. The kidney was a center for pain, a fact Javier had become all too familiar with. Being smaller came to his advantage, making it easier for him to deliver the blow.

Jaime staggered, unsteady on his feet for a split second. Then the pain connected to the short circuit in Jaime's brain that made him deadly. His fight reflex engaged. Javier saw the violent veil come over his eyes and braced himself for what was coming.

Jaime struck, leading with the bull rush of his rage. The punch to the throat was quick, debilitating. Javier lost his breath long enough to open himself up to the onslaught of Jaime's fists.

Javier kept his feet. With a quick ball change, he used the first pause in Jaime's advance to deliver a blow between the eyes, then another one low, near the groin.

Jaime didn't keel, but grunted and backed away several steps, allowing Javier to take stock. His shoulder throbbed. His nose was weeping blood again and his ribs protested when he filled his lungs. His kidneys felt as if they'd swapped sides. Still, he kept his hands up.

Jaime's punches were devastating, but he wasn't accustomed to close contact. Once he was on the ground, he threw his weight around, but fought without finesse.

Javier waited for his next charge. Then he went low.

They landed in a sprawl in the dirt. Javier heard Jaime's expensive shirt tear. He heard the wind leave his lungs. Before the man could recover, Javier put him in a wrestler's hold.

Jaime fought like a snake. The men shouted unheard advice. They closed in so that the lights from the vehicles glowed in the stripes between their legs.

Javier didn't let up. His stitches ripped. The blood on his face blinded him. His ribs screamed, but he didn't release the pressure. He could hear Pia weeping, Sloane screaming...

He could see Grace. And his mother. Both of them battered but strong.

Javier locked his arm over Jaime's throat. He applied more pressure. Enough to make Jaime gasp, then flail... There was rushing in Javier's ears now, roaring, drowning the men's protests.

Something sank into his thigh and pain razored through him. The hold broke. Jaime twisted. A knife gleamed in his hand. It arced up to meet the line of Javier's throat.

Javier stilled. He met Jaime's gaze. The knife nicked the skin. His leg was agony. Blood soaked the denim of his jeans.

Jaime spoke, baring his teeth as he did so. "You learned *nothing* in the ring, hermanito."

Javier should've known. He should've had Jaime turn out his pockets.

"I wonder what Pablo would say if he knew," Jaime ventured.

"Knew what?" Javier wheezed. The wound in his leg hadn't just crippled him. The amount of blood soaking his pant leg indicated that Javier would likely bleed out if the knife at his throat didn't kill him first.

Jaime made a satisfactory noise. "That the son he didn't want turned out to be the last one standing."

Javier lowered his head back to the ground. He closed his eyes.

The knife lifted ever so slightly. On the wind, Javier heard a familiar *twump-twump-twump*.

The men shouted and scattered. Jaime gained his feet and lunged after them.

Javier grabbed his retreating ankle.

Jaime fell in a resounding heap. He kicked. Javier rolled to avoid a foot to the face.

The oncoming hum of the helicopter closed in on the trucks pulling away from the scene. The spotlight from above replaced the flagging headlights, pinpointing the tangle of limbs that were Jaime and Javier. Dust blew up from the abandoned airfield, blinding them.

Jaime coughed. He gained his feet again and attempted to flee.

Javier missed his ankle. He flopped onto his back, bracing his hands over the wound on his thigh. The pain was a red-hot poker. It was bigger than he could comprehend. It would rend him in two.

The dust storm and helicopter noise escalated. Javier stayed down. He thought he heard the distant cacophony of gunshots.

Then he heard a voice screaming over the whirring engine. "Javier!"

Sloane dropped next to him, holstering her weapon. She looked him over. "Christ!" she cursed. Turning her head, she barked at someone over her shoulder. "Hold on!" Her hands replaced his on the wound on his leg. "Lie back!"

Javier wished she and the helicopter would stop screaming at him.

Other figures circled him. Men in gleaming black helmets. Hands busied themselves on his leg. His pant leg was torn away. "Pressure!" someone shouted. Another yelled, "Stretcher!"

Together, they strapped him onto a board and rushed him toward the noise of the helicopter.

As they boarded, he looked for Sloane and saw her crouching near the open door, watching some point in the distance as the helicopter lifted, engine whining. When she finally drew her attention back to him, he asked, "Did you get him?"

The grim set of her mouth told Javier everything. He turned away from the sight. Failure twisted alongside pain.

Someone touched his arm. He looked down to see that it was her. She was no longer looking at him, but she held on as the airfield fell away beneath them and the darkness of the countryside swallowed everything else.

Chapter 19

Grace found Sloane leaning against the wall outside the operating room, arms crossed, eyes far away.

Remy stood against the opposite wall. He met Grace's gaze and shook his head.

Grace was weary. Surgery had gone as expected. The doctor in charge had generously let her sit on the operation. They'd had to close the wound on the front of Javier's shoulder again and repair the damage to his thigh.

She shuddered at how close he'd come to bleeding out. Jaime's knife had penetrated deep. The road to recovery wouldn't be short or easy. Javier was stable, however, and would be moved to post-op just as soon as he regained consciousness.

Grace wanted to be there when he did, but she'd needed to step out for a minute. Center herself. Just breathe.

Her hands had been steady in there. Now, with the gloves off, not so much.

She leaned against the wall next to Sloane, wrapping her arms across her middle. She let out a long breath, closed her eyes. "He's going to be okay."

Sloane made a noise.

Grace turned her head to study her friend's profile. "Before the anesthesiologist put him under, he told me you saved his life." When Sloane didn't stir, Grace pressed. "Well? What do you have to say for yourself?"

The frown deepened. "I must have lost my mind."

Grace turned her shoulder to the wall. Bracing her elbow against it, she cradled the side of her head. "Let me see if I've got this straight. You had Jaime Solaro in your sights. And you let him go to save the man I love?"

Sloane made another noise, this one just as expressionless as the last.

Grace moved to her, throwing her arms around her.

At first, Sloane stiffened. Slowly, she eased, and her arms rose to link around Grace's waist.

Grace pressed her face into her friend's shoulder. "Thank you," she breathed.

Sloane's arms tightened. "When it's my turn," she stated, then stopped because her voice wasn't steady. She started again. "When it's my turn to fall for some good-for-nothing guy, you owe me."

"Damn right I do," Grace agreed. Over Sloane's shoulder, she could see Remy. His head tipped back against the wall and relief painted his face. Sloane had torn off into the night without either of them after word got back to her that the Suburban from the parking garage's location had been pinpointed near the border between Mississippi and Louisiana.

Together, Grace and Remy had ridden out the wait. When Remy's phone finally rang, she hadn't wanted to hear the news trickle in that Javier or Sloane, or both, were dead.

Jaime was once again unaccounted for. But having Sloane and Javier back, alive... It was a bright spot.

Sloane's cell phone rang. The tension surged back into her frame. She nudged away, drawing the phone out of her pocket. She checked the screen. "I need to take this."

"I know," Grace said. "We'll talk later."

Sloane nodded, then headed off, answering the call as she went.

Grace looked at Remy as her voice faded down the corridor. "Any news of Pia and Babette?"

He shook his head. "Sam's out looking for them. He may know to look somewhere no one else does."

Grace nodded slowly, clutching her elbows. "I hope he finds them." If Sam couldn't locate them, then who could? She scanned Remy as he eased his hands into the pockets of his jeans. "You may still get your shot."

"What do you mean?"

"You want to be the one to put Jaime Solaro in the ground," Grace noted. "Javy tried and failed, from the looks of things. Sloane missed her shot to save him. Once Javy and I are tucked away in whatever safe houses Sloane puts us in, it'll be your turn."

Remy lifted his chin in understanding. "There's a silver lining."

"If you do get that shot," she told him, "don't just take it for Sloane. Take it for me. And Javy. Pia, too. And Babette. And *don't miss.*"

He regarded her in all seriousness. "I won't," he pledged.

"I should get back inside," she said. "See that Sloane gets something to eat?"

Now he smiled and tipped his fingers to his brow in a small salute. "Consider it done, Dr. Lacroix." And he left, too, to go after her.

Grace waited until she knew she was steady. Then she pushed through the doors and went back into the OR.

Morphine did wonders. It swam through his bloodstream, chasing pain and painting pictures of beautiful dark-skinned women at his bedside. Women that looked an awful lot like Grace.

His mouth was cotton dry. He parted his lips, licked them. "Bonita," he muttered.

The visions of Grace and her doubles coalesced into one. Her features sharpened as she sat up in her chair at his bedside.

Her scent washed over him, lovely and intoxicating. He closed his eyes and rode the wave. He rode it until she tapped his cheek, making him blink at her again.

Her face was above his. Concern webbed between brisk doctor's eyes. She peeled the lids of his eyes back. After a moment's perusal, she decided, "Your pupils look good."

She stared at the machines beeping nearby. "Your vitals are holding steady. Though your pulse is up."

Could she not understand why? She'd need to assume from now on that if she was close enough to take his pulse, it would be racing.

"Take a few deep breaths for me."

He did so. She watched the machines. He wished she would look at him.

Finally, she nodded. Her fingers wove through his. Together, their hands lay on his sternum.

"Grace," he whispered. "Look at me."

Her gaze returned to his. She drew closer. "Are you in pain? Do you need something? What is it, Javy? What do you need?"

He just looked at her, unable to draw the words out. All the doubt and heartbreak he'd felt leaving her hotel room muted him.

She seemed to realize what he was thinking. She eased down onto the bed at his hip. "I'm not going anywhere."

"Why?"

Her chin wobbled. On an inhale, she said, "Because I love you."

The words echoed through his head, but they didn't register. "You...love me?"

"Yes," she said, drawing the word out patiently.

"I'm a Solaro," he blurted.

"Javy," she began. "Not now."

He sat up, eager to prove that his condition had no bearing on his ability to converse sensibly. Halfway, white lights popped in front of his eyes.

She scoffed. "Back down," she admonished, helping him settle once more on the pillows. "And thank you for proving my point."

"I left without telling you why," he reminded her.

"I know why you left," she replied. There was no sting of reprimand. She smoothed his blankets over him, then brushed the hair back from his brow. "You thought you could play chess. You thought you could check the king."

"I did," he revealed. "I did check him."

Grace's throat moved in a swallow. She was smoothing his hair in repetitive motions. Her face had gone taut, her eyes wet.

He hadn't thought she would touch him like this again. Javier's chest tightened.

Gathering herself, she spoke again. "If that's the case, then why isn't he the one in the hospital bed? Because he brought a knife to the fight?"

"Because he doesn't know how to fight fair," Javier told her. "I thought I could end it—for you. For my mother."

"I never asked you to finish it," Grace pointed out.

"So you are angry with me," he surmised.

"Not for the reason you think I am," she argued. "I don't care that you're Jaime's or Alejandro's brother. I don't care that your Pablo's son. It hurt knowing you lied. But I can understand why you felt you had to hide it."

"Lying meant losing you," he said. "Deception was the one thing you couldn't forgive. You deserved the truth about who I am. From the beginning."

"I know who you are," she murmured. Again, she had her hand in his hair. She couldn't seem to stop herself from running her fingers through it. "I've always known."

It sounded like forgiveness. It looked and felt like forgiveness. But the morphine drip was doing its work. He wasn't certain if the dream was reality. "You wanted me to leave."

"I wanted you to go back across the hall," she corrected. "Not run off into the night sacrificing yourself. That's twice now I've nearly lost you. You have to stop trying to get yourself killed."

"I'll never stop protecting you, Grace," he said. "I'll never be sorry for it."

She shook her head at him. Again, there was no admonishment. Her eyes circled his face, swimming.

The first tear slipped away. Before it could slide, he intercepted it with his thumb, and smeared it. "Where's Luis?"

"With Agent Sapello," she said, sniffing. She ran her hand under her nose. "Turns out, she's quite the cat person."

"She can't have him," he warned.

She let out a watery laugh. "She promised to return him."

Releasing a quiet sob, she asked, "Can we at least put a lid on the heroics until you make a full recovery?"

He looked down at his battered body. "I don't have much choice." By then, Jaime could get away. He could find Pia and escape to whatever hideaway he'd already arranged for them. He could kill Sloane and could try for Grace again.

"Sloane wants to turn us both over to the US Marshals," Grace said.

"What does that mean?"

"It means a new place to live," Grace said. "It means a new life, at least until they apprehend Jaime. New identities. Everything."

Javier didn't like the sound of that. "We have names and lives already. Homes, too."

"My home's been destroyed, Javy," Grace pointed out. "My friends have gone into hiding. I can't go back to New Orleans until this is over."

"Come with me," he urged.

She frowned. "To New Mexico?"

"My boss has fourteen hundred acres of cattle lands," Javier explained. "There are places we could hide out there. He'd help us. We'd be safe. And if Jaime ever found us, I know the territory. I know how the land works. I would defend you."

"I don't doubt that," she murmured. "Sloane won't like it."

"Isn't it your decision?" Javier asked. "She can't force you to go with the marshals, change your name, be someone else. Is that what you want?"

"Are you asking me to come with you because you know witness protection means we'll likely be separated?" she asked carefully.

That was part of it, he had to admit. He couldn't imagine being separated from her again. If he had beaten Jaime and his men at the airfield...if he'd walked away and they were both free, he couldn't contemplate a life without her. Not if he'd earned her forgiveness. Not if she loved him as much as he loved her. "Grace," he whispered. "Come home to New Mexico with me. I'll keep you safe."

"I know you will," she murmured. "I know that, Javy. But

if we didn't have to worry about Jaime…if we were free to do whatever we wanted… If I asked you to live with me in New Orleans—would you leave everything? Would you come live with me?"

"Si." The choice would have been simple. "If that's what would make you happy, I'd join you and Luis in the apartment on Saint Peter."

"A cowboy in the Crescent City?" she asked with a small smile.

"There are stranger things to be found on those streets, no?" She had to nod.

"If you want to come back when this is all over," he said, "we'll come back. I'll follow you. I'll follow you anywhere."

She paused, tracing his knuckles as she held his hand between hers. "Maybe I *should* change my name," she considered.

He felt another wave of heartache coming on. "Is that your choice?"

She nodded. "Yes."

That cabin in the mountains—that vision of living side by side on the desert plain—vanished in an instant.

She leaned in, stretching out beside him in the hospital bed. "Don't look so sad, vaquero," she told him. "It's not every day a woman agrees to be Señora Rivera."

"What?"

She laughed at his utter lack of understanding. "I'm telling you I want to run away with you. I'm telling you Luis and I are coming with you to New Mexico to hide away with the horses, rattlesnakes and cougars. Bon Dieu."

"You're…coming with me." It dawned slowly—like light breaking into the world for the first time. It touched everything, taking its time, bringing clarity and life.

"I'm coming with you," she repeated. "And I'm going to be your wife. How does that sound?"

He had multiple wounds on his body. He'd just come out of surgery for the second time in a week. But he'd never felt happier. "It sounds like I'm going to have to ask Tante Lalie for your hand. And Sloane."

"Your battles aren't over," she warned, and she laid her head snugly on his unbandaged shoulder, curling her body into his as she draped her arm over his waist. "But at least you won't have to fight them alone anymore."

"No," he said, and couldn't fight the grin that had overtaken his face. He drew her chin up so her eyes yawned, dark and vivid for him. "Neither of us will fight our battles alone again." It was a pledge. "Te amo, Grace. Mi sol."

"Javy," she murmured, angling her mouth to his. "Cher. Te amo."

* * * * *

Romantic Suspense

Danger. Passion. Drama.

Available Next Month

Colton's K-9 Rescue Colleen Thompson
Alaskan Disappearance Karen Whiddon

Stranded Jennifer D. Bokal
Bodyguard Rancher Kacy Cross

LOVE INSPIRED

Christmas K-9 Guardians Lenora Worth & Katy Lee
Deadly Christmas Inheritance Jessica R. Patch

LOVE INSPIRED

Christmas Cold Case Maggie K. Black
Taken At Christmas Jodie Bailey

LOVE INSPIRED

Dangerous Christmas Investigation Virginia Vaughan
Colorado Christmas Survival Cate Nolan

6 brand new stories each month
Romantic Suspense
Danger. Passion. Drama.
MILLS & BOON

Keep reading for an excerpt of a new title
from the Intrigue series,
UNDER LOCK AND KEY by K.D. Richards

Chapter One

Maggie Scott looked around the dimly lit museum gallery, exhausted but content. She'd done it. The donors' open house for the Viperé ruby exhibit had been a rousing success. The classical music that had played softly in the background during the night was silent now, but the air of sophistication and sense of reverence still filled the room. Soft spotlights lit the priceless paintings on the wall while a brighter beam shone down on what was literally the crown jewel of the exhibit. The Viperé ruby glowed under the light like a blood red sun.

Maggie stood in front of the glass case with the almost empty bottle of champagne she'd procured from the caterers before they'd left and a flute. She poured what little was left in the bottle into the flute and toasted herself.

"Congratulations to me." She downed half the liquid in the glass. Her eyes passed over the gallery space with a mixture of awe, satisfaction and pride. The night had been the culmination of a year's worth of labor. A decade of work if she counted undergraduate and graduate school and the handful of jobs she'd held at other museums before joining the Larimer Museum as an assistant curator three years earlier. It had taken a massive amount of work to ensure the success of the display and the open house for the donors and board members, who got a first look at the highly anticipated exhibit. As one of two assistant curators up for a possible promotion to curator and with the director of the British museum who'd loaned the Viperé ruby to the relatively small Larimer Museum watching her, she was under a great deal of pressure from a great many people. But the night had been an unmitigated success, so said her boss, and she was hopeful that she was now a shoo-in for the promotion.

Maggie stepped closer to the jewel, reaching out with her free hand and almost grazing the glass. The spotlight hit the ruby, creating a rainbow of glittering light around her. She raised the champagne flute to her lips and spoke, "To the Viperé ruby and all the other pieces of art that have inspired, challenged and united humanity in ways words cannot express."

She finished the champagne and stood for a moment, taking in the energy and vitality that emanated from the works around her.

Maggie was abruptly yanked from her reverie by the sound of a soft thud. She and Carl Downy were the only two people who were still in the building. Carl was the retired cop who provided security at night for the museum. Mostly, that meant he walked the three floors of the renovated and repurposed Victorian building that was itself a work of art between naps during his nine-hour shift.

A surge of unease traveled through her. She gripped the empty champagne bottle tightly and called out, "Carl, is that you?"

A moment passed without a response.

Unease was replaced with concern. Carl was getting on in years. He could have fallen or had a medical emergency of some type.

Maggie stepped into the even more dimly lit hallway connecting the rooms, the galleries as her boss liked to call them, on the main floor. The thud had sounded as if it had come from the front of the museum, but all she saw was pitch black in that direction. She knew the nooks and crannies of the museum as well as she knew her own house. Normally, she loved wandering through the space, leisurely taking in the pieces. Even though she'd seen each of them dozens of times, she always found herself noticing something new, some aspect or feature of the pieces she'd overlooked. That was one of the reasons she loved art. It was always teaching, always changing, even when it stayed the same.

But she didn't love it at the moment. The museum was eerily still and quiet.

Suddenly, a dark-clad figure stepped out of the shadows. He wore a mask, but she could tell he was a male. That was all she had time to process before the figure charged at her.

Her heartbeat thundered, and a voice in her head told her to run, but her feet felt melted to the floor. The bottle and champagne flute slid from her hands, shattering against the polished wood planks.

The intruder slammed her back into the wall, knocking the breath out of her. Before she had time to recover, he backhanded her across the face with a beefy gloved hand.

Pain exploded on the side of her face.

She slid along the wall, instinct forcing her to try to get away even as her conscious brain still struggled to process what was happening. But her assailant grabbed her arm, stopping her escape.

Her vision was blurred by the blow to her face, and the mask the intruder wore covered all but his dark brown eyes. Still, she was aware of her assailant raising his hand a second time, his fist clenched.

Her limbs felt like they were stuck in molasses, but she tried to raise her arm to deflect the blow.

Too slowly, as it turned out.

The intruder hit her on the side of her head, the impact causing excruciating pain before darkness descended and her world faded to black.

KEVIN LOMBARD'S PHONE RANG, dragging him out of a dreamless sleep at just after one in the morning.

"Lombard."

"Kevin, hey, sorry to wake you." The voice of his new boss, Tess Stenning, flowed over the phone line. "We have a problem. An assault and theft at the Larimer Museum, one of our newer clients. Since you are West Investigation's new director of corporate and institutional accounts, that makes it your problem."

Kevin groaned. He'd only been on the job for three weeks, but Tess was right, his division, his problem. It didn't matter that he hadn't overseen the installation of the security system at the Larimer. He'd looked over the file, as he'd done with all of the security plans that West Security and Investigations' new West Coast office had installed in the six months since they'd been open, so he had an idea of what the gallery security looked like.

West Security and Investigations was one of the premier security and private investigation firms on the East Coast. Run primarily by brothers Ryan and Shawn West, with a little help from their two older brothers, James and Brandon, West Security and Investigations had recently opened a West Coast office in Los Angeles, headed up by Tess Stenning, a long-time West operative and damn good private investigator. If he'd been asked a year ago whether he would ever consider joining a private investigations firm, even one with as sterling a reputation as West Security and Investigations, he'd have laughed.

But staying in Idyllwild had become untenable. A friend of a friend had recommended he reach out to Tess, and after a series of interviews with her and Ryan West, he'd been offered the job. Moving to Los Angeles had been an adjustment, but he was settling in.

He searched his memory for the details of the museum's security. Despite West Security and Investigations' recommendation that the museum update its entire security system, the gallery's board of directors had only approved the security specifications for the Viperé ruby. Shortsighted, he'd noted when he'd read the file, and now he had the feeling that he was about to be proven right.

Tess gave him the sparse details that she'd gotten from her contact on the police force. Someone had broken into the museum, attacked a curator and a guard and made off with the ruby. He ended the call and dragged himself into the bathroom for a quick shower. Ten years on the police force had conditioned him to getting late night—or early morning, as it were—phone calls. The shower helped wake him, and he set his coffee machine to brew while he quickly dressed then pulled up the museum's file on his West-issued tablet. A little more than thirty minutes after he'd gotten the call from Tess, he was headed out.

He arrived at the Larimer Museum twenty minutes later, thankful that most of Los Angeles was still asleep or out partying and not on the roads. He showed his ID to the police officer manning the door and was waved in. Officers milled about in the lobby, but he caught sight of Tess down a short hall toward the back of the Victorian building, talking to a small man in a rumpled suit and haphazardly knotted blue tie. The man waved his hands in obvious distress while it looked like Tess tried to console him.

Kevin made his way toward the pair. In the room twenty feet from where they stood, a police technician worked gathering evidence from the break-in.

"This is going to ruin us. The Larimer Museum will be ruined, and I'll never get another job as curator again." The man wiped the back of his hand over his brow.

Tess gave Kevin a nod. "Mr. Gustev, this is my colleague Kevin Lombard. Kevin, Robert Gustev, managing director and head curator of the Larimer Museum."

Gustev ignored Kevin's outstretched hand. He pointed his index figure at Tess. "This is your fault."

"West Investigations is going to do its best to identify the perpetrators and retrieve the ruby."

Gustev swiped his hand over his brow again. "I can't believe this is happening."

The man looked on the verge of being sick.

"Mr. Gustev—" Tess started.

"You were supposed to protect the ruby."

"If you recall, we did make several recommendations for upgrading the museum's security, which you and the Larimer's board of directors rejected," Tess said pointedly.

Gustev's face reddened, his jowls shaking in anger.

"Mr. Gustev," Kevin said before the curator had a chance to respond to Tess. "We are going to do everything we can to recover the ruby. It would help if you took Tess and I through everything that happened up until the time the intruder assaulted you."

"Me? No, it wasn't me that the thief attacked."

Kevin frowned. On the phone, Tess had said the guard and the curator had been attacked.

"It was my assistant curator who confronted the thief." Gustev frowned. "She's speaking with the police detective in her office right now."

"Oh, well, why don't you tell us what you know, and we'll speak to her once the police have finished."

Gustev ran them through a detailed description of the party that had taken place earlier that night. Kevin pressed the man on whether anything out of the ordinary happened at the party or in the days before, but Gustev swore that nothing of note had occurred.

The curator waved a hand at Tess. "I have to call the board members." He turned and hurried off down the hall, ascending a rear staircase.

Tess's eyes stayed trained on the retreating man's back until he disappeared on the second-floor landing. She let out a labored sigh. "This is going to turn into a you-know-what show if we don't get a handle on it fast."

Kevin's stomach turned over because she was right. "I'm not sure we can avoid that, but I'll do my best to get to the bottom of things as quickly as possible." He turned to look at the activity taking place in the room to the right of where they stood.

Glass sparkled on top of a podium covered with a black velvet blanket. A numbered yellow cone marked the shards as evidence. A crime scene tech made her way around the room, systematically photographing and bagging anything of note.

Tess groaned. "Someone managed to break into the building and steal the Viperé ruby, a ruby the size of your fist and worth more than the gross domestic product of my hometown of Missoula."

His eyebrow quirked up. "Sounds like a lot."

"Try two hundred fifty million a lot."

Kevin gave a low whistle. "That's a lot."

Tess cut him a look. "A lot of problems for us. I'm afraid Gustev—" she nodded toward the staircase that the curator had ascended moments earlier "—is going to throw himself out of a window."

The curator was more than a little bit on edge, but who could blame him. "The thief attacked the assistant curator but left her alive?"

Tess nodded. "The night guard and one of the assistant curators were knocked unconscious by the thief, apparently."

Kevin frowned. "What was an assistant curator still doing here so late?"

"That I don't know." Tess shrugged. "But the museum had a party tonight to kick off the opening of the Viperé ruby exhibit. The board, donors and other muckety mucks, drinking, dancing and, undoubtedly, opening their wallets."

"Undoubtedly," he said, turning his attention back to the crime scene technician at work.

Tess shook her head. "The guard was out cold when the EMTs arrived. They took him to the hospital. He's on the older side, former cop, though, so he's tough. The curator is in her office. Declined transportation to the hospital."

"Sounds like she's pretty tough, too."

Tess shrugged. "Or stupid. Detective Gill Francois is questioning her now."

He frowned. He hadn't had the pleasure of working with Francois yet, but he'd heard of him. The detective was a bulldog.

Tess chuckled. "Don't do that. Gill's good people. I've

already talked to him. He's agreed to let us tag along on the case, as long as we play nice and keep him in the loop regarding anything we find out."

He felt one of his eyebrows arch up. "And he'll do the same?"

Tess rolled her eyes. "You know how it goes. He says he will but…"

"Yeah, *but*." He did know how it went. He'd been one of the boys in blue not so long ago.

"Listen, I made sure West Investigations covered its rear regarding our advice to the board of directors of the museum to upgrade the entire system." Tess waved a hand in the air. "I told them that the security they'd authorized for the Viperé ruby left them open to possible theft, but they didn't want to spend the money and figured the locked and alarmed case along with the on-site twenty-four-hour security guard was enough."

"Didn't want to pony up the money?"

Tess tapped her nose then sighed. "Still, this is going to be a black mark on West Investigations if we don't figure out what happened here quickly. I know you've barely gotten settled in, but do you think you're up for the job?"

"Absolutely," he answered without reservation. "The first thing I want to do is get the security recordings and the alarm logs and get the exact time when the case was broken. We'll also need to figure out what the thief used to break the glass." He pulled the same type of small notebook he'd used when he was a police detective out of his jacket along with the small pen he kept hooked in the spiral. His tablet was in the computer case that hung from his shoulder, but he preferred the old-fashioned methods. Writing out his notes and thoughts helped him remember things better and think things through. "Of course, shatterproof glass isn't invincible, but it would have taken a great deal of force and a strong weapon to do it." He scratched out notes on his thoughts before they got away from him.

Tess cleared her throat. "The alarm went off just after eleven, triggered by the curator after she'd regained consciousness. Getting more specific than that is going to be a problem, at least with regards to the alarm logs."

Kevin looked up from his notebook. "Why?"

Tess looked more than a little green around the gills.

His stomach turned over, anticipating that whatever she was about to say wasn't going to be good.

"Because the alarm didn't go off," she said.

"The alarm didn't go off." Kevin repeated the words back to Tess as if they didn't make any sense to him. Then again, they didn't. "How is that possible?"

"That is a very good question."

He and Tess turned toward the sound of the voice.

A man Kevin would have made as a cop no matter where they'd met descended the back staircase.

Kevin's gaze moved to the woman coming down the stairs next to him, and his world stopped.

The man and woman halted in front of him and Tess.

"Hello, Kevin." The words floated from Maggie's lips on a wisp of a breath.

"Hello, Maggie."

Maggie Scott. His college girlfriend and, at one point, the woman he'd imagined spending his life with.

Subscribe and fall in love with a Mills & Boon series today!

You'll be among the first to read stories delivered to your door monthly and enjoy great savings.

WE SIMPLY LOVE ROMANCE